Monta_____ _____ ___ barn door,
pull___ ___

True to f___ _____ _____ in her
heels and ___ ___ _____ ___ed and
scowled at ___ ___ ___ _____ _intedly
looked at her arm, clamped in ___ ___ ___nd. He
pulled her over to the discarded rain slicker. "Put
that back on." He heard her breathe. "Now!"

She jumped, then bent down, pulling the huge
slicker around her small shoulders. She straightened and turned around, a defiant look still creasing her features. She took one deep breath and her
lips quirked slightly. "Yes . . ."

His eyes narrowed.

". . . master."

That did it. His arms shot out around her. He
slammed her up against him. She looked up, surprised yet a bit triumphant.

He bent his head, staring into her glistening
eyes. "Shut up."

His mouth hit hers hard, intending to punish her
silent. She gasped. He buried his tongue in her
warm mouth. For once, she didn't fight him. . . .

He bent his knees and clamped his arm under
the slicker and beneath her bottom, lifting her so
her mouth was even with his. Her hands gripped
his shoulders, and his left hand spanned her damp
head. She groaned and gripped him tighter.

His mind flashed the thought that this was
heaven, but she tasted like sin. . . .

Books by Jill Barnett

Bewitching
Just a Kiss Away
The Heart's Haven
Surrender a Dream

Published by POCKET BOOKS

Surrender A Dream

JILL BARNETT

POCKET BOOKS

New York   London   Toronto   Sydney   Tokyo   Singapore

This book is a work of fiction. Names, characters, places and incidents are either the product of the author's imagination or are used fictitiously. Any resemblance to actual events or locales or persons, living or dead, is entirely coincidental.

An *Original* Publication of POCKET BOOKS

POCKET BOOKS, a division of Simon & Schuster Inc.
1230 Avenue of the Americas, New York, NY 10020

Copyright © 1991 by Jill Barnett Stadler

ISBN: 0-671-72341-3

First Pocket Books printing March 1991

10 9 8 7 6 5 4 3 2

POCKET and colophon are registered trademarks of Simon & Schuster Inc.

Printed in the U.S.A.

Dedication

To the staff at Sharpe Memorial Hospital, San Diego, California, who were so kind to us when we needed kindness and care; to Dr. Sidney Smith and Dr. Pat Daily and their surgical teams for giving me back my husband; to José Verdugo of the Playa Hermosa for helping so fervently; to the medic who got there first; to the cardiologist in La Paz, Haydee Contreras, who *made* the hospital help Chris; to Jim Stadler for sticking to his brother's side, even in a Mexican ambulance, and to his wife Debbie for trying to make sense of all those frantic Spanish phone calls; to Dr. Scott Bingham and Critical Air Medicine of San Diego for their evacuation and emergency care; to Gerry Stadler, who does more than any man should have to, and for being the foundation in this family; to his wife Linda, who never complains when we need him; to Louise Stadler for trying so hard when everything around her was crumbling apart; to Mark Stadler for traveling hundreds of miles to give me his shoulder to lean on; to his wife Jeannine, a special lady who let me have that shoulder at a time when she needed it herself; to Mike and Donna Stadler and their children, Sarah and Nathan, for opening their home and their hearts to our daughter so I could be there for Chris; to my friends and family for their prayers and wishes; to Lisa Snyder for being

v

the best neighbor and friend in the world; to Ruth and Penny and Kristin for talking me through one of the most difficult moments of my life; to Jane, who just let me sob on the phone when I couldn't be strong any longer; and to my husband, Chris, who fought so hard and was, thank God, too stubborn to die. I wish I could give you all what you've given me.

Surrender A Dream

PROLOGUE

Mussel Slough, Tulare County, California
May 10, 1880

THE SUN WAS HOT, HOT ENOUGH TO BLISTER PAINT. DOWN from the broad, blue western sky the heat smoldered, baking cracks in the rusty red clay of the irrigation ditches. Just four hours earlier those same hard-dug ditches swelled with water from Tulare Lake, water that fed wet relief to acre after acre of tawny California wheat. As if daring the noonday sun, the wheat stood tall, and still, except for a small patch near the dirt road where two fourteen-year-old boys hid.

Willie Murdoch crawled forward, craning to see past the battered crown on his friend's straw hat. "Psst, Montana? Do ya see anything yet?"

"Uh-uh. But if you'll keep your trap shut, maybe I'll hear 'em coming." Montana Creed slipped off his hat and wiped the sweat from his forehead. His damp hand slicked back a wet thatch of brown hair and he laid his ear on the hot ground. A few flies buzzed around his head and their drone hung in the sweltering air. But Montana waited. A long, silent and blistery few minutes passed before he heard it—the distant tremor of horses' hooves pounding down the road. Turning to Willie, he whispered, "Here they come."

Both boys edged forward, peering through the golden labyrinth of tall wheat shafts. Within minutes a murky

1

cloud of burnt-orange dust rose up from the road. The dust cloud billowed toward the crest in the road, and suddenly a rider and two buggies came into view, rumbling their way toward the Creed homestead.

"That's Marshal Poole," Willie whispered, nodding at the lone rider. "Who are the others?"

"The land agent for the railroad's in the first buggy, but I don't recognize the men in the other one." Montana squinted, trying to get a better look at the two men in the second buggy. Nothing in their appearance gave a clue to their identity. Both wore flat-brimmed Stetson hats, dark woolen coats, and white shirts, all coated orange with the dry dust of the San Joaquin Valley. They looked no different than any of the local men, and no different from the group of armed settlers, an even dozen, that suddenly confronted them, riding out from between the house and barn, led by Montana's father, Artemus Creed.

No one said a single word. The twelve settlers formed a wall across the drive. Both black buggies stood side by side, and the marshal's horse shifted uneasily in front of the buggies. A nervous twitch appeared on the marshal's face. Unarmed, he slowly approached the group. "I've got a writ of dispossession for an Artemus Creed."

"I'm Creed." A tall, lean man with the same brown hair and square jaw as Montana brought his mount forward.

The marshal held out the writ. "This is a federal court order. You're to vacate this land immediately."

Montana, still hidden with Willie in the field, held his breath, scared silent when his father raised his right hand and aimed his gun at the lawman. His father's deep voice echoed in the turgid air. "I'm not leaving my land."

Bill Murdoch, Willie's father, rode forward. "Look, Marshal, you know the Settlers' Rights League is appealing that order. The case will be before the Supreme Court in the next few months. Can't you delay serving that writ until the court rules on the appeal?" Bill tipped his hat back and nodded toward the other men. "We've all worked this valley for eight long, back-breaking years. The railroad promised us the land at two dollars and fifty cents an acre, and instead they're selling it out from under us for over forty

2

dollars an acre. We can't pay it, and we shouldn't have to!"

The other settlers grumbled in agreement.

"I'm just doing my job. In the eyes of the law, the railroad owns this land, and they can sell it to anyone willing to pay their price." The marshal pointed toward one of the men in the second buggy. "Mr. Crow, here, has paid it."

Crow leaned back against his seat, revealing a gun belt.

The marshal continued, "According to the railroad, he's the new owner of this section. Mr. Creed, you have to clear out, now."

Twelve guns cocked, their barrels aimed at the marshal and the men in the buggies. The settlers were not going to back down. The land agent in the first buggy was silent, but in the second buggy Crow and his friend exchanged some quiet words.

Montana watched his father move even closer to the marshal. With the settlers holding the railroad men at bay, Artemus Creed grabbed the writ. He struck a match, lit the court order, and threw it on the dry ground where it curled into a pile of dark ash. "No railroad-bought judge is gonna force me off my land. Hand over the reins and we'll escort you and your friends here, out of Tulare County . . . alive."

The unarmed marshal exchanged a brief look with the land agent in the front buggy. Shrugging, the agent handed Artemus his gun and the buggy reins.

Another settler, reins in hand, was just leading the marshal away when Bill Murdoch, Willie's father, rode over to the second buggy. He looked at the man named Crow, nodded at his gun belt and said, "Give me your gun."

Crow, a hired gun for the railroad, had his own answer. He raised a double-barreled shotgun and blew away Bill Murdoch's face.

Willie screamed just as shots exploded from both gunmen in the buggy. Montana rolled on top of him, trying to keep him from leaving the protection of the wheat field and running to his father's faceless body. The boys struggled and rolled in the furrows, Willie driven by shock and grief, and Montana by instinct to save his best friend.

3

Neither boy saw the other gunman fall nor the speed with which Crow shot Coley Jackson two times in the belly, killed Johann Swenson with one shot, drilled Ben Burnett through the head, blasted Ross Parker in the throat, and then fired a bullet into the chest of Artemus Creed.

The impact of the shot sent Artemus reeling off his horse. He hit the ground and rolled. He must have seen his son because he scrambled up and, shouting a warning, tried to run toward the field. Crow dropped his empty revolver, grabbed a rifle from the buggy seat, and downed Montana's father with one shot in the back. In just two minutes the railroad gun called Crow had cut down six men and then fled into the wheat field.

It was the thick silence of death that brought the struggling boys to a halt. With Willie still pinned beneath him, Montana stared in shock at his father, bloody and lying facedown only ten short feet away. But Willie, his strength still driven by grief, heaved Montana off him, grabbed a gun that had fallen nearby, and looked around for Crow. He spied him halfway across the wheat field and took off after him.

Montana couldn't will his limbs to move; he was still dazed, not comprehending what he had seen. Finally he was able to stand, and two deep breaths later he raced after Willie, following the trail of trampled wheat. Willie was wiry and fast, and he had a good head start. Montana's long legs churned and he tightened his fists, trying to drive himself faster. He hit the end of the field at a full run, cleared an irrigation ditch in one leap, and was into the next parcel of wheat when he heard the shot.

The sound rang through his teeth, signaling that whoever fired the shot was close by. He stopped, trying to listen for another sound. All he heard was the hammering of his heart and the taut wheeze of his panting breath. He moved deeper into the wheat. As he neared the end of the row, another shot sang out from the edge of the furrow. He rounded the corner and saw a sobbing Willie trying to take aim, his hands shaking so with anger that Montana could see the gun barrel weave.

Across another water ditch he saw Crow, scurrying up

the side. Willie's shots had missed, but as Crow made it to the crest of the dirt canal, Montana caught a flash of metal. Instinctively, he threw himself against Willie's back, and on impact Willie's gun resounded. In the same instant Crow spun around and fired.

Crow's shot missed; Willie's didn't.

The boys laid on the hot, cracked ground, panting. Montana opened his eyes and followed Willie's cold stare. Crow's body, his chest stained red with blood, lay sprawled in the dry ditch. Montana rolled off Willie and sat up, gulping deep breaths of hot air that dried his mouth and burned down his throat. His eyes began to burn too, from the rising sting of the tears he couldn't control. He looked at Willie, whose face was tight with grief and pain—a pain kindred with Montana's.

They were two friends who had grown up together, laughed and fought together. Together they had idolized their fathers, and a few minutes ago they had watched those fathers die. So they sat, side by side, at the edge of a golden wheat field, and together they cried.

Two days later the victims of the Mussel Slough Tragedy were buried. The railroad hid the truth, and the first public accounts of the battle were published in a railroad-controlled newspaper. The settlers were painted as villains and murderers, encroaching on the railroad's land, and while other newspapers investigated the incident, the fact remained that in the eyes of the law, the settlers were at fault. But public sentiment sided with the settlers, those hard-working farmers and ranchers who, eight years earlier, had been enticed by the railroad's false promises. These men and their families had taken an area of miserable, dry land and made it bloom.

In the Tulare district no one else stood up to the railroad. Most people feared such action would only produce more men like Crow. The Settlers' Rights League dropped their Supreme Court appeal for lack of funds. The people who could, paid between forty and seventy dollars an acre for land originally contracted to them for two dollars and fifty cents an acre. The others, the ones who couldn't pay and the families of the men killed, were evicted.

But the people cared. Over two hundred buggies, carriages, and wagons trailed behind the hearses that carried the victims of Mussel Slough. Buried deep were the men who gave up their lives for their land. But that same day a new emotion was born: public contempt for the railroad.

Montana Creed stood on a small slope, watching the wagons and buggies leave. He had his father's horse and the few belongings that meant something to him. Packed in his saddlebags were his father's ivory-handled knife, his mother's cameo, photographs of his family—all of them dead now except him—and a small sampler his mother had made when they first settled in California. She had died a year later from a rattlesnake bite, but the sampler had always been special to Montana and his father. His father, a descendant of hard-working sharecroppers, believed that a man's wealth, or a nation's, came from the land. So for the Creed family, the sampler stood for their dreams. It read: *Our Hearts Are in the Land*. The words reflected what Montana had been taught to value. The land.

Montana looked down at his hand and rubbed his fingers together. They were gritty, still dusted with the earth he had sprinkled on his father's wooden coffin. The box was now buried deep in the earth his father so loved, and that thought should have made Montana feel better. It didn't. He still hurt.

Willie left the group that lingered in the small cemetery and he joined Montana. "What'll you do now?"

Montana wiped his hand on the worn denim of his pants and continued to watch the procession of wagons weaving their way into the horizon, his face thoughtful. After long seconds he turned to Willie and answered, "Leave."

"Leave!" Willie's voice reflected his surprise. "Why? There're plenty of folks around here who need a hand. I'm working for the Rileys, and they've even got a place for Ma and the girls. I'll see if you can work there too. You know livestock and farmin' better'n any of us. I know—"

6

"Don't bother, Willie," Montana interrupted. "I can't stay here."

Willie's face turned stubborn. "Then I'll go with you."

"No." Montana's expression was just as unyielding. "You've got your family to think about. They need you."

"But—"

Doc Henderson, the man who'd tried to save the victims of Mussel Slough, and Jake Riley, owner of the largest spread in the valley, joined them, cutting off Willie's argument.

Riley turned to Montana and said, "I need another good hand, if you want a job."

The kindness in Jake Riley's eyes almost cracked the cold wall surrounding Montana. He turned away, his pride and pain not allowing him to bend. "Thanks for the offer, Mr. Riley, but I can't. I need to be on my own for a while."

"You ought to take Jake up on his offer, son," Doc Henderson advised. "There's not a soul in this town, in the whole county, who wouldn't help you out."

Montana looked at Willie, the friend who was closer than a brother, and at the two men who were willing to help the son of Artemus Creed. "I know that, sir, and I thank both of you, but I can't stay here."

Doc Henderson eyed Montana's horse and the saddlebags that appeared half empty. "Where will you go?"

Montana's shoulders straightened. "As far away from the railroad as I can."

Jake and Doc exchanged a look of understanding. Willie stepped forward and offered Montana his hand. The two fourteen-year-old boys shook hands. It was the gesture of men, and of two youths who had been forced to grow up fast by the events of the last two days. They said goodbye.

Doc Henderson gave it one last try. "What will you do, son? Your father didn't leave you anything."

Montana mounted his horse and took one last look at the lush valley below. "Oh, he left me something, all right." He turned and pinned the doctor with a pair of determined gold eyes. "He left me a dream."

7

1

Chicago
Spring 1894

A BLACK ENAMEL OVERMAN SAFETY BICYCLE ROUNDED THE corner. The silver spokes flashed in the sunlight, and the rubber ball-bearing pedals propelled the bike at an outlandish speed of twelve miles per hour. Air-filled pneumatic tires absorbed the shock as the wheels bounced over the deep ruts and steel cable-car tracks that checkered the busy intersection.

Ringing like Quasimodo's bell was the cycle's newest doodad—a sparkling London chime with a genuine nickel gong. It sat atop the handlebars next to a black leather tool bag and a lollipop-shaped oil can that swung from its chain and clanged in ear-ringing discord against the steel bar post. Despite its annoying sound, the can was necessary, for its contents—the Dynamic Cycle Oil—made the chain mechanism glide like a yacht on Lake Michigan. Speeding through the morning air, the bicycle made another turn and then sailed down Randolph Street, right into the path of an oncoming bakery wagon.

The wagon team reared and the bicycle swerved right, jolting over the curb and cleaving its way through the crowded sidewalk. Women shrieked and men yelled, but the bicycle plunged onward, brakeless and out of control. Suddenly the cycle veered left, heading straight for an iron street lamp. The cyclist released the handlebars and, with both arms, grabbed the lamp post. The front wheel dropped down the curb, and with a loud crunch the bicycle dumped over, leaving its rider clinging like ivy to the cold iron post.

Adelaide Amanda Pinkney slowly slid down the lamp post. Her pent-up breath whooshed out the moment her kid pedaling shoes touched the granite sidewalk. She let go of the lamp post and looked at her bicycle, lying across the curb at a twisted angle. Its front wheel was still spinning. Stooping down, she tilted the cycle upright and stared at her pride and joy.

It was crooked. She stood and rolled the crippled bike up onto the walk and then watched helplessly as her special plaster-cast, custom-fitted saddle fell to the ground with a sickening thud.

"Hey, lady! Get a horse!"

Her gaze shot up. A crowd had gathered and stood back a bit—her audience. Some of the men were smirking and the women shot her horrified looks before they regained their composure and scurried away. A few men mumbled something about women drivers before they went on. Not one gentleman offered her assistance. So she ignored them, figuring they were just angry at the thought of being run down by a *woman*. Then she saw the driver of the bakery wagon and she heard *real* anger. He stood with his arms waving like a flag. German curses bellowed from his mouth as he stared at the mess in the street.

Addie stifled a groan at the sight. The wagon doors must have opened when the horses reared, and all the wooden trays, filled with loaves of bread, golden doughnuts, and crusty muffins, were scattered in the street. The bread loaves looked like oval pancakes, and the muffins were crumbled chunks. Whole doughnuts rolled along the cobbly gray street until they chanced into the path of speeding carriage wheels.

A Chicago policeman, appearing solemn-faced behind his thick gray brush of a mustache, walked toward her. Clenched between his teeth was a whistle whose shrill trumpet could be heard even over the clamor of the busy street. His long, dark coat had double rows of brass buttons. They sparkled, but not half as brilliantly as the star that was pinned on his left breast pocket.

Addie wanted to run.

Instead, she leaned her bicycle against the lamp post and managed to appear busy as she tucked a few loose strands of raven-black hair back under her straw hat. She tugged

9

her boned shirtwaist back into its proper position and fiddled with the braid on her jacket. Just as she began to dust off the chalky dirt from her navy serge skirt, the policeman arrived. Unable to ignore him when he stood only a scant two feet away, she took a deep breath and looked up, ready for battle.

Under the shade of his tall helmet, his eyes were kind, and familiar. Every Thursday for the last few months, Officer O'Grady had come to Addie's counter at the Mason Street Library and she'd given him the latest books on California, the golden land of opportunity. They shared an easy friendship, and a dream.

"May the saints be singing, Miss Addie! What brings you out in this mess?" He gestured toward the street in the heart of the business district, where every morning a jam of trolleys, wagons, and carriages crammed in a fifty-foot-wide jumble.

"Oh, Officer O'Grady, I'm so glad it's you. I had to deliver some of the library's loan books to the Ryder Street School this morning and I, uh . . . I seem to have had a little mishap."

The officer eyed Addie's bent bicycle and then turned toward the teamster, who yelled while he tried to shoo away a couple of loose dogs that scavenged through the remains of his baked goods.

Addie, her face in a half grimace, peered around the officer's shoulder, secretly hoping the teamster would have vanished. He hadn't. Instead he turned and stomped straight toward them.

"Better make a quick getaway," O'Grady said, and with a wink he added, "I'll handle him."

Addie smiled in relief.

"Get along with you, now!"

A quick thank-you and Addie rolled the hobbling bicycle into the sidewalk crowd, moving along as best she could with the heavy bike and the awkward cadence of its bent wheel. She thumped around the corner and stopped to rest and get her bearings. She inspected the wheel, knowing she needed to get to a repair shop, but the shop she usually used was in the riding academy near her small apartment, which was all the way across town. There was a sister riding club somewhere on Water Street but she wasn't sure exactly where. Taking a deep breath, she crossed her fingers—hoping she was going in the right direction—and she and her bike headed away from the business district.

Half an hour later, as the sweat drizzled down her face and onto her soaked clothes, Addie stared at her crossed fingers and wondered why she kept doing something so silly, especially when it didn't seem to work. The riding academy was nowhere to be seen. She sagged back against the cool bricks of a nearby building and searched through her jacket for her handkerchief. It wasn't there.

The sweat drops trickled down her nose, making it itch so much that she swiped at it with her sleeve. Then she saw her hankie. A small lace corner of it was sticking out of her cuff. She removed it, straightened, and wiped the moisture from her face and neck. She fanned her face. The humidity was awful.

It was a Chicago spring day, typically unpredictable. The morning had been cool, so Addie dressed accordingly. But now, in only a couple of hours, the weather had changed. The air swelled thick with humidity, and the wind that had breezed by earlier was gone.

Whenever the wind halted, the people of Chicago had to swallow her industrial waste. Addie could taste the brackish taint of smoke seeping closer. Vulcanian fumes belched from the city's smokestacks, and the sky turned into a dark and billowing cloud. Drifting downward, the smoke cloud mixed with the rising stench of the stockyards, the black, gritty soot that spewed from the elevated trains, and the heavy, moist air. Soon, a gray fog coated the city.

This was progress, and Addie hated it.

She grabbed her bicycle and headed east, away from the fog, and two blocks farther she found the riding academy and its repair shop. A short time later she left, having made arrangements for her bicycle to be delivered the next day. She pulled on her leather gloves and made her way to the trolley stop.

It was not a good day. The first three cars were so crammed with passengers that they didn't even stop. She

11

was so flustered that when one did stop, she just jumped right on, not bothering to check the number. The trolley rumbled on before she remembered. She glanced up; it was trolley No. 613. It was common knowledge that No. 613 was the worst car in the city, and not just because of its unlucky number. This car's route went through the most hellacious area of Chicago.

Addie released the trolley pole and eyed an empty seat. She plopped down on the hard wooden bench. At least she had a place to sit. She was short and hated to stand on these things because everyone was always taller. She never got any air. Standing on 613 would be horrid. This route would take her to work the long way. The car bucked over an intersection, and she hung on tight as the electric trolley-car rattled over the streets.

The car jerked to a stop every few blocks and more people squeezed in, until Addie was pinned against the window side of the trolley. Apparently, the majority of Chicagoans were not superstitious. The car was packed and the odor of unwashed bodies was so strong that she turned her face to the open window, preferring the dirty outside air to the stink inside.

She looked at the street. They were in the slums. Filthy children crowded the stoops of the tenements. Some of them were little more than babies, naked and toddling through the street muck. Gangs of boys, angry and cocky, stood and stared, until one began to throw pieces of broken tenement brick at the trolley. The others joined in, jeering and swearing. A health cart slowly made its way down the street, spraying the walks, and anything on them, with disinfectant. Buckets clucked against the cart's barrel pump where they hung, waiting to be filled and handed out to anyone who wanted the disinfectant. No one did.

Piercing through the trolley racket was a baby's wail. It had a hungry sound. Garbage was thrown in the gutters, and the desperate ones rummaged through it, looking for something that resembled food. These people were starving, hundreds of them. It was then that Addie remembered the doughnuts, rolling out in the street. The street dogs of the business district ate better than most of these people.

She felt a pang of guilt, yet she knew she couldn't help. Chicago was her hometown, and now its growth had gotten out of hand.

Just one short year ago Chicago's Exposition had drawn people from everywhere, and many of them never left. Suddenly it wasn't a prairie cowtown whose only claim to fame was that it had burned down twenty years earlier. The Exposition boasted everything, from the splendid architecture of the different state buildings to the amusements and racy sideshows of the Midway Plaisance. In that one year almost two million people, natives and tourists alike, were lured to the specter of George Ferris's giant wheel, and Addie had been one of them. At night, adorned with electric lights, the wheel was something to see. She had watched as it turned, making the sky above the Midway glow as if the stars had fallen to that one special place on earth. The Exposition had proved that the city could compete with the best of them. Its industry, transportation, and services rivaled New York City, but so did its slums.

For Addie, Chicago wasn't special anymore. The crowds and filth seemed to worsen. She had been born here, twenty-four years ago, and had only left to go to Columbia University and attend Melvil Dewey's School of Library Economy. Other than those two years, Chicago had been her home. When she returned, she had seen the city through different eyes, but she'd gotten along fine. Only an occasional yearning sprouted, usually spurred by one of Aunt Emily's letters, for someplace different—a new kind of life. She had always managed to push those thoughts into that little part of her mind where she hid her secret dreams. A new life seemed like a dream, just like her other girlish dreams—dreams of wealth, and of success, and of the man she would marry. But in the three months since her mother's death, Addie had trouble dispelling those dreams. They kept creeping into her thoughts at the most inopportune times. And sometimes, she would cry. It was hard to admit, but she was lonely, and unhappy.

Her father had been dead twelve years, and with her crippled mother's recent passing, Addie had no one, except her aunt who lived in California, miles and miles from Chicago. Aunt Emily was the last of Addie's family, and she missed her, missed that bond and the knowledge that there was someone who would love her just because she was Adelaide Amanda Pinkney. She missed it so much that when she sent a letter to her maternal aunt, notifying her of her sister's death, Addie had secretly hoped that Aunt Emily would ask her to come and live with them on their farm. But she'd heard nothing, and though that was odd, Addie assumed that maybe things had changed for her aunt and uncle. Times were hard all across the country, and from what she'd read, even the California farmers hadn't had an easy few years.

She should be happy, with a comfortable home and a job. Her mind flashed with an image of those hungry people. Lord knew she had enough to eat. Addie glanced at the straining buttons of her skirt. Maybe she had too much lately. Whatever, there was something eating at her. It was an itch to do something other than her monotonous routine. She had always been a methodical person, yet lately nothing seemed right. And Chicago, well, it just wasn't home anymore.

The trolley bell clanged and she saw the familiar sight of the Mason Street stop. She stood and wormed her way to the door. The car jammed to a neck-whipping stop, and the horde of passengers was sent waving backward. All except Addie, who'd had the foresight to grip the trolley pole for all she was worth. She stepped off the car and walked the short distance to the Mason Street Library. Halfway up the stone stairs she stopped and looked up. There was no sun, only a smudged sky. She wondered if she would ever see a blue sky again. Her shoulders sagged a bit and she turned and went into the library. Maybe, once at work inside, surrounded by the books she loved, she'd be happy. Maybe.

The next night another gray cloud of smoke blew into the sky—a vast and moonless California sky. The dark vapor chugged out of the smokestack of Southern Pacific No. 11. The locomotive groaned up the grade, churning to pick up enough steam to crawl toward the crest in the track that

14

led to Modesto, the train's next stop. Near the top of the grade two men jumped onto the coal tender. They wore masks.

The smaller man, wearing a red shirt and armed with a pistol, lowered himself into the cab. He pointed the gun at the engineer. "Stop the train."

The engineer paled, grabbed the brake and jammed it back. No. 11 squealed to a stop.

The bandit in the blue shirt jumped down from the coal box and ran back to the express car. He yanked on the doors. They were locked from the inside. He banged on the side of the car. A small slot in the observation window opened.

His steady gun pointed at the messenger who peered from the slot. The blue bandit spoke, "Shove out the safe."

"No!" The messenger slammed the slot shut.

The bandit fired two shots, into the air, and a few minutes later his partner led the engineer and fireman over to the express car.

"You have two minutes to send out that safe or we'll shoot these two." The blue bandit raised his gun and rested the barrel on the engineer's sweaty temple.

When the red bandit did the same to the fireman, a sudden scurrying erupted from within the express car. The loading door creaked aside and the heavy iron safe toppled onto the dirt.

"Thanks." The blue bandit lowered his gun. "Now get outta there."

The express messenger, a pudgy man with thinning blond hair, leapt from the car. The minute his feet hit the soft dirt his hands were in the air, waving frantically. All his bravado had apparently been left behind his little slot.

"Get in that cattle car," the blue bandit ordered with a wave of his gun.

With their hands held high, the railroad men walked to the next car. Covering them was the red bandit, with his gun cocked. They climbed into the car, and the bandit rolled the door closed. He slid the iron lockbolt into the latch.

The train robbers walked back to the safe. Shoving his

hat back with the barrel of his .44-caliber Schofield, the red bandit pulled off his dusty mask and swiped at the damp blond hair that fell on his forehead. Then he smiled. "Well, we did it!"

The other man grunted behind his bandanna mask and turned, lifting his gun. He unloaded the rest of his bullets into the safe's lock. Jerking open the riddled door, he pulled out five money bags. The two men stuffed them into their shirts and ran down the hill. Behind a giant crag of a rock stood two horses, tethered and waiting. The men mounted and rode off, with five thousand dollars of the railroad's payroll.

Topping the front page of the San Francisco *Tribune* was the headline on the robbery. Many speculated on the identity of the bandits, but there were no leads, only the descriptions of the men, and those were vague at best. The man dressed in red was under six feet, small in build, and was thought to have light hair. The other man's hair was hidden by his hat. "Maybe brown, maybe black," the engineer had told the reporter, before adding, "but he was tall, whip-thin and very tall."

Two weeks later Addie stood on her tiptoes, straining to reach the volume on the shelf. She was just too short, and someone had pilfered her step stool. This happened all the time, even at Columbia. But then, most of the women at school had had to use stools. It was beyond Addie as to why the men who designed libraries *had* to make the shelves so darn high. One would think only Amazons could read.

And she was not all that short. Well, at least not the shortest. Her classmate and current superior, Hilary, was an inch shorter. She was four feet eleven and had never forgiven Addie for being an even five feet. Because of one silly inch Addie was still suffering. Both women came home to Chicago and were placed in the newest library facility on Mason Street. Hilary made Addie's life miserable. She'd misfiled books and then blamed Addie. She'd dumped coffee on Addie's salary draft, and it took three weeks to get it reissued; and one day, after Addie had spent almost five hours cleaning up the misfiled catalog cards, she'd seen Hilary go through and purposely dump out three of the wooden drawers. Addie had to start all over again.

Her job wasn't fun anymore. Ever since the library board had made Hilary head librarian, she had done her best to make Addie feel inadequate. Hilary could never stomach the fact that Addie had graduated with honors, far above her on the dean's list. She belittled Addie's work, drilled her with more fruitless orders than Napoleon at Waterloo, and generally threw her weight around, which must have been a monumental effort.

Addie had worked hard for the library and had loved her work, even with Hilary's antics, until the last few weeks. The woman had gotten worse. Now she was deducting the cost of lost books from Addie's pay. Addie didn't understand the girl, but knew that she couldn't take much more. She didn't care if Hilary's brother did chair the board. Each day was getting worse and worse.

Addie had marched to the end of the aisle and was busy combing the sections in search of her stool when she heard the familiar sound of Hilary Dappleton's infamous "Pssst."

"Pssssst!"

Addie started to turn, but then she remembered how Hilary had purposely blamed her yesterday for the lost set of Collier's Encyclopedia. *Once more, just to irritate her.*

"Pssssssst!"

She sounds like the old steam boiler in the basement. Addie squelched a grin and turned around slowly. Hilary's dimpled hands gripped the scrolled edge of the mahogany issue desk. Her buxom torso obliterated a large portion of the counter as she leaned over it. Addie glanced at her face. It was so strained with her effort to fuel her next pssst that it was deep purple, like one of those newfangled red onions.

Addie pointed to her own chest, her face the picture of innocence, and mouthed the word, "Me?"

Hilary's onion head bobbed up and down in agitation.

Addie widened her eyes and blinked.

One queenly arm, encased in green taffeta ruffles, waved her over. The abundance of green flounces on Hilary's arm

17

continued to ruffle, like a tossed salad. The action made the black fringe of her shoulder epaulets sway as if windblown.

They probably were windblown, Addie thought. All that hot air had to go somewhere; it probably came out her ears. Addie sauntered over to the desk. "Did you need me, Hilary?"

"I swear, Adelaide, you must be deaf!" Hilary straightened and shoved her wide belt back into its proper place, crowning her royal-sized hips. "What do you expect me to do, shout? You know the rules about quiet."

"What do you want?" Addie couldn't hide her perturbed tone.

"Just a minute." Hilary started to rummage through a stack of paperwork that sat on her desk. "I found something that belongs to you."

Now what?

"Ah! Here it is!" Hilary held up a tea-stained envelope. She handed it to Addie. "I hope it's not bad news," she added in a honeyed tone so false that it rang warning bells in Addie's head.

It was a telegram, which had obviously seen some wear. She turned it over. The flap had been opened and badly resealed. She looked up at Hilary, whose round face couldn't hide her wicked glee. It was all Addie could do not to slap her silly. Instead, her voice cloaked in ice, she said, "Thank you," and turned. With her head held high, she walked away. Almost immediately she heard the thunder of Hilary's feet, scrambling to catch up with her.

"Wait! Aren't you going to open it?" Hilary huffed along, right behind Addie, who turned and marched toward the ladies' necessarium. She flung open the door and spun around just in time to slam it, hard, in Hilary Dappleton's Cheshire-cat face.

She looked for a place to sit, other than the obvious one, and spied her stool, sitting in a corner of the pink-tiled room. She walked past the pedestal sink and sat down. The envelope flap was half open and she ripped it the rest of the way. Unfolding the telegram, Addie stared at the date: March 20. The telegram was over a month old.

That witch! She'd bet that Hilary had kept the cablegram on purpose, just to be mean. Then Addie read the message and knew how really mean the other girl was. Both Aunt Emily and her husband were dead, killed in a freak accident. A flash flood had swept down the road and overturned their buggy. Both had drowned.

Oh God, now I really am alone. Addie sagged back against the wall and stared at the rest of the message. She was the only relation. The farm was hers.

She took a deep breath and tried to control the tight ache in her chest. For the second time this year, and for the third time in her short life, Addie had to accept death. It hurt. The accident that killed her father had happened so long ago that the grief had lessened with time. Her mother's passing was painful, but since she had been an invalid for so long, bedridden and crippled, Addie had worked through the loss by justifying it as an end to her mother's suffering. And it had been expected.

This wasn't. Her mother's sister was special to Addie, and though she hadn't seen Emily for almost eight years, they had always written. Her mother could never understand her own sister's wanderlust. Marrying at almost thirty-five and then taking off for some godawful place in the wilds of California. But Addie had always envied her aunt's gumption. Her vivid descriptions of the farm, the town, and the people, had always made Addie laugh. And the space. When Aunt Emily wrote of the openness of the land, Addie's dreams began.

She read on. The telegram was sent by a lawyer named Levi Hamilton, and he requested that she contact him as soon as possible regarding the disposition of the farm.

A sudden pounding rattled the door, followed by a "Psssst!"

"Yes, Hilary?"

"Are you going to stay in there all day? You have no right to hog the room, Adelaide!"

Addie stood up, put the message in her pocket, and went over to the sink. She washed the grief from her face and walked back to the door. She flung it open and looked the woman in her squinty eyes. She wanted to tell her off, but common sense told her that nothing she could say would do any good. So, she walked right past her, heading over to clean up the card catalog, again.

Two hours later she was just finishing with the D's when she felt Hilary walk toward her. Addie didn't look up.

"Aren't you finished yet?"

"No."

"Well . . . ?" Hilary's foot drummed on the wooden floor.

Addie sighed and looked up. "Well what?"

"Are you going?"

Going where? Addie thought. Then it dawned on her. Hilary wanted to know if she was going to California. Addie took a deep breath and ran her tongue over her teeth before she replied, "Do you find other people's mail more interesting than your own, Hilary?"

The witch smiled. "I've been thinking, Adelaide. A farm would be a good place for you, working in all that dirt. It would suit you . . ." Hilary examined her nails. "And you wouldn't have to be able to spell." She gave the card drawers a pointed look. "Make sure those are all in the right order. I hate it when the cards are misfiled." With that five-pounder of an order, Hilary rumbled away.

"A farm would be a good place for you," Addie mimicked under her breath. All that dirt, humph! After working with Hilary, farming should be a breeze. Hilary had sure flung enough dirt at her lately.

Setting her elbows on the desktop, she rested her chin on her hands. Could she do it? Work a farm alone? She did have some money, so she could hire help. There were plenty of books on agriculture and farm life. She'd read enough of them.

Books had always been a source of learning for her, so why not learn farming? God knows she didn't want to stay here. There certainly was nothing left for her in Chicago. And she had no future here at the library. Working with Hilary had dampened any enthusiasm she'd had for her profession. This was a chance for a whole new life. She might never get an opportunity like this again. It wouldn't be easy . . . But her aunt had done it, and so could she. In fact, that's exactly what she would do. But first . . .

Addie looked over at Hilary, who was lording over the issue desk. *So you hate misfiled cards?* She grabbed a stack of cards from the D drawer and another from the R's. With the dexterity of a riverboat gambler, she shuffled the catalog cards. For the last fifteen minutes of the library's operating hours, Addie went, at random, from card drawer to card drawer, shuffling Hilary's beloved catalog cards. The library closed and Addie grabbed her belongings. With the happiest smile she'd worn in months, she walked past Hilary's throne.

Hilary glanced up, her face in one of its pouts—the one that made her look as if she'd been sucking on pickles. "You're not leaving? There's still too much work to do."

"Yes, I am leaving. For good."

Hilary smiled in triumph.

Addie glanced at the card files and smiled back. "Goodbye, Hilary." Then she walked out the door.

2

HEAT FROM THE MIDDAY SUN BEAT DOWN. ABOVE THE bleached pine planks of the station platform, the hot air waved. A white cloud of steam spit from beneath the train and was swallowed by the thirsty air. The conductor slammed open the door and a load of passengers debarked. Soon the platform filled with train travelers, all anxious to get about their business. Addie grabbed her hat and stepped off the train.

A man walked past her, carrying a white, handwritten sign that said:

HOTEL HAMILTON
BLEEDING HEART'S BEST!
ONLY TWO DOLLARS A NITE, WITH BREAKFAST.

Next to Addie a child cried, its overeager grandparent hugging it too tight. A couple of buggies for hire were tied to a iron hitching post that stood at the platform's north end. But no one approached Addie.

Stepping up to the ticket cage, she looked through the bars, searching for a clock. She spied one on the back wall and it read: 2:25. The train had arrived early, by five minutes. Addie smiled. This must be California. Nothing was ever early in Chicago.

The lawyer, Mr. Hamilton, was to meet her train, but no one was left on the platform, except the stationmaster, who was deep in conversation with a couple of men. Addie sat down on a shaded bench and waited.

A loud thud rumbled from the south side of the platform. Addie peered around the roof support beam. Another bang echoed from the baggage car, and a second later a large suitcase catapulted from the open doors. A volley of valises clunked onto the plank platform, landing by two boxes with their bands broken. A myriad of clothing spilled from the open boxes. Whoever was in that baggage car had all the finesse of a stable mucker. Addie watched in horror as one of her trunks was shoved to the car edge. It teetered for a long moment and then crashed to the platform.

Oh, my God! she thought. My bicycle's in there! Addie shot to her feet and marched to the baggage door. "Hello!"

A grunt sounded from the dark corner of the car.

"Yoo-hoo! Hello, I said!" She leaned farther into the dark car. A scraping noise grated from within, and the back end of a baggage man appeared from the recesses of the car. He tugged, with what looked like an immense effort, on another large trunk. As he hauled it into the light, Addie could see the markings blazoned on the side. It was her brand new Crystal Gibson barrel trunk. The one that held all her farming books.

"Oh sir! That's mine." Addie raised her gloved hand, waving a pointed finger at the trunk.

The man placed his hand on his lower back and creaked upright. He turned and, from under his bushy, white brows, stared at her. His face was weathered by sun and age and his chin and cheeks were completely obliterated by a full white beard. He had a barrel chest that was covered in red plaid flannel, and a big fat stub of a cigar hung from his mouth. If he'd had a jolly hat, he'd have looked like Santa Claus.

He rolled the cigar to the side of his mouth. "Ya say this here thing is yers?"

Addie nodded.

"Whatcha got in here, lady, anvils?"

She frowned. "No. It's filled with books."

"Books?" He sat on the trunk. "I ain't got no use fer them things."

"Well, I do." She raised her small chin a notch.

"Waste a time, I say." He pulled a match from his shirt pocket and struck it on her new trunk. Puffing on his tobacco stub, he asked, "Whatcha gonna do wit'em?"

Addie watched him inhale a mouthful of the smoke and then she smiled proudly. "Learn to farm."

The man convulsed in a fit of hacking coughs. He finally got his breath and looked at her as if she were standing there naked, and with two heads. "Jesus H. Christ! Not another one. Damn fool easterners ain't got 'nough sense to spit downwind!"

So much for Santa Claus. Addie's smile faded. She wondered briefly if maybe her plans were ridiculous. She had wired the lawyer of her decision, and his response hadn't been the least bit discouraging. This old geezer sure made his opinion clear. He thought she couldn't do it. Well, she could, and she'd make sure he was one of the first people to see it. But for now she changed the subject. "Sir, there should be a bicycle in there somewhere. Would you please find it for me?"

He gave her a long, crusty look before he moseyed back

into the depths of the car. She heard a loud crunch and a string of curses that could sizzle bacon.

She cringed. "Yoo-hoo, sir? Please be careful. I need that bicycle."

She heard some more grousing and then he appeared, rolling her bike toward the door. His look had changed. It was even more stunned.

"What in the Sam Hell are ya goin' ta do with this here contraption?"

"Ride it."

He leaned back, looked her up and down, and then eyed her bicycle. "Now that I'd like ta see."

Addie sighed, looking for patience. "You probably will. Now please put it down here . . . *gently!*"

His forehead wrinkled into even more of a frown. "Why?"

"Because I wanted to make sure it doesn't end up like these." She pointed at the broken bandboxes and the clothes strewn around them.

He glanced at the clothing and shrugged. "That's not what I meant. Why are ya gonna ride this here thing? A horse is a helluva lot easier, 'specially on them there dirt 'n' gravel roads." He nodded toward the dusty road that intersected the north end of the train station.

Addie swallowed hard. "I don't like horses."

"Uh-huh . . ." He nodded. "But yer gonna learn ta farm, right?"

She'd had it with this meddling old coot. "Look, Mr. . . ."

"Custus . . ." He doffed an imaginary hat. "Custus McGee."

Custus? His mother must have been a prophet. "Well, Mr. McGee, I don't see how my plans are any of your business. Now if you—"

"I make ever'thin' my biznuss, missy. Ain't much gits past ol' Custus." He rolled the bike over and put it down next to Addie, mumbling something that sounded like "damn fool female." Then he disappeared once again into the car, and before she could blink, two more bandboxes

24

bounced across the station deck. Addie rolled out of the line of fire.

The stationmaster stood by the gate to the baggage room, and Addie turned her bicycle over to him and made arrangements to have her belongings held until she finished with her aunt's lawyer. After getting directions to the law office, she made her way through the small town of Bleeding Heart.

By the time she arrived at the yellow clapboard building that housed the office of Levi Hamilton, Esq., Addie was absolutely sure that moving here was the right decision. Unlike that coot Custus, the rest of the townspeople appeared so friendly. Five people had wished her a good day as she passed them on the narrow plank sidewalk. Five people! The only people who greeted her in Chicago were drunks or pickpockets, both with ulterior motives. She was sure going to enjoy this small-town life.

Addie opened the office door and stepped inside. A lone desk sat in the middle of the small room. It was stacked high with ledgers and papers, and a dusty Remington Rand typewriter sat at a cockeyed angle. Tangled across its keys were the unraveled remains of three ribbons, and the spools hung like pendulums over the backside of the desk.

Although the room was empty, a door beyond the desk stood open just a crack. As Addie neared the door she could hear voices coming from the back room. It sounded like some sort of argument. She hesitated and then took a deep breath while knocking on the frosted glass of the door.

The voices stopped and a moment later the door flew open. A small man with thinning brown hair and a red face stared at Addie. His gaze shot to a regulator clock on the back wall and he groaned. "Miss Pinkney?"

Addie nodded. "You're Mr. Hamilton?"

"Yes, yes, and I'm so sorry! I forgot all about the train. Please, please come inside." He stood back so she could enter the room.

Inside, there were two other men. Both of them turned and stared at her. One of them, a gentleman, stood up almost immediately, but the other man continued to look right at her, gauging her. He had deep, bay-brown, curly hair that hung over his collar and shoulders and looked as if it hadn't seen a pair of scissors in months. His square jaw was dark with thick beard-stubble, and his upper lip was hidden by a thick, light brown mustache that was just as scruffy as his hair. His skin was tanned and his cheekbones high, a face that seemed to be all sharp angles. But his eyes were what froze Addie's steps. They actually looked yellow, timber-wolf yellow, and just as raw.

Slowly he stood, and as he did, Addie's head went up, higher and higher, until she could feel the knot of her hair rest against her own shirt collar. Her knees locked. Suddenly she had the same sensation she'd had when riding Mr. Ferris's giant wheel. The dizzy feeling swelled, and she looked away, hoping to dispel it.

"Please sit here." The other man smiled and gestured to his chair.

"Thank you." Addie returned his smile and sat down. He had dark hair. His brown eyes were kind. They had crinkle lines in the corners. That and his smile convinced her that this man was more . . . civilized.

Mr. Hamilton scurried around his desk. He seemed high-strung, nervous. He glanced at them, rubbing his forehead with his fingers as if the gesture would help him find his lost words. When he dropped his hand, his forehead was covered with ink smudges.

Addie smiled. He looked at the black ink stains on his fingers, flushed, and pulled out a handkerchief. He swiped at his fingers and then took a deep breath.

"M-Miss Pinkney, this is Mr. Parker . . ." He gestured to the civilized man, who gave her another smile. "And this is Mr. Creed."

Addie turned her head toward the tall one, the carnivore. She looked at his shirt button, gave a quick nod and turned back around. It was the best she could do.

The room was absolutely silent. She gnawed at her lower lip. Then it dawned on her that she must be barging in on some kind of meeting. "Mr. Hamilton . . ." Addie started to rise. "I don't want to intrude on your meeting. If you'll—"

"No wait!" Hamilton shot out of his chair. "You can't leave!"

Startled, Addie plopped back down.

"These men are here for you."

"Me?" she said, unable to keep the squeak out of her voice.

"N-No. I mean, because of your aunt and uncle." Levi Hamilton ran a hand over his balding head. The smudges smeared. He shook his head in exasperation. "I'm making a muddle of this. Miss Pinkney, Mr. Creed, would you excuse us, please? I'd like to meet with Mr. Parker outside for a moment."

The two men left, and Addie realized she'd be left alone with the man called Creed. "But—" As the word slipped past her lips, the office door closed. She sagged back in the chair and kept her eyes straight ahead.

The room was so quiet. She waited, playing with the little pearl buttons on her gloves. He said nothing.

The clock ticked. She twisted the buttons. Second after interminable second went by, and still not a word. But she could feel him looking at her, with those yellow eyes. A button came off in her hand and she stared at it.

His chair creaked and she popped open her purse and hid the button inside. All was quiet again, so she fiddled with the contents of the small bag until she could feel his gaze finally leave her. A sigh escaped her lips.

She glanced at the door. *What is taking them so long?* Her eyes went from the door to the wide mahogany desk. Like the one outside, it was covered with bound ledgers. A thick law text encased in tan leather lay open next to a box labeled Simplistic Typewriter Ribbons, guaranteed not to smear. The box was empty, and Addie smiled. Her mind flashed with the picture of a jittery and ink-stained Mr. Hamilton, tangled in spools of Simplistic typewriter ribbons.

Lawyers were cool, calm people. At least she had always thought of them as such. Mr. Hamilton destroyed that image. He was sure a nervous little man. She twisted another button and it popped off her glove.

Just like you.

She stared at the button and the three-inch gap on the

wrist of her glove. She was acting silly, nervously twisting off buttons just because of Mr. Creed's looks. She did wonder what a man like him could possibly have to do with her aunt and uncle. Maybe he was some long-lost relative of her uncle's. After all, Addie had never even met her uncle Josiah, but from Emily's letters she knew her aunt had been happy. Josiah Mitchell, a bachelor in his forties and a grizzled, western farmer, had swept into Emily's life, and in less than two months Addie's aunt had married and moved to California. But in all her letters Emily had never mentioned any other relations. Then Addie remembered that the telegram had said she was the only living family member, which meant this man couldn't be a relative. More than likely she was just letting her imagination get away from her, all because this Mr. Creed had scruffy hair, yellow eyes, and apparently no voice. Maybe he worked for them. That would make sense. He was most likely the hired help. And he was probably a really nice man, when he talked.

The button slipped out of her fingers and bounced onto the wooden floor, rolling loudly, like a cannonball instead of a small little pearl. Addie leaned down and grabbed the button. As she bent over the side of the chair, upside down, some little urge made her sneak a peek at him. He was dressed in black, dusty black, except for his gray shirt. His legs, which seemed to go on forever, were stretched out in front of him. His dirty leather boots were crossed at the ankles, and dried mud speckled the floor where his heels rested. Addie's gaze slowly drifted up the length of his legs. No wonder he was so tall, she thought. She had never seen anyone with legs that long.

Suddenly he switched ankles and his chair cried out a late warning. Addie bolted upright, too fast. Darts of light danced before her eyes. She blinked, trying to clear her spotty vision. Dadgummit! She'd bet he caught her gaping at his legs. Her heart drummed hard so she folded her hands, prayerlike, in her lap. Maybe a heavenly plea would help ease this awkwardness.

But instead of praying, she strained to get a glimpse of him out of the corner of her eye. Slouched in his chair, he stared out the window. She wondered why he didn't say anything. Even in Chicago people would converse if they were stuck in a room alone. Maybe he had trouble talking to a lady. Some men did. She remembered the shy boys in college. Many times she and her female classmates had to initiate the conversation.

Yet this man in no way resembled the shy college men she had known. In fact, he didn't look the least bit shy, or reserved, or even approachable. There was a tense air about him, something primitive. She debated a minute, and then decided she was being foolish. It was up to her to break the icy silence.

Addie took a deep breath and forced a smile. "Lovely weather, isn't it?"

Nothing moved but his head, as he turned to pierce her with those eyes. "No."

Her smile died.

"It's too damn hot." The sound of his deep voice seemed to echo in the room.

She gaped at him, his words not registering because of the rich sound of that voice. It didn't fit him, the tall man with the shaggy hair. She'd expected him to have a raspy voice, as hard and weathered as his looks. Instead it was clear, and so incredibly resonant that the timbre of it sounded like the bass section of the Chicago Symphony, playing something bold, like Vivaldi.

But his words were sure raspy enough. She should have been insulted. But he was right. It was hot. And the room was getting hotter. It had been a stupid thing to say. Of course, a gentleman would have never contradicted her. She should have trusted her first impression. He was uncouth, a real toad of a man. But what a shame, because the toad had the voice of a prince.

Montana stared out the window. She annoyed him, pestering little fly of a woman. And the last thing he needed was to be shut up in some room with a foolish female. Especially one who had nothing better to do—when she wasn't staring at him—than chatter about the weather. He bit back a yawn and resisted the urge to lean his head back against the chair. His eyes burned, but if he dared to close them, he'd fall asleep. He was exhausted.

It had taken over two long hard-riding days to get here from the Tehachapi hills. Wade Parker's telegram arrived the day after he'd promised to help an old friend. He had wired back to Parker that he'd be delayed and wouldn't be in Stockton for two weeks.

It was still hard for him to believe the news in the telegram. Old Doc Henderson had left him a plot of farm land. He hadn't thought about his pa's friend in years, let alone seen him. But apparently the doctor had remembered him. Montana's hand gripped the chair arm. Or maybe the doc remembered the injustice done to Pa.

Burned into Montana's memory was that day, fourteen years ago, when he had watched his pa gunned down so the railroad could line its already gilded pockets. Every time the weather got hot, that dry California hot, he remembered that day. And it was so real he could almost smell the sharp loamy odor of baking dirt, hear the drone of the flies, feel the taut, scorching air, and smell death.

And today it was that damn hot.

He glanced at the woman. Her fingers fiddled with something and she stared at the clock, probably doing her best to ignore him, which was just fine with him. Prattling about the lovely weather when it must have been a hundred in the shade. Christ! He had no use for her chitchat. He didn't rightly understand what the hell she was doing here anyway.

When he'd finally ridden into Stockton, Parker had left a message for him to come to the town of Bleeding Heart, another half day's ride. He'd ridden hellhound to get here, and no sooner had he sat down than Wade and this other fellow, Hamilton, had started arguing about some stupid case involving this Pinky woman. All he wanted to do was find out where the land was and get the deed. Then he could wash up, eat, and get some sleep before riding out tomorrow to survey his property.

His property. God. After years of going from one small western town to another, from one farm, one ranch, to the next, never staying long because he couldn't let himself take root. He knew damn well that the land he worked would never be his. He'd had no claim to any land, no wealth, no home. Until now. Montana rubbed his fingers over his tired eyes. He was afraid this bequest was a dream. One in which he'd wake up and find it snatched away. But as he glanced about the room, he knew he wasn't dreaming. Montana Creed was sitting here, in a strange lawyer's office, and in less than an hour from now he'd have it—land, his own land, his father's dream.

The door finally opened and Parker and Hamilton returned. Neither face showed much emotion. Hamilton sat down and Wade pulled a chair up alongside the large desk. Both men looked at each other for a moment, then Hamilton suggested Wade start.

"Although I'm representing Mr. Creed, this concerns both of you, so I'd appreciate it if you'd hear me out." Wade looked at the Pinky woman and she nodded. "My client, Benjamin Henderson, M.D., received a plot of farm land. I believe it's almost a section, approximately six hundred and forty acres. The gift was in payment for saving the life of a young girl, the only grandchild of Agostin Bernal, first landowner in the Del Valle Valley. Dr. Henderson died in April and he left this land to Mr. Montana Creed."

Montana watched as the little wisp of a woman finally turned her dark head and city-pale face toward him. She looked him in the eye. He couldn't read her expression. She had huge dark eyes, almost black, that seemed to hide what she was thinking. It was odd. Montana had an uncanny knack for pinpointing a person's train of thought by looking them right in the eye. But at the moment her eyes were unreadable.

"It took some doing to locate Mr. Creed," Wade continued. "With the help of an old friend of his, I found him, and notified him by wire of the terms of the will. These were clear and simple. Mr. Creed was given full and sole title to the section of land."

Montana breathed a silent sigh of relief. Since he was included in this explanation, for a brief second he was afraid that Wade would say that this woman had something to do with the land, his land.

"Then the problem arose . . ." Wade announced.

A problem? Montana pulled himself up in the chair and waited.

". . . I came out to inspect the property. Doc's property had no improvements. It was just a section of land, never-farmed land. But what I found was a fully improved, working farm, complete with fences, barn, well, and house."

Slowly, Montana turned and glared at the woman. Somehow, she was involved.

"This is where I come in," Levi Hamilton interrupted, fiddling with a pencil. "The farm was the Mitchell place, your aunt and uncle's, Miss Pinkney."

Her look was still blank, but Montana could feel the land slipping from his tight fingers before he even had a chance to hold it.

Hamilton stood, jamming the pencil behind his ear. "The Mitchells purchased the land with land coupons, a legitimate purchase." He ran a nervous hand around his collar. "Unfortunately, the seller was a s-swindler, because their deed to the farm is fraudulent. Mr. Creed's benefactor held the true title."

Thank God! Montana watched her face pale more, and although he couldn't see into her eyes, he could tell the woman was distraught. He felt some pity for her, but not much, because he was so damn glad that the mix-up was her problem and not his. A smile of relief kept itching forward. It wasn't easy to hide.

Her voice was quiet. "So I didn't inherit anything?"

"Yes," Hamilton answered. "You did inherit the farm, but because the property wasn't truly theirs to give, we have a little problem."

"Oh."

Christ! She sounded like she was going to cry. That's all he needed. Montana uncrossed his legs and leaned forward. This was uncomfortable as hell. Three men watching this little wisp of a woman, waiting for the watery outburst.

It didn't come, which surprised him. He even felt a bit more pity for her. After all, he'd won; she'd lost. As the winner, he figured he should say something . . . sort of polite. He looked at her again. "Sorry, Miss Pinky. You win some 'n' you lose some."

Her head flew up. Her eyes narrowed. "Knee . . . Pinkney," she corrected.

"Uh . . . excuse me," Hamilton interrupted. "We have a problem here because Miss Pinkney does have a legal claim to the land."

Montana shot out of his chair. "What the hell do you mean she has a claim to the land? Her deed's no good!"

Hamilton craned his neck upward. "There's a legal term known as 'adverse possession.' The doctor's land was unimproved. The Mitchells improved it, innocently thinking it was theirs. They made the land worth more, by building a profitable farm, complete with outbuildings. There was nothing dishonest in their actions. Because they made the land more valuable, legally, Miss Pinkney has as much right to the land as you do." His eyes darted to the little woman and he gave her a nervous, toothy smile.

Montana wanted to drive those teeth down his throat. Instead he turned to Wade and shouted, "Is he right?"

"Calm down, Montana." Wade stood up and looked him directly in the eye. "We're gonna fight for it. Judge Beck will be here in a couple of days. We'll let him settle this. He's a fair man and you have legal title. Don't worry. Even I think Hamilton's claim is a bit farfetched."

Hamilton jumped to his feet. "It is not. Johnson vs. Wright, 1872. Beckman vs. Haines, 1888."

The woman had been sitting there quietly watching them. She continued to look back and forth from one man to the next. When her eyes lit on Hamilton, he said, "Don't you worry, miss." He raised his fist. "You have a right to that land and we're going to get it for you." His fist slammed onto the desktop. A brass pencil holder bounced off the desk and the pencils scattered onto the wooden floor. Levi Hamilton disappeared behind his desk.

Wade looked at Montana and shook his head.

Hamilton stood, brushing the dust off his knees.

"What were you saying, Levi?" Wade asked, poorly suppressed mirth tingeing his voice.

Hamilton's face flushed with embarrassment, or anger,

Montana couldn't tell which. "I said, we're going to win that land." Hamilton glared up at Wade.

Wade crossed his arms, as if to say, *just try*. Then he returned the little lawyer's stare.

Montana would not lose this land. He gripped the desk edge and bent down so he was almost nose to nose with her lawyer. "I am *not* gonna let a bumbling lawyer and some fool of a woman take *my* land!" He turned and pinned the Pinky woman with his iciest look. "Especially one who looks like she doesn't even know where to plant a grain of seed!"

She jumped, obviously stunned by his angry words. Montana saw the anger that glowed from her face. Then she smiled, and he could see her mind working, could almost smell the smoke. She slowly turned to Hamilton. "As my attorney, you speak for me, correct?"

Hamilton nodded.

"Then please tell Mr. Creed that I am sure I can tell him where he can plant his seed."

Hamilton choked and Montana could feel the blood rush to his face. Even Wade's professional look of confidence broke into a slight smirk. Then they all looked at her, unable to believe what she had said.

She stood, calmly, as if she'd just showed them, and she tugged on her gaping gloves. Then she added, "I'll be at the hotel until the judge arrives." She looked right at Montana. "I'll see you in court, Mr. Creed."

Struck dumb, Montana watched her parade out the door, wondering if she could possibly have known exactly what she said.

Addie paced the small hotel room, wishing for all the world that she could have punched that Mr. Creed in his belligerent face. Her fists knotted at her sides and she could feel her nails cutting into her palms. She didn't care. She was too doggone mad. How dare he talk to her that way! As if she set out to steal his land—rather, *her* land.

Her land. It might not be hers. That toad might get it. Then what would she do? She'd sold the small apartment she'd lived in all her life, sold the belongings, and come west with only essentials and a few of her favorite things. She had some capital, but there was no way she could build a farm all alone. She wasn't even sure she could handle an existing one. But she was sure going to give it a try. And she would not let that man take her land.

She would have been willing to try to come to some agreement, maybe offer to buy him out, until he called her a fool. Twice in one day she'd been labeled such, and she didn't like it one bit. Just because she was a woman, he thought her . . . inferior. She could tell. Well, she wasn't, and she'd show him.

She sat on the bed. It was hard as the wooden train bench. She sighed, suddenly feeling the weight of the world on her small shoulders. She was worried. If the judge didn't rule in her favor, she wouldn't have a place to live. Lord knew she didn't want to go back to Chicago, but neither was she prepared to start from scratch. At least Aunt Emily's farm made her feel as if she had roots, even if they weren't her roots.

She walked over and opened the window, hoping some breeze would slip through. It didn't. It was perfectly still outside. The window overlooked the hotel's back street. An ice wagon pulled up and began to unload. Hay spilled onto the street as the iceman used his iron tongs to lug the blocks from inside. That would be the only job to have in this heat.

Addie licked her lips, imagining what the ice would feel like melting in her dry mouth. A couple of kids ran up to the wagon. She watched one of them, a boy in cut-off pants and a straw hat, pull out a small knife and chip off some ice. He handed it to the smaller boy, the one with bright red-orange hair. They laughed, and then the iceman chased them off. A small dog yapped at their heels as they ran down the narrow street, and Addie remembered the dog and doughnuts.

It was different here. The children she'd just seen weren't mean and they weren't starving. Both had looked healthy, plump, and like children everywhere, they were into mischief. The gangs of Chicago kids would have probably beaten up and robbed the iceman.

35

Although it had only been a few hours, she knew she wanted to stay, despite that obnoxious Mr. Creed. Addie wanted the farm, and she had to find a way to ensure that she'd get it. The judge would be here in two days, so she had two days to come up with a surefire way of getting the land.

Addie paced and then sat, paced and sat, until she couldn't think anymore. Nor could she stand that board of a bed. Walking back to the window, she peered out just as a wagon barreled down the street. It pulled to a dusty stop at the hotel. The driver jumped down from the seat and whipped off his hat. He had a head of familiar white hair.

It was Custus McGee, delivering her things. He beat his floppy hat against his leg, and then the wide-brimmed hat sailed onto the wagon seat. He walked around the wagon, untying the tarp that covered her possessions.

Possessions. That was it! One look at her trunks sitting in the wagon and Addie knew exactly what she would do.

She leaned out the window. "Yoo-hoo! Mr. McGee!"

He stood, rooted to the ground, and stared up at her. Addie could see him chomp on his cigar stub while he watched her.

"Leave those things there, please. I'll be right down!" Addie grabbed her purse and ran out the door, right into Mr. Montana Creed.

His hands gripped her shoulders. She looked up at him. He looked as startled as she was. She raised her chin and gave him her haughtiest look.

His hands dropped from her shoulders as if they'd been burned. "You oughta watch where you're going, Miss Pinky." Then he walked right past her and unlocked the room next to hers.

"Knee. Pink-ney." She tightened her fists. She would have flung her purse at him, except that might ruin her plan. So instead she turned and walked away. She had just reached the stairs when she heard him.

"Miss Pinky!"

She jerked to a stop.

"I'll see you in court." Then she heard the door close.

36

Addie stomped down the stairs and out through the back of the hotel. Custus still stood there, waiting for her.

She started to walk toward him, but heard a window open above her. She leaned back against the building and looked up. It could have been the toad's room. Turning back to Custus, Addie waved at him, while she stayed flush against the wall.

He was folding up the tarp.

"Psssst!" *Good Lord, I sound like Hilary!* "Mr. McGee," she whispered.

He looked up, and she gestured for him to come over. The man moved like a snail.

When he finally stood in front of her, she asked, "How much would you charge to take me to the Mitchell place?"

"Why?"

She counted to ten. "Because I own the place now." One little lie wouldn't hurt. Besides, she did have a claim to it. "Emily Mitchell was my aunt," she added, icing the fib with some truth.

He leaned against the building. "Ya don't look like 'er."

"I look like my father. Now how much?" She opened her purse.

"How much ya got?"

"Mr. McGee, here's two dollars. Will you or will you not take me there?"

He took the money and turned around. He spread one bill flat against the hotel wall and smoothed the wrinkles out of it. Then he held it up toward the west and scrutinized it.

"It's real." Addie crossed her arms.

"Sure is." He folded the bills up and put them in his shirt pocket. "Woulda done it fer one, though. Ya easterners sure throw yer money 'round." With that bit of western wisdom, he strolled back to the wagon and retied the tarp. He hopped up onto the seat and turned toward her.

Addie glanced up at the window and then made a dash for the wagon, making sure she didn't get too close to the horses. She grabbed onto the side of the wagon and tried to get her foot up to the running board. She was too short.

Looking around, she spied a crate by the hotel door. She

37

flung her purse on the high freight wagon seat, turned and marched over to get the crate. Setting it down by the wagon, she stepped up and then pulled herself aboard. She dusted off her gloves and smiled at the old coot.

"Ya know, ya might be able ta farm that land after all." And Custus gave her a wink before he whipped the team into a full run.

Half an hour later Addie was sure she should have stayed at the hotel. Custus had yet to slow down, even on the curves and the ruts. At one point she had grabbed onto him to keep from being flung out.

He finally slowed and pointed up the road. "That's the Mitchell place."

Just as the sun was setting, Adelaide Amanda Pinkney had her first glimpse of the farm. Custus turned onto a dirt road that was scattered with gravel. As the wagon wheels crunched along, she looked at her land and smiled. It was lovely.

The fields were barren, recently plowed under, but the dirt was a rich sienna-brown. A big two-story barn stood at the end of the dirt road, and sitting back a bit was a tall white windmill. Between the barn and the house were a few empty pens and a small fenced chicken yard. A wide porch encircled the small white farmhouse, and Addie could see the remnants of a flowerbed that had once edged the porch rails. Wooden storm shutters, painted a deep green, framed the narrow windows, and a small red-brick chimney topped the shingled roof. But the best thing there was the tree. A giant, sprawling oak tree stood near the front of the house. Its wide, fingery branches clawed outward, and from the width of its leathery trunk, Addie knew it must have been there for decades. There were other trees, a grove of tall eucalyptus that sat behind the house, and a few rows of fruit trees could be seen behind the henhouse. But the massive beauty of the oak made it stand out.

She smiled, thinking of her aunt and remembering her letters about the tree. Aunt Emily had loved it, had made sure the house was built just behind it.

Custus stopped the wagon. "Well, here ya are, missy.

This here's yer farm. The stock's done spread 'tween the Latimers and the Johnsons. I'm shor they'll be bringin' em back jus' a soon as they hear'd ya done moved in.'' He jumped down from the seat, untied the tarp and started to unload.

Addie remembered her bicycle. She lowered herself to the running board, but the ground was still a long way for a short person. She had to get down, so she grabbed onto the side of the freight wagon and swung down. Her feet still didn't touch the ground and she slammed into the side of the wagon. The horses nickered in protest, which made Addie immediately let go. The high squat heel on her button-top, Goodyear welt shoes gave way. She hit the dirt, fanny first.

As soon as her teeth ceased to ring she turned to freeze Custus with her iciest look. He completely ignored her. Her clothing trunk hit the white wooden porch with a thud, and Custus began to pry off the boards that were nailed across the front door.

She stood up, dusted herself off, and went to get her bicycle out herself. She grabbed the front wheel and pulled it down, inspecting it for damage. Amazingly, there was none. She rolled it toward the house.

Ten minutes later everything was unloaded and in the house. Addie lit the kerosene lamps and watched old Custus the coot drive off. She unpacked a few things, fetched some water from the pump, and found some clean bed linen in her aunt's cedar chest. She washed, changed, and crawled into the bed. It was a feather bed, as soft and comfy as a sweet dream. Within minutes she was sound asleep.

The sun rose early, and as it crept over the eastern foothills, its first light cracked through the east window. Addie pulled the covers tighter around her and she grinned. She was here, on her land. Sneaking out here was the best idea she'd had. Surely the judge would be hesitant to throw her off the land where she lived, even if she only lived there for a couple of days. She'd heard that possession was nine points of the law, and she had possession, not Mr. Creed.

Throwing back the covers, she got up and slipped on her dressing gown. She went to the washstand, poured some water, and scrubbed her face and teeth. A couple of stretches and she felt wonderful. She walked outside and stood on the front porch, watching the sunrise. Against the foothills the sky was brilliant pink, and it melded upward from pale purple to a rich, rich blue—the blue she'd thought she'd never see again. She felt so good, listening to the peace, the quiet wonderful peace.

Then something clicked in the silence.

Addie turned toward the giant oak.

Montana Creed leaned against the tree, with a gun pointed right at her.

3

"WHAT THE HELL DO YOU THINK YOU'RE DOING?" MONTANA pushed away from the tree trunk, with gun in hand, and slowly walked toward the Pinky woman. Her dark eyes, wide open and shocked, looked like coal chips against her white face. She was scared, which was exactly what he wanted. He would scare the living hell out of her if he had to, anything to get her off his land.

He stopped, no more than three feet from her. "I said, what are you doing here?"

She took a long, deep breath. He could see it condense into a white fog in the cold dawn air. Her hands gripped her robe lapels, pulling them together, and she masked her fear by sticking that noble little nose of hers high in the air.

"I'm living on *my* farm."

"Like hell."

"My my, but you have a such a way with four-letter words."

He holstered the gun and made for the porch steps. She ran along the porch and stood directly in front of him. His boot hit the first stair.

"Move it!" he ordered.

"No." She put her arms out to her sides to try to block him from stepping around.

He took another step and now stood on the stair just below her. Even though she stood on the higher step, he was a good head above her. He glowered down. She glared up.

She was something. He put his boot on the next step, right between her bare feet, and he paused, giving her the chance to move. All the while his eyes bored into hers, challenging, daring. She didn't budge, so he stepped up. The sheer size of his tall body against hers forced her back. So he kept at it, walking right into her while she shuffled backward with her head cocked back, returning him icy glare for icy glare. He marched her right back against the front door. The wooden screen door clattered against its frame when she hit it. She straightened and took a sharp breath.

"Move," he ordered.

Her arms went out again, trying to block his entrance, or shield the farmhouse, he wasn't quite sure which. He started to move left.

She grabbed the doorframe with her right hand, still trying to block him. "I was here first."

"It's my farm," he gritted.

"No it isn't."

"I have the real deed."

"The judge will decide that."

"You can't win." He moved right.

"I can't lose." Her hands gripped both sides of the doorjamb.

"Let me by, Miss Pinky."

Her chin jutted out. "Knee . . . Pink-ney!"

He smiled, knowing that got her every time.

41

"It's my house. My aunt and uncle built it. You can't go in!"

"I can go any damn place I want." He grabbed her by the waist and picked her up. She screeched. He had caught her off guard, and satisfaction swelled through him. He plopped her down behind him, turned around and opened the screen door.

An instant later she grabbed a hold of his shirt—he could feel her little claws—and she pulled back. His shirt buttons flew through the air like buckshot, bouncing off the weathered doorjamb. Cold air hit his chest and Montana looked down; his bare chest stared back. He let go of the screen door and turned around, slowly, counting to that long, long number ten.

She dropped his shirt and panic flashed in her black eyes. Just as he reached for her, she shot under his arm and through the door, quicker than a cut cat. The screen door banged against the frame, and before he could open it, the front door slammed shut, then the lockbolt. And Montana saw red.

Addie used the wall for support while she tried to catch a full breath. Her heart pounded and the throb of it beat drumlike in her ears. Her breath slowed. She'd done it! She'd locked him out. For a few moments there she'd thought he'd had her. She blew out a cleansing breath and pushed her tangled hair back from her face. Sweat beads dotted her hairline; it was nervous sweat from trying to mask her fear.

All was quiet, too quiet. She wondered if he was still there. She edged toward the narrow window on her left, inching along with her back pressed against the front wall. She turned slightly and pinched the floral trim of the kettle-cloth curtain. Pulling it back, she peeked around the window frame just enough to try to see the porch.

The door splintered once . . .

She panicked.

Twice . . .

Addie pushed away from the rattling front walls and

grabbed the nearest chair to barricade the door. But it was too late.

The wood cracked; the hinges broke; the door wobbled and crashed to the floor. Montana Creed was inside, glowering, all six feet four of him. It was not a pretty sight.

"Like I said . . . I go any damn place I want."

Addie clamped her gaping mouth shut. He started toward her, and she could feel his anger. It shot toward her like Apache arrows. She was going to die. Right here and now. She knew it. He looked mad enough to kill her, and he wouldn't use his gun. He'd use his bare hands—the ones that were clenched so tightly in front of him that his knuckles were white.

She stepped back and felt the edge of a table behind her. Her hand reached back and grabbed the first thing it touched. It was hard metal, tin of some sort, and it was tall. Her fingers gripped the wooden stem and she lifted it. The wooden base was heavy. A perfect weapon.

He closed in from her left. She flung the thing at him and ran to the right, behind a fringed sofa, heading straight for the kitchen door.

Three bullets hit the door before she took four steps. Addie dropped to the floor, instinctively covering her head with her arms. She was wrong. He *would* use the gun!

The shots stopped and she lay there, eyes squeezed shut while she waited, waited for him to round the sofa and finish her off. This was it, she thought. She'd pushed this long-haired madman too far. She'd die in the parlor of her aunt's farmhouse, with no one to mourn her, except Mr. Hamilton, her lawyer. All her schooling was for nothing, wasted on someone who wouldn't live past twenty-four short years. No new life out west. No dream come true. Just death. She'd traveled all this way to die. But maybe they'd bury her under the giant oak with a marble marker, etched with the words: *Adelaide Amanda Pinkney died fighting for her land.*

Well, at least the murdering toad wouldn't get it. They'd hang him for this. Then Addie realized that she hadn't heard him move. Slowly, she removed her arms and opened her eyes, half expecting him to be standing over her, ready to shoot. All she saw was the deep brown velvet of the sofa back and a few months' worth of dust balls that covered the bare wooden floor. She looked up, expecting to see those mad, gold eyes laced with the need to kill.

Instead, the plastered ceiling stared back, complete with a few cobwebs hanging from a bronze lamp. She pushed up onto her hands and knees and listened. There wasn't a sound. Maybe he was waiting for her to stand up, then he could drill her full of bullets, just like the door.

She looked around for an escape, someplace she could crawl to, but the sofa was the only protection between her and the kitchen door, the bullet-ridden door. Then she heard the creak of leather, and a few seconds later the sound of metal. Oh Lord! He must be reloading. Suddenly, in vivid color, she could picture him pulling the deadly, metal bullets from his gun belt, sliding them into the chambers of his cold, cold gun.

Our Father, who art—

Glass clinked and Addie stopped praying. She heard the glass again, scraping. Now what was he doing? Not more than a second or two later she heard it again, plain as day. It was glass scraping metal. A moment later she heard it again. No matter what, she couldn't make sense of those sounds. She thought for a second, fought an inner battle of good sense versus her curiosity.

Her curiosity won. She was going to die anyway, so she might as well see what sort of torture he was readying. With her shoulder against the sofa back, Addie crawled on all fours over to the end of the couch. She sat back on her knees and very slowly peered over the top edge of the sofa.

The toad stood, gun in holster, completely entranced by a stereoscope. It must have been the weapon she'd thrown at him. His hand gripped the oak spindle of the tin viewer just above its wooden base, and he slid the glass picture slides around as if he had never seen a magic lantern before.

Addie eased upward and began to back toward the door. "What is this thing?" His voice stopped her dead in her tracks. It was still deep as thunder, but for the first time calm threaded through its sound instead of rage, and for some reason she felt no need to run.

44

"A stereoscope. Some people call them magic lanterns."
She cautiously stepped forward. "Don't tell me you've
never seen one?"

He shook his head and grabbed another slide, turning the
viewer to focus on the new slides.

Addie walked around the sofa and stood there, watching
him. Where had he been? Hiding in the hills for thirty
years? Stereoscopes had been around when her mother was
a child. A vast number of slides were available throughout
Chicago. The Mason Street Library alone had box after
box of lantern slides that showed almost every major city
in the world.

Curiosity piqued, Addie watched him, this man who was
so tall, so intimidating with his gun and those yellow eyes
that seemed to burn holes right through a person. And now
those same scorching eyes were fascinated with a toy. A
toy, for heaven's sakes. She shook her head and wondered
what kind of life the man led, where he had been raised,
and by whom. For a brief moment she asked herself what
it would have been like to have been raised without toys.
Did the land mean so much to him because he'd never had
anything? Maybe, but that wasn't her problem, and there
was no way on God's green earth that she would give him
her land.

It was bad enough that he held the legal deed. The judge
could easily decide in Mr. Creed's favor. Chances were
better for her if she could stay on the property, of that she
was sure. So, she needed to fight him at every turn because
she couldn't lose, not now, not when she had nothing left
and no one in her court except her aunt's lawyer. She had
to stand up to him.

He finished with the viewer and set it down by the slide
box. Now he was glaring at her again. The toad was back.

"Please leave." Addie purposely stuck her nose up, so
she'd feel taller, and grasping her robe she swished by him
in a starched, regal manner that was the exact opposite of
what she felt inside. Inside, she felt like soggy bread.

"I'm not going to leave. It's my land, legally."

Addie spun around, ready to start again, but he was leaning against the wall, as if he owned the place.

"In fact, Miss Pinky . . ."

He paused, and she knew he was waiting for her to correct him. She gave him a sugary smile.

He shrugged, suddenly calm as a toad in the sun, and he looked around the room. Pushing away from the wall with his boot, he strolled around the parlor, stopping here and there to scrutinize a particular item.

"What are you doing?" she asked, puzzled and worried because she couldn't figure out what he had planned.

He walked over to the mantel and ran his finger over the bronze top of a cupid's wreath clock. "I'm just looking at my property."

"It's not yours!"

He ignored her. "I'm going to like living here. It's all . . . homey." He picked up a thick, leather-bound book that Addie had noticed last night. It was a copy of *Nutall's Standard Dictionary of the English Language*.

She watched him skim through it. "Don't bother. Most of the words have more than four letters."

He didn't look up, didn't acknowledge her. He slowly closed the book and turned around to put it back on the mantel. He tilted his hat back with a casual nudge of his thumb, then he spoke, "Well, crap, damn, and hell, Miss Pinky, you're right."

He got her, every time. Sauntering over to a small walnut table, he stopped and picked up an English majolica vase. It was trimmed in gold and midnight-blue and had pink raised flowers and green leaves. He frowned at her. "Can't stand this gaudy stuff though. You can take this with you when you leave."

"I'm not leaving."

"We'll see." He reached up and pulled down the polished bronze hanging lamp and examined the dust-covered glass dome, shaking his long-haired head. Then he eyed the crystal prisms that fringed the globe before flicking them with his fingers. The glass pinged like chimes in the wind, and he nodded. "Nice. Very nice."

For a brief, angry instant, Addie wondered if hanging for murder could possibly be so bad.

Now he strolled toward the bedroom, so she scurried after him. "Get out!"

Again he ignored her, walking over to the iron bed, still unmade. He stared at it, then looked around the room, his gaze landing on each item of disarray. He looked at her trunk, open and draped with clothing. Her shoes were piled nearby and all of her farm books were stacked in front of the mirrored armoire. Next he zeroed in on the pile of clothes she had tossed on the floor last night. Her drawers were on top.

He bent and picked them up by the waist ties, dangling them out in front of him. "Yours?" He smirked.

She jerked them out of his hand and, face flaming, stuffed them in her robe.

He waved his hand around the messy room. "Sloppy little thing, aren't you?" His look was just as goading as his words. "Didn't your mama teach you to have more respect for other people's property?"

Addie just glared at him, not willing to let him know he was getting to her.

He shrugged and turned, tossing his hat on the still-rumpled bed pillows. Apparently it was now the bed's turn. Ornamented in gold, with enameling in black japan, it sat there, innocently. He ran his hand over the brass top knobs and then sat on the plump mattress, bouncing slightly to test its softness.

"Feathers. Real comfortable. I'll sleep great in here." With that he lolled back against the pillows, locking his hands behind his head and making a big to-do about crossing his booted ankles, complete with spurs which dug into the crocheted coverlet—her aunt's crocheted coverlet.

That did it. Without a thought, Addie grabbed the washbasin, still filled with last night's cold wash water, and she baptized the toad.

"Goddammit!" He swiped his long, dripping wet hair off his purple face.

"Sleep well, Mr. Creed!" Then Addie and the basin made for the kitchen.

*　　*　　*

Montana stopped in the bedroom doorway, dripping. He took aim and shot the hanging lamp from the ceiling. It crashed to the floor. That stopped her, but then so had the bullets in the kitchen door, and she'd recovered from that episode. She turned around, dropped the basin, and what little color she had drained away. Her eyes locked on the gun, then she looked right at him. He was sure that this time his plan had worked, and he'd scared the hell out of her. He didn't smile with satisfaction, although he felt like it. Instead he shook his wet hair out of his face, then slowly walked toward her, the gun aimed right at her chest.

It was working. He had her good and frightened, if her wide eyes were any indication. She backed up slowly, until she had backed out onto the porch. She stopped suddenly and looked around, as if surprised to be outside again.

Then she turned back, looked at the house, then at him. Her eyes turned black with determination and she did the strangest thing. Instead of stepping back, like a fearful woman should, she stepped toward him. He couldn't believe her. Suddenly, as if the air outside had fortified her, she didn't appear the least bit frightened. She just looked right at him with those unreadable black eyes of hers.

"You will not drive me off *my* land. Here's another four-letter word for you, Mr. Creed. Mine. The farm is *mine*." Her look was pure determination.

He raised the gun higher. She just stared at him, as if he had no gun and wasn't threatening her at all. Her reaction made him stop and think. She'd been so skittish before, Montana had assumed she'd be easy to frighten. She wasn't, or at least she didn't show it now. He eyed her, assessing her face, her huge, dark eyes, anything that would give him a clue to her fear. Still nothing, no hint of fear. He'd bet she played poker. No one could be so unintimidated by a loaded gun. He'd better push her a little more.

"My deed isn't a fake. Get off my land." He took one step closer.

"No. I won't leave."

She stared him down; he closed the gap. Now they stood

eye to eye, she on his porch and he in his doorway. The Pinky woman still appeared to have no fear of him.

Just to remind her, he lifted the gun.

She didn't even blink. He moved closer, but deep inside it gave him the chills, the way this woman acted as if his gun couldn't harm her, couldn't end her life in a fast second.

Slowly, he placed the gun barrel against her chest. *That ought to scare her.*

"Go ahead." She smiled at him. It was an icy smile, a poker smile.

Damn stubborn woman. His teeth clamped together, hard. His shoulders tightened under his wet shirt and he could feel his neck veins throb, could feel his blood race and pump through his body. Seconds crawled by. It was as if she had turned to stone. With her eyes, her look, her stillness, she challenged him. And he didn't dare blink. He wanted her to do it first.

Slowly, ever so slowly, he drew the gun barrel up an inch, then another. She didn't flinch. With deliberate slowness he traced her collarbone with the barrel, dragging the cold metal sight over her skin. Her lips parted.

He trailed the gun up her white, white neck, pausing right on the bluish spot where her pulse beat. She licked her lips. His gaze dropped to those lips, heart-shaped, full, and now moist from the only nervous action she'd displayed.

The air sizzled and as they stared, fire darts of tension shot all around them. Mistrust, desperation, intensity, and something odd—something akin to passion—seemed to crackle above them, like green wood in a camp fire.

Montana could feel the sunlight glare onto the house. It beat against the left side of his face. He began to sweat, but it wasn't from the sun. There was a thrill in the battle with this woman, something intense and powerful, almost sexual. Her expression defied him, invited him to counter her. It was a provocation, and his mind flashed with the image of her . . . under him.

"Do it."

Do it? He blinked. *Dammit.*

"Pull the trigger," she dared in a whisper.

He blinked again, and she smiled a winner's smile. Beaten for the moment, he lowered the gun and shoved it into his gun belt. Then he stood there a moment more, watching the triumphant grin on her small face. She'd won.

He jerked the dripping hat off his head and threw it as he stormed past her. His brand-new, wet Stetson hit the dusty, dry ground with a hollow thud. He stomped down the stairs and all around the hat, a cloud of orange dirt drifting up in his wake and then settling on its damp crown.

"Damn hard-headed female!" Back and forth he paced, trying to vent his frustration. "She's crazy, damn fool crazy," he mumbled, madder than hell at her for beating him. Then he stopped and glared at her.

She smirked back. Finally he could see her thoughts reflected in her eyes. She had that *I've bested him* look, and he didn't like it.

"You're crazy, lady." He shook his head. "You could have been killed."

Her smile disappeared and she shrugged. "I have no one, and nothing to lose."

He just stood there, contemplating her words. Jesus, he thought, she was as desperate as he. No wonder she didn't fear him. She was alone with nothing to lose, just like him. Or she was bluffing. Whatever, she'd earned a notch of his respect. He watched her for a second or so, reassessing his rival. It was obvious that she wasn't going to back down. He'd have to find another way to run her off. A threat with a gun wouldn't do it. She was a worthy adversary, determined, stubborn, and willing to take risks, a good poker player. But so was he, and he'd have to call her bluff.

He spun around and headed straight for the big red barn. He went around the back and untied his horse, Jericho, and walked to the edge of the barn. She wasn't on the porch, so he figured she must have gone back inside. He rounded the corner of the barn, leading his horse back to the oak tree. He could see the Pinky woman, peering through the flowery-edged curtains, watching him.

He decided to put on a show. He flipped up the saddlebag

flap and began to unpack, dropping a few small things onto the ground.

The window squeaked open.

"What are you doing?" she yelled.

He untied his bedroll and then pulled out a bundle of clothes wrapped in a red union suit he wore on cold winter nights.

"Answer me!"

He continued to ignore her and untied the clothes. The window slammed shut. Montana picked up the union suit and held it up in the air, where he knew she couldn't miss it. She now stood in the broken doorway. He watched her, around his longjohns, shaking them some more. She stepped, tentatively, onto the porch, then she paused while he fiddled with the buttons on the backflap of the longjohns. She walked to the porch railing and he turned the under-wear this way and that, letting her get the full effect.

He'd just let her think she won, lull her into a state of confidence. He shook out the union suit and hung it over the low branches of the oak tree, where it couldn't be missed. Its bright color would wave like a red flag when there was a breeze. He smiled at the image.

She padded down the porch steps, barefoot, and did her best to march toward him. Bending over, he pulled a clean shirt—a dry one with buttons—from his clothes bundle, and watched her out of the corner of his eye. The wrap thing she wore flapped behind her, and her nightdress clung to her legs. It outlined them perfectly. He straightened. Now this was getting interesting.

Carefully, she tiptoed over the gravel of the front drive, hopping once or twice when her bare foot hit a stone. That was even more interesting since when she'd reached down to grab her foot, Montana could see her legs, clear up to the knees. She looked up, scowling, and then followed his gaze to her exposed leg. She jerked down the gown, stuck her nose up, and closed the few feet between them.

While she heaved her indignant self forward, Montana made a big deal of shaking out each of his clean shirts. She had nice legs, although they weren't very long since she was such a little thing.

She stopped in front of him. "What are you doing?"

Silent, he took off his shirt and dropped it onto his pile. Then he turned around. Her belligerent face stared up at him. She was so short her stubborn chin was about even with his chest hair. Purposely, he took a deep breath and heard her gasp.

"Unpacking," he finally answered while he shrugged on the other shirt and unbuckled his gun belt, tossing it over his saddle. He undid the buttons on his fly and watched her face flame.

"Stop!"

He flicked open the last button. "No."

She spun around. "You can't stay here!"

He tucked in his shirt, all the while smiling at her indignant back. Stepping around her, he headed for his saddlebags. "If you can stay here, so can I." He pulled out a pair of denims and shook them. They snapped in the morning air with the same tone as his answer.

Now she faced him, her hands landed on her hips. "You are not staying in my house."

He glanced over his shoulder. "You're right, I'm not staying in my house. I'm going to be a gentleman."

She snorted.

"You can stay in my house, Miss Pinky." He removed a piece of canvas from the bag.

"Knee, Pink-ney!"

He got her.

"Where are you staying?"

"Right here." He shook out the canvas and then pulled out his tent stakes. Within a matter of minutes he had erected a small canvas tent. She still stood there, silently fuming.

He uncinched his saddle and pulled up the stirrups, hooking them over the horn. Then he lifted the saddle and turned, calculating just what height to hold it so it barely missed her hard head. She ducked anyway.

He hid his smile and dropped his saddle on the ground near the head of the tent. He was having a good time, egging this little woman on, more fun than he'd had in a long time. He turned, planning to mispronounce her name again, but his horse nickered and nosed over to munch on some new grass near her feet. Before he could say a thing, the Pinky woman gasped and ran hellhound for the porch.

Montana stared at the empty spot where she had stood only a moment before. He glanced at Jericho, grazing peacefully beneath the oak.

She was afraid of his horse.

He chuckled. Hooking his fingers into his belt loops, he rocked back on his boot heels, grinning like a weasel at the henhouse door. One nudge from his gentle old horse could do in one minute what all his blustering and bluffing couldn't. Here was a woman who could stare down a gun barrel and dare him to shoot her, but good old Jericho scared the hell out of her.

He walked over and picked up his hat, dusting it off. He stopped and flicked at the mud on its crown before he walked back to his camp, mulling over this new information. He was desperate to keep this farm. He had to drive that woman away, and he wasn't opposed to playing upon her weakness to do it. But she was a smart one, and he'd have to think about this. He needed to use her fear to his best advantage.

That was how to win in life. One had to bide his time, take however much time was necessary to appraise an adversary, and use that time, whether it be hours or years—whatever was needed to lull the enemy into a sense of security. Then go for the throat. Get them right in their weakest spot.

But right here and now, he needed to think and he needed some strong black coffee to turn the wheels of his mind. He started a fire, then poured water from his canteen into the small, graniteware coffeepot he carried with him. Rummaging through his chuck bag, he found the Arbuckle sack and threw a handful of the coarse, black grounds into the pot. Then he sat down, leaning against the sturdy oak and waiting for his coffee. Time was his.

When the coffee was done, he poured some in his tin cup and sipped it, his eyes now appraising Jericho, who was still munching on the grass nearby. He glanced at the farmhouse, and then his horse. He eyed the doors and windows, then his horse. He stared at the porch, and then at his horse. Leaning back against the hard oak tree again, he drank the coffee and rubbed his chin. It might possibly work . . .

The toad was right, she was crazy. She had just done the craziest thing of her life. She had no idea where she'd dug up the nerve to stand there and have a staredown with a gun.

It was his fault. If he wasn't so . . . irritating, she'd have probably acted more rationally, maybe bargained with him. Instead, he pricked a devil within her that just made her want to anger him. No, anger was too mild a word. What she wanted to do was stick in his craw, like a month-old biscuit.

But why? What was it about him that made her want to drive him crazy? Probably his attitude. Never had Addie been able to tolerate someone with a superior attitude. It grated on her. That was what destroyed her position at the library. Hilary's attitude had become so intolerable for Addie that she just had to fight back. For some reason this Mr. Creed scratched that same spot of irritability in her.

In each of their three encounters she had felt challenged, as if he were daring her. And finally she had to stop backing away. But that wonderful deep voice would be her downfall if she didn't watch it. She'd practiced ignoring it, which was much easier when he shouted at her. It was when he spoke without cynicism or anger that she let her guard down.

He is your enemy, she reminded herself. He wanted her land and he had the chance to take it away, too good a chance for her to just lie back and trust that justice would be served. She needed to fight, to ensure that she would get the farm. She had to; she had nothing else, nowhere else to go. All she had left was determination, and nothing, not a gun nor a gun-toting madman, was going to chase her away.

His horrible horse chased me away. Addie groaned. The huge animal had nudged her foot, and she didn't even think. She just reacted, like she always did when one of those deadly animals made a sudden move. She ran as if the devil were after her, that devil of a horse.

She shivered and rubbed away the chills that flickered through her arms. It had been a pair of horses that killed her father. A raging team of eight deadly hooves that snuffed out all the light in Addie's youth. Her father had been everything to both her and her mother. They adored him, and he never abused that adoration. He had always loved them and never ceased to show that love in his every action and every word.

Not one day that Addie could ever remember had her father not told her how much he loved her. His teasing, his charm and wit had taught her to laugh. It was on his secure lap that he'd first showed her the rain ring that sometimes framed the moon. He called it a rain ring because, he told her, the ring meant it would rain soon. Addie could remember watching for the rain, and sure enough, three days later a storm had come blustering through the city.

It was on that same secure lap that Addie'd learned the power of prayer, the gift of knowledge, and the ideal that nothing was beyond her reach, if she really wanted it. Her father had taught her that if she wanted something, she should go after it. Nothing kept you from succeeding except yourself, he'd said. Self-doubt was the one obstacle man constantly creates. And it's what keeps man, or woman— he'd laughed at her frown—from achieving his or her dreams.

But even self-determination could not bring back the father whose wife and daughter had been his world, a happy world that had died on a cold Sunday in February. Her parents had dropped Addie off at a skating party, then planned to go for a sleigh ride in the park. They never made it. A skittish pair of horses had run wild, overturning a wagon and dragging it into her parents' buggy. The animals didn't stop; her father didn't live. He died, slowly, in agonizing pain, and her mother, crippled forever, had been forced to live a lonely twelve years confined to a husband-less home.

Financially, she and her mother had been comfortable. They owned the flat in Bishoptown, a middle-class section of Chicago. They could even hire care for her mother, who was insistent upon Addie continuing her education. While she attended college, they'd hired a woman to care for her mother. Her father had left them secure enough to afford a few luxuries, one of which was college for Addie. Her mother had said it was what her father would have wanted.

But when Addie graduated, with honors, she'd been alone. Her mother couldn't travel to New York; her weak condition wouldn't have allowed it. So she had received her degree as part of the third graduating class of Dewey's Library School at Columbia University, but she was the only one in her class who graduated alone, with no relations to look proud, no congratulatory hugs, only the hope that maybe her father was watching, was with her in soul if not body. It was that thought that always kept her going, drove her spirit.

She wondered what he would have thought of her today, standing up to a loaded gun. Those chills got her again. Sometimes she amazed herself with the bounds of her own gumption.

The smell of smoke seeped through the walls of the farm-house, and she pulled back the curtains, peering out at the toad. He had started a camp fire, under her aunt's tree. She frowned and watched as he poured some coffee from a gray-speckled graniteware pot. Then he lounged back against the gnarled tree trunk, sticking those endless legs of his out in front of him as if he was just as comfortable as could be.

He sipped his coffee. It was obvious that he wasn't going to leave. She released the curtains, pausing to brush the wrinkles left from crunching up the printed muslin in her tight fist. There was no reason to damage her belongings just because the toad was out there.

Two could play at this game. She'd just go along her merry way, doing what she'd have done if he'd not found her. Which reminded her. How did he find out she was here? She paced across the dusty plank floor. He must have seen her leave with Custus and her trunks and realized what she intended. In the future she'd have to be sneakier—no . . . *discreet* was a better word. She'd be more discreet.

He was a sharp one, but she would not allow him to take what was hers. It was hers; Aunt Emily wanted her to have it. After all, he'd started this land war, and she'd make good and sure he got his fill of battles.

She glanced down. She wasn't dressed for war. She was still in her bedclothes, and she needed to get going on this neglected house. She'd get dressed and working. But first she sneaked a peek outside, through the opening in the curtains. She was reconnoitering the enemy. He still sat there propping up the tree, and all over the tree's thick and knobby branches were his clothes; in particular, one set of bright red longjohns that waved like a knight's battle standard from her aunt Emily's wonderful old tree.

4

By noon the sun was high, hanging in the sky like a plump spiced peach. A few clouds, fluffy and white as marshmallow creme, floated slowly across a California sky that was the exact same color as fresh blueberry ice cream. In the distance golden breadloaf-shaped foothills sliced through the western edge of the valley, where fields of butter-yellow grain stood proud. At the base of the hills giant oak trees sprouted up like clusters of dark green broccoli.

Addie was starved.

She closed the back door and glanced around the empty pantry, admitting to herself that she was not half as bright as she'd thought. In her haste to sneak out to the farm, she'd forgotten about food, and there was none in the farmhouse. She went to the kitchen pump, her third trip in the last five minutes, and she drew another cup of water, hoping it would assuage the gnawing in her stomach. Her mind flashed with the image of the Chicago bakery wagon and its doughnuts—the ones that had rolled down Randolph Street. What she wouldn't give for a doughnut right now, even a crumb. She sipped the water and stood at the sinkboard, trying to block out the food images that plagued her mind.

After a few long seconds of staring out the open window, Addie's eyes were drawn to her aunt's tree. Hanging from the lower branches were at least a dozen pieces of that man's clothing, the most prominent piece being those red longjohns, and he sat just below them, with one of his long legs drawn up, an arm casually resting on his knee. He looked at home, and that, more than anything, disturbed her. His faded, blue-checked shirt, the worn denim pants, the muddy hat, all were the image of a western man. Even the dusty boots fit him, looked right on him.

Good Lord. What was she doing? Gawking at her enemy and softening? She was slipping, letting her guard down, and that wouldn't do. She had to remember his goal—it was the same as hers; he wanted the farm. She had to remember how he had tried to scare her off, had even shot at her until she called his bluff. She had to remember how he'd acted, rough and obnoxious, with the manners of a toad—a term that fit him just like those boots.

Addie's black eyes narrowed with renewed anger as she watched him rise, rummage through his pack and pull something out. He went straight to his camp fire and squatted, stoking it up with a small stick.

Oh no . . . She moaned. He had a pot. He was going to cook something.

Rising on tiptoe, she tried to get a gander at what he was tossing in a small black kettle. *It's probably a few flies— toad food.* Of course at this very moment she'd eat about anything. A minute later Addie groaned. It was bacon— sizzling, smoky bacon. She closed her eyes and breathed in the smell. Her stomach rumbled. He strolled over to a small sack and pulled out a tin can. Beans, she thought, noticing a red and yellow label. Fat little beans in a thick, brown sauce . . . She chugged down another tasteless cup of water.

The smell of bacon and beans wafted into the room and her mouth began to water. Sweet and savory, the aroma drew her, and she leaned toward the window, gripping the sash and licking her lips. Her stomach growled again. She wanted those beans, wanted to wolf them down. But they were his, so she wanted to cry. She slammed the window shut and marched into the parlor, intent upon continuing her cleaning, to take her mind off food. Instead she scoured the room, searching for something edible.

She could still smell it, the fragrance of his meal, now seeping through the broken doorway. She turned and moved toward it. Standing in the shadows of the house, she looked out longingly. There had to be a way to get some of those beans.

Her pride wouldn't let her ask for them, but maybe she could barter. She turned around and tried to think of something she had, that he didn't, something he needed . . .

She marched in the bedroom and over to the oak washstand, where she snatched up a black leather shaving case. She snapped open the case and noted the contents. Inside were a man's comb and brush; he certainly needed those. A nickel-plated lather brush sat next to a celluloid soap box and a straight razor and strop. She remembered his thick, reddish-brown mustache and the scruffy shadow of hair on his face that was beyond stubble and wasn't quite beard, just hairy. He needed these things too.

A buttonhook sat next to a small whisk broom. He wouldn't need the hook since he wore those leather boots. Somehow, Addie couldn't picture those infinite legs of his ending in high-top, button shoes. But then she had no business "picturing" him in any way, except long gone from her farm.

Her stomach growled a protest. She'd delayed too long, thinking when she should be getting her hands on that food. She noted the last few items, the tooth and nail brushes, a small can of peppermint tooth powder, and a bottle of bay rum hair oil, but one necessary item was missing. There was no mirror. She paused, her face thoughtful. No mirror? Hmmm . . . If he tried to shave without one, maybe he'd slit his throat. Then her problems would be over. She smiled. It made her feel better, even if she couldn't really do something like that. Besides, didn't toads have green blood?

Rummaging through the top drawers of a dresser, she found a round, nickel mirror with a folding handle. It was perfect. Now she had her bartering booty. At the porch steps she slowed down. It wouldn't do to look too eager. She relaxed her hold on her booty, suddenly aware that she had been clutching it to her breast like a sackful of rare oranges. She needed a plan here, but unfortunately she'd have to think fast because he'd already spotted her.

She approached him, her march now a casual stroll. Her deep forest-green skirt swished around her legs as she sauntered over, making sure she kept plenty of distance between herself and his grazing horse. She told herself to act as if they were casual acquaintances, just meeting at church. She moved closer and the mouth-watering smell of beans almost brought tears to her eyes.

She stopped in front of him, trying not to lick her lips. He still squatted in front of his camp fire, stirring those wonderful beans. She forced her eyes away from the pot and held out the mirror.

He ladled the beans into a tin plate and she almost groaned aloud.

"Here." She held out the mirror even farther.

He stopped ladling and looked up, not saying a word, but staring at the mirror.

He was not going to make this easy, but she had to have those beans, so she took a deep breath and said, "I thought you might need this."

His gold eyes burned into her. "Why would I need a mirror? I know what I look like."

Lord, give me patience. Addie wanted to hit him over the head with the mirror. It would give her such pleasure. But then she wouldn't get the food, unless she grabbed it and ran. Her mind flashed with the delightful image of her bopping him, grabbing the beans and running. She couldn't do it though, because there was no way on earth she'd let him know just how badly she wanted that food.

She swallowed a small chunk of her pride. "These were

my uncle's. I have no use for them and thought you might. Maybe we could work out a trade."

He appeared enthralled by his food, and shoveled another spoonful into his mouth before asking, "What's in the case?"

"Toiletries."

He coughed. "What?"

"Toiletries," she pronounced slowly, as if she were speaking to Rip Van Winkle just awakening from his twenty-year nap. "You know, tooth powder, soap and a razor, hair oil . . ."

He grunted, then set down those precious beans and stood. It was all she could do not to drop the case and grab the plate. She could almost taste them now . . .

He took the case and snapped it open. "What sort of trade?"

Addie pulled her eyes away from the bean kettle. "Oh, I don't know. Maybe . . . uh, well, is there something you might have too much of?" She refused to look at those beans, so she looked at him. It was a mistake, because he pinned her with a stare that almost went right through her. She had the strangest feeling he could see her thoughts as clear as the California sky.

From the case he pulled out the straight razor and turned it this way and that, letting the sunlight glare off the bright stainless steel.

"I can't think of a thing I could trade." He slid the razor back into the case and then rubbed the hairy stubble that probably hid a weak chin.

The beans! You have too many beans! Addie bit down on her tongue to keep from shouting at him.

"The only thing that comes to mind is that measly pot of beans . . ."

Thank you, God!

". . . But then a city lady like yourself would never eat plain old canned beans." He shook his shaggy head.

"Yes I wou—" She stopped midword. She'd almost given herself away. "I mean, if that's all you have, I suppose I'll have to take them." There, she thought, that was casual enough.

61

"Nope." He heaved a heavy sigh. "I couldn't take advantage of you that way."

"But—"

He held his hand up in her face. "No, no, something this valuable, well, I just wouldn't feel right."

His face suddenly took on a look of pure integrity, underscored by a bit of stubbornness. The look assured her that her trade idea wasn't going to work; she'd have to be sneakier.

"Maybe we could find something else, to add to the beans. . . ." Her hungry eyes lit up. "That's it! I'll take the beans and something else. Now that's fair."

"Well, I don't know, Miss Pinky."

Addie clamped her teeth together, trying to keep from correcting him again. After all, she needed to be amiable.

"Just look the case over. I'm sure you can find something else to trade. Her eyes were drawn to his plate, almost full of beans and lying on the ground, lonely and forgotten and probably cold, but she didn't care. "Take your time."

She moved closer to the tree trunk. This isn't going well, she thought, pushing the flapping arm of a shirt away from her head. She needed some insurance. The plate still sat there. She watched him out of the corner of her eye. He seemed oblivious to her. She stepped back closer to the tree, and the plate. As he examined the shaving kit, she scooted right in mincing little steps, until her left shoe just touched the rim of the tin plate. Very slowly, she pushed the plate closer to the side of the tree. It stopped against one of the nubby roots that protruded from the ground. She swore silently.

She gave him a quick furtive glance. He was unscrewing the hair-oil bottle. She turned slightly, and with a quick flick of her pointed-toe shoe, lobbed the plate over the root and behind the tree.

"Phew!"

Addie spun around, sure she'd been caught.

He was scowling. "Now I understand why they call this stuff 'toiletries.' It smells like it belongs in a toilet."

"Most gentlemen like bay rum. We ladies find it pleasant," Addie informed him in a superior manner that covered up her fear of being discovered.

He snapped the case closed. "Well, I'm not a 'gentleman' . . ."

No, you're a toad.

". . . And I don't want to be one if I have to smell like a sissy. You can keep it." He set the case down and moved toward the tree. He was heading for the place where he'd set down the beans, her beans. She stepped up on the root, hoping her skirt would help to protect her hiding place. She'd had it now. Her humiliation was complete. He would know that she was trying to swipe his food.

But a second later she was saved. A buggy rattled up the drive and captured his attention. Addie sagged back against the tree trunk and blew out the breath she'd been holding.

Her lawyer, Levi Hamilton, drove, and his passenger was the other lawyer, Wade Parker. Levi reined in the buggy.

"So this is where you two are," he said, sounding annoyed. "We've been trying to find you all morning!" He bobbled down and walked right past Mr. Creed and straight toward her. He was supposed to be on her side, but right now he didn't look too happy.

She had better explain why she'd left the hotel, especially since in her rush to get out here, she'd completely forgotten about him.

"I thought I'd have a better chance before the judge if I was already living here, but I had no idea he'd do the same." Addie pointed an accusing finger at Montana, who was deep in conversation with Mr. Parker.

Levi took her arm and led her toward the other two men. "The judge was here this morning—"

"Oh good!" She interrupted, picking up her pace. "Just give me a minute and we can leave. What do you think my chances are? Do you think he'll rule in my favor?"

Mr. Hamilton stopped her.

"He's already ruled." The comment came from Wade Parker. He stood with his client by the buggy.

Her stomach dropped. She looked from her lawyer, who

nodded, back at the two tall men. Oh God, she thought, he's won.

She turned to Levi and asked so quietly her words were almost whispered, "Who won?"

"Both of you."

"What?" Addie and Montana shouted in unison.

"He found you both had legal claims," Wade Parker explained.

"So what are we supposed to do?" Montana asked sarcastically. "Pretend we're Solomon and slice the place in half?"

"The judge already did that," Levi answered. "In fact, that's one of the reasons we're here." He gestured to Wade. "As your attorneys, we have to inventory each client's holdings to submit for the court's records."

"What did I get?" Addie asked, dying to know but scared at the answer.

"The buildings," Levi answered with a satisfied smile.

Addie's heart jumped. She'd won! She'd been awarded her aunt's property!

"Then what the hell did I get?" Montana shouted.

"The land."

She hadn't won. He had, and when she caught a glimpse of him, she could read on his angry face the same confusion she felt.

Wade explained. "Miss Pinkney, you own the farmhouse and Mr. Creed owns the land. Montana, you own the water, but she owns the well. She owns the fences, but you own the pasture. She owns the barn, windmill, chicken yard, and so on, but you own the land on which they sit. The orchard is divided equally, as will be any crops grown in the fields."

"But the fields are mine! Goddammit! Wade, this land is mine. She has no right to it. How could any judge in his right mind come up with something so damn stupid?"

"It's not stupid!" Addie shouted back. "It's very fair, and wise." She was so happy she'd gotten the place, even if it was only the buildings. At least she could live here, in her aunt's home. She didn't have to leave, and that was such a relief because she had been really worried she'd lose and have no place to go. She wasn't quite strong enough to face that prospect, and now she wouldn't have to.

Addie looked at Mr. Creed's red face and yellow eyes, glaring at her as if he could melt her. She couldn't stop herself from goading him. "I'm perfectly happy with the decision."

"Well, if I were you Miss Pinky, I would be too. You've just stolen my farm!"

"Knee! Pink-ney! And it's mine! Even the judge thought so!" She planted her fists on her hips and glared back at him, giving him her most scathing look.

He rudely turned his back on her. "When can we appeal?"

Mr. Parker looked uncomfortable. "The circuit judge won't be back in this area until after the first of the year."

"That's eight months!" Montana jerked his hat off his head and slammed it to the ground, just as he'd done earlier, only this time he swore through his teeth. "Son of a bitch!"

Then he did the most awful thing. He stormed over to his simmering camp fire and kicked over the pot of beans. She watched in famished horror as they spilled over the fire, the rich brown sauce steaming and sizzling before it bled into the dry dirt. Instinctively she hugged her middle, as if she were protecting her poor empty stomach from the appalling sight. The palm of her right hand began to rub her stomach soothingly.

There was still the plate, hidden behind the tree. Her stomach growled as if in relief.

Mr. Parker had walked over and was speaking quietly to his client, their backs turned toward Addie and Levi, who had been strangely quiet during all this. She turned to him. "Thank you."

His expression changed from one of uncertainty to a cream-whiskered grin. "I'm glad you're happy. I don't know how the judge would have decided this case if you two had been there." He shook his balding head. "We took him right over to the hotel the first thing this morning, but neither of you were there. We looked around, but the judge had to be in Stockton by this afternoon and Angel's Camp tonight, so he insisted on trying the case with only Wade and myself serving as your representatives. We might have won, Addie, had you been there."

"He could have won too." She nodded to the other men. "Maybe I can buy him out. I was willing to do that before."

"Farming isn't easy."

"I'll hire help if I have to, but I'm staying. Besides, I figure to start out slowly, restocking the farm. I can get by just raising chickens at first."

"Okay, then we might as well get on with the inventory." Levi turned and asked Wade if he was ready to start. Mr. Creed came with Wade.

Levi turned to Addie. "You want to come along while we do this?"

"I am." Mr. Creed crossed his arms and pinned her with his "dare you" look.

Her stomach rumbled, reminding her of the hidden beans. "I trust *my* lawyer. All I need is a written copy of the inventory. I have things to do." *Food to swipe.*

She watched them head for the barn, and after an agonizing few minutes they disappeared.

Now was her chance.

Addie spun around and made for the tree, only to go about five feet and then stop dead in her tracks. His horse was nibbling on the grass right next to her beans.

"Dadgummit!" she swore.

The horse glanced up, giving her an annoyed look.

"Shoo! Horsey! Shoo!" She waved her hands in front of her, hoping the horse would take the hint. He didn't; he just kept gnawing closer and closer to the plate.

She panicked and bent down, grabbing a handful of gravel from the nearby drive. She fingered a few of the pebbles.

"Shoo! Shoo!" She tossed a couple pebbles near him.

He moved closer to the plate.

She clamped her teeth together and tossed the rest of the gravel right at the horse's backside.

He looked up, narrowed his big brown eyes, and stuck his muzzle right in her plate of beans. He ate; she groaned.

He licked his fat, pink lips, and her stomach shriveled like a raisin. Then the cruel brown devil lapped at the plate with his giant tongue and nonchalantly gazed up at her. He smacked those fat, freckled pink lips right at her.

It was almost more than she could take. She rubbed her face with her hands, as if she could erase the whole incident. Just as defeat began to creep through her, she remembered. There was one last hope.

She walked over to the small pot, lying on its side in the dirt. She grasped the handle and peered inside. One lone bean stared back. She sighed and reached in to pick it up, but something zipped past her face and landed right in the pot—on the bean. It was a big, black fly.

Toad food.

It was four o'clock, three long hours since Levi Hamilton had left with Addie's supply list. After the men had finished their inventory, she had cornered Levi and explained her food problem. He'd offered to take the list to town and have her supplies delivered that afternoon, but the afternoon was almost over.

She stepped out onto the porch and looked eastward, toward the road. Still nothing. She walked along the porch that ran across the front of the farmhouse, making sure she didn't look at the tree. She'd had enough of that man for one day. Rounding the corner of the farmhouse, she spotted the woodpile. There were two stacks of wood, a large pile of split logs perfect for the fireplace, and next to it, a smaller stack of stove wood.

Since the food was coming, Addie figured she might as well get the stove fired up; that way her meal would be ready all that much faster. She went over to the smaller pile and began to fill her arms with wood. She'd gathered only a few pieces when she felt it—the burn of his eyes. He was watching her.

She forced herself to concentrate on gathering the wood and she kept filling her arms, until her chin held the last piece in place. She turned and caught him out of the corner of her eye. He stood by his horrid horse. And he stared.

Moving with exaggerated indifference, Addie made her

way to the back door, not an easy task. It was hard to see with her chin propped on top of the wood, and nigh on impossible for her to look down. She lifted her foot and felt around for the bottom step. Once she had her foot firmly atop the step, she pushed up. She made it. Only three steps to go, but she could still feel his eyes on her. It was as if he were waiting for her to fall or drop the wood. The thought made her all that more determined not to do either one, even though she realized now that she'd overloaded her small arms.

Pretend they're books, she told herself, stepping up one more wooden step. That was it. She needed to pretend they were heavy books, like encyclopedia. She had always amazed the library staff with her ability to juggle the heaviest stacks of books. So she called on that talent now, when her pride needed it the most. It was tough though because she was out of practice, so she leaned her right shoulder against the wooden siding on the house and made it up one more.

There was only one left. Taking a deep breath, she put her foot on the porch platform and pushed upward.

She made it.

It was the sudden applause, snapping loudly from the direction of the tree, that made her drop the wood.

"Dadgummit!" She turned and glared at him, the wood sticks scattered around her feet like pages from an unbound book.

The rich deep sound of his laughter filled the farmyard. Addie bent down and picked up a few pieces of wood. It helped to hide the red she could feel flooding her cheeks. When she straightened, he was walking toward her, still chuckling, and leading that devil of a horse of his. The horse plodded along behind him, looking innocent but full. All that horse had done since she first saw it was eat, something she hadn't done since midday yesterday. They ambled by and the horse looked right at her and snorted.

She spun around and went inside, dropping the wood into an empty box by the stove. She went back outside to gather the rest of her spilled wood, and she saw where they were heading. The sated horse stood at the empty water trough while his owner began to work the pump—her pump.

Holding one of the stove sticks up to her forehead to shade the setting sun, Addie yelled, "What do you think you're doing?"

"Watering Jericho." He kept right on pumping while the rusty pump sputtered and burped a small trickle of brown water.

"Stop! Stop it, I say!"

He ignored her and pumped away.

She tossed a piece of wood at his feet, and his horse shied.

He pinned her with an angry, cold glare. "What the hell do you think *you're* doing?"

"Get away from my pump!"

"Like hell. It's my water!"

"But it's my pump and my trough."

"How am I supposed to water my horse?"

"I really don't care how, but you will not use my pump." She crossed her arms and stuck her nose up, looking down at him with what she hoped was the same smug look he'd worn. "Maybe you should dig your own well, Mr. Creed, or find a convenient river."

She picked up the last few pieces of wood. "If you wish to lease the use of my well, you can contact Mr. Hamilton, and after we set a price, he can draw up a contract. Until that time, you cannot use my pump. Should you try to use it without my permission, I will have you arrested for appropriating my property. Good day!" With a swift kick, Addie closed her door behind her, shutting out the string of curses that filled the farmyard.

5

It was late in the afternoon, and still the temperature must have been ninety. Montana dumped the last of
his canteen into a tin plate. He set it on the grass in front
of the tree and watched as Jericho lapped it up.

"Dig your own well," he mimicked. "As if digging a new
well was as easy as licking butter off a knife." He paced
around the tree, slapping a flannel shirt out of his way and
ducking beneath a low branch. Hell, he thought, the job
would take a good two days with a well-digger.

They needed water, so he'd have to sneak over at night,
when she was asleep. He'd steal his own water just like
she'd tried to steal his beans. He'd seen her eyeing the
beans, even heard her stomach growl like thunder. He
smiled at the memory of toying with her when she was
trying to be so smooth. She'd been as obvious as a prosti-
tute in church.

It hadn't taken him long to figure out that she had no
food, none at all, and it made his day. He needed something
to make his day since it had already been so bad. No judge
in his right mind should have considered her claim legitimate. The land was legally his. He had the deed, the legal
deed, and still the damn court upheld her stupid claim. It
wasn't his fault that her aunt and uncle had been duped. It
wasn't his fault they'd picked Doc's land for a farm. They'd
been using the land for all those years, and it seemed to him
that they should have had to pay him rent or something,
but instead that woman ended up getting half his farm—his
land.

There was no other land available in the valley, according

to Wade Parker. Except for a few dozen small farms like this one, the majority of the land was still owned by descendents of Bernal, who had claimed the land in a Spanish land grant. As Wade had informed him, the Bernals didn't sell their land, ever.

He would not give this land up. His father had fought for his land, even given his life for it. Doc gave him this place, Montana thought, gave him his dream, and he'd be damned if he'd give up without a fight. That Pinky woman and her lawyer had no idea just who they were tangling with. He was a Creed, and Creeds didn't give up.

He began to pace again. Judge's ruling or no, he'd get the farm. He would make her life so miserable, so unlivable, that she'd give up. She would take her little city fanny and hightail it back to wherever she'd come from. He would drive her away any way he could. There was no way he'd let that pesky little fly of a woman beat him. No way on this earth.

The jangle of harness bells sounded from the road. Montana turned and watched the cloud of orange dust billow along the eastern border of the farm. He grabbed Jericho's mane, mounted bareback, and rode to the end of the drive.

It was the same old codger and wagon that the Pinky woman had used to sneak out here. The wagon bounced over the road ruts at what must have been a tooth-rattling speed. The driver pulled back on the reins only a few feet from the farm entrance, and the team skidded to a dusty stop, the barrels, boxes, and cans banging and rolling on the wagon bed.

Montana fanned away the dust and leaned forward, resting his arm on Jericho's damp neck. "What can I do for you, mister?"

The driver rolled a fat cigar stub over to the corner of his mouth. "I'm s'pose ta deliver this here stuff ta the little missy."

Montana stretched his neck to get a look at the wagon load.

"Yoo-hooooo! Mr. McGeeeeee!"

Montana turned at the sound of her voice, and watched

71

"the little missy" run down the steps and hurry toward them.

So he waited.

She crunched toward them on the gravel, and as each step brought her closer, Montana's anticipation heightened. This time he had her.

She stopped, well away from the horses. "Mr. McGee—"

"Custus," the old man corrected.

"Uh, Custus, I'm so glad you've finally arrived. It's getting late, and we need to get the supplies unloaded before dark. Just drive right around to the back door there." She pointed toward the farmhouse.

"I'm afraid that's not possible," Montana informed her.

Her dark eyes narrowed. "And just why not?"

"It's my land, and I don't choose to let this wagon on it."

"You can't do that!"

Montana purposely nudged Jericho forward.

She took two quick steps back. "I have a right to use this land. My lawyer wrote it into our papers."

Sitting back on his horse, Montana tipped back the rim of his hat and looked down at her. "As I understand it, Miss Pinky, you do have that right. But he," Montana thumbed at the old man, "doesn't."

Her mouth dropped open.

Montana loved it. "I do not choose to let this wagon nor your friend here on my property." He smiled and nudged his horse closer.

Her lips pursed together as she stepped back again, and she glared daggers at him.

He couldn't help it; he laughed.

"Decide what yer doin'. I ain't got all day here." Custus pulled the cigar from his mouth and spat on the ground.

She spun around toward the old man. "Unload here please, Custus."

Custus lit his cigar. "All of it? Ice and all, right here, huh?"

She mouthed the word "ice," closed her eyes for a brief second, and then looked right at Montana, her prissy little nose up so high he figured she'd drown if it rained.

"Yes." The word clipped from her mouth. "Here, on the *public* road. Don't touch his precious land."

Custus hopped down from the wagon seat and unbolted the chains that held the tailgate. He puffed on his cigar and dropped the gate. A few dozen bright colored cans thudded to the ground. She marched over, waving the clouds of cigar smoke out of her way, Montana decided to take up cigars. Then she frowned at the old man. He shrugged, puffed some more, and grabbed a sack of flour, swinging it onto the ground. It looked to be about a hundred-pound bag.

Montana chuckled to himself. He doubted if she weighed that much. This was going to be good, real good. So he sat back and watched, just to annoy her, as Custus unloaded the entire wagon. Two ice blocks, about two feet square, solid and heavy, were packed in protective straw. He stacked them to the side. Crates of canned goods, jars, and tins were soon stacked up three high on the dusty road. Sacks labeled Spreckles Sugar, Arbuckle Coffee, and Great Northern Beans soon lined up next to a large crate of Washington State Apples.

The old man unloaded a bag of Quaker Oats and set it on the apple crate. Jericho whinnied and the Pinky woman grabbed the bag faster than chain lightning. Hugging it to her chest, she scurried to the other side of the wagon, all the time giving his horse a wary look.

The hot sun was almost behind the western foothills by the time the wagon was empty. Custus dusted off his hands, swiped the sweat from his face with a old bandanna, and closed the wagon's tailgate. The Pinky woman put her hand deep in her skirt pocket and pulled out a small pouch. "How much do I owe you?"

Custus lit another cigar and puffed. "Forty-three dollars for the supplies and two dollars for the delivery."

She pulled some bills from the pouch and paused in her counting. "I thought you only charged a dollar?"

"Ya hear'd of supply and demand? Well now, ya needed them there supplies, so I'm demandin' two dollars." He took the bills, counted them, held one up to the setting sun and scrutinized it, then tucked them in his torn shirt pocket.

She pulled out another bill and handed it to him after he

hopped back in the wagon seat. "Please tell Mr. Hamilton that I'd like to see him." She eyed Montana. "First thing tomorrow morning."

Custus tucked the bill away with the others and, puffing on his cigar, turned the wagon back toward town and took off at a full run.

She just stood there a moment, waiting for the dust to settle and staring at the mound of foodstuffs. Montana watched her take a deep breath and pick up the closest crate. Her small arms went straight as fence posts from the weight of the heavy crate and she started toward the farmhouse, shuffling along the drive.

He had to do it. Montana kneed Jericho forward and they walked along the opposite side of the drive, staying parallel with her as she did her best to carry the crate. It took only a few minutes for her to notice.

She stopped and set the crate down. Pulling a splinter from her hand, she scowled up at him. "Don't you have anything better to do?"

"Nope." He smiled and tipped his hat. He'd done it, given her the first installment of trouble. A few days of this and she'd be long gone, scurrying back to the city where she belonged.

She finished rubbing the circulation back into her hands and bent down and picked up the crate. Without a backward glance she took off, muttering something. Montana tried to decipher her mumbling. He shook his head, trying to make sense of what he thought she'd said. It sounded like she'd said "toe."

The back door slammed shut. Addie dropped the crate and grabbed a jar. She scurried into the pantry, seized a jar wrench, and pried off the sealed lid. Two seconds later her cheeks bulged with a whole, plump, spiced peach.

It was heaven, pure heaven, except for the pit.

She spit it out and eased onto a small pine bench, her back against the pantry shelves. And she chewed. Her eyelids drifted closed and she savored the fruit, all juicy sweet and spicy with cinnamon . . . and nutmeg . . . and allspice. It tasted like sunshine.

As she stuck her fingers into the jar for another one, she vowed to never, ever take food for granted again. Chewing with the delicacy of a masticating cow, she set the jar down and wiped her hands on her skirt. She stood and walked to the crate, determination driving every footstep. Now she wanted beans.

She plucked each item from the crate: Fanny Purdy's Pickles, Dr. Goody's Curative Rhubarb Relish, Mrs. Todd's Mincemeat, and Prince Albert Marmelaide, but no cans and no beans. There must have been ten cans of Charles River Baked Beans bouncing off the wagon and rolling around the dirt road. She remembered seeing the distinctive yellow and red labels right before that carnivorous horse had whinnied after her oatmeal. It was just her luck to grab the wrong crate. Well, she had to bring in the supplies anyway, so she might as well get started. Of course to do that she had to tolerate *him* and his devil horse.

She crept to the window and peered out. She couldn't see him. He wasn't by the tree, although all his clothes still decorated it like a ragman's tinsel. She leaned to the other side, but she couldn't see the south end of the farmyard. Why was she suddenly uneasy?

The water! Addie barreled out the back door, sure she'd catch him.

The farmyard was empty. He wasn't there.

With her eyes narrowed in suspicion, she descended the steps. Just because he wasn't there didn't mean he hadn't been there already. She wouldn't put it past him. She walked over to the pump. It appeared untouched. She looked into the trough; it was damp, but no more so than it had been earlier, when she'd stopped him from using the pump. She looked around the back of the farmhouse. The orchard held nothing but full, plump green trees. No sign of anyone. The chicken yard stood empty as a church on Saturday night, and the big, weathered, two-story barn appeared untouched. He must have gone to find a river, because it was quiet, so, so quiet, and peaceful.

The sun had sunk below the western foothills, turning the blue sky into a fiery silver-pink, just like the inside of a seashell she'd once seen. A flock of birds, flying in an arrow, shot across the pearly sky, and the evening's first cricket chirruped through the silence. Addie relaxed and smiled. She was home.

She walked along the back of the house, just looking at the south end of the farm. Not far from the back of the house was a small staked area. She hadn't seen this before. As she stepped closer she could see the remains of some small furrows and a few brown, sunburned plants. This must have been her aunt's garden. Addie bent and plucked one of the dead plants. A small, shriveled brown carrot dangled from the liver-colored leaves. It should have been a fat, crisp carrot suitable for a raisin salad or a spicy cake, but now it was mottled and limp. She sat down on a small vegetable cart and stared at the carrot, lying so lifeless in her palm. Then she gazed out toward the fields, plowed under, barren, and brown. This place was her aunt's dream, and through the letters and years, it had also become her dream. She remembered every color, every bit of life of which her aunt had written, and at that moment she knew that the farm needed its own renaissance, to come to life again. No more barren fields, no more empty chicken yard, no more dead garden. She was here and she would breathe life back into this farm.

Tossing the dead carrot on the ground, she stood, filled with renewed determination. She needed to get those supplies inside, get settled as quickly as possible, and shape up this farm. She dusted the dirt from her derriere and glanced down at the cart. It was almost a miniature version of a hay cart, with two front wheels and back legs and long wooden handles with which to roll it. Her aunt must have used it to haul manure or fresh dirt. In fact, it was coated with a thick layer of dirt. But the cart was sturdy.

She smiled, her eyes alight with a new idea. Grasping the wooden handles, she lifted the cart and rolled it to the back door. She ran inside, through the kitchen, dining room, and parlor, and down the small hallway to a storage closet. She flung open the door and grabbed her bicycle, pressing down on the handlebars and testing the tires for air loss as she rolled it back to the kitchen. They needed more air. She snapped the tire pump off the shaft and attached it to the tire valve. She pumped that plunger over and over, imagining the toad's face when he saw her. She would show him. No one would stop Adelaide Amanda Pinkney.

A few minutes later she thumped her shiny black bicycle down the back landing, and propped the cycle against the railing. She was ready to attach the cart. She found some rope near the barn and looped it through the metal pull rings on the cart handles. Then she tied it around the seat post. Mounting the seat with an experienced cyclist's ease, Addie tested her invention. It worked fine empty, but good sense told her that she'd better test it loaded.

At the woodpile she stopped and filled the cart with enough wood to weight it down. For momentum she pushed the cycle forward a few yards and then used a running mount. She made it about ten feet before the rope caught in the spokes. She stopped dead, straddling the crossbar with her green serge skirt hiked up past her knees and her shoe heels buried in the soft dirt.

Dadgummit! It didn't work. She gripped the handlebars and shoved forward, looking over her shoulder as she hobbled along, trying to see the problem. Sweat dripped from her head before she realized that the rope was too taut. It needed some give, bouyancy like seat springs, to allow for the bumps in the ground.

But what? She glanced down and, like an answered prayer, her eyes locked on her stocking supporters, her pink elastic stocking supporters. Fifteen minutes later, with her cart bouncing behind her like a baby buggy, Addie rounded the corner of the farmhouse, gravel spitting in her wake and her myrtle-green hose sagging around her ankles.

The toad was standing in front of her supplies, and his horse stood behind them. Still aiming to show him, she pedaled faster and lifted her nose a notch higher.

She skidded to a stop right in front of him. The gravel crunched and sprayed at his boots, just as she'd hoped. She dismounted and leaned the cycle by a stack of crates. Wiping her sweaty hands on her skirt, she turned. "Couldn't find a river?"

He shook the gravel off his boots, tilted his hat back and smirked.

She hated that smirk.

"I didn't need a river." He nodded at his horse. "Jericho found what he needed."

Addie walked around the supply pile and screamed. "He's licking my ice! For godsakes, stop him!"

"He was thirsty."

"That . . . is . . . my . . . ice."

"Well then, maybe you ought to get it off the public road." He leaned back against her supplies, crossed his arms—and his boots—and watched that damnable horse of his.

The two ice blocks, packed in straw, were stacked, and the horse lapped up the insulating straw, melting ice with a long stroke of his huge tongue. He turned his head toward Addie and chomped; his brown eyes appeared almost gleeful. Then he swallowed and licked the drops of water that were dripping down the sides of the block.

"Get him away from there!" she said, frantically waving her pointed finger at the horse.

"It's your ice. You get him away."

"It's your horse!"

"He's thirsty because you won't let him have my water. Animals find water when they need it. He's only acting naturally."

"Then he can act 'naturally' near a river, but get him away from my ice. That's stealing, Mr. Creed."

"You should know. You stole my land."

"I did not. It's my farm—"

"On my land," he interrupted.

Addie spun around and grabbed a crate of cans. "The court didn't see it that way."

"That court couldn't 'see' through a barbed-wire fence."

She loaded her crate in the cart and looked him straight in the eye. "How much do want?"

"For what?"

"For your precious land."

He stood stiff as a banker's collar. "It's not for sale."

"Why not? I'll pay you a fair price, though heaven knows why I should."

He stepped closer to her, and she could almost see him shake with fury.

"It's not for sale."

He was mad again. She could tell because he'd been shouting for a good three minutes. She'd gotten him.

"Why not just sell me the land and go buy your own farm?"

"This is my own farm."

"Half of everything grown will be mine. The court decreed it."

He strode to his horse, grabbed a handful of his mane and mounted. Then he turned to her, and she could have sworn she'd never seen anyone so furious.

"You'll only get half if you last here that long." With that threat he rode off.

"I'm staying here all right, mister." Addie shouted after him. "I might even be here to see you become human!"

She turned and began to load her supplies, muttering, "Although I doubt either of us will live that long."

Addie wiped the last dish and set it on the counter. She untied her apron and looked around the kitchen. It smelled wonderful, like the beans, bacon, and biscuits she'd eaten earlier. She put the apron on a peg near the pantry door and she stretched, pulling all the stiff, tired muscles she'd used to get her supplies into the house. Washing the ice blocks hadn't been easy either. She'd had to lift them to the sink and pump water over them. Then, after wrapping them in cheesecloth, she'd lugged them over to the Arctic Ice Box and loaded them in the top compartment. The perishables were inside the lower box, cooling, in spite of that awful horse. The crates, cans, sacks, and jars all sat in the pantry, waiting for her to organize them—something she planned to do first thing in the morning.

Her pitcher sat on the sinkboard, and she pumped it full of water, grabbed the lamp, and left the kitchen. She passed the parlor and checked the front door. It was about as secure as she could get it. Pushing the broken door up into the splintered frame hadn't been easy either. She'd used the andirons from the fireplace to prop the door up, and tried to get the hinge pins back in. She wasn't very good at that; the door still wobbled. But at least she had some privacy.

Entering the bedroom, she set down the lamp and wash water. She pulled down the holland shades and stripped to her smallclothes. She washed the day's heat from her skin, and the cool water felt like heaven in the still air. It had been another hot day, and lugging all that stuff into the house hadn't helped.

She pulled out her muslin nightdress with the little tucks—it was her favorite for warm summer nights—and slipped it on. Then she removed her drawers, crawled into the big feather bed and turned down the lamp wick.

Fifteen minutes later her hair was wet with sweat. It was hot, and there was no air in the room at all. Throwing back the thin sheet, she left the bed and went to the window. She lifted the shade and opened the window, hoping some air would drift inside. When it didn't, she went to the other window and opened it too. Then she returned to bed, where she lay there, sweat still eking from her skin.

Finally reaching a point of desperation, she pulled the sheet up to her chin and glanced around the room. *Silly, there's no one in here.* Under the sheet she unbuttoned the nightdress and wiggled out of it, still keeping the sheet tucked firmly under her chin.

She was now naked. She'd never slept naked before. In fact her mother had even worn her undergarments under her nightdress, but Addie had always slept better without restrictions. Between the chemise, corset, cover, drawers, and an occasional bustle or hoop, she felt constricted all day. She didn't want to feel that way at night too, especially when it was hot.

Addie reached down under the sheet and pulled out her nightdress. Tucking the sheet neatly under her arms, she laid the dress across the foot of the bed; that way it was within reach for morning. She plopped back against the pillows and giggled, feeling a little bit wicked, lying there under the sheets, stark naked. She closed her eyes, remembering this feeling from before, at the Chicago Exposition, when she'd sneaked a peek through the opening in the Little Egypt tent.

Within the tent, in splendid, wicked glory, had been a small young woman clothed in layer after layer of colored veils. Oh, how she'd danced, spinning and turning and wiggling. With each deep movement the woman had dropped a veil, and the audience, mostly men, had cheered and clapped. Their enthusiasm made the woman's movements even more . . . native. Addie had been a bit embarrassed, but enthralled, and in the back of her mind she'd always wondered what it was like for a woman to dance like that for a man.

Soon Addie fell asleep, dreaming of herself in a hot, torrid desert, where she, an exotic creature clothed in a coin-covered belt and sheer veils of red, yellow, and purple, danced before her sheik. She swirled and spun and her veils drifted toward the man whose face was only a dim image, but he sat beneath a date palm and he wore all white. When she spun to a stop before him, her head thrown back in submission, he stood, picked her up and carried her to his horse—a big brown thing with pink-freckled lips and beans on his breath.

She woke up with a start. A nightmare had butted in on her dream. She glanced at the window; it was still dark. She could probably get a bit more sleep before the sun rose. Lying in the darkness, she listened to the night sounds: crickets, and an occasional thud on the front porch, which was the loose door in the wind.

Turning over, she punched the feather pillow a couple of times, and went back to a sound and dreamless sleep, never remembering that there was no wind.

6

A LOUD CLUMPING SOUND FILLED ADDIE'S SLEEPY HEAD. All cozy, with her face buried in the pillow, she did her best to block it out. Sleep was much more important. She'd started to drift off again when the bed shook like a Chicago trolley. Holding a breath, she opened her eyes, waiting to see if maybe she'd dreamed it.

She counted four more clumps on the wooden floor. Very quietly she exhaled. Something banged against the foot rail and rattled the whole bed. Addie shot upright, her eyes wide as imported ripe olives. She clutched the sheet in her tight fists and pulled it over her naked chest. Her mouth froze halfway through her scream, which came out in a croak. Her body froze, her hands still holding the sheet, and her breath froze in her throat at the sight that greeted her.

That devil horse stood in her bedroom!

Its brown eyes blinked at her and it snorted, then rubbed its muzzle on the foot rail of the iron bed. Addie scooted back, pinning the bed pillows between the head rail and her naked body as she watched it.

Slow as a snail she moved to the right of the bed. The horse moved with her. She moved back to the center. So did the horse. She leaned left, and the horse edged around to the left side of the bed. The horrid animal was stalking her.

She eyed the windows on either side of the bed. They were open and beckoning, and a few too many feet away. And she was naked. She clutched the sheet a bit tighter and judged the distance to her nightdress. It was lying against the foot rail, only inches away from the horse.

Scooting down farther on the bed, she tried, under the covers, to kick the gown closer to her reach. The horse watched her; the gown didn't move much. A few more tries and she gave up. She glanced back at the horse. Its long neck was bent around, chewing at an itch on its back.

Now was her chance. Addie leaned forward and grabbed the sleeve of the nightgown. The horse's head twisted back around and its knowing eyes met hers. She jerked back on the sleeve and the horse bit down, clamping a hunk of the nightgown in those huge yellow teeth.

"You . . ." She pulled. "Obnoxious . . ." She pulled harder, her words gritted through her teeth. "Beast!" The sleeve ripped half off.

With one hand she reached out and gripped the bodice as tightly as she could. The bodice wouldn't tear; there were no bodice seams, but she could feel the tuck threads snap.

The horse snorted and shook its head. The sheet slipped. She clamped her elbows hard against her sides, trying to keep the sheet up. Still she tugged back.

The horse began to gnaw on the gown.

"You're not going to eat my nightgown too!" She leaned back, still trying to get him to release it.

The horse walked backward; Addie slid forward. Cool air hit her exposed backside. He moved back again and her feet hit the iron rungs on the foot rail.

Using the rail for leverage, she bent forward and moved her grip up the nightdress, hand over hand. The sheet fell; the horse let go; and Addie's bare back hit the mattress with such force she bounced.

Glaring at the damnable horse, she pulled the torn gown over her exposed chest and sat up. She untwisted the gown and slipped it over her head, shoving her right arm through the gaping armhole. The shoulder seam of the sleeve hung down near her elbow. She tugged it up and began buttoning the front of her gown. All the pristine little tucks were crushed with teethmarks and beginning to unravel, and three of the little pearl buttons were missing. The horse lifted its lips, pushed its huge tongue against the roof of its mouth a few times, and spit out two pearl buttons.

Then it butted its forehead against the rail and banged the bed against the wall. Addie closed her eyes, imagining exactly how she was going to kill Mr. Creed—slowly, very, very slowly. Then she could send this horrid creature to the closest glue factory. But right now she had to get away from this horse. The animal rocked the iron bed, and she watched the window from the corner of her eye. With each whack, she moved closer to the right edge of the bed.

The window was maybe three, four feet away. If she moved fast, she could do it. The horse lowered its head and hit the rail. Addie's bare feet hit the floor.

She vaulted out the window, black hair flying, right into Montana Creed's chest.

His arms clamped around her. "Damn!" he swore. They both hit the ground, dust curling up around them and slowly sifting down.

Her face rested in the dirt above his head. She coughed. His hands gripped her derriere and he mumbled something against her chest. She lifted her head and shook the dust from her face. He mumbled again. She looked down, horrified to find his nose buried in the middle of her bosom. Then his hands squeezed her bottom.

She brought her knee up, catching him right between the legs.

"Jesus Christ!" He let go, fast.

She scrambled to her feet and spun around to face him.

He rolled on his side, hands between his legs and his face all scrunched up.

"What do you think you're doing?" she demanded.

"Trying to breathe," he groaned, and then sat up, resting his head on his knees while he took some deep breaths.

"How dare you! How dare you do this to me! Peeking in the window like some . . . Peeping Tom!" She crossed her arms and looked down at him. "You're a sick man."

He got to his feet, slowly, and picked up his hat, dusting it off on his pant leg. "I wasn't looking in your window."

"Sure." She tapped her foot in agitation.

"I was looking for my horse." He swiped the dust off his neck.

"In my bedroom! You knew he was there."

The awful horse stuck its head out the bedroom window and whinnied at its master.

"Get that animal out of *my* house, now!" Addie waved her pointed finger at the horse.

"Why, Miss Pinky . . ." His mouth crept into that awful smirk. "You aren't afraid of a poor dumb animal, are you?"

His tone told Addie that he darn well knew she was. "Get that beast out."

He walked to the window and reached up to stroke the horse's nose. "Why, Jericho here wouldn't hurt a fly."

So says the toad.

The horse spit out the other pearl button. Montana bent down and picked it up.

"Lose this?" He tossed the button to her and she caught it. Then he pulled out a pocketknife and opened it.

"Get him out, now."

Holding up the knife, he examined the blade. "Why should I?"

"Because he's trespassing."

He leaned back against her farmhouse window, and with his devil horse looking innocently over his shoulder, he began to clean his fingernails with the knife. "It'll cost you."

"Pardon me?" She'd swear she'd heard wrong.

"I charge for horse removal."

"But it's your horse!"

"Like you keep reminding me, it's your house."

"You put that horse in there."

He started cleaning the nails on the other hand, grinning. "Now why would I do that?"

"Because you're a toad!" Addie screamed before she could stop herself. Her hand flew to cover her mouth.

He threw his head back and laughed out loud.

She planted her hands on her hips and waited for him to stop laughing. A bee buzzed around her face, and she shook her head. When she looked at him again, his gaze rested just below her neck. Addie glanced down. Half her bosom fell through the bodice gaps and her dark nipples were budding against the thin nightgown. Her arms clamped over her chest and she felt her face flush red.

"Cold?" he asked.

She wanted to die. Instead she turned and walked away, heading around the corner and straight for the porch. The front entry was wide open and the wooden door lay on the porch, as if it had just fallen there. But it hadn't. She knew that as well as she knew her own name.

The toad was outside and the horse inside; she didn't know which was the worse evil. She decided to bear the beast inside, since he couldn't speak, but she paused when Levi Hamilton came up the drive. To Addie, his arrival was like manna from heaven.

Remembering her state of dress, she ran up the stairs and stepped over the broken front door. She ran into the parlor and grabbed the woolen throw off the sofa, wrapping the throw around her shoulders before going out to greet her lawyer.

She ran down the steps. "Oh, I'm so glad you're here."

Levi wrapped the buggy reins around the brake shift and hopped down. "Custus gave me your message. What do you need?"

"A gun."

"What for?"

"To shoot that man and his horse!"

Levi bit back a smile and shook his head. "What's the problem?"

Addie lifted an arm and pointed toward the broken doorway. "He put his horse in my bedroom and won't remove it!"

"That's not true." Mr. Creed stood a few feet away while he looked her lawyer straight in the eye, and lied.

She faced him and crossed her arms again only tighter. "Then how did he get inside?"

He shrugged. "He was probably thirsty. She refused to let me use her pump to draw any water."

Looking surprised, Levi turned to Addie. "You did?"

She nodded. "I told him he had to lease the use of it. I

said we'd decide on a price and draw up an agreement." She looked from Levi to Mr. Creed. "That was why I asked you out here." She tugged up on her drooping sleeve. She could lie too.

Mr. Creed muttered under his breath.

Levi spoke. "Addie, you really should let him use the pump. This whole thing with the farm isn't the horse's fault. He's just a poor animal."

Her lawyer was defending that deadly horse. "That horse is an animal, all right. He attacked me."

"How did he attack you?" Montana asked.

"Well, he—he—"

"I wouldn't call rocking your bed 'attacking.' "

"How did you know that's what he did?"

"I saw him—"

"Ah-hah! So you *were* peeking in my window." She turned to Levi. "He's a Peeping Tom! Have him arrested."

"Arrested for what? Looking for my own horse?"

"For looking in my bedroom window!"

"You've just got a bug up your little city-white butt because you were buck naked."

"See, you did look!" She was mortified, so she covered it up by adding, "And how I sleep is none of your business."

"I looked for my horse. Your lily-white body just happened to be part of the scenery."

"I hate horses! You knew it and you put it in there!"

He smirked at her. "Prove it."

"Get me a gun, Levi."

Fists up, she started to go for him. Levi grabbed her arms and held her back. "Calm down, Miss Pinkney, just calm down. I'll take care of this. I have to before you two kill each other."

She took a deep breath, all the while glaring at that horrible man and wishing her eyes could shoot poison darts.

Levi let go of her arms. "Let's get the pump lease worked out. Now what do you feel is fair?" he asked her.

"He doesn't have that much." She glared at Mr. Creed.

"I think five dollars a month is fair. That's sixty dollars a year." Levi looked back and forth between them.

"Make it two hundred," Addie spat.

Mr. Creed didn't even blink. He just gave her that smirking look that said he didn't care how much she charged. It annoyed her.

Levi frowned at her. "I think that's too much—"

Mr. Creed interrupted, "Two hundred is fine, Levi. Draw up the lease." As he spoke, his eyes drilled her.

Two hundred was not fair, and she knew it. It was a ridiculous amount. What was going on? She didn't trust him, or that horse of his. But what did she care if he wanted to pay the price? It was payback for all the splinters she'd picked out of her hands the night before. Lugging the supplies hadn't been easy, even when she'd used her cycle. In fact her thighs still ached from all that pedaling, and the muscles in her arms were killing her, especially after she'd had a tug-of-war with that devil horse. And she had things to do, but she couldn't do them with that horse inside.

"Get the horse out," she ordered.

"I'll do it," Levi volunteered.

"Fine." She spun around, stuck her nose up and marched up the porch steps. When she stepped over the door, she paused, giving Mr. Creed a knowing look. She knew that he'd removed the door to get the horse inside, but she couldn't prove it. She stepped inside and let Levi precede her. Mr. Creed followed her.

They approached the bedroom. The horse stood by the washstand, drinking last night's wash water. Its big tongue lapped at the water, and it sounded to her as if the animal was purposely making drinking noises. It looked over its shoulder at them once, its tail swishing, and then went back to slurping.

That deep, princely voice sounded over her shoulder. "See, he was thirsty."

Addie turned and blessed him with her best scoff.

Mr. Creed leaned against the bedroom doorjamb, looking happy as a toad on a warm rock. He smiled at his horse.

Levi went over and started to lead the horse away. The animal tried to bite him.

Both Addie and Levi looked at Montana. He shrugged.

"Sorry, he doesn't like strangers." He pulled out that knife again and cut a string from his shirtsleeve.

Levi reached for the horse, whose ears flattened before it nipped at him. He turned to Addie. "He's not going to let me do this."

She faced Mr. Creed. "You do it."

"Sure, Miss Pinky, but for horse removal I charge two hundred dollars."

Levi began to cough, and Addie bit back the nasty name she wanted to shout at him. He'd gotten her. No wonder the lease fee hadn't bothered him. Whatever amount she demanded for leasing her pump would be what he would charge her.

She took a deep breath, swallowing a bit more of her pride. "Just get him out."

"I want it in writing. One horse removal in exchange for a year's lease of your water pump *and* trough," he said, still leaning against the doorframe.

"Fine." She agreed under duress. "But if that animal 'wanders' in my house ever again, I want 'free horse removal.' "

"Agreed." Mr. Creed sauntered over to his horse. "I can almost guarantee this won't happen again." He patted the horse on the neck. "Will it, boy? You were just thirsty, weren't you?"

The horse flicked its ornery head and blew out its nose, as if answering its master.

He led the horse out of the room, and by then Addie had moved to the far end of the hall. As he passed by, he said, "After all, we have water now. Don't we, boy?"

Acre after acre of rich, reddish-brown land encompassed the farm buildings. It was twice as much land as Montana and his pa had farmed, and lost. They'd had a barn, but it wasn't much bigger than the three-room farmhouse his father had built, and the railroad had stolen. But this farm had a real barn, a two-story structure of California redwood, with three stalls, complete with manure gutters. There were two large grain bins and three smaller ones, a sturdy hayloft built under the high gabled roof, and big hay doors to load the bales. A large area, perfect for a future silo, lay vacant between the barn and the two feeding pens enclosed by split-rail fences. Someday he'd build a silo to store the grain that would grow so well in this fertile soil.

A smokehouse was partially hidden behind the barn, and a tall, white windmill stood between the barn and the house. The water cistern sat on a white wooden building nearby, and pipes led from it to the back of the farmhouse. This place had water plumbed from the cistern right into the kitchen. It was a prosperous place, a farm to be proud of. And Montana intended to make damn sure it was his, all his.

He watched Jericho drink from the trough. He smiled, feeling so damn proud of himself. He'd gotten her, gotten his water, and she hadn't even seen it coming. He resisted the urge to rub his hands together; he chuckled instead.

He hadn't thought it would be so easy, getting his horse in her bedroom. He cut some burlap he'd found in the barn and tied pieces of the cloth to Jericho's hooves to muffle the sound. It worked, but the best part had been Jericho's own creation—butting up against her bed. When that happened, it had been all he could do not to jump in the open window and kiss that horse.

He reached out and stroked old Jerry's mane, reliving the whole incident in his mind. A small part of him—a very small part—had to respect the woman. She'd put up a good fight, just as she had when he'd tried to scare her with his gun. She had gumption, he had to give her that. She was like a jigger tick, small and harmless but a real pain when she got under your skin. And as much as he hated to admit it, he had to respect her strength, both in character and physically. Her small arms had lugged the wood and hauled those supplies. He would have expected a woman to be sapped dry. But not the Pinky woman. She'd come out the winner in her tug-of-war with Jericho.

He started laughing again, remembering the way she'd slid down that bed, her whole backside exposed. He'd had to look twice because her skin was as white as those sheets, and it had looked even whiter with all that black hair hanging down her shoulders.

It dawned on him then that she wasn't bad-looking, although he'd always preferred redheads, tall, buxom redheads, not miniature black-haired city prisses with skin like buttermilk. For such a little thing, she had some curves too, at least from what he'd seen of her. And felt of her, he reminded himself. Her round little butt had fit right into his palms. He remembered squeezing her, then he remembered her knee.

He groaned. She had spirit too. Even when she was afraid of him and his horse, she'd not broken down. That amazed him more than anything. Women always cried. And it always got to him when they did. She hadn't cried. He'd yelled at her, shot at her, taunted her, and done his all-around best to send her packing. Not once had she shed a tear.

Driving her off was not going to be as easy as he'd thought. The gun hadn't worked, neither had the bullets, and the horse in the bedroom hadn't worked either, although he had gotten his water. He'd have to watch her, find another weakness and use it. He hoped it wouldn't take too long because in a couple of months he had to get his wheat planted. It would be his first crop, and he'd be damned it he'd share the profits with her. No city-born and -bred female, stubborn though she was, would beat him. Of that he was sure.

Addie glued the last label on the pantry shelf. Standing back, she admired her work. Every jar, every can, every single one of her supplies was put away, in order. Melvil Dewey would have been proud of her. The huge sack of flour sat on the floor just below the label 641.021. Next to that label sat the lard can, 641.022, and the other baking ingredients: Durkee's Perfectly Pure Gauntlet Brand Spices, 641.0231 through 641.0239; Rhumford's Baking Powder, 641.024; Arm and Hammer Saleratus, 641.025; Charles Fleischmann's Austrian Quality Yeast, 641.026.

It was an organizational masterpiece, and good solid use of the Dewey Decimal System. She had decided against using a card catalog. After all, she would be the only one using the kitchen. The class and division numbers were inbred in her. As a librarian, and honor graduate of Library Economy, she had prided herself on her ability to guide the library's patrons straight to their desired books. As Professor Dewey had always said, "Da card catalog is for da laymen's usage."

Wiping her hands on her muslin apron, she left the pantry, ready to start unpacking her farming books. Once in the parlor, she opened the barrel trunk and began to shelve the books.

Three hours later she tucked the last book into its section. It was a little-known volume titled *Swine Husbandry*. She was sure that one day she'd raise pigs, but first she'd start with chickens. They supplied meat and eggs, both of which Levi assured her she could sell in town. There was already a sturdy henhouse. She had everything she needed at her fingertips, except the chickens. Custus had told Levi that there were a few chickens with the other farm stock, and a neighboring family, the Latimers, would bring them back in a few days. But Addie wouldn't do things halfway. "A few" chickens wouldn't be enough. She intended to be a prosperous farm woman, and she'd brought her books to help teach her how.

Three volumes over from the swine husbandry book was the one book she needed to read: *Makers of Millions; Or the Marvelous Success of America's Self-Made Men*. And women, Addie thought. She took the tooled-leather book over to a large, brown velvet-covered armchair that matched the sofa. She sat back, pulled her reading spectacles from a chain she'd hung around her neck and propped them onto her nose. She began to read.

It was late when she finally set the book on the lamp table. Yawning, she stretched and let the spectacles drop from her nose. She wiggled, rubbing her shoulders against the back of the chair. The book had been an inspiration. Mr. Wendell T. Gates had started out just like Addie. He'd moved from Trenton, New Jersey, to Eli, Nevada. He bought a large brood of chicks, and within a few years he had expanded, and expanded, all the time investing in his chicken ranch and eventually earning over a million dollars. The man retired with a fortune. And that's what she would do, earn her millions through chickens. It sounded simple enough, and she was an intelligent, college-educated woman. And she didn't give up. Tenacity was her middle name, just like Mr. Wendell T. Gates.

Through the open parlor window the night sounds drew her attention. She released the window shade and settled back in the chair, gazing at the night sky. It had been dark for some time, and there was a certain peace that came with the dark. Life was different here, on this farm, different from anything she'd known. The sharp, earthy smell of dirt was something pleasant here. One could smell it so clearly once the night settled in and cooled the hot ground. The trees smelled too. With her bedroom windows open she could almost taste the tangy, clean odor of the eucalyptus trees that stood behind the farmhouse. It was wonderful. And the sounds were so different, somehow quieter and softer. The cricket's song and the hum of the locust were peaceful, lulling sounds, unlike those of rattling trolley cars or the constant clicking of the hooves of so many wagon teams on a paved street. Those, Addie thought, were noises, but these were sounds, and there was a difference. One could soothe, while the other annoyed . . .

A horse's nicker rent the air, sending all her benevolent feelings straight to Hades. In her active day, she'd been able to block out the existence of Mr. Creed and his horrid horse. Now she couldn't.

She leaned over the edge of the chair arm and peered out the window. He sat in front of the tree with his horse alongside. She could see the outline of that devil's snout in the glow of their camp fire. The animal looked hell-sent. After today, she was sure that was exactly where that horse had come from, the horse from Hades.

Addie knew that the Devil himself had had something to do with her humiliation. Never in her entire life had she slept nude. Yet the one very night she did, that foul fiend put his obnoxious horse in her bedroom. But she'd gotten away. She'd showed him.

You showed him all right. You showed him every inch of you.

She felt her blush coming, and buried her face in her

93

hands, as if that would make the whole incident go away. The very thought of that man ogling her just made her want to . . . scream? No.

Cry? No.

Hide? Never!

Get even? Yes!

Of course that wouldn't be easy. The man obviously had no shame. He'd probably dance naked through a church social. After all, he hung his clothes, red underwear and all, out in broad daylight for the whole world to see. He didn't care a fig for a woman's sensibilities, of that Addie was sure.

And where had he come from? He was rude and crude, and a loner. He didn't much care for people. She could tell. What sort of woman had raised a man like that?

What sort of life had he led that he'd never seen a stereoscope? The viewfinder sat next to the glass lamp. She picked it up by its long, wooden, candlestick-shaped base and noticed her uncle's initials, J.M., carved on the base. She fiddled with the double glass slides that were magnified by the viewfinder's binocular-type eyepiece. It had been a wonderful invention, allowing people to focus three-dimensionally on the picture depicted on the slides. The stereoscope viewer had opened a whole new world for people.

So where had he been? He must have some upbringing, because he had said something biblical when he'd been so mad about the judge's ruling. He'd referred to Solomon, dividing that poor babe in half. What sort of Christian man turned out so . . . hard? The bible said there's good in all men, but she had yet to see any in him. It could be that she was being unfair. Somewhere in that long, lanky black soul was some good.

The Christian in her was trying to think of something good about the man while she absentmindedly looked into her uncle's viewer.

"Good God!" She whipped it away from her face and stared at it as if it was something foul. She threw on her spectacles and looked again. This time she gasped. With her eyes never leaving the eyepiece, she felt around on the table for the stack of glass slides. She examined each and every slide, all the while becoming more and more stunned. No wonder he'd been fascinated. They were not travel slides, not slides of exotic animals like elephants and zebras. The slides were of women, naked, buxom, women.

It was then Addie realized that Mr. Creed's long, lanky black soul held absolutely no good.

7

TWO DAYS LATER ADDIE PEDALED DOWN THE DIRT ROAD toward home, her cart bouncing along behind her, the charming chirps of two hundred, week-old baby chicks echoing in her wake. This was it, the first day of her new venture. She looked over her shoulder at her large brood and smiled. They were the cutest things she'd ever seen. They were all toasty-brown balls of fuzz, with little round heads and tiny beaks. Buying them from that nice old woman and her son was the smartest thing she'd done, although she'd let the son talk her into twice as many as she had planned. But then she'd also saved twenty-five dollars.

Levi had told her of a chicken farmer in Pleasanton who sold his broods and was very reliable, but Addie had done better. She'd seen a big old place off the Livermore road that had chickens everywhere. Granted, it wasn't as well equipped as she'd have had her place, but there were sure enough chickens. So many roosted on the outbuildings that at first glance she had thought the buildings had red roofs.

A gnarled old woman had stood near the road, and Addie, starting to feel like a real Californian, had stopped to chat. When she mentioned she was off to buy chickens from the Sycamore Ranch in the next town, the woman, a

Mrs. Potter, told her, gesturing to the dilapidated farm behind her, that her son had more chickens than he knew what to do with. So Addie, thinking she should at least take a look, had followed the woman, and an hour later left with her chickens.

Pedaling down the dirt road with renewed vigor, she hummed "Joshua Fought the Battle of Jericho," feeling quite proud of herself. By purchasing the chicks from the Potters, she had cut five miles off her trip and gotten two hundred chicks for the same price she'd have had to pay for one hundred fifty at Sycamore Ranch. She had done well, just like Mr. Wendell T. Gates.

She could see it now. The huge sign she'd have on her farm someday, touting her prosperous business. *Addie's Chicken Ranch*. No, that didn't sound right. She pedaled faster, her mind working with the same speed as her feet. Maybe *Pinkney's Perfect Fowls*? That wasn't right either. It reminded Addie of baseball fouls, which in turn reminded her of the Chicago Cubs, who hadn't won the National League pennant since 1886. She was mad at them, so to name her future million-dollar endeavor after them didn't sit right with her.

California Capons. She swerved to miss a rut. Too stuffy, she thought, shaking her head.

Ah-hah! She had it. *Pinkney's Pullets*. It was perfect!

It was a few moments later when she reached the drive. She jammed her heels into the gravel to stop the bicycle and she stood back, staring at the entrance to the farm and imagining what it would look like someday.

Oh, she could see it now. The huge barn painted red with crisp white trim, and in bold letters across the facia would be *Pinkney's Pullets* in letters a full yard high. The farmhouse would be expanded, a second and even third story added with some lovely turrets and gables, maybe even a round window. She loved round windows. They were so . . . not square. She'd always liked light, so maybe she could add some of those glass skylights that had become so popular recently. Everyone in Chicago had been installing them.

Nestled in the third story would be a sewing and workroom. There would be a Kruse New Crown sewing machine—the one that was completely enclosed in that lovely burl cabinet. Montgomery Wards in Chicago'd had one, and she'd fallen in love with it on sight. She could have a big oak table where she'd cut out dress patterns, and she could use it to make some of those lovely tissue-paper flowers, in all colors. Then she'd put them everywhere. She could even make some to match her aunt's majolica vase, the one the toad hated.

She smiled. Maybe she'd order about six or seven of those vases from Montgomery Ward and place them everywhere he could see them. She could get giant majolica urns, the ones that came up to her waist, in the brightest colors around, and put them right in front of her bedroom windows, for privacy and just to irritate him. She'd even set some on the front porch, right across from his tree, where he would have to look at them all the time. She giggled; that's exactly what she would do. In fact she might just order them tomorrow.

She checked the chicks, all snug in the cart, her deep plum, knitted shawl tied over the top to serve as a tarp and protection from the dusty road. Then she pushed her bicycle down the drive, heading for the chicken yard and the beginning of the prosperous venture, *Pinkney's Pullets*.

She leaned her cycle against the wire fence that surrounded the chicken yard and untied the cart, rolling it through the gate and over to the short wooden ramp that led to the henhouse. It was dark and stuffy inside, so she opened the west window to help ventilate the small wooden room. Fresh straw covered the raised wooden floor, and the room smelled grainy from it. Addie had cleaned the building yesterday afternoon and filled it with nice, clean straw. Mr. Wendell T. Gates had advised that cleanliness was an important factor in chicken keeping. No diseased chickens for her, no sirree. She was going to have the cleanest, healthiest chickens in Northern California, maybe in the whole darn state!

Her little chicks sang from beneath her shawl, and she untied it and began lifting out the fluffy little darlings. As she set each one down on the floor or in one of the nests, she cooed and stroked the little dear as if it were her own child. She smiled at them—her little babies.

She filled the small waterers made from quart jars inverted into tin bowls, and the narrow tin feed trough that ran floor level along the south wall. She had found these items when she'd cleaned the henhouse, and it had been a lucky find because it seemed that Mr. Gates had neglected to explain how to make either the waterers or the feed hoppers. Addie scattered handfuls of feed throughout the straw, just as the wealthy Mr. Wendell T. Gates had instructed. She turned to leave, pausing to take another look at her chicks. There were a lot of chickens. In fact, there seemed to be chickens everywhere; so, very carefully, she tiptoed to the door. It wouldn't do to squish one. Then she shut the large wooden door, leaving open only the small chicken door that was cut into the base of the henhouse door. She crossed the chicken yard and went through the gate, latching it behind her.

An hour later Addie sat at the kitchen table, surrounded by the smells of her dinner—black-eyed peas and ham—while it simmered on the stove. With pen in hand she opened her poultry ledger—the one that would help her keep track of her hens, eggs, and profits. According to Mr. Wendell T. Gates, it was important for a businessman—or woman—to keep good records. So she entered: *14th of April, 1894; 200 chicks purchased, $75.00; one bag of chick-grain, $1.40; yield, $.00, but just wait! A. A. Pinkney, Pinkney's Pullets, est. 1894.*

Montana stood and dug through the pocket of his pants. He flipped the man a quarter, picked up his bundle and left the Bleeding Heart Barberorium. He went to the hitch post and put his bundle of dirty clothes into his saddlebags. It wasn't hot today. The air had cooled the night before and a breeze had started to drift in from the west. He looked skyward, searching for clouds. Only a few white ones moved across the sky. At least it wasn't going to rain, he thought. Jericho turned and stared at him for a long moment.

"What's wrong, old boy? Don't you recognize me?"

The horse snorted, dipped its head in recognition and turned back around. Montana rubbed his smooth cheek. It felt good to be clean-shaven, although what the hell had possessed him to cut off his mustache was something he didn't want to think about. He'd had that brush of hair on his lip for over two years, then suddenly he'd looked in the mirror and told the barber to cut it off. There was nothing he could do about it now. The hair on his face was gone. He mounted and shook his head, his trimmed brown hair now brushing his shoulders. He still wore his hair long, the way he liked it.

Bathing had been the best of that day's pleasures. You just couldn't wash right from a bucket. It was better to sit in a big old tub, and that was exactly what he'd done too, sat in that tub for over an hour. He had propped his long legs against the end of the tin bathtub and smoked a whole cigar. He couldn't remember when he'd last allowed himself those pleasures. Now there were only two more pleasures that needed tending.

He led Jericho through town, heading for the Enchantress Saloon, a place that should fill both his needs. A few minutes later he was sipping a whiskey, his arms resting on the dark mahogany bar. Seven tule elk heads hung on the bar wall, and cobwebs draped down from the antlers. He rested his foot on the bar's brass foot rail. Like most saloons, the rail was tarnished with street muck left from the patrons' boots. He kicked the rail and some of the dried soil flaked onto the plank floor nicked from too many years of spurs.

He'd been in enough saloons in his day, but this was one of the shabbiest he'd seen. Beneath the elk heads was a wide, wood-framed mirror dingy with grime and hanging drunkenly. The assorted liquor bottles lined up on the back counter were coated thick with dust, and the lamps hanging from the rafters were so gray he doubted if they'd give off any light at all. The floor was covered with cigar butts, ashes, and brown gunk. He glanced around the corners of the room. There was no spittoon.

A tinny piano sat by a small wooden platform that served as a stage, and a man was passed out on a nearby table, snoring. Montana turned back to the mirror and stared at his foggy reflection. He removed his hat and placed it on the dingy bar, next to his drink. How could his upper lip have thinned? He didn't remember looking like this. He ran his fingers over his square jaw and examined his chin. That blasted hole was still in it, the one that gave him hell when he shaved.

A door slammed and, at the scrape of a wooden stool, he turned toward the stage. A small, crowlike man in a red shirt and brocade vest began to beat out a tune on the piano. It sounded like glass breaking. Then a woman in pink satin and feathers strutted across the stage. She burst into a lusty rendition of "I Have a Wild Yearning for You."

Montana changed his mind. *She* sounded more like glass breaking. She clumped across the stage and threw in a few can-can kicks, not once coming close to keeping time with the music, either with her legs or her lungs. He turned back to his drink, hoping it would help drown out the racket. The woman screeched out two more songs, plucking feathers from her pink fans and tossing them in his direction.

Then she moved in for the kill. As she came closer, Montana decided she looked as if she'd canned one too many cans. Her eyes, what he could see of them through all the black goop, reminded him of an old hound dog he'd once had. They drooped. He eyed her body. It drooped too.

"Buy a drink for a thirsty lady, stranger?"

"Give her what she wants," he told the barkeep, digging into his pants pocket and throwing a coin on the counter. The man poured her a whiskey and set it on the bar.

She snuggled closer. "You're what I want." She rubbed her shoulder up against his chest.

He laughed and shook his head. It was just his luck to stop at a saloon with the most sorrowful-looking whore east of the Pacific Ocean. "Sorry, Miss . . ."

She fluttered her droopy lids at him. "Jessie Joan."

"Well, uh, Jessie Joan, I'm afraid I'm gonna have to pass." He turned back to his drink.

She was silent for a moment, and he expected her to leave, but she didn't.

"Why?" she asked a moment later, all the forced seductiveness gone from her voice.

He looked at her, surprised by her directness.

She stood back a bit, her hands on her hips, her sad eyes drooping more. She stuck her lower lip out. "Ain't I good enough?"

She looked up at him the same way that old hound dog did, whenever he hadn't gotten a bone. Her eyes were moist, looking more than rejected. She looked hurt, and he felt sorry for her.

"It's not you, Jessie Jane—"

"Joan. Jessie Joan." She blinked back the moistness.

Jesus Christ, he panicked, don't cry.

Her shoulders started to shake. Montana rammed his hand in his pocket and fished out a bag of gold coins.

"Aw, don't cry. Please don't cry." He pressed the coins into her shaky hands while she gazed up at him, tears running from her wrinkly eyes.

"It's not you. You're . . . you're very pretty," he lied. "It's me. I have a problem." His mind searched for some excuse to fend her off without hurting her pride.

"A big, tall bull of a man like you?" She sounded doubtful.

A bull . . . That was it. "It was a bull that did it to me. Pinned me up against a wall, and I haven't been right since," he said, thankful that he was a fast thinker.

She sniffed again and stared at his fly, as if she could gauge the damage. Then she glanced at the gold coins he'd pressed into her hand. He had to get out of there before she started bawling again. He grabbed his hat off the bar, holding it over his fly, and he started to back out. "And you know what? Right now, you're so pretty I don't think I can take being around here. It'll just remind me of my . . . affliction," he told her as he passed by the table with the drunken man.

Montana turned, slamming his hat on his head. Then he bent down and lifted the drunk by his arms and walked him back to the tearful whore. He shoved the man at her along with a few more coins. "Here, you two have fun on me."

The drunk draped his arms over the woman, burying his

101

face in her neck. Then he snored again. A second later Montana was out the door.

He rode Jericho out of town, heading back to the farm. It hadn't been in his original plan to go back so early, but now he didn't feel like drinking or carousing. His urge for female companionship was gone, long gone. He couldn't stand a crying woman. Their sobs always made his gut wrench, and he'd do anything to stop the tears. It was a real weakness, and one he'd learned to hate, because of the times he'd gone and done stupid things just to get a woman to stop. Hell, one gal in Placer County had almost had him up before a preacher, all because her tears had turned him to mush.

No, he'd go back to the farm where he could think, and he'd plan his next round with the Pinky woman. He needed a good battle. And, he reminded himself, she didn't cry.

The sun just settled behind the foothills when Montana heard it—a scream and then the most godawful wailing he'd ever heard. He spun around toward the sound.

The Pinky woman ran toward him, howling like a jackass in a tin barn.

"My chickens!" she sobbed. "My chickens! You have to help meeeee!"

He looked down at her face, wet with tears, and his insides knotted.

"Look at my babies." She held out her apron. "Look! They're dying!"

He looked in her apron. It was filled with dead chicks.

"What the hell?" He looked from her to the chicken yard, then ran toward it.

Baby chicks were blindly stumbling everywhere, dropping to the ground faster than sinners at a revival meeting. He flung open the gate and told her, "Get me something to put them in!"

She knelt down and emptied her apron, then ran for the house. He walked around the small chicken yard, trying to salvage some of the chickens. The back door slammed and she ran down the steps toward him, carrying a laundry basket and still crying for all she was worth. He cringed. She was the noisiest crier he'd ever heard. It killed him.

He entered the henhouse. There were a few dozen chicks inside and they looked salvageable. He closed the west window, cutting off the cool draft. She came inside hiccuping while she tried to catch a breath. Gritting his teeth, he grabbed the basket out of her hands. "Help me put them in here."

She got down on her hands and knees, her shoulders heaving and wheezing while she scooped up her chicks. The sound she made pulled from deep in her throat, and he hurried to get the rest of the chicks.

It was so pitiful he couldn't take any more. He stood and said, "You get these and I'll see if I can save the ones in the yard."

She nodded at him while squatting on the floor, her shoulders working up and down with her wheezes as she gathered her chicks. He ducked out the door and looked around the chicken yard, shaking his head. There must have been near a hundred dead chickens, keeled over in the dust. What had possessed the woman to buy so many chicks, and too young at that? Hadn't she ever heard of a brooder? Christ! He walked around the yard and found about twenty or so live ones which he put inside his shirt to try to give them the warmth they needed. Then he went back to the henhouse. She was still at it.

He stooped down and put his chicks in the basket, which was now filled with sick chickens, pecking and squeaking at each other. She finally lifted her quivering head and looked at him, her white skin all blotchy red and her huge, wet eyes full of pain and hurt and shame. It was like a fist in the gut.

He turned away. "Go heat up the stove. I'll bring the basket."

"It's al-al-read-dy h-hot," she sniffed. "I w-was c-cooking di— Hic! Din-ner."

He tucked the basket onto his hip and anchored it with his arm. Putting his hand on her heaving shoulder, he guided her out of the henhouse. The minute she looked at the yard, it started again—the loudest caterwauling he'd ever heard. His hand clamped down on her arm and he almost dragged her out of the yard, up the stairs, and inside.

"Go get some blankets and as many roasting pans as you have. We have to warm them up or we'll lose them." He set the basket near the big black range and tried to mentally block out the howling that echoed from the back of the house.

She shuffled back a few minutes later, her wails preceding her, her arms piled with a bobbing stack of woolen blankets. She dropped them on the floor beside him, sniffing, then brought out the roasters. There were only three of them.

Montana lined one of the graniteware pans with a blanket and gently placed the weakest chicks inside. "Open the warming oven for me."

She hurried over, sniffing, and using her apron to protect her hand, she opened the shallow door above the oven.

Montana eased the pan inside. "Leave the door open."

She nodded and stepped back, her crying now down to a pitiful blubber. He filled the next blanket-lined pan, and she began to help and, thank God, cease her wailing. They worked together, putting all the chicks in the warm confines of the oven.

Montana bent and slid the last panful inside. Something brushed his shoulder. It was her hand, barely touching him. He glanced up at her small, pale face, her eyes rimmed bloodred and her cheeks all raw-looking. Her lips were puffy from biting them while she sniffed. It was the most helpless, pathetic little face he'd ever seen, and something deep inside him twisted. It scared the hell out of him.

"Thank you." Her eyes began to fill again.

He shot upright. "Don't cry."

She sniffed, swallowed, and took a deep, shuddering breath. It was almost harder for him to watch her try to hold back her tears. Feeling awkward and confused as hell, he looked around the room, knowing he couldn't look at her much longer or he'd do something really stupid. His gaze locked on the table, set for one.

"Would you like something to eat?" she offered a moment later.

She must have been about ready to eat dinner, and he suddenly noticed that it smelled damn good. "Will you stop crying?"

She nodded.

"Okay." He walked over to the table while she set another plate and fork down. She dished up his meal and set a plate of fresh cornbread next to the butter crock. They ate in awkward silence. He had three helpings while she pushed her food around the plate, looking sorrowful, drained.

He leaned back in the chair and she glanced up, staring at him for a long moment before she said, "You shaved."

He only grunted in response.

The silence dragged on; the only sounds in the room were the sickly peeps from the chickens in the oven. He waited a moment longer and then asked the question that had been hovering in his mind for over an hour. "What the hell were you doing with all those chickens?"

She raised her bowed head. "I'm starting a chicken business."

"You?"

Her chin shot up. "Yes. I can raise chickens."

"What do you know about raising chickens?"

"The book said it wasn't difficult," she said defensively.

The book? "What book?"

"The one by Mr. Wendell T. Gates. He said raising chickens is a profitable enterprise."

"Not if you kill them the first week."

Her face crumpled.

"Don't cry!" His hands flew up. "You had too many chickens anyway."

She sniffed loudly. "I did?"

He nodded, assured that this woman could never raise chickens, although her crying might raise the dead.

She frowned. "That's not what the book said."

"Just what did that book say?"

She stood. "I'll get it."

He watched her scurry from the room. She came back with a big brown leather book and set it down on the table.

It was something about making millions. He hoped they meant dollars, otherwise she might have bought a million chickens.

She opened it to a page, removing a tin bookmark, and pointed. "See, Mr. Wendell T. Gates explains the way to make a fortune with chickens."

Montana skimmed the page and shook his head in disgust. "Did this Mr. Gates mention that chicks under three weeks should be placed in a brooder?"

"A brooder?"

"To keep them warm. They're too weak and susceptible to disease when they're this young."

"Oh. He must have forgotten." Her face appeared thoughtful and she asked, "Can I buy one of those brooders?"

"You can make one out of a wooden box and gas lanterns. I spotted some old ones out behind the barn."

She was quiet for a moment, staring at his empty plate.

He needed to leave. After all, he reminded himself, it wouldn't do to get too friendly. He still wanted her gone.

He put his napkin on the table and started to rise.

"Wait!" she said, her little face hopeful. "If I make all your meals, will you build the brooder? And anything else I need for the chickens?"

He paused. If he helped her, he'd never get rid of her. He glanced down and the empty plate stared back at him. The food was good, though, and he was tired of beans and bacon. He spotted the pile of blankets and remembered the changing weather.

She sniffled and her lip began to quiver. "I know I don't deserve your help," she wailed. "I'm a chicken killer!" Then she started crying all over again.

Montana shot upward, his chair banging against the kitchen wall. "You said you wouldn't cry."

He stood there feeling ridiculous while she laid her head in her hands and went at it.

"Please." He finally reached out and touched her shoulder. She stood, wiping her eyes on her sleeve. "I'm sorry."

106

She looked up at him, all teary and pitiful and looking as if she didn't have a soul in the world.

He stared down at the pale little face, drained of all its fight, all its gumption, and he felt odd, a little sad and a little protective. She blinked back the rest of her tears, sniffed, and licked her lips. He suddenly felt something else—the same twisting sensation that signaled his need to taste a woman, this woman. Not her, he thought, please. He fought the urge to lower his head, fought like the very devil to keep from burying his lips on hers . . . moving his hands on her small body . . . losing himself deep inside her.

"I'll do it," he agreed quickly, grabbing his hat and backing away, "if you throw in a couple of those blankets too."

She nodded, her face thankful, her lips tilting slightly. At his pause, her tongue darted out, nervously licking those lips. He had to get out, now, before he did something stupid. He picked up the blankets, tucking them under one arm, and crossed to the door and opened it, pausing in the doorway, careful not to look back at her for fear of his own actions. "Keep the chicks warm tonight. I'll get the brooder done tomorrow."

He left and moved across the yard, wondering what the hell was wrong with him. He called himself a fool for reacting to her tears. He hated that flaw in himself.

The more he thought, the more he stomped, straight toward his camp beneath the tree. He threw the blankets down, angry at himself for giving in to his adversary, all because she cried. He jerked off his boots, hopping on one foot and swearing when he landed on a rock. How could he be so damn stupid? He'd almost fallen under the spell of her tears. He'd acted like he had Cupid's cramps. Throwing his boots down, he crawled into his bedroll, telling himself that he needed help and a better plan. He grabbed her blankets and shook them out, pulling the ends over his shoulders as he turned onto his side.

"Goddammit!" he muttered. The blankets smelled all flowery, woman flowery.

He was a fool, a fool who had wanted to kiss her, touch her, taste her . . . do more to her. He took a deep cleansing breath. He was a fool, all right, one who should have never left town when it had saloons and women—and he needed to find a woman, bad. And not that woman, because she was the one hitch in his plans. She could keep him from ever having the farm. He needed to get rid of her. He needed to drive her away. He didn't need that woman. He turned onto his back, crossing his arms behind his head and staring up at the night sky. His mind flashed with the sad image of that sorrowful whore. No, he thought dryly, as his hard body throbbed inside the bedroll. What he really needed right now was to find a bull and a wall.

Thud! Thud! Thud! Addie shot upright, blinking. He wouldn't dare! she thought, peeling her puffy, burning eyes open and expecting to see that horrid horse. The room was empty and she was in the kitchen, not her bedroom. Letting the blanket drop, she sagged back against the pillows she'd propped against the wall, and rubbed her sore eyes. Lord but she was tired! She glanced at the stove. The oven doors were open and the birds' incessant chirping poured out into the room. She'd stayed up most of the night, watching the chicks, keeping the stove fire going just enough to warm her poor birds. Only five had passed on, and the rest appeared to be recovering fine, if their noise was any indication.

Yawning, she wobbled to her feet and shuffled over to check on the chicks. With her left hand on her sore back she bent slowly and peered inside the top warming ovens.

Thud! Thud! Thud!

She looked toward the sound, frowning. What was that? She yawned another jaw-cracking yawn, went to the back door and opened it, squinting in the morning sun.

Mr. Creed was in her chicken yard, hammering. He must be building the brooder, she thought, tucking some loose strands of black hair out of her face. She planted a hand on her hip and stood there watching him for a while. He was down on one knee, looking at something on the side of the wooden box. His legs were so long and lean, even in his kneeling position. And when he stood, well, it did something to her, staring up at him. From her height, Addie was used to staring up at everyone. But somehow, when she looked at this man, it was different. She felt even smaller, and she always had this odd urge to prove she wasn't. Maybe small wasn't exactly what she felt. Weak would be a better word. She felt weaker in the presence of this man, which made him seem all that more intense and powerful. Then the need to fight that power would crackle all around her until she found something, some way, to best him.

He'd look down at her and something inside triggered. She wondered if those strange-colored eyes of his were the catalyst. When he looked at her, she was sure he could read her every thought, and it made her so uneasy, antsy—until last night.

She looked back at the chicken yard and realized that the dead chicks were no longer in the yard. He must have gotten rid of them for her. She crossed her arms and leaned back against her back porch rail. Last night there had been a change between them. It was an uneasy truce, never voiced by either of them, yet they both knew it existed.

Just before supper, when she'd walked out to check the waterers and had seen all those dead chicks, she was so appalled that she'd instinctively run for help. He was the only person there. The truly amazing thing was that he'd helped her, after all their bickering and after she'd been pretty petty about the water pump and all. Part of her felt awful, especially as she watched him build that brooder.

She bit back another yawn. She couldn't remember feeling so tired. Of course two hours' sleep wasn't much. Well, tired or not, she had a chance to maybe make up for her behavior by cooking for him. She was an exceptional cook, and as soon as he finished and they could get her chicks into the brooder box, she'd make him a breakfast to remember—farina with apples, biscuits and honey, fried potatoes with fresh green onions she'd found growing wild behind the orchard, a thick slab of ham and perfectly fried eggs. It would ease her guilt.

He stood and for the first time noticed her. He pushed his hat back and looked at her. What had ever made her think that his scruffy beard had hidden a weak chin? The man had the strongest, squarest jaw she'd ever seen. It looked as if it was honed from granite. His cheekbones were Indian-high and his mouth was wide. It was a nice mouth, when it wasn't quirked into that obscene smirk, and without all that bushy brown hair he didn't look so wild. Even with his hair just tipping his shoulders he was pleasing to look at. More than pleasing, as much as she hated admitting it. He was downright handsome. Neat men had always appealed to her—men who had their hair trimmed short and who smelled of bay rum. The fact that she found this man attractive surprised her. Adelaide Amanda Pinkney finding a long-haired man attractive. *Humph!*

There had been one time, though, when she'd been stunned by the illustration of a prince in a book. He'd had long hair, a noble nose, and a strong, square jaw. She looked at Mr. Creed's profile; it looked like that prince in Grimm's Fairy Tales, but that wasn't what amazed her. She thought of him, last night, as he sat across from her at the dinner table. She remembered looking at his clean-shaven face and thinking that his beard hadn't hid a gump chin; it had hidden a dimple. Imagine that! She shook her head. The toad had a dimple. She smiled at her thoughts. The toad prince.

She heard the metally clink of the chicken gate latch, and she watched him walk toward her, long, lean, with power in his stride, command and confidence in his step. Confidence oozed from him like hot lava from Mount Etna. As he neared, she fought the urge to run from him, to keep from getting burned. Then she remembered the way he'd been last night. He'd been nice to her, and she wondered if maybe they really had achieved a truce. They might be able to work out something with the ownership of the farm. For the first time Addie felt as if that might be the case.

"Good morning," she said, smiling.

"What the hell's good about it?"

Her mouth dropped.

"It's damn near eight in the morning and I'm starved. I like my breakfast at six, Miss Pinky." Then he scowled at her, as if she had purposely reneged on their agreement.

"Now see here—"

"I don't want to see anything but breakfast."

"Well, excuse me, master, but it's a little hard to cook

110

with a stove full of chickens," she informed him in her most sarcastic tone.

He stepped closer and tried to burn her with his eyes. "I wasn't the one who was fool enough to buy chickens when I knew nothing about them."

"I did too know! I read that book. Mr. Gates must have forgotten the part about their age. I can learn to raise anything from a book, mister!"

"Lady, the only thing you could raise is someone's temper."

"You horrid toad! And to think—"

"Don't think anything," he interrupted. "Just get that white butt of yours inside and bring me those chickens. The sooner I get them in the brooder, the sooner you can make my breakfast." With that royal pronouncement, he turned and went back to the chicken yard.

And she had worried about being burned? He'd scorched her. They had no truce and never would. She had forgotten who she was dealing with—the toad. She stormed inside, slamming the door in her wake. The worst thing was, now she had to cook for him, three meals a day. She fumed, and then gently slid a pan of chicks out of the oven, setting them on the stove top. The little chickens chirped up at her and she watched them squirm inside the pan. She wouldn't have them if he hadn't helped, so she couldn't in good conscience renege on their agreement. No, she'd have to cook his meals, but if he started demanding them at certain times, well, then she'd show him! She removed the other pan of chickens, wondering how on God's green earth she would be able to stomach cooking for that man. Her mind searched for a way for her to tolerate her agreement yet give him a little trouble at the same time.

The thought of sitting across from him and watching him gobble down the meals she worked so hard to prepare was more than she could handle. He'd probably eat three helpings of everything. Unless . . .

Addie smiled, a wonderfully wicked little smile. She took a deep, prideful breath. Oh, she'd live up to their agreement—she'd cook his meals, yes sirree, but . . . the meals didn't necessarily have to be good.

111

8

With two hands Addie lugged the heavy pail of chick mash to the brooder box. She wrapped her arm around the pail and carefully leaned over the box, letting the mash flow into the feed hoppers that lined three of the brooder's wooden walls. Even before she'd finished filling the hopper, the little golden-brown chicks were trampling and pecking at each other to get to the feeders. The empty pail dropped to her side as she straightened. She blew some loose strands of damp, black hair out of her face and arched her back, wiggling out the kinks of her shoulders while she watched the birds feed.

Lord, those chicks could eat! Five times a day she filled the hoppers and the water jars, and both were empty again in less than ten minutes. It seemed to Addie that all she'd done for the last day and a half was fix and serve meals, to the chicks—which she enjoyed doing even though it was hard work—and to the toad.

She grinned a wicked little smile. Unlike the chicks, he wasn't gorging himself. Of course, the meals she'd prepared were not the sort of dishes that would make one want to overeat.

Yesterday morning after they'd silently loaded her chicks into the brooder—she too angry to speak to him, and he sulking because his breakfast was late—he'd explained the way the brooder worked. She didn't understand that man at all. He had been so helpful the evening before, saving the chicks and all. He'd lulled her into a sense of camaraderie. Then suddenly the next morning he was back to his toady old self.

His belligerent tone still galled her. He had arrogantly rattled off the brooding instructions with the speed of a Gatling gun, then informed her that she had exactly fifteen minutes to get his breakfast, after which, he also demanded dinner at noon and supper at six, "and no later."

So, Addie was exacting her revenge slowly, by completely ruining only one or two items per meal. She knew he'd figure out her plan if everything she served him was inedible, especially since she'd fed him one of her best prepared meals the night before. She'd thought this out and planned to use strategy. She'd even decided to make black-eyed peas and ham once more, and to make it perfectly. Then he'd think that was the only thing she could cook, and afterward she'd make sure never to fix it again.

So far her plan was working. Yesterday she'd made his late breakfast—farina that was just cold enough to become gluelike. Since the eggs were too precious to ruin, she'd made them the regular way, except when she fried his she'd made sure the yolks were broken. The ham was cooked just a tad too long.

At dinner she pretended that the stove heat was almost impossible to regulate, justifying the lumpy mashed potatoes with the little raw chunks. They had crunched in his mouth. She'd heard them. Whenever he hit one, they sounded like carrots. It had been all she could do not to look up. Instead she had blithely taken another forkful and acted as if they were just fine, crunch and all.

The roast was black on the outside, cold and purple in the middle. Addie ate very little because she had eaten the end cuts, which were cooked perfectly and very delicious, before she'd stoked up the stove fire. Of the three perfectly baked apples she'd served, she had eaten two. She'd beaten him to the serving spoons, and when he frowned, she explained about the article she'd read once in *Harper's*. It said women needed to eat more fruit, to encourage their delicate nature. When he choked and coughed and turned a little blue, she then explained that the same article suggested men should eat more meat, since it fortified their animalistic nature. He'd left soon afterward, making some excuse before beating a path to the water pump and drinking away his cough.

All she did at supper was to add just a teeny bit too much salt to the soup. He hadn't appeared to notice, except he'd made quite a few trips to the water pump that night. She had known because the pump handle must have squeaked over a dozen different times.

At none of these meals did she serve bread of any kind, knowing that most men loved breads. She wanted him to crave bread, to be wanting it so badly that he couldn't stand it, because she had a biscuit revenge recipe all planned—a pleasure for today's dinner.

Tilting up the face of her watch pendant, Addie checked the time. She needed to finish making dinner. Grabbing the feed pail in one hand and the water pail in the other, she left the chicken yard. In two hours she'd have to feed the chicks again. Raising chickens was not easy, but she wasn't afraid of hard work. She'd do whatever was needed to make this venture successful, and to show the toad she could do it.

Once inside her kitchen, she washed up, checked the parsnips and the brisket, and went to the pantry, taking down a big, brown earthenware bowl. She set it on a thick pine work table that stood in the middle of the kitchen. She gathered her ingredients and brought them to the table too. Glancing at the wall across from the table, she smiled at her aunt's collection of potchamania.

Most ladies had taken up the art since true porcelain had become so scarce and dearly priced, and Aunt Emily had been a master at the craft. She'd showed Addie once, how one could cut out small colorful pictures from cards and advertisements and then paste them on the inside of a clear glass dome or vase. Once they dried, she'd applied a thin coat of plaster of paris, which hardened to form a white, porcelainlike background. The final look was one of hand-painted porcelain, and Aunt Emily had at least a dozen prime examples displayed on a mahogany whatnot right across from the kitchen worktable.

Addie hummed as she opened the Rhumford's Baking Powder and measured it into the bowl. Next she added a pinch of salt, and then she grabbed the large, rectangular tin flour sifter. Holding it over the bowl, she scooped out a cup of the lumpy, coarse flour and dumped it into the sifter, turning the iron crank so the fine flour soon drifted downward from the sifter's mesh bottom. As she repeated the process, her eyes locked on the small, yellow sack sitting next to the flour bin. She smiled, opened the sack and scooped out a half cup, adding it to the flour she was sifting into the bowl. Was a half cup enough? She scooped another half cup and dumped it in. *Three parts flour to one part plaster of paris . . . that ought to do it.*

She had just added the three walnut-sized balls of lard when she heard the crunch of wagon wheels on the drive. Wiping her hands on her calico apron, she hurried to the front door and out on the porch.

The wagon, a two-seater with three ladies and a child, rolled to a stop. The driver, a stout older woman with a floppy straw hat, turned to Addie. "Good day to you! You must be Emily's niece. I'm Hettie Latimer," she said with a smile, then she ruffled the bright red hair on the boy next to her. "This is Abel . . ." She pointed at the women in the back seat. "And these two are my daughters, Elizabeth—we call 'er Lizzie—and the oldest, Rebecca—"

"She don't let no one call'er nuttin'," the little boy interrupted, grinning around his mother's broad back.

"Maaatherrr! Make him hush!" Rebecca whined, putting her hands on her hips and glaring at Abel. Addie thought she was a little old to be acting so put-out with a little boy's sass. The girl appeared to be in her early twenties, about Addie's own age. She looked tall and slim, and long, auburn curls fell like dark red apple peelings from beneath a broad-brimmed pink straw bonnet adorned with cornflower-blue ribbons and pink and blue silk flowers. The hat hid the girl's face in shadow, but Addie thought it was a lovely hat, one that would have looked just awful on her.

Remembering her manners, she dropped her apron and descended the stairs, smiling. "It's a pleasure to meet you, all of you. I'm Adelaide Pinkney, but please call me Addie."

Hettie backed down out of the wagon, swiped her hands on the front of her green dimity dress, and she took Addie's outstretched hand. Hettie's hand was as warm as her smile, and Addie immediately liked her. Lizzie, who appeared to be about seventeen, joined her mother. They had the same heart-warming smile, only Lizzie's was a bit shyer. She wore a pretty yellow hat, with green ribbons to match her forest-green skirt and green calico shirtwaist. Her features were plain but pleasant, and her skin was almost as pale as Addie's. Every square inch of her face and neck was covered with freckles, hundreds of little brown freckles, and when she raised her head and looked toward the road, Addie caught a glimpse of some short, carrot-red curls around her forehead.

Rebecca stood behind her mother, completely ignoring Addie and swatting at some flies that buzzed around her face. As she shook her regal head, Addie got a closer look at her. She was beautiful, with a classic straight nose, full, pink lips, and clear blue eyes. Her skin was absolutely flawless. But she didn't smile, not once, and that bothered Addie. Also the woman was very tall, full-bosomed, and elegant. From the way she ignored her, Addie felt like a shorty, squatty, gray pigeon standing next to a peacock.

"Here comes my John," Hettie said, pointing at a heavy wagon that was just making the wide turn onto the gravel drive.

The wagon was loaded high with rough wooden cages that looked to be filled with . . . chickens, more chickens to feed. Addie stifled a groan.

"Those are Emily's prize hens. Lizzie's been keeping them until you could get out here. They're the finest, fattest, layingest hens you've ever seen. Well over fifty of 'em."

Now she did groan, but it was drowned out by the rattle and crunch of the wagon wheels on the gravel. Then she saw the cows, two of them, moseying along behind the wagon, tied to the gate.

Was she ready for cows? Looked like she had no choice. *What do cows eat, and how often?*

The wagon stopped and the big man on the seat tipped his straw hat at Addie.

"This is my John," Hettie said with pride in her voice.

Another boy, a bit older than Abel, peered around his father. Abel raced by. "I'll beat ya to the loft!" he shouted, and the older boy bolted from the wagon and ran.

"Amos!" Hettie yelled. "You get back here and pay your respects!"

"Aw, Ma!" He turned around and reluctantly walked toward them.

"That's all right, Hettie, I'll meet him later. Let them go," Addie suggested, noticing that Abel had already disappeared through the barn doors. A strange, guttural sound came from the wagon bed, and she whipped her head around and stared at the cages. She'd never heard chickens sound like that.

"All right, Amos, go on." Hettie relented, shaking her head. "Those two will be the death of me. John? Why don't you get Mabel and Maude settled in the barn so Miz Pinkney doesn't have to."

"Mabel and Maud?" Addie asked.

John Latimer laughed as he untied the lead for the two cows. "That's what your aunt named her cows."

With a strained look on her face, Addie watched them lumber by. She thought cows mooed and lowed, and then the sound gurgled again from the wagon.

Hettie yelled after her husband, "Have the boys come get Teddy and his friends."

"Teddy?" Addie asked, a high squeak in her voice. "And his friends?" She turned her horrified eyes to the wagon bed. How would she ever remember the names of fifty chickens? "Don't tell me she named all the chickens too."

"Oh my, no. Those are the turkeys," Hettie explained.

Turkeys? Two more guttural gobbles pierced the air. Addie closed her eyes, wondering how often *they* ate. She nodded her head slightly, pinching the bridge of her nose. "Turkeys," she stated.

Her head hurt.

"You know, my dear," Hettie said, "you've been the talk of the town."

Addie plastered a strained smile on her face. "Why is

that?" she asked, intuition telling her she wouldn't like the answer.

"You and that Mr. Creed fellow."

Hearing their names linked together for the first time stunned her to stone, horrified stone. Oh, my God! she thought, assuming the worst, that the town thought they were . . . were cohabiting, without the sacrament of marriage. "They think he . . . uh, I mean . . . me . . . they don't think we . . ."

Hettie's hand flew to her chest. "No! Oh no, my dear, that's not what I meant. The town's just downright bedazzled with the judge's ruling . . ."

Rebecca snickered, then gave Addie a thorough once-over, making it obvious she found her sadly lacking, and probably incapable of cohabiting with any man, let alone "bedazzling." Before Addie could blink, Lizzie stepped back, bumping her sister and pushing her against the dusty wagon wheel.

"Ohhhh! Look what you've done!" Rebecca glared at Lizzie. "I'm all dusty."

Lizzie swatted at an imaginary fly. The exact imitation of Rebecca's earlier gesture. "Sorry, I didn't know you were there." She turned slightly and winked at Addie as Rebecca pulled her skirt around and swiped at the dust.

"You girls behave!" Hettie ordered before continuing. "We all knew Emily and Josiah, and this was their farm, the Mitchell place. We watched them build it. Heard tell that some doctor owned some land around here, but we had no idea it was the same property. Every woman in this town loved your aunt, and we're all rooting for you, my dear. The grange men are taking bets on how you two will work this out."

"Where is Mr. Creed?" Rebecca asked, looking pointedly at the oak tree, where his clothes still hung and his camp was still set up.

As if summoned from hell, he and that horse ambled around the corner of the barn. He stopped when he saw them, then slowly walked the horse to the group of women. Addie could have sworn that both he and his horse wore the same cocky grin. They stopped a few feet away and he sat back in his saddle, tipping his hat ever so slightly. "Ladies."

His voice would have melted an ice block.

"Well now," Hettie said, "speak of the devil."

"How true," Addie muttered, disgusted with the way he and Rebecca eyed each other. The woman looked like she'd just been served dessert.

It annoyed Addie, for some odd reason, but what really got to her was that she had to admit Mr. Creed did look good enough to eat.

His long legs gripped the horse, and the faded denim of his pants pulled tightly across his thighs, so tightly that she could see his thigh muscle tighten when he leaned back. She looked away briefly, then found her gaze drawn back to him. He still lounged in his saddle, looking like the world was his for the taking. She focused on his shirt pocket but was soon staring at the place where his dark shirt was unbuttoned. She aimed her eyes at his neck, trying not to gape at the hair that covered his chest. She didn't think it was proper to look at body hair, but her curiosity, and some little devil within her, almost pulled her gaze back. She took a deep breath instead.

His face and neck were tanned, even darker than before. The ends of his brown hair curled slightly around his collar, framing his square, hard jaw. He smiled slightly and the dimple deepened. His look was warm, as were those yellow eyes of his. Her stomach fluttered, just as it had on George Ferris's wheel. She'd never had a thrill like this, sparked by a man. The woman in her yearned for a man to look at her like that, just like that.

He slowly tore his gaze away from Rebecca. "Aren't you going to introduce me, Miss Pinky?"

Addie's lips tightened, holding back the need to correct him. She watched him sling his long leg over that obnoxious horse and slide onto the ground. It was done without thought and with a horseman's ease. She could never get down from a horse like that. Her legs were too short. Of course she'd never get on one of those beasts, so she needn't stand there mooning over the fact. She was afflicted

119

with this fear. It was a weakness, and she needed strength, not weakness, when she was around this man.

He turned around and waited, silently. He knew darn well what her name was, but he was baiting her. She was forced by common social decency to introduce them to him. It galled her.

"These are the Latimers, Hettie, Lizzie, and . . . Becky." Addie couldn't resist.

He smiled, a wonderful, handsome, princely smile that Addie had never before seen. "Rebecca, what a pretty name . . ."

The woman preened. Addie suppressed the sudden need to kick him in the shins.

"And Elizabeth . . ." He blessed Lizzie with the same smile. She shyly nodded back.

How dare he bamboozle that sweet girl! Acting like he was the new preacher in town, the epitome of the gallant gentleman, when he really was a . . . a toad.

He removed his hat. "Mrs. Latimer, it's a pleasure. Wade Parker has spoken very highly of you. Is your husband here? I've been wanting to meet him."

The toad really had manners.

Hettie gestured toward the barn. "John's inside with our boys. He's getting the stock settled in."

"Come along, Mr. Creed," Rebecca said, linking her arm with his. "I'll be happy to introduce you to Father." She started leading him toward the barn.

He stopped and turned to Hettie. "With your permission, ma'am?"

Not only did the toad have manners, he could be a gentleman. She had never seen that side of him—she bit her lip to hide the hurt—not even once.

That awful horse snorted and the couple stopped. Mr. Creed turned and whistled and that devil of a horse pranced right over to them. It'll nip at her, Addie thought, remembering her experiences and that he'd said his horse didn't like strangers.

She stood there, quietly waiting. Rebecca said something to Mr. Creed and he laughed. He had a wonderful, deep laugh when it wasn't being snide. The girl said something and then held out her hand. Addie winced, now a little afraid for the other woman, and she waited for the horse to bite.

It lifted those awful lips and then took something from her hand, chomping away. Then it nuzzled the woman while she scratched its ornery ears. The horse rubbed its head upward, like it was in pure heaven.

Addie really hated that horse.

They walked away, Rebecca chatting away as if she and Mr. Creed were old friends. The horse trailed behind her like a royal page. It made Addie mad, because it brought home the fact that he really didn't like her. Even his horse didn't like her. But worse yet, she was hurt. Hurt because all Mr. Creed did was shout or swear at her. Hurt because he never treated her that way. Hurt because he didn't treat her with the same respect as he did the other women. She was a woman too. No man had ever looked at her like that, and the woman in her wanted a man to look at her like that, just like that.

Her jaw went up a notch as she masked her feelings. She forced a smile and said, "Please, come inside. I'll fix something to drink and we can have a nice chat. I'd love to hear about my aunt."

Hettie and Lizzie followed her through the house and into the kitchen.

Addie looked at the messy worktable and at the oven. "Oh my Lord! I forgot about dinner!"

She ran to the oven and opened it. The brisket was dry as jerky. She lifted the pan out with her apron and set it on the stove top, next to the smoking parsnips. They were stuck to the bottom of the cast-iron pot. She turned and sighed. "I'm so sorry. I can't even ask you to stay and eat."

Hettie marched over to the pan and examined the meat. "Now don't you worry about a thing. I've burned more dinners in my day than I care to mention. We'll just whip up some gravy and boil some potatoes and everything will be fine." She marched over to the water pump and began to wash her hands. "Come along, Lizzie, Addie can get the potatoes and you can peel them."

Addie went in the pantry, filled her apron with potatoes

121

and brought them to the women. Returning to the stove, she jabbed a serving fork into the brisket, jerked it off the bottom of the pan and held it up, eyeing the thing. She didn't think gravy would help this dry, black meat, but she was willing to try.

"Now what is this?" Hettie asked, standing over the earthenware bowl on the worktable.

"Biscuits," Addie answered without thinking. *Oh Lord, the plaster of paris!*

She rushed over, leaning over the bowl and blocking Hettie's view of the plaster sack that sat next to the sifter. "I'll have to redo these. They're probably ruined." Addie wrapped her arms around the big bowl and heaved it off the table. "I'll just throw this old dough out and make some fresh."

"It looked fine to me, my dear. There were only dry ingredients in that bowl. They can't go bad. Why, you hadn't even cut in the lard or added any liquid yet." She reached out for the bowl. "Here, now, that's way too heavy for a little thing like you." She plucked the bowl from Addie's arms before she could get away.

The little yellow sack of plaster sat right on the table, next to the flour, and with the label facing Hettie. As the woman set the bowl down, Addie grabbed the tin sifter and, turning it upside down, she whipped it over the plaster sack. Hettie was rolling more little lard nuts and smiling at her. Addie smiled back, but it felt more like a wince.

She quickly slid the sifter off the table and covered the bottom with her hand to keep the sack from falling out. Just as she spun around to head for the pantry, Hettie spoke, "Wait, Addie, I'll need the sifter for more flour and for the gravy."

Addie froze. How was she going to get out of this? "Uh . . . let me wash it first." She sped toward the dry sink. But she forgot Lizzie was there, peeling potatoes into a big tin garbage pail. Addie just stood there, her mind a blank.

Hettie picked up a jar and sniffed its contents. "There's nothing a man loves more than good old-fashioned buttermilk biscuits."

She turned and watched in horror as Hettie poured some

buttermilk from the jar into the bowl. Liquid would set the plaster. She closed her eyes, her hands still gripping the sifter and its bottom. *Think!*

"Get a move on girl. I'm gonna need that sifter."

Addie's eyes flew open. Lizzie stared up at her with a puzzled look on her sweet face. Trusting her judgment and praying she was right about Lizzie, Addie very slowly lifted the sifter, showing Lizzie the sack. The girl's green eyes bugged and then she started to laugh, but slammed her hand over her mouth to keep the noise from escaping.

"You know, this dough is really stiff, Addie. I've never seen anything like it."

Now Lizzie was really laughing hard, but very quietly. Addie could feel her own laughter coming. Lizzie pointed to the garbage pail. Addie dropped the sack inside, and Lizzie bent over the pail and covered the sack with peelings, all the while making these odd little snorting sounds.

Addie watched Lizzie's shoulders shake. She was going to lose control. Any second she was going to burst into laughter. Addie raced past the table, dropping the sifter by the bowl as she hurried into the pantry. She sat down on a pickle barrel, with both hands over her face, and she rocked, silently laughing so hard her shoulders shook and tears streamed down her face. The look on Lizzie's face had been priceless. She wiped the tears and tried to catch her breath.

"There, there, my dear . . ."

Addie slammed her hands over her face. Hettie stood right behind her, patting her shoulder.

"There's nothing to cry about. One ruined meal isn't the end of the world. Besides, it's been my experience that men will eat anything. There's two things men are fools about: women and food. Like with women, most men can't tell good food from bad. You watch, they'll never even notice."

Addie nodded and stood, but she could still hear Lizzie muffling her laughter.

"Uh . . . Ma?" Lizzie called out. "I think they'll notice these."

Hettie and Addie peered around the corner. Lizzie stood

there grinning and holding the bowl up by the spoon that was stuck in it.

"What in the world?" Hettie stared at the bowl. "Well I've never, in all my born days, seen anything like that!"

Lizzie and Addie shared a knowing grin. "I must have gotten the measurements wrong." Addie grabbed the heavy bowl and made for the pantry. As she rounded the corner she added, "I'll get you another bowl, Hettie."

An hour later everyone sat around the big table. Abel and Amos sat on barrels they'd rolled out of the pantry, the adults sat on the six oak chairs. Rebecca had waltzed in with a man on each arm, her father and Mr. Creed, both men laughing at something she had said. Then she'd sat them down next to each other and plopped into the chair next to Mr. Creed. When her mother suggested she help, she made some lame excuse about just being in the way. Then she'd rested her elbow on the table, planted her perfect chin in her slender hand and stared at the conversing men, appearing enthralled with their every word.

Addie really disliked Rebecca, which bothered her because the other Latimers were so pleasant, some of the nicest people she'd ever met. Hettie reminded Addie of her aunt, and she adored Lizzie. They thought alike. The only consolation Addie had was that the men appeared to be talking about crops and not paying much attention to adoring Rebecca. And Mr. Creed no longer had that enamored, Prince Charming look on his face.

The meat was served, covered in a dark brown gravy. The potatoes were perfect, the biscuits light, fluffy, and without plaster. Addie cut into her meat. It was still awfully tough. She gripped her knife and sawed into it, finally managing to carve off a piece. She swabbed it in gravy and stuck it in her mouth, looking up and smiling. She chewed, and her smile slowly died. The meat was tough as hide, but on she chewed, and chewed, and chewed.

The table was completely silent, every one of them masticating like cattle. The men had pained looks on their faces. Rebecca, her cheeks bulging slightly, politely lifted her napkin to her lips. A moment later her mouth was empty. She sipped her water. "Do you remember the time you burned that roast, Mama?"

"Not now, Rebecca," Hettie warned.

"Oh I'm sure Mr. Creed would like to hear the story, now wouldn't you?" She smiled at him.

Addie's foot itched again. She reached down to scratch it, glaring at Mr. Creed, daring him to answer the woman.

He winced while he chewed, looking as if chewing was a painful experience. Rebecca continued to look at him expectantly. Addie stared at her plate, waiting for the story she knew would make her look more foolish than she already did.

She heard John Latimer's voice. "Quiet, Becky."

Addie looked up and Hettie gave her a reassuring smile. She smiled back, a bit unsure, a lot grateful.

Rebecca buttered a biscuit, handing it to Mr. Creed. "I've been told I make wonderful biscuits. Isn't that right, Mama?"

"You ought to, I taught you myself," Hettie answered.

"Too bad it only took you ten years to master the craft," Lizzie mumbled at Addie, who bit back her grin.

"Did you hear about the train robbery?" Amos asked.

"Oh! Do we have to talk about that awful thing again?" Rebecca piped up, her voice the same irritating tone as wheel metal scraping gravel.

"Get some more coffee please, Rebecca," Hettie ordered in a no-nonsense tone.

"I'll get it." Addie started to rise but Hettie stopped her and stared at her eldest daughter. Rebecca reluctantly obeyed, flouncing over to the stove and returning with the coffeepot. She poured some into her father's cup and then sashayed over to Mr. Creed and, bending over his shoulder, slowly refilled his mug. He spoke to her, quietly, and she murmured something back.

Addie looked away, trying to ignore the scene. Every word he spoke to her was an order, or was taunting her. He didn't like her. Addie wondered if it was because of the farm or because she was . . . unlikable. The other Latimers seemed to genuinely like her. She was sure of that. But despite all her bravado when it came to dealing with Mr.

Creed, something deep inside, something she didn't really want to admit, made her a bit jealous of Rebecca and the way the man treated her, and looked at her.

"They took ten thousand dollars!" Abel exclaimed, looking right at Addie.

"Who?"

"Some bandits done robbed the S.P. again, two nights ago. Just a few miles outside o' town," Abel said, his young eyes alight with the excitement.

"They said it was the same two as before," Amos added. "Only about ten miles from here."

"That's just horrible!" Addie said, imagining how frightened she'd have been had her train been robbed.

"Not really," John Latimer informed her. "The railroad's been driving out half the farmers in California for years now. They started in the central valley and now they're doing it up here. Ever since that Mussel Slough incident years ago—"

Mr. Creed's coffee mug slammed down on the table. Steaming hot coffee sloshed out of the mug, over his hand.

The whole table stilled. He didn't say a word, just stared off, over Addie's shoulder. His expression was harder than stone, his lips thinned, the muscles in his neck so tight that Addie could count the throbs of his pulse. His nostrils flared slightly and his eyes were hot, angry, and gleaming like gold. And he didn't move. He didn't flinch. She had never seen anything like it. His look was deadly, filled with such pure hatred that she felt like running away, even though he wasn't looking at her. She silently prayed that she was never the recipient of that look, because if she ever was, she knew she'd soon be dead.

Hettie and Rebecca fussed over him, tending the dark red burn on his hand, but he didn't seem to notice. Finally he glanced down and stared blankly at his hand. Hettie covered it with a wet towel. Rebecca had the butter crock in her hand, apparently waiting to put butter on the burn.

His eyes cleared and he took a deep breath. "I'm okay."

Addie stood and went to the pantry, taking down the box that held the medicines and bandages. She came out and set it on the table. Hettie treated and bandaged his hand while Rebecca fawned over him. Her behavior didn't bother Addie anymore. All she could think of was the lethal look in Mr. Creed's eyes.

John sent the boys to milk the cows, claiming Mr. Creed couldn't do it with his burned hand. Addie didn't comment that he wouldn't have done it anyway, since they were her cows. She didn't want to start anything with him after what had happened. She wasn't that stupid. He hardly said much, just went outside with John while the women cleaned up. The boys brought in the milk, and the Latimers were soon all packed up and driving down the road.

Addie stayed on the porch, watching Mr. Creed. He stood at the end of the drive, where it met the road. He stared off to the southeast. She went to feed and water the chicks. It was twilight when she'd finished. As she left the chicken yard she looked down the drive. He still stood there, as if he were carved from the heaviest stone, unable to move.

The sky darkened and deep purple clouds crept over the western hills, consuming the brilliance of a burning pink sky. The breeze picked up, flicking dust and leaves around the farm yard. The air cooled. She turned, lifting a hand over her brow to block the wind, and she watched the clouds continue to pour over the hilltops, growing darker, as if a door from hell had suddenly opened up.

Now the wind blew; it caught the barn door, slamming it hard against the barn. Addie ran to the doors and remembered the turkeys. She went into the barn and fed them some chicken mash, hoping that would suffice until she could read about the big birds. The doors banged again, and she ran through the dank darkness of the barn, out the wide-open doorway. She grasped the left door, shoving it closed and anchoring it with her hip while she grabbed at the other door. Her hairpins flew and her hair tumbled down from its topknot. Her eyes teared from the blasts of air. She lowered her head and finally grabbed the other door. Pulling with all her might, she tried to fight the power of the wind, ramming her small body against the doors, holding them while she slid home the wooden latch.

The wind almost howled now, whipping her loose hair across her face, over her eyes, into her mouth. She peeled it away and turned around, expecting to see him still standing there, statuelike, oblivious to the wind. His spare clothing blew from the branches of the tree and tumbled down the drive. His packs slid from the force of the wind, butting against the tree trunk. Ash and burnt wood chips spun upward in a small dark cloud, the remnants from his last camp fire.

She glanced at the water trough. The horse was gone. She looked at the tree. The saddle was gone. She looked down the drive, where it met the road. He was gone.

9

COME ON, BOY. IT'S NOT MUCH FARTHER." MONTANA BENT low over Jericho's neck as the horse plodded through the deep mud of the north field. Rain pelted against his back, covered only by the thin shirt he'd worn that day. An icy blast of wind blew right through him and he shivered and hunkered closer to the horse's wet mane. His hand throbbed beneath the sodden bandage, so he let it fall, holding the reins in only his left hand. The rain and wind whipped at him and he felt the bandage unravel. The burn ached but he ignored it and tried to see through the rain.

Jericho stumbled and Montana knew he had to dismount or risk injuring the horse. He slid from the slick saddle, his boots plunging into mud that almost reached his knees. The rain streamed down; the mud sucked at his feet; the wind bit through his bones. He shivered, growing colder and colder by the minute. Lightning cracked through the black sky, breaking open its darkness for a brief, silver instant before it blackened again, shuttered closed. Thunder bellowed high above him, as if protesting the hiding of light.

His horse shied. Instinctively Montana pulled the reins with both hands. The leather pushed into his raw burn. He wanted to yell. He didn't. He went on, unaware of the way his jaw clamped, unaware of the gritting pressure of his teeth, aware of only the need to keep going. In weather like this, flash floods surged over fields and roads. He remembered Wade saying that the Pinky woman's aunt and uncle had died in one, swept away, buggy, horses, and all.

He looked to the west, half expecting a wall of black water to swallow him at any second. He saw nothing but a curtain of pounding rain, until he looked to the south. There he caught the flicker of a dim light. Swiping the water from his eyes, Montana stopped and tried to focus. Again the lightning split the sky, and he saw it—the outline of the farmhouse.

He jerked on Jericho's reins. "We're home, boy. We're almost home." The horse snorted, shaking his head. They both dragged on. They crossed the edge of the north field and closed the few hundred yards to the oak tree, pausing under the protection of its wide branches. For the first time, he breathed through his open mouth, not having realized his jaw was so tight until he relaxed it. Now it ached like his hand.

Again the lightning stabbed down, only it was so close to them the light from it almost blinded him. Soon after, the thunder boomed. Jericho brayed, rolling his eyes and flattening his ears. He reared up, pulling the leather reins right through the wet, straggling bandage on Montana's hand. He sucked a breath, bending and grabbing his white-hot hand. The bandage fell off. The rain poured into his eyes, and when he could focus again, he lifted his head.

Warm, filtered light bled through the windows of the farmhouse as the curtains split aside. The front door wobbled open. She stood, a lamp in one hand while she called out to him. He couldn't understand her over the howl of the storm. She disappeared for a moment, then she ran down the porch, wrapped in a rain slicker twice her small size. She flew at him, this pestering, little bug of a woman, all cloaked in yellow oilcloth, feet scurrying across the sodden farmyard like a water weevil. She neared, yelling something about the barn and pointing at it.

The wind gusted and she slowed, sloshing forward with the lantern under the voluminous protection of the slicker. "Put your horse in the barn!" she yelled over the scream of the storm.

He nodded and led Jericho across the gravel toward the barn. A moment later he stopped, unable to believe what he saw. She whipped past him, a flash of yellow oilcloth, and ran ahead of him, lighting his way with her lantern. "Get back inside!" he shouted.

She ignored him, as usual. *Damn her!*

Before he could reach for the door, she shoved her small shoulder under the wooden door latch and somehow rammed it up, out of the bolt. The door flew open, almost taking her with it as it swung wide. He blocked it with his body, pinning her between him and the edge of the door. He straightened his right arm, using it to hold the door, keeping her covered, protected by his body. She wiggled and he could hear the mumble of her voice. He pressed closer; she squirmed some more, making the oilcloth crackle between them. He jerked once on the reins and Jericho loped inside. He wrapped his arm around her middle, lifted her off the door and hauled her inside, slamming it behind him. He stood there, water pouring off them both.

Her wet head poked out of the slicker. "Put me down!" She kicked at him and slipped out of his arm, landing on the ground with a hard thud. "Dadgummit!" He heard her swear as he bent and picked up the fallen lantern.

"Why the hell didn't you get back inside?"

The slicker crackled again while she tried to dig her way out, her arms waving like a drowning swimmer. All the while she mumbled, something about curses "upon his black soul." Then she said something about his horse. Finally she whipped the slicker off and scowled up at him.

Her hair, wet and black as the sky outside, hung around her face. Her cheeks were flushed red from anger and the bite of the wind. Her skin looked whiter, and almost breakable. Her eyes, black as her hair, glared up at him. Dark and round, they glistened with anger. Her black brows winged upward with her frown, but it was her mouth—red, full, and pouty—that made him suddenly want to taste her, feel her, and do battle with her—in a bed, atop her.

He shook the image from his mind and repeated his question. "Why didn't you go back inside?"

"You looked like you needed help." she said, managing to sound aggravated and doubtful at the same time. She pushed herself up, shaking the water from her soaked hair. She wore some nightgown made of cloth so thick it would take one of those telescope things to look through it.

He breathed a relieved sigh. He didn't want to think of her sexually.

Then she bent and wrung the water from her long hair. Her gown was wet; it clung to her, outlining her butt perfectly. He remembered her bare backside, lily-white and sliding down her bed when she had that tug-of-war with his horse. His hands itched, and he thought of the feel of it, when she'd jumped out the window right into him. He loved a round butt.

Then he reminded himself just who the round butt belonged to. This woman was trouble for him, and for his future. He needed to get rid of her, not bed her.

"If I need your help, I'll ask for it." He spun around and walked past her toward Jericho. Picking up the reins, he led him to a nearby stall. Hay bales were stacked in a corner and he shoved one under the stall railing. He needed wire cutters, and looked to the wall, where a few tools were haphazardly hung on some rusty nails. No wire cutters. He squinted, trying to see in the dark corner of the stall. "Bring that light over here."

He heard her breathe, hard. Then . . . "Asking for help?" Her voice was threaded with feigned innocence.

"Hurry the hell up!"

She bent and grabbed the lantern. "Yes, master."

He ignored her, continuing to slam around the barn, looking for a toolbox.

She held up the lamp.

He forgot to ignore her, and glanced up. It was a mistake. She held the lamp out and its light proved better than a

131

telescope. He could see the silhouette of her body beneath the fabric. Her naked body.

"What are you looking for?"

"Tools." He moved a barrel aside, swearing. *And a bull and a wall.*

"I saw some stuff in there." She pointed toward a small doorway, hidden in a dark corner.

He strode forward. It was too dark to see anything. He took another breath, glad for a moment that he couldn't see her. But the sooner he found the cutters, the sooner he could get rid of her, at least for now. And he needed the light to find the cutters. "What are you standing there for? Bring that light here."

"I thought you wanted me in the house," she said, her tone dripping with sarcasm.

No, he thought, that's not where I want you.

He waited a long, long moment. "Well, now that you're here, you might as well be useful."

Light preceded her into the small workshop. He turned, expecting her to mouth off again, but she stood there, looking aghast at the room. "Lord, what a mess."

He grabbed the lantern and hung it on a hook from one of the low rafters, well away from her small, perfect body. He looked around the room. She was right. Rakes, shovels, and hoes were scattered over piles of farm and shop tools. Wooden-handled planes lay on the damp ground, with hammers, rusty saws, and every other tool imaginable strewn chaotically across the room. Nails and screws spilled from a barrel, and tangles of rope crisscrossed the room.

He shoved aside an overturned wheelbarrow and found a wooden chest. He kicked the top open and found the wire cutters. He grabbed them and walked past her. "Follow me."

"Of course, master."

"Knock it off." Or, he thought, *I'll master you, all right.*

He made it a few feet into the dark barn and remembered the light. He swore, spun around, and ran right into her. His hand shot out, instinctively grabbing for something to hold.

132

He held a soft, full breast. The nipple hardened. *Sweet Jesus*. So did he.

She gasped, then slapped his hand away.

Their breathing echoed through the silence of the room.

He didn't dare look at her. He stared over her head, focusing on a harness that hung on the shop wall. She didn't move, and he could feel her staring up at him. He didn't want to see her face. "Move. I need to get the lamp."

He heard her step aside, and he walked by, grabbed the lantern and left the room. He could hear her shuffling behind him, her mouth quiet. At least there were no more "master" comments. He set the lamp down inside the stall and cut the baling wire; then he began to break up the hay for his horse. "You don't have to stay."

"No . . . I don't . . . do I?"

He counted slowly to ten. It took forever. She fought him, every damn time.

He kicked a flake off the hay, waiting for a smart remark. It never came. Unable to resist, he said, "What's wrong, no more master comments?"

She looked away. He followed her example and tried to ignore her as he uncinched the saddle and lifted it off the horse. He looked around, then set it on the stall rail. He next removed the bridle and Jericho went straight for the hay.

The Pinky woman stood next to it. Jericho closed in and she gasped, jumping back. She stood plastered against the stall, her eyes as scared as a bug in a chicken yard. He felt sorry for her, for about a second.

"Where's all that fight now, Miss Pinky?"

She didn't say a word.

"He won't hurt you. Come on."

"Uh-uh." She shook her fool head.

"If you'd learned to ride, you wouldn't be so afraid." She looked skeptical and fearful. He'd try one more thing. "It's just your ignorance."

That did it. She glared at him. "I'm not ignorant."

"Then how come you never learned to ride a horse?"

"I don't like them." Her chin shot up, but she still hugged the stall. Jericho's tail swished while he ate, and

133

she kept one eye on him while she moved her head out of the path of the bushy, black tail.

"Well, I don't like dances, but that doesn't mean I never learned to dance." He shook his head, unable to reason like this crazy woman. "Come on." He started to leave the stall.

She didn't budge.

"For Christ's sake!" He spun around and grabbed her arm, almost peeling her away from the stall. He made for the barn doors, pulling her along with him. "Come on, now, you need to get back to the house before the farmyard floods." And I'll be damned, he thought, if I'll stay stranded in the barn all night with her.

True to form, she fought him, digging in her heels and pulling back. He stopped and scowled at her. She glared up at him; then, when she knew he watched her, she pointedly looked at her arm, clamped in his left hand. He pulled her over to the discarded slicker.

"Put that back on." He heard her breathe. "Now!"

She jumped, then bent down, pulling the huge slicker around her small shoulders.

Finally she obeyed him. Satisfaction swelled through him.

She straightened and turned around, a defiant look still creasing her features. She took one deep breath and her lips quirked slightly. "Yes . . ."

His eyes narrowed.

". . . master."

That did it.

His arms shot out and around her. He slammed her up against him. She looked up, surprised yet a little bit triumphant.

The battle was on. He bent his head, staring into her glistening eyes.

"Shut up." His mouth hit hers, hard, intending to punish her silent. She gasped. He buried his tongue in her warm mouth. He tasted her as he'd imagined. For once she didn't fight him, so he ran his rough tongue over hers, waiting to see what she'd do. Damn if she didn't stroke back.

He bent his knees and clamped his right arm under the

slicker and beneath her bottom, lifting her so her mouth was even with his. Their tongues battled. Her hands gripped his shoulders and his left hand spanned her damp head, holding it so he could thrust deeper. She groaned and gripped him tighter, moving her lips. He stroked her teeth, pulled back and licked at her lips.

His mind flashed with the thought that this was heaven, but she tasted like sin.

Slowly, like rainwater, he let her warm, little body slide down his. It took forever for her feet to touch the ground. All the while his mouth mated with hers. His hand still held her, gently kneading her butt and pressing her closer. He raised his hand and slowly drew the tips of his cold fingers over her neck, remembering the gun trailing over it and pausing to let his fingers feel the pulse beat in her neck. Her skin was smooth, like cornsilk, and softer than a ripe cotton bud.

He watched her, rainwater beading near the curls that framed her face. Her lids closed, her lashes black and thick, her cheeks colored. The Pinky woman had passion, hot lusty passion. He wanted more. His mouth left hers and her breathing labored. He smiled and drew his lips across her forehead, kissed her eyes. He bent lower and rested his open mouth against the pulse in her soft neck. He licked her, then blew a small slow breath on the damp spot. She moaned. She moved. His lips brushed her ear. He wet it and sucked in a breath. She cried out and shook her head away from the thrust of his tongue.

Her black eyes shot open. Panting, she stared up at him as if he'd just grown horns.

"Oh, God!" Her hand covered her mouth and she spun around, out of his arms. Before he could gather her or his senses, she'd fled to the door and run out into the storm.

"Addie, wait!"

The barn door banged shut.

He ran to the doors and shoved them open. The kitchen door slammed shut and he caught a flash of yellow through the window. He gripped the door, and stared out at the rain for a very long time, calling himself every kind of a fool. He'd forgotten. In his need to battle with this woman,

135

he'd gone and forgotten the purpose of their fight. His land.

Nothing was going right. He'd foolishly thought he could drive her away. She'd proved that wasn't the case, so far. She'd proved to have a stubborn streak as wide as his. There were times, however, when he'd actually looked forward to goading her. Fighting with this woman was . . . stimulating. He laughed to himself, thinking about his physical reaction to her. Sometimes it was too stimulating. Something about her fueled his ire, and an odd need to make her react. He liked to see her mad, good and mad.

But he had to admit that part of his interest was because she could surprise him. Just when he thought she'd do one thing, she'd turn around and do just the opposite. He was intrigued, and a little worried. She, unlike anyone he could remember, came close to touching a part of him that was better left untouched.

He watched the rain, his face thoughtful. The lights went out, one by one. Montana stared at the dark windows, wishing this could be easily done. The house should be his. It was on his land. He didn't need to have some little female causing him trouble. He needed to rid himself of her before he started to care about what happened to her once she was gone.

He tried to think, to conjure up his anger at the whole situation. Then he could direct that anger at her. Instead his mind flashed with the image of her face, lost in a world of feeling. Within a second, though, her passion had changed to horror. Her face had worn the same look she'd had when Jericho scared her. She was frightened, all right. He had finally frightened her, or his lust had. But now she was safe inside her farmhouse, protected from him.

The rain had lessened, and he listened to it flicker on the wooden roof. The water that drizzled from the farmhouse roof changed to a fine trickle. He really looked at the wooden farmhouse, feeling deep inside that it was rightfully his. It wasn't a woman who should be dominating his thoughts. He needed to secure complete ownership of the farm. In the past few hours his goal had been forgotten, waylaid.

But not now. He knew he had to drive off this woman—this woman who fought him at all the wrong times. And he had to do it soon. He leaned against the barn door, letting the water cool his face. Maybe it would help him think of how to get rid of her once and for all.

The gun hadn't worked. Neither had the horse. She seemed immune to her own fears. He'd learned that he could only push her so far. Then she fought back. Now he had learned something new—the Pinky woman had passion. It was something new he could use against her.

An idea sprouted in his mind. He smiled, and stared at the bedroom window. It might work, using her own passion against her. Suppose he chased her, like some love-starved fool. Suppose he scared her with his advances, hot lusty ones. She was inexperienced, that much he could tell from the caution in her kiss. It was great ammunition.

A devious smile creased his face. His eyes glowed golden. He turned back, closing the barn doors, and suddenly he laughed out loud. It was a great plan. After the way she'd run, he was sure it would work. He'd start tomorrow, very slowly, and he'd build that fear to new heights. It would surely send her running. But if it didn't work, he was sure of one thing. He was going to have one hell of a good time.

Addie sat in the dark parlor. The wet rain slicker hung on a wooden hall tree, and she could hear the water drip onto the wooden floor. The plop, plop droned on. It soothed her, and Lord knew she needed soothing. She tried to rub some warmth into her cold face. She ended up slicking back her wet hair. Water drops trickled down from her hairline, trailing over her mouth. The water felt cool on her warm, swollen lips; they still burned from his kiss. She ran her fingers over them, feeling the sensitive surface. She wondered if they'd ever be the same. She closed her eyes.

Her emotions warred. Part of her was embarrassed, part of her puzzled. All of her was confused, and a very little, very wanton part of her was still shaking, because she liked it. She shivered, despite the fact that she sat in a soft chair, in a warm room, with a warm throw slung over her damp clothes.

Never, as long as she lived, would she be able to look at that man without remembering the way he'd kissed her. With his tongue. No pursed lips, no puckered mouth. The devil had descended on her open-mouthed and used his tongue the way one savored a treat.

When he'd kissed her, she'd felt like a dish of ice cream on a hot Fourth of July. And nothing, not the chaste smooches of a college classman, not the freewheeling joy of her first bicycle ride, not even the thrill of Mr. Ferris's wheel, had ever made her feel the way she felt in that barn. She grabbed a copy of *Harper's* and fanned herself. Just the memory had her all hot and bothered.

Addie, girl, are you ever in trouble. Toad trouble.

Her fist slammed onto the padded chair arm. Why him? She'd been held in a man's arms before. She sprang out of the chair and paced the small room. She'd been kissed, and those experiences had been pleasant and cozy, like the men who had done the kissing. Those men had slowly courted her. They had been gentlemen, with neat, trimmed hair. Men who smelled of bay rum, instead of rainwater, leather, and something else, something earthy.

Tossing the throw on the chair, Addie went into the bedroom, changed into a dry nightgown and crawled under the downy covers of the feather bed. She laid back, thinking of her first kiss. It had come from an upperclassman named Sam, who had spent most of their six-month courtship sitting on a proper settee in the dormitory parlor, fidgeting like a three-year-old in church. She'd finally got tired of waiting, so she'd asked him to kiss her. She had thought for a brief moment that he was going to run out the door. He twisted his tie, pulled at his collar, and nervously swallowed big gulps of air. It still took him ten minutes. Then he'd plastered his dry, tightly closed lips on hers; but not for long, because he pulled away, burping from all the air he'd swallowed. Addie could remember thinking that it was like kissing a wall, a belching wall.

Unlike tonight. Chills tingled up her neck. She prayed they were from her damp clothes. She knew better. Just like she knew she'd been asking for it, pushing him like she had with her smart mouth. But she'd gotten far more than she'd asked for. She'd done it to irritate him; it never really crossed her mind that he'd react so ruthlessly. She'd forgotten, because of the chicks, how he'd treated her before. She should have trusted her instincts. The first time she laid eyes on him she'd seen the wildness in his eyes. She'd seen it again at the dinner table. Her mind flashed with the image of his eyes just before he kissed her. They hadn't been the same. His eyes had burned with anger and power. The look wasn't lethal, as the others had been. It was dominant.

And the last thing Adelaide Amanda Pinkney needed was to be dominated, especially by him. She had a farm to mind, chickens to raise, and a few more meals to ruin. And now she had a man to avoid, intriguing or not. It didn't matter that he made her feel odd. It didn't matter that he sparked in her a need to be a woman, a cherished, respected woman. It didn't matter that he kissed her senseless, with his tongue. What mattered was her future and her farm, and she'd just have to learn to ignore him, for her own good.

A hard hand hit her smack on the backside. "Whack!"

Addie screamed and shot straight up. Her hand covered her burning bottom.

"Time for breakfast . . . Addie."

The toad prince stood by her bed, grinning. It was the most lecherous grin she'd ever seen.

She jerked the covers to her chin. "What do you think you're doing?"

He loomed over the bed, his hair brushing his shoulders, his fists pressing into the bed, his leering face closing in. "I'm hungry . . ."

"Get away!" Addie scooted back.

His knee edged onto the bed. ". . . so hungry."

He crawled closer, his mouth was parted, his gold eyes half closed. His expression that of an animal, seeking its mate. She dodged his lips. They landed on her neck, nibbling. She dropped the sheet and tried to shove him away. "Stop that this instant!"

He pulled her hand from his shoulder and lifted it to his warm lips. "You don't mean that . . . sweet Addie." He held her hand fast, planting little kisses all over it while he grabbed the other one. He nuzzled open one palm. She tugged back on her hand.

"Don't fight this," he mumbled into her hand. "It's stronger than both of us." He licked her palm.

"Stop that!" She kicked at him, but the covers restricted her. His other knee eased onto the bed and he crawled closer. All the while, his lips trailed over her wrist, sending traitorous chills down her weak spine. She managed to jerk one hand away and swatted at him. He dodged her swishing hand and buried his hot face in her neck. He made deep little wheezing noises into her neck, and she could feel his shoulders shake. Did men laugh when they were in the throes of passion? She'd never been in the throes before, so how would she know?

"Get off me!" She shoved at him and kicked furiously beneath the covers, afraid of what was going to happen.

He put a knee on either side of her legs, pulling the covers so taut that her legs were pinned. He bent over her, resting on his elbows on either side of her stiff shoulders while his face and mouth chased hers.

"I'll scream," she threatened.

He blew in her ear, then whispered, "Do it. Let all that passion out." His tongue circled her ear. "My sweet . . ."

Chills whisked down her neck and she twisted her head away.

". . . hot . . ."

Desperate, she grabbed fistfuls of his hair.

". . . Addie . . ."

She pulled, hard.

He grunted, then swore under his breath. He twisted his head.

She wouldn't let go. "Get off me!"

He kept his mouth against her neck. He began to suck on it.

She pulled his hair again.

His hands splayed over her breasts, and squeezed. "Such soft, pearly globes," he said through gritted teeth.

She twisted his hair. He reached up and grabbed her hands. He lost his balance and fell, full force, on top of her.

A loud crack sounded. The mattress buckled and they crashed to the floor, the iron foot and head rails collapsing.

He was still sprawled over her, one knee wedged high between her legs. He moved it.

Addie's eyes flew open. Feathers floated everywhere, and the more she wiggled to get free, the more they puffed up into the air. She waved them away and Montana began to sneeze. Addie wormed free and crawled over the remains of the bed, tilted at an odd angle with the floor. Just as she reached the edge, the last side rail gave way, dumping her out onto the feathered floor.

She heard his muffled voice between sneezes. Grabbing half of a broken wooden bed slat, she scampered up and raised it high over her head.

She remembered her bottom.

The slat came down, right on his backside.

A muffled, unrepeatable male word was all she heard. He rolled through the feathers and out the opposite side of the broken bed.

Addie brandished the slat at him while he waved the feathers away. "Get out of here, you, you weasel!"

"You'll love it." He leered at her. "I promise . . ."

She grabbed her hot chocolate cup from the bedside table and flung it at him.

He ducked and put his hands out, backing up a bit. "Now, sweet . . ."

She waved the slat in one hand, and with the other, spun the saucer at him. "Don't you 'now, sweet' me! Get out!"

He was smiling, actually smiling at her.

A vase hit the wall beside his head. She moved forward, swinging the slat like the Count of Monte Cristo—she'd loved that book. She parried and lunged forward. He stepped around the rocker, backing straight toward the window.

"There, there, sweet, now don't get upset." He still had

that smile on his lascivious face. "I understand. It'll take time for you to overcome this shyness." He was almost laughing.

Her face turned purple. She couldn't speak. Instead she looked for something else to throw, and spotted the heavy gilded bronze inkstand.

Her hand reached toward it.

His gaze followed her hand. "Oh shit!" He dove out the window, and the stand, ink and all, sailed out after him.

Addie stormed to the open window, glaring out at him. He was lying, thigh high, in the mud, Peyton's Indelible Ink spotting his face and dripping from his dimpled chin. He grinned at her, his teeth sparkling milky-white in his ink-splattered face.

His deep voice echoed in the farmyard. "Does this mean I won't get breakfast?"

Addie threw the broken slat at him and slammed the window shut.

10

MONTANA BENT UNDER THE PUMP AND LET THE WATER SPILL over his head. He shook the water from his hair and then washed his hands, one at a time, under the spigot. His stomach growled, and he smiled. It was dinnertime, close to noon if the high sun was any indication, and he was hungry. He'd missed breakfast, but he didn't mind because he'd had too damn much fun, attacking the Pinky woman.

Laughing at the memory, he dried his hands on a towel. One whack on that round little butt of hers and her dark head had shot up from the pillow. Her black eyes had all but swallowed her prissy-white little face. It had taken every ounce of his restraint to keep from laughing out loud, especially when he had laid on the sugar stuff.

He pulled a comb from his pocket, drew back his wet hair and tied it behind his neck with a thin leather strip. Then he leaned on the pump, watching the smoke burp from the roof's stovepipe.

She was in the kitchen now, cooking—on second thought, burning. The woman wasn't much of a cook, although anything was better than the beans and bacon he'd lived on for weeks, and some things she cooked weren't too bad. Others—well, he thought, remembering his sore jaw, others tasted like his saddle. Maybe he'd get lucky and she'd make black-eyed peas and ham again. That meal had been great.

Food, however, was not his concern. Driving her off his land was, and it looked as if he was finally succeeding. Feeling his small triumph, he whistled "A Man Without a Woman." He remembered her fear-filled face, and the sweetness of her flowery smell. The whistling slowed. He could almost feel her stiff little shoulders, and the soft whisper of her skin against his lips. The tune died on his lips. He remembered how she'd quivered beneath him. It had been in fear, but he savored it, just like he savored the way she'd shivered when he'd licked her ear. But it was the memory of her scooting around the bed like it was on fire that told Montana his plan was working.

And now it was time for more—if he wanted to be a man without *that* woman. He grinned and the whistling began again. With the towel slung over a shoulder, he pushed away from the pump, then walked across the muddy farmyard, heading for the back steps. It was dinnertime, and time to seduce the determination right out of little Miss Pinky.

The mud clung to his boots and covered the sound of them on the wood of the back steps. He looked down at the muddy boots. Anticipating her reaction, he pulled them off and set them by the back door. He straightened and tried to look through the door's window. The glass was dirty, so he wiped the dust off with the towel and tossed it over the stair rail. The flowery curtains dulled the scene but he could see her moving around the room. He reached for the knob and turned it, slowly,

The image of her angry, horrified face still brought a smile of satisfaction to his lips. Then he remembered the inkwell and wondered if he'd have to dodge a fry pan. He frowned; fry pans were heavy. He looked in the window again. She wasn't near the stove, but just to be safe he quietly cracked open the back door and reconnoitered the kitchen.

Something smelled like heaven. Maybe he'd get lucky again, like the black-eyed peas and ham. He stepped inside, quietly closing the door. He turned at the sound of her heels clicking across the hardwood floor. She walked from the table to the stove, never even glancing at the door. Lifting the lid on a cast-iron pot, she peered inside. The savory smell of stew filled the room.

He loved stew. His stomach rumbled. Then he remembered her cooking. His face contorted, and he wondered if she'd thrown in a pound of salt. His stomach groaned again. Apparently *it* had no discretion. He lounged back against the doorjamb and crossed his arms over his belly to cover the sounds.

Pot lid in one hand and spoon in the other, she stirred the stew, humming. She released the spoon and reached for the salt shaker. He winced. She hammered it through the air a few dozen times, then set it down.

Montana was suddenly thirsty.

She replaced the lid, still unaware of his presence, opened the oven door and peered in. He wondered what gastronomical horror lurked inside that hot, black oven. No doubt it would give his stomach hell. She poked her hand inside. His gaze left her head and wandered to her small, round backside. He savored the view, then remembered his plan.

He stared at her through lowered lids and searched for the slow, deep voice he used to calm Jericho. "Hello, sweet Addie."

The oven banged shut. She shot upright. Her eyes swallowed her face again.

He pushed away from the wall and slunk toward her.

She held the wooden spoon in front of her, swordlike. "Stay away!"

"I'm still . . ." He slowly traced the edge of his lower lip with the tip of his tongue. ". . . hungry."

"Dinner is almost ready." She spun around and started banging pan lids, conveniently holding the largest one in her right hand. It was her shield.

"It's not food I'm hungry for."

"Well, food is all you're getting." She spun around, ignoring him, but she raised the pot lid another inch.

He watched her fiddle with her pans, then closed in. She looked over her shoulder at him and gulped. He loved this. Bent on entrapment, he placed a hand on either side of her and leaned down. He was so close he could feel her quick breath against his lips.

"Feed me."

She rammed her bony little elbow into his ribs and ducked under his arm, brandishing her spoon. "Now you stop this!"

He rubbed his ringing ribs. His stomach growled. It was desperate. She waved the spoon under his nose. He wasn't sure how to handle this charade yet, so he decided to pull back a bit and lull her into a sense of security. He'd eat—hopefully there'd be one or two things edible, as usual—then he'd move in for the kill. He'd seduce better with a full stomach.

"If you wish to eat in my home, you . . . will . . . behave . . . sir." She shook her spoon with each staccato word.

He let his gaze rove over her, slowly. Then, when she looked about ready to heave dinner at him, he nodded, but smiled, hoping to make her wonder and worry.

"You can help, since you're so 'hungry.' You may get the butter crock from the icebox," she ordered as she waved the spoon around some more. It made him dizzy. She reached up to grab a platter off a cupboard shelf, but transferred the spoon to her other hand, still waving in his direction.

No use getting his eye poked out, he thought, and started toward the oak icebox near the back door.

Then she added over her shoulder, "And then please put

the flour tin back in the pantry. Third shelf on the left, look for the label 620.0212."

He stopped midstride. "What?"

"The pantry." She set the platter down and waved her other hand at the pantry wall as if that explained what the hell she meant.

He stared blankly.

She sighed. "Just get the butter, please." She marched over to the wooden worktable and plucked up the flour tin, then wedged it onto her hip. She grabbed a couple of small sacks and another small, orange tin and disappeared into the pantry.

Montana put the butter on the table and crossed to the little storage room next to the kitchen. His curiosity was piqued. She walked along the row of shelves, placing each item in a certain spot. Then he spotted the white labels.

He walked up to the closest one, beneath the flour tin. The figures looked like money sums except she'd put the damn decimal in the wrong place. He stared at the flour label, 620.0212. He shook his head. There was no way that the flour could have cost her six hundred twenty dollars. Maybe it was cents.

She placed the orange can on a lower shelf, then she raised a corner of her apron and wiped a smudge from the label.

Montana scratched his ear, trying to decipher her sums. It didn't help. He still couldn't make sense of those numbers. His confusion must have shown all over his face, because she pointed to the labels. "Dewey was a brilliant man."

Dewey who? And he couldn't have been too brilliant since he can't even add sums right.

Montana told her so.

Her nose shot up and she took on her fighting stance—hands on her hips, chin high, lips all prissy. "For your information, this is the Dewey Decimal System of Cataloging. It's an organizational masterpiece, created by Melvil Dewey, the creator of the Science of Library Economy. I was honored to learn from the master himself, at Columbia

University." She ended this nonsense with a curt and superior nod of her snippy little head.

Well, la-tee-dah, he thought, but resisted the urge to say it. He'd like to wipe that smirk right off her face, and he knew how too. His tongue in her mouth would take the prissy look off the Pinky woman's smug face.

He looked around the small room. Christ Almighty, what was wrong with him? He'd been slipping. There was no back door in this room, and he stood by the entrance, blocking it. He had her! Stepping toward her, his raised his arms out, reaching . . .

She must have read his intent, for he felt the wind as she whizzed past him and out of the room.

He snapped his fingers. *Damn!* He'd lost his chance. He'd have to be sharper next time, he thought, rounding the corner of the kitchen. She set the meal on the table. He looked for a corner to back her into but she had already scurried back to the stove. Montana moseyed over to the table and took a closer look, hoping to find something that she might not have ruined.

The stew had to be in the covered dish sitting in the middle of the table, by the biscuits. He loved biscuits. She hadn't cooked those yet, so he had a chance that maybe, like her cornbread, they would be great. She set a small pitcher of cream on the table. Ah-hah! She'd served cream just like that when she'd made those baked apples. She'd hogged most of them, but the one he'd eaten had been good, really good. His mouth watered. Things were looking up. Yes, he'd wait a bit before he moved in for the kill.

She approached the table, her hands filled with a bowl of spicy baked apples. His stomach cried. She set them on the table, nearer his side. She went to the sinkboard, filling a water pitcher before she started back for the table.

Thinking quickly, he rushed over and plucked the heavy pitcher from her hands. "I'll help you with that," he said. "It's heavy."

Her mouth fell open. He'd caught her off guard. He set the pitcher on the table and then again acted the gentleman and pulled out a chair, one that was farther from the apples.

"Miss Pinkney," he said, indicating that she should be

seated. He'd used her real name. It was the only way he'd convince her he was really being a gentleman.

She must have grown roots. She still stood there, looking at him in an odd way. He waited. He wanted those apples. The only thing he liked better than baked apples was apple pie, hot, warm, and flaky . . .

He caught her movement out of the corner of his eye. She still stood rooted to the same spot, but now her arms were crossed. Her look had changed too. It was no longer stunned; now the look was suspicious. She didn't trust him. A smart woman.

"I'll behave," he lied.

She searched his face. Something twisted inside him. He ignored it. She walked to the chair and sat, her movements slow and apprehensive.

"I promise I won't pull the chair out from under you."

Her head tilted back as she looked up at him. An eternal second passed, and then she laughed. He found himself smiling back. Her eyes sparkled up at him, like those jet beads women wore, and with her head back like that, he could see her long, white throat. All that smooth skin. He remembered its flavor, could almost taste the musky sweetness . . . Then he remembered the game he must play.

He quickly sat down by the apples, and while she placed her napkin in her lap, he loaded three of the four apples on his plate. As he reached for the creamer he tried not to gloat. He failed.

At the sound of her gasp, he didn't even blink, but he could feel the burn of her glare. Ignoring her, he removed the lid from the stew and ladled it into his bowl. Finally he looked up and smiled, real friendlylike. Her nose was up again.

"Would you pass the water please?" he asked, acting casual as could be.

She clunked the pitcher down next to him. He shoveled in the apples. He'd been right. They were perfect.

With ladylike delicacy she ladled a small, select portion of stew into her bowl, scowling.

Time for more, he thought. Slowly, he moved his foot over near hers. He lifted his glass to his mouth and drank.

At the same time, he inched his foot under the hem of her skirt. He watched her over the glass rim. She shifted in her chair but didn't appear to notice what he was doing. She was in for a big surprise. She lifted her spoon to that prissy mouth of hers.

He rubbed his sock-covered toes up her calf. She shrieked and dropped the spoon. Her chair skidded back a good foot and she looked under the table.

He wiggled his toes.

She fumed. "You said you'd behave!"

This was going to be good.

He set the glass down and rubbed his forehead, "Sorry. I guess I couldn't control myself." He donned the sick swain look. "I couldn't help it. Must be my animalistic nature." He ate half an apple.

Her eyes narrowed.

He stabbed another hunk of apple with his fork and lifted it up, waving it like she had the spoon. "These ought to help. Isn't that what you said? If fruit 'enhances a delicate nature' then it ought to counteract an 'animalistic' one." He chomped down on the piece and chewed, grinning like an idiot.

She scooted her chair back to the table and replaced her napkin. She stared a moment, then she smiled. It was an odd smile. She picked up the plate of biscuits with both hands and offered them to him. "Here, have some biscuits." She still smiled, which was a strange reaction, considering . . .

Montana grabbed the plate. She let go and he dropped his fork, ramming his other hand under the plate. It must have weighed ten pounds. He set it down, amazed that a dozen biscuits could be that heavy.

He stared at them. Maybe the plate was cast iron. He picked up a biscuit. No, the biscuit was cast iron.

He tossed it in his palm. It slipped and fell. His dinner plate chipped. She passed him the butter crock and then proceeded to eat, occasionally peering up at him.

He sawed at the biscuit. His knife stuck. He set it down, biscuit still attached, and he ventured a taste of the stew. It was a little salty, but not bad. His next bite was a big, man-sized spoonful. He crunched down on something. His tongue burned and his nostrils cleared—permanently.

"Water," he gasped, grabbing the whole pitcher and gulping down the water.

She lifted her napkin to her lips and patted them. "Oh my, did I forget to take that hot chili pepper out? I put it in for flavoring. It's supposed to give it a little spice." She grabbed one of those iron biscuits and held it out to him. "You shouldn't drink water, you know, it'll only make it burn worse. Here, have another biscuit."

Now his ears were hot. The burn was spreading through his senses like prairie fire.

She waited for him to take the biscuit. God, he'd try anything.

He put the biscuit to his mouth and bit down. It crumbled like talcum powder as he chewed. It did help, since it turned into a thick paste that clung to the roof of his mouth. The paste cooled the burning. He pushed at the roof of his mouth with his tongue. Montana decided that if he were to ever eat a hatbox, it would taste like this. The burning subsided, so he didn't feel compelled to eat more of the iron biscuits. Besides, his tongue was numb. When she wasn't looking, he crammed them into his pockets, figuring he'd dispose of them later.

Now how the hell was he going to lust-scare her with a numb tongue? She'd gotten him again. But he had plenty of time, so he'd back off and try again later.

Just as he was about to rise, he heard the crunch of horse's hooves come down the drive. He looked at the Pinky woman. She'd heard it too. They both rose at the same time. He went to the back door, and while he pulled on his boots, she went out. A few minutes later, boots on, he rounded the corner of the house.

There stood Miss Pinky, head craned back as she looked up at Rebecca Latimer. Tall, bosomy, and regal, the redhead sat astride one of the finest pieces of horseflesh Montana'd ever seen. It was a dark bay with black points and the strongest quarters he'd ever seen. The stallion looked as if he could turn on a biscuit and never break the crust, even the Pinky woman's biscuits. Montana moved in for a closer look. The animal stood about sixteen hands and looked to be maybe four years. He wasn't sure, but from the way it backstepped and pulled at the bit, he was sure it wasn't much older.

Rebecca controlled him, though, which brought his respect for the woman up a notch. Little Miss Pinky, however, was busy backing toward the front steps. Neither woman noticed him. They were too busy sizing up each other, the way one bulldog eyes another. . . .

"Hello *Adelaide*."

"Rebecca," Addie said with a curt, uneasy nod. This woman made her uncomfortable, very uncomfortable. Her horse shifted backward, straining against Rebecca's control. It sidestepped and blew a wheeze of air out its muzzle. Addie saw its nostrils flare. A fanciful part of her mind wondered if the chafing animal would suddenly breathe fire.

Instinctively she stepped back, wanting to put as much space as possible between the spirited horse and her cowardly self. Her heel hit the bottom stair. She backed up two of the stairs. This was better, she thought, now I don't have to look up at the woman.

Rebecca pulled back on the reins, controlling the horse with a skill Addie envied. Then the woman scanned the farmyard. "Where's Mr. Creed?"

"Right here, ma'am." He sauntered forward, looking long . . . and lean . . . and loose. The temperature seemed to jump a good ten degrees.

Addie sucked in a deep breath as she watched him walk forward, unable to tear her eyes away. The man emanated confidence, and something else. There was a hardness about him, as if his whole being were as callused as his hard hands. And they were callused, all right. She'd seen them when he'd reached out for her. She'd felt the hardness when he'd whacked her derriere and then crawled all over her, touching her . . .

Lord that sun was hot! She'd felt those callused hands when he'd squeezed her bottom, and her bosom. No one had ever squeezed her bosom. Or licked her ear, inside. She pulled at the tight lace of her collar.

"Why Mr. Creed," Rebecca was saying. "I'd swear you look thinner."

The woman practically shouted the word "thinner." Addie's back stiffened.

"And you look even prettier, Miss Latimer." He smiled up at her, oozing all that . . . that gallantry stuff he never oozed at her. *Well,* she thought, remembering the chair, *almost never.*

She stepped up another stair, just for good measure.

"I'm here to offer you a *good* meal." Rebecca gave her a disparaging glance and then blessed him with a gorgeous smile.

Addie decided Rebecca Latimer had too many teeth.

"Mother sent me to invite you to dinner Friday. Papa wanted to talk to you about the next grange meeting." Her huge blue eyes were riveted on Mr. Creed. Addie had the feeling she'd faded into the porch.

Mr. Creed looked up from what appeared to be his inspection of Rebecca's horse. He smiled at Rebecca and, in a voice tinged with admiration, said, "A beautiful animal."

For some stupid reason, Addie's chest tightened. She watched the other two, feeling completely left out, and a little hurt. They were both so confident and friendly and . . . tall.

Rebecca was a beautiful woman, and even more stunning in the blue she wore today. Her short jacket was a deep sapphire cutaway basque, made of bouclé, and it covered a stark white lace blouson. A split skirt of black serge allowed her to sit astride the spirited horse, and in the stirrups her black calfskin boots shone leather perfect. And they matched her riding gloves. The woman would have turned heads without the horse, but the contrast of her clothing against the dark bay of her mount was even more striking.

Addie shook her head. Leave it to Rebecca to have a horse that matched her hair. And how did one ride a horse down a dusty road and come out without a speck of dust? Addie knew *she* would no doubt be coated red-orange. But of course she didn't ride.

Mr. Creed hunkered down, running those callused hands

gently over the horse's flank. Addie's mouth went dry. He straightened and walked slowly around the horse.

Rebecca leaned down, positioning herself closer to Mr. Creed's face while she patted the horse's long neck. "His name's Diablo. He's the fastest horse in the county." She sat up in the saddle and then slid off the horse in one easy, smooth movement. She handed Mr.Creed the reins. "Here, ride him."

The toad looked like he'd been given a platter of flies. His face took on a boyish glee, and in a flash he was on the horse. With a spit of gravel, the animal took off down the drive.

Ignoring Rebecca, Addie lifted her hand to shield the sunlight as she watched man and horse fly, hooves eating up the distance to the road. At the end of the drive they dipped and turned, riding back toward the farmhouse as though they were drinking the wind. His body movement flowed with each stride of the horse, and his long legs gripped the animal with complete control. They flowed as one—this wild, long-haired man and the spirited horse.

She heard Rebecca's quiet gasp of appreciation, but she didn't look at her. She couldn't take her eyes off Montana. The sight even thrilled Addie. The animal's hooves pounded faster and faster on the ground. It beat in her ears, and was the same rapid thud as her heart, which suddenly felt as if it were lodged in her dry throat. For the first time Addie felt respect for and not fear of a horse.

He reined in and smiled, leaning over the horse and speaking to it in that quiet, soothing deep voice. His hand stroked the animal and it calmed immediately. She expelled her breath. She hadn't even realized she'd been holding it.

Rebecca smiled up at him. "I'll tell Papa you'll come to dinner." Her eyes turned pleading. "You will, won't you?"

He dismounted, still admiring the horse. "Sure."

Once again Addie was left out. She moved back into the shade of the porch, and as if the woman read her mind, she turned. Her eyes were suddenly cool. "Oh, you may come too, Adelaide, if you'd like."

Addie's pride prickled. "I'm sorry, Rebecca, but I have

too much work to do. Please thank your mother for me, though."

The woman's look brightened. "Fine," she said with a wave of her slim hand. She moved to her horse.

Addie had the feeling she'd been dismissed.

Rebecca started to grab the saddle, but Mr. Creed stopped her. "Here, I'll help." He grabbed her waist and lifted the laughing redhead high in the air. Addie closed her eyes and swallowed a lump of air. Then she opened the front door and stepped through.

Rebecca's laughter sang through the doorway, and Addie turned back.

"Thanks for the ride, Miss Latimer." Mr. Creed crossed his arms. Addie stared at his broad back, imagining for a brief, silly second what it would be like to have his callused hands hold her waist and lift her high in the air, above that face that could change with a real smile, the face with the dimple.

"Any time, Mr. Creed," Rebecca answered. "He's a wonderful animal."

Addie looked at a smiling Montana Creed. Yes, she thought, he is. And she quietly shut the door.

11

ADDIE CLOSED THE GATE ON THE CHICKEN YARD, PICKED up the empty pails and headed for the barn. Just as she passed the turkey pen she heard it—the loud bawl of a cow. She turned as one of the cows meandered around the corner of the barn.

Oh good Lord, she'd forgotten to milk them! She dropped the pails and ran to the house. Up the back stairs and through the kitchen she sped, until she reached the lamp table in the parlor. A thick red book sat facedown on the table. She grabbed her spectacles—flinging the chain around her neck—and the book on cows, then raced back to the barn.

Both animals stood, abandoned in the yard, bawling for all they were worth. The poor things. She'd forgotten all about them. She opened the barn door, using a wood wedge to keep the door propped open. This was her first milking experience, and she needed all the light she could get.

After yesterday's dinner the Latimer boys had taken turns explaining what she needed to do. It sounded easy, and after all, the boys were only ten. She figured if ten-year-olds could do it, then so could she. After reading her book, some of her confidence had slipped.

She stood by the door and waited for Mabel and Maud—she couldn't tell who was who—to trot inside. Both of them just stood there, blinking their huge, sorrowful eyes and making some horrid groaning sounds.

"Get inside you two!" Addie ordered.

The only movement from the cows was the swish of their long tails and a twitch of an ear. Addie stuck her spectacles on the bridge of her nose and whipped open the book, thumbing through the thin pages. She skimmed the columns, and found it.

To bring the cows in, one can use a cattle prod. If none is available, a stick will suffice.

She looked around for a stick. There was none. She read on.

Switch the back of the bovine's legs or "prod" the hind quarter with the implement.

She had no implement, so she walked around the cows and stared at their backsides. The animals bawled again; it was an awful sound, almost a painful plea. Improvise, she thought, so she tucked the book under her left arm, and

155

with her right arm extended, index finger pointed, she edged toward the closest cow.

She poked it in the rump. It didn't budge. She poked it on the other side. Its tail slapped up and whacked her on the arm.

"Ouch!" She rubbed her red forearm. "Move, you two!"

The only parts of them that moved were their ears.

"Get along!" She remembered reading that phrase somewhere. It had something to do with little dogs, but maybe cows would respond.

These cows didn't. She raised her hand high and squeezed her eyes shut. They bawled again so she did it. Her palm slapped hard on the cow's rump. She cracked open one eye, just in time to see both cows lumber inside.

She'd done it. Smiling, she followed them inside, the book once again propped on her arm, reading as she was going. "Let's see," she told the cows, "it says that you're supposed to go to your stanchions . . ."

Addie glanced up. Both cows were in respective low stalls, their heads stuck between wide openings in the end walls. *Those look like stanchions to me. Whoever said cows were dumb animals?*

"Thank you, ladies," she said, and then read on.

Ten minutes later the water and feed troughs at the end of the stanchions were filled and Mabel and Maud were gnawing away. According to the book, Addie had to wash the udders and the teats, clean milk being essential to its longevity. She planted her derriere on a small milking stool she'd found hanging on a nail and grabbed a cloth from a pail of clean water. She dabbed at the bulging milk sack. The cow groaned, and Addie jerked her hand back.

The cow turned its big brown eyes and slobbery face toward Addie and stared.

"Now Mabel, or Maud, whichever you are, this isn't easy you know. I need your cooperation here."

The cow blinked and turned back to the trough. Addie took a deep breath and leaned down under the cow until her cheek rested against the animal's hairy hide. She held the huge udder with her left hand and cleaned it with the cloth.

A few minutes later, dropping the cloth into the bucket, she said, "There, now that wasn't so bad, was it?"

Mabel/Maud ate on.

Addie hooked her squat heels over the stool rung and placed the open book on her knees. With an elbow planted on each leg, she rested her small, determined chin in her hands and read about milking technique. Sufficiently educated, she placed another pail under the cow and rubbed her hands together.

Time to give it a try, she thought. She leaned down and pinched the teat between her thumb and forefinger, then squeezed, rolling her other fingers down the length of the teat. Milk pinged against the tin pail and she giggled. It worked!

Minutes later she'd mastered the rolling pull technique—with both hands—and the once-quiet barn was filled with the clean ring of milk hitting the pail.

Milking, she found, soothed her, much more so than chicken feeding. Resting her head against the warm, coarse hide of the gentle cow, she closed her eyes and just listened to the squirt, ring, squirt, ring of the milking sound. Lulled and loose, she eventually opened her eyes, gazing around the barn.

Sunlight spilled through the barn doors, and inklings of it sparkled through the cracks in the wood walls. The clean, spring smell of hay washed out the dull tinge of old manure. It smelled like earth and country and home. She was happy here, and busier than she'd ever thought possible.

Farming was hard work. Levi Hamilton had been right. She had her hands full with the chickens and her future plans for them. Right now, literally, she had her hands full with the cows too. The milk products from two cows were more than she could ever use, but Hettie had explained that her Aunt Emily had sold the extra milk and cream to Peabody's Mercantile, who'd credited the dairy money against her supply bill. That sounded good to Addie. She intended to do the same.

But she wasn't sure what to do with the dadgum turkeys. She supposed she could eat them, like the cockerels. Those were the male chickens. Addie learned the chicken lingo fast. In the meantime she'd just keep feeding the gobblers.

She finished with the first cow and lugged the full milk pail to the barn door. One down, she thought, one to go, and she started the process all over again with the other Mabel/Maud.

Head against the other cow, Addie sighed. She was tired today, and as much as she hated to admit it, she didn't think, right now, she could work a farm alone. Of course with the judge's ruling, she didn't have to. Mr. Creed would be growing the crops.

However, if he'd had no claim to the land, she would have had to hire someone to work the land, or at least lease it to a neighboring farmer. And how were they going to coexist on this land? She supposed that eventually he'd be able to build his own structures, but for now she would have to share hers with him, especially if she wanted her half of the crops.

Oh, she knew she could learn to farm and even handle it alone in time. She'd teach herself, like she had the milking. But from the little she'd read and heard, the winter wheat planting would have to be done soon, and she had yet to learn much of anything about crops, not to mention handling a plow.

The milk stopped squirting. Oh good Lord! There was a major flaw in her plans. To plow a field, you needed a horse.

A horse. She shivered, her face in a grimace. She hadn't thought about plowing and horses. At least she hadn't put the two together. But maybe that was good, because she'd always harbored a fear and dislike of the animals. That weakness might have been the one thing that could have kept her from ever coming west. It was the one thing she had run from for years.

Maybe it was time to stop running. It wouldn't be easy, that she knew. She'd always thought of horses as horrid and mean and deadly, like that devil horse of Mr. Creed's, and she had good reason too, long before that animal'd attacked her. She'd adored her parents. The loss of her father was something she had to accept, but watching her mother's pain, day in and day out, had escalated that fear. It hadn't been easy for Addie.

Of course, nothing in life was easy—her father had taught her that too. He had taught her that life was challenge, and that she should attack it head-on. Her fear of horses had been the only thing she'd sidestepped.

For the first time Addie thought of what her father's reaction to her horse fear would have been. He would have hated to be the cause for any weakness in his daughter, or anything that caused her pain. He wouldn't have wanted her to suffer forever because of the way he died, and if the truth be told, if she really wanted to do him proud, Addie knew she shouldn't let that weakness, that flaw in her character, affect her life.

This was not an easy thing to admit, but admit it she must. She was weak, though she'd thought herself strong. She loved her father, but she'd done him an injustice by not living every bit of her life as he'd taught her. By not confronting her problem. She'd forgotten to look at her own weakness as a challenge.

Her father was the one who'd taught her to take everything life offered, and never, ever believe that something was unattainable. If you wanted something, then you had to reach out and grab it. In everything else, Addie had treated each obstacle as a challenge. She loved a challenge.

She'd handled going off to college, alone, and handled the competition with the others, good old Hilary included. She'd stuck it out at the Mason Street Library, allowed Hilary to belittle her, purposely dock her pay, and make her life pretty miserable all the way around. She did leave, which some might say was running away, but in her mind she hadn't run away from Hilary. She'd just exchanged one challenge for another. To Addie, the challenge here on her aunt's place was like a dream come true. She couldn't let a chance to live that dream go by. It wasn't in her.

But now she had a new set of challenges. The farm and Mr. Montana Creed. Learning about the farm would be a self-taught lesson. It would take time. Mr. Creed, on the other hand, was a whole other story, possibly an unending one.

She sighed and tried to block the image of that man—half toad, half prince—from her mind. She failed miserably. The trickle of milk tapered off, so she grasped another teat, squeeze rolling until the milk sprayed out again in a steady, ivory-colored stream—the exact same color as the toad's teeth.

That man confused her. Everything was easy when she thought of him as the toad. Her conscience hadn't eaten at her when she'd thought of him as her enemy. Any man who'd point a gun at a woman, then trail it over her, didn't deserve any water. She'd thought it the perfect comeuppance at the time. Now she felt petty.

Of course, keeping Custus from delivering her supplies wasn't exactly the royal act of a prince. Neither was sneaking that horse of his in her bedroom. He had definitely behaved worse than she.

He helped you with your chickens.

I know, I know, she thought. The chicks were healthy and plump already, seeming to grow with every feeding. And there were certainly plenty of feedings.

How did you repay him?

Addie closed her guilty eyes. She wasn't very proud of the answer. She'd fed him burnt meat, chili peppers, and plaster of paris biscuits.

But I let him, and his horse, move into the barn, she reasoned, grasping for something that didn't make her feel so ashamed. But she knew that the minute the storm had blown in that night, she couldn't let him stay out in that weather. The lightning was deadly.

Then what did you do?

Addie swallowed. She'd goaded him, "yes mastering" him until finally he'd kissed her just to shut her up. Her gaze flashed to that spot in the barn. The spot where she had learned all about tongues.

She'd asked for trouble, and she'd gotten it all right. The man couldn't keep his hands and lips off her. She sighed. Never in all her born days did Adelaide Amanda Pinkney think that she would inspire lust in a man. Desire, maybe love, but this was too . . . too thrilling to be those emotions. Love was something warm and comfortable, like lying in a feather bed. The feeling she got from kissing this man was more like lying in a bed of fire, and enjoying it.

That's what really scares you.

It is not, she argued with her mouthy conscience. *What scares me is this man. He's confusing, and a little shady.* The man did have a black side to his soul. She had a right to be a little afraid of him. This man ogled pictures of naked women, for God's sakes! He was probably easier to spark lust in than most. He looked in her bedroom window too. And she'd foolishly kissed him. She didn't fight him at all. All because she was curious.

Good Lord. She had to live near this man, eat meals with him. They were both forced into farming this land together. By not fighting him, she had surely given him the idea that she welcomed all that canoodling.

What a dadgum, foolish, idiotic thing for her to do. Of course he'd slithered into her bedroom. He'd probably thought she'd welcome him with open arms. But then, he should have caught on when she resisted. If someone threw things at me, she thought, I'd figure I was doing something wrong. Men could be hardheaded, though. She'd bet he figured he could wear her resistance down.

He might do it too.

"*Oh shut up!*" Addie yelled into the empty barn.

He won't do it, because I'm going to explain things to him, she decided.

She stood, dragging the heavy milk pail out from under the cow. She would apologize for making him think she wanted his attentions. Lugging the pail forward, she justified everything. She really hadn't meant to encourage him; so, she thought, trying to balance both of the heavy pails on the neck yoke she'd discovered, she would apologize. It was the proper thing to do. She'd take the blame, even though it was his fault too. After all, he did encourage his lecherous side by goggling at naked women. But she'd overlook that and make him see that they had to work together, so they could make this farm into the best, most lucrative farm in the valley, maybe in all of California. It was the smartest thing for both their interests.

Yes, Addie thought, trudging under the weight of her yoked milk pails, that's exactly what she would do, at the first opportunity.

Before Montana opened the door, he looked down at his boots. No mud this time. He opened the door and braved the culinary beast. The kitchen was empty, but a clatter sounded from around the corner and he moved into the pantry.

"Dadgummit!" she muttered, standing on a small milking stool while she reached toward a can on the top shelf. Her back was to him and he found himself eyeing her butt. Then his gaze slowly drifted up her waist, her back, up the small little buttons that traveled to her hairline.

She muttered again and he watched her strain to try to grab a can, her small hand swiping at the top shelf. He wondered how long it would take her to inch the can forward. A hairpin fell out of her hair and pinged onto the wooden floor. Her black hair was jammed into some knot thing high on her head, and one long piece fell, then another, and another, then the knot slid halfway down her back.

Montana silently padded across the small room until he stood beneath her. He reached up and grabbed her waist.

She shrieked, and a stack of cans clunked onto the floor. Her head jerked and she frowned down at him over her shoulder. Smiling, he plucked her off the stool.

He heard her inhale and felt her stiffen, so he waited for the fight. Nothing happened.

Surprised at her lack of reaction, he tossed her slightly, turning her so he held her high above his face. He wanted to see her face. This should be good.

Her eyes were squeezed shut. He waited. She slowly peeled open her huge, black eyes. It was the strangest thing. They looked a little foggy. Then she stared at his chin. Before he could figure out her reaction, she started to squirm.

"Put me down!"

"No." He held her fast, closing his hands tighter around her small waist. His middle fingers touched.

Her feet looked like she was pedaling that bicycle of hers, so he locked his elbows and held her up even higher. He had been right. She didn't weigh much more than a sack of flour. This was fun, holding her high above him and watching her feet pedal through the empty air. She muttered the whole time, and when her words registered, he was impressed. She really could come up with some inventive curses. His poor "black soul," he thought. The madder she got, the faster her feet went. He couldn't help it; he laughed out loud.

To throw her off, he lowered her slowly toward his face. Panic flashed in her black eyes before they bore into his. This was his best plan yet.

"Release me, at once!"

"Now if I do that, you'll land right on that sweet, little white butt."

Her fist flew at him. It missed by a foot. Her cheeks turned darker than apples.

"I'll put you down . . ."

"Good." She crossed her arms, as if she weren't airborne, and waited, indignation spitting from her little red face.

"It'll cost you." Very slowly he let his tongue wet his lips. Her eyes almost popped out of her head and her mouth gaped open.

"A kiss. One sweet kiss . . ."

Her mouth clamped shut. Her hands grabbed his wrists. "You are a sick man. Put me down."

"I said it'll cost you a kiss."

The little witch dug her nails into his wrists. He just smiled and drew her down toward his mouth. She puckered up her little face and pursed her lips together so tight that they all but disappeared. He didn't laugh this time, but it was tempting. She looked like she was about to kiss a frog.

He watched her scrunched-up face, and when their mouths almost touched, he stopped, waiting a long moment. The determined Miss Pinky didn't open her eyes. He slowly drew his tongue across her tight lips.

It worked. Her eyes flew open and her lips relaxed. He kissed her; she squirmed, so he backed her up against the pantry shelves. He had her pinned, his hands still gripping her small waist. Her feet still moved, so he moved his leg between hers, wedging his knee against a pantry shelf. Her hands left his wrists and pinched into his shoulders. She twisted her head away from his mouth. There was her soft neck, presented to him like a succulent Christmas goose. He concentrated on nibbling over her neck.

It was a mistake. Her fist slammed into his left ear.

"Ouch!" He dropped her and grabbed his ringing ear. She landed astride his thigh.

He shook his head and rubbed at his ear, so he could better hear her tirade.

"Keep your lecherous lips off me!" She threw her leg over his and slid off, bending to pick up the stool. She held it in front of her like a shield.

He still rubbed his ear, but then remembered his goal. He let his gaze rest on her lips and purposely moved forward. "I'm hungry . . . Addie."

She raised the stool. "Well, I'm not dinner! Your meal is out there." She nodded toward the kitchen.

"I wasn't talking about food." He winked.

She was so scared, Montana could tell she was about one more clench away from packing. Her jaw worked in and out and she finally sputtered, "F-Food. Our agreement was for food. I'd promised to feed you because you helped me save my chickens. That's all we agreed on."

"Feed me, now." He took a step toward her.

"Stop that!" Her stool waved around his nose and he stopped, praying to keep from smiling.

He purposely lowered his lids, giving her a look that should have scared the drawers off her. "You were hungry last night . . . in the barn." He gave her what felt like a good suggestive leer. "Remember?"

"I—I—" Her face reddened again and she raised a hand to her forehead and swiped the hair off it. She had begun to sweat. Some damp black hairs began to curl around her bright face. She absentmindedly fanned herself.

Little Miss Pinky was hot. He loved it.

She took a deep breath. "Mr. Creed. Uh . . . I . . . I think you misunderstood what happened."

Montana schooled his look. Her eyes searched his face, and then she did the one thing that stopped him cold.

"I'm sorry. It was all my fault."

She had just apologized. He couldn't believe her. She was accepting the blame.

She sighed and shook her head. "I'm afraid my actions led you to believe that I . . . I feel a special—" She stopped, searching for the right word. ". . . a special regard for you. I'm afraid that's not the case."

He could see her trying to gauge his response. He didn't even blink.

She went on. "I've been thinking," she said, setting the stool down and locking her hands behind her little butt while she paced the small room. "This whole farm-sharing thing is difficult. I've tried to do the right thing." She stopped and looked up at him.

He wanted to throttle her. Do the right thing. . . . She hadn't done anything right. If she'd wanted to do the right thing, she'd have gone back to Chicago.

She raised her hand. "Now don't get all boorish again. I was wrong about the water." She crossed her arms and waited for his response.

He'd be damned if he'd give it. He wanted to see what she was up to. With a casualness he was far from feeling, he leaned back against the pantry shelves. He waited.

Apparently it was enough because she began to pace again. "It was very kind of you to help me with the chickens. That's why I said I'd fix your meals. Last night, I realized how dangerous it was for you to be camped outside. That's why I let you use my barn."

Her barn. He wanted to wring her neck.

"I've decided to make up for my pettiness about the water. You and that . . . that animal can use the barn." She stopped her pacing and gave him a tentative smile.

When he didn't respond, she went on. "I feel we should come to some agreement. Since you will be planting our crops . . ."

Montana took a deep breath. *My crops.*

"I feel that you should have use of my uncle's farm implements. Therefore, I will give you free run of the farm. Oh, not the house, of course. You may have your meals in here, but you'll have to sleep in the bunkroom in the back of the barn.

"You must understand that we will be business partners, nothing more. If my actions in the barn made you think that maybe we could be . . . something else, well, I apologize." She awaited his response, that little nose of hers sky high again. Little Miss Pinky had spoken.

His mind raced for something to say. He supposed he should let her believe he was thankful, but it would kill him. This was his farm. She didn't belong here. Still, the only way he could see to solve the Pinky woman problem was to continue. The lust angle did scare her. Although she seemed to have come to grips with it, for now anyway. Hell, she'd blamed herself. That was fine with him. Let her believe it's her fault, he thought. Meanwhile, he'd have to do this more subtly.

"Don't you have anything to say?" she asked.

He couldn't do it. He knew she was waiting for him to thank her, for her benevolence. He'd never get the words past his lips. They'd stick like her roast in his throat.

"Do you think that you can forget about last night?" Her voice was suddenly quiet and threaded with a little worry. "Can you treat me like a business partner?"

Not on your life. Instead of saying what he thought, he tried to look like a spurned swain. He wasn't sure he succeeded.

"I'll try," he finally said, realizing this was a new angle to his old game. He could continue the act, but this time he'd have her sympathy. Every time he'd get all lovey-dovey, she'd think he couldn't help it. If he hounded her enough, she'd still run. He tried to look contrite, then added, "It won't be easy, Addie, but I'll try to control myself when I'm around you."

"Good. Let's eat." Her face lit up with her smile, and for some stupid reason, Montana's chest tightened. He watched her walk from the room, but he didn't follow immediately. He stood there, telling himself that he must be catching a cold from the storm.

12

"I WANT YOU TO TEACH ME TO RIDE A HORSE."

Montana decided he was hearing things, and continued to work on the old wagon he'd found behind the barn.

"Well?" she asked.

He turned and looked at her. Her arms were crossed and that nose was up again.

"Will you do it?"

He turned back and tightened the hub on a wagon wheel, thinking he intended to *do* more to Little Miss Pinky than she knew. He stretched his arm through the spoke so he could test the bolts on the axle.

Her foot tapped an impatient beat on the dusty ground. He smiled. "Why this sudden change of heart? I thought you were afraid of horses?"

"I'm not afraid of them—"

He grunted, then pushed hard on the wrench.

"I just don't like them."

Her foot still tapped.

"Then why learn now?" He turned onto his back and slid under the wagon, scanning the undercarriage for loose boards. He heard her resolved sigh.

"If I'm going to become a prosperous farmer . . ."

Don't bet your farm on it, he thought, then grabbed a hammer and pounded in a few nails.

". . . I need to learn to work with horses," she shouted over the hammering.

He raised his head slightly, so he could see where she stood. Her black, button-top shoes were only a few feet from where his dusty, old boots rested, toes up, on the ground. The boot leather was a dingy gray-brown and wrinkled with time and wear. Hers were dusty, but the clean, shiny newness of the leather still glistened through the fine coat of valley dirt. From the square, pointed toes all the way to the top of the shoe, there wasn't one crease in the black leather, not even where the leather tongue swelled over the rim and buttoned tight and high above her ankle. Montana shook his head. *Not even one crease.*

She didn't belong here, this city woman with her grand plans and her books. "I thought you had books to teach you everything you needed to know. Why do you need me? Use a book."

She called him a toad again under her breath.

He smiled, locked his hands behind his head and watched that foot tap up a little dust again.

"I don't have a book on horses," she admitted. The confession was spoken so softly that he'd had to strain to hear it.

"Huh?" He made her repeat it.

"I said," she raised her voice a full octave, "that I don't have a book about horses!"

"Why not?" he asked, grinning to himself. He liked this game.

"Mr. Creed! It is very difficult to converse with you under that wagon!"

I know, he thought, *but it's so much more entertaining.* Then his mind flashed with all the possibilities of entertainment offered by giving Little Miss Pinky horseback riding lessons, which might prove to be a better game. He just couldn't pass it up.

Still lying on his back, he grabbed his tools, pushing them out by the wagon wheel. He scooted partially out from under the wagon and grabbed the old, splintered edge of the wooden bed, pulling himself completely out into the bright sunlight, and into her view. He blinked at the brightness, then stood and plucked his hat off the wagon seat. He dusted the hat off out of habit, then dropped it onto his head.

Leaning as indolently as possible against the wagon bed, he pulled a bandanna from his back pocket and wiped the axle grease and dirt from his hands. His eyes had adjusted to the sunlight and he got his first glimpse of her. Her black hair was up, all snottylike, without one hair out of place. She wore a stark white shirt that looked crisper than fried chicken. Her skirt was black and made out of some shiny stuff that looked like it belonged at a church social instead of on the back of a horse.

He let his gaze drift over her. Her nose went up. He needed to bring it down a notch. "You'll learn to ride astride, Miss Pinky, so unless you want the world to see that city-white little butt of yours, I'd suggest you change clothes."

She sucked in a quick breath and her face began to flush. Her small fists knotted and he'd swear he heard her teeth grind. Then her nose went up again. "Fine." She almost spat the word. Then she spun on her heel and marched toward the farmhouse, leaving Montana to savor his plan.

Addie didn't have a split skirt like Rebecca's. All she had were her biking knickerbockers from her riding club. She rummaged through her barrel trunk and pulled out the official riding uniform of the Bicycling Belles.

She removed her corset, wearing only a chemise. One never wore a corset when riding a bicycle. It inhibited one's breathing. Riding corsetless was one of the female luxuries of the riding craze, and almost two years before, Addie had joined the women cyclist reformers who advocated "rational dress."

She tied her drawers and buttoned the small pearl buttons up the front of the corset cover she used for riding. It was a full size bigger than she used with her corset, but the cambric fabric modestly concealed her body through the sheerness of her uniform's white linen shirt. The shirt was piped in black and had a high-standing collar, like the ones worn by the cadets at West Point. There was a black cap with silver-cord trimming on the visor, and for the shirt's French cuff she had matching silver cuff links shaped like bicycle bells.

Addie fastened them with care. The cuff links were earned by the club riders. She'd won hers in the Annual

Ladies' Pullman Race, a ten-mile course sponsored by *Harper's Weekly* and the Ladies Associated Cycling Clubs. She smiled proudly and grabbed her castor-colored stockings with the black diamond inserts, sliding them up her legs and fastening them with a pair of black elastic stocking supporters. She unfolded her knickerbockers. Some of the women's clubs called them bifurcated garments, but the Belles didn't like distinguishing the female garments from the male. Most of Addie's clubmates felt that cycling had given them a new freedom and a sense of equality with men. Before she left, many of the men's cycling clubs had begun treating their female counterparts with respect—for the ladies' cycling skill, not their gender.

Sitting on the bed, she put one leg through each "compartment," just like her Columbia University gym bloomers, buttoned the short, blossomy pants below the knees, and fastened the waistband. Lastly, she pulled on her trimmed knee boots, slid into the short, black jacket with its silver-braided epaulets and the club's monogram on the breast pocket, and grabbed her riding gloves. Then, hat in hand, she was all set, except for a little bit of lost courage.

A horse whinnied in the farmyard, and Addie edged over to the bedroom window. With one finger she inched open a little peep crack in the shade. She bent closer and squinted through the opening. Mr. Creed stood in the yard, his saddle at his feet and that devil horse running loose in the yard. She watched the animal prance around its owner in what looked like some sort of game. Mr. Creed laughed as the horse trotted by, nodding its head and flashing its tail. It went right by him and kept going, all the way to the smokehouse gate, then suddenly it turned and galloped straight at him.

The horse was going to trample him! Addie held her breath and squeezed her eyes shut. She waited for the scream of pain.

The man laughed. Her eyes flew open. The horse skidded to a stop barely a foot shy of him. She dropped the edge of the shade and leaned against the wall, searching for courage. She needed to do this, brave the devil beast and conquer her silly fear. Her heart beat in her chest like an overwound clock and her breath came in small pants. She actually felt dizzy for a second. She thought of that horse running straight at its master. Maybe her fear wasn't so silly after all.

Then she pictured her father's proud face when she'd won the school spelling bee, heard the pride in his voice one Thanksgiving when she'd sat at the top of the stairs, eavesdropping, and heard him boast to a business associate that his daughter could do anything she set her mind to.

That memory was all it took. Addie walked through the farmhouse and out to the yard, mentally assuring herself that she could do this. It really wasn't any different than conquering the cows.

Her reassurance lasted only as long as a match in the wind.

"I'm ready," she announced, standing right in front of Mr. Creed.

He tipped his hat back and stared, forever. Then he moved like a snail, circling her. She slowly turned with him, could feel his gaze on every inch of her, up then down, up then down, like a yellow flame licking at dry wood. She raised her nose a notch to see him better from under the flat visor of her cycling hat.

He laughed.

"What's so all-fired funny?"

"Well, that getup ought to cover your butt."

"So delicately put. You have such a way with four-letter words," she shot back, angry because he was laughing at her uniform—the one she was so proud of.

Her eyes narrowed. He kept laughing.

Somewhere near her stomach a part of her ached like it was filled with too-green apples. He hadn't laughed at Rebecca Latimer, but he was laughing at her. It hurt, but she refused to cry. Instead, she remembered what a toad this man was and told herself she shouldn't give one fig about him. She slapped her glove against her palm and waited until he had finished his annoying attempt to humiliate her.

"Are you through?" she asked when his laughter subsided and he appeared to finally realize his baiting wasn't working with her.

He tightened his lips, obviously holding back a big grin, and nodded.

"Good." She eyed the horse, then him. He bent and picked up a knotted rope thing. Her mind flashed with the image of a hangman's noose. Her throat tightened and she paled, then the image vanished. Taking a deep, brave breath, she said, "Okay. Let's start."

He straightened. "The first thing you have to learn is how to catch a horse."

"Why?"

"Because if you want to ride a horse, you must catch him first." His sarcasm wasn't hidden.

"I know that! I meant why can't you catch it for me?"

"Do you want to learn to ride?" he snapped.

"Yes."

"Then you'll have to learn everything from step one." He stood there waiting, as if he thought she'd give up. That just spurred her on.

"Continue please," she said with a wave of her hand.

He held up the rope thing. "This is a halter. You'll use this to lead and tie him."

"It," she corrected.

"What?"

"It. The horse."

"Him," Montana corrected. "Jericho is a gelding, a male horse."

"I thought male horses were stallions."

"He was." The man had an odd smile on his face.

Addie tried to think, and although she'd avoided anything that had to do with horses, she remembered hearing something about the terms filly and mare. Age had something to do with those terms, so she figured the terms stallion and gelding must be similar. "Oh, I get it. Male horses are stallions until a certain age and then they're called geldings, right?"

He shook his head, grinning.

She didn't understand.

"Give up?" he asked, his voice hopeful.

After a few long seconds she nodded.

He stepped very close to her and leaned down, as if he were about to divulge a government secret. She waited.

The toad told her in three- and four-letter words.

Addie turned bright red. She could feel her whole body burning with embarrassment. He laughed again.

She spun on her heel, her hands in such tight fists that she wadded the leather gloves into a tight ball. She wanted to march straight for the cool safety of the farmhouse, but she took one step then stopped, remembering her father's faith in her.

When she didn't move, his laughing stopped.

Nose up, she turned, giving the horse a thorough inspection. Then she looked the toad straight in his yellow eyes and said, "Technically, I was right. *He* is an *it*." She looked up at him from beneath the visor, her nose up just enough. "No wonder he's so ornery." She paused for emphasis. "Is that your problem too?"

All the humor vanished from his face. Until now Addie had never really seen a purple face.

He dropped the harness and came at her. She ran; so did he. She scurried toward the giant oak tree. Her heart beat fast, she dropped her gloves, and her hat flew off. She looked over her shoulder. He pounded after her, closing in. She reached the tree and jumped the large roots, swinging around to the other side to place the big tree between them. She'd thought she'd succeeded. She was wrong.

His arm hooked around her waist and Addie felt the cool air as he swung her around. Her back hit the tree trunk; his body hit her front, pinning her hard against the tree. She squeezed her eyes shut and waited, panting into his damp neck. With every shallow breath, she smelled his scent. He smelled of anger.

Her chest moved into his, rubbing. The chemise didn't shield her from the feel of his chest. Her breasts tightened. His hands closed over her shoulders. She couldn't look up. She wasn't that brave. His breathing deepened and his hands moved slowly across her narrow shoulders, closing in, then stopping at the base of her neck. His thumbs brushed the skin of her throat right where the neck opened on her high West Point collar. Over and over, higher and higher, he moved his lethal thumbs on her throat, his strong fingers holding fast on the back of her neck. If she moved, he could snap her neck. Her eyes grew large with the thought.

His lips brushed over her hairline near the temple. Goose pimples blistered down her arms. His body pushed harder into hers, until her fanny pressed flat against the tree. Addie could feel the pinch of rough bark through her clothes. His breath brushed closer and closer to her ear. She shivered. The breath grew loud, like the crash of a storm wave, powerful, thrilling, uncontrolled, yet somehow distant. Then his knee wedged between hers. He pushed up with his body. She skidded a couple of inches up the tree trunk. Her eyes grew wide.

She'd done it again, pushed the man too far, just like she had with her "yes mastering." He scared her, but not because she thought he'd actually harm her. She was scared because of what he made her feel, of how he awakened a devilish side to her that made her want to push him into reacting. And when he reacted, it was a carnal reaction, which should have scared her. It didn't, exactly. Instead she felt that it gave her some power over him, and that excited her. She'd never felt powerful before. He moved his face so close to hers she could feel the soft brush of his breath. "Want to find out for yourself, sweet Addie?"

Good Lord, did she? She looked up into his piercing eyes. The game had suddenly changed, and she, a novice, wasn't ready for it. *No,* she thought, *I can't.* But she couldn't find her voice.

She had just wanted to test and push. And she'd pushed him too far, which had been too easy and too fast. He must have been staring at naked ladies again. That must have been it. So it was his fault too, she reasoned, having no problem suddenly shifting the blame.

When she finally found her voice, she tried to sound as if he and their position had no effect on her. "I want my riding lesson." She swallowed her pride. "I'm sorry I insinuated that you were like your horse." *You're worse.*

As if the animal had heard her, it moseyed over near the tree and stared at them, then it bent and began to gnaw on the grass. Montana watched it for a long moment. His body still pinned her but his breath slowed, then the anger left his face. His gaze was still on the horse, but she could see him thinking. The serious, sensual line of his lips changed, replaced by a cat-and-the-canary smirk. It changed too fast, giving her the sudden urge to examine his mouth for feathers.

He grabbed her waist, distracting her caution, and lifted her, purposely not setting her down. His eyes took on the same randy look he'd worn in the pantry. "You're sure?"

"Of course I'm sure. Put me down!"

"I can give you some *other* riding lessons."

"Riding what?" she frowned. The lecherous grin he wore told her that she shouldn't have asked. "Never mind!" she said before he explained in four-letter words. "Just put me down and give me that halter thing!"

She could see him thinking again, and then his look changed to amusement. He thinks I can't do this, she thought. He set her down, so she donned a confident air and promptly marched over to the halter, picking it up, turning it this way and that in an effort to figure out how to hold it.

Montana's tall body blocked the warm sun. "Unhook it."

"I could have figured that out. I'm not stupid."

"You were the one who asked for lessons," he reminded her.

"There are some things, Mr. Creed, that are just common sense." She glanced up at him. "Please don't treat me like an idiot just because I'm a woman. My brain is just as big as yours, sir!"

"Fine." He turned and sauntered over to the tree, leaning back against it. He tipped his hat back, crossed his arms over his puffy chest and waited.

She'd show him. With an air of false confidence, she approached the horse. It looked up at her, chewing. She closed in from the right. Its head shot up and it whinnied just before loping away.

Addie fanned the dust away from her face. The devil horse now stood near the empty pen by the barn, innocently staring at her.

She slowly walked toward the barn, swinging the halter at her side and giving the animal a wide berth. She moved in from the right again and heard Montana laugh. His horse took off again.

"Look what you did!" Addie planted her hands on her hips and glowered at the man. "You scared him away!"

He kept laughing. "Want some advice, or would you rather use your 'common sense'?"

"What advice?" She drew a long breath and prayed for patience.

"Always approach a horse from the left, saddle him from the left, and mount from the left."

"Why?"

"So you don't get that big brain of yours knocked 'common senseless.' " His smile said he'd gotten her. And he had, with her own words.

"Funny." She crossed her arms and slapped herself with the halter. She waited for him to stop laughing. "If I'm going to learn, I need to understand everything. Now, why the left side?"

"Well," he drawled, "I seem to recall it had something to do with knights and the size of their swords."

"I don't have a sword," she reasoned.

"I do." He hooked his thumbs into the top of his pants. "Wanna see?"

She could feel her face flush, so she stiffened her spine and turned, calling out over her shoulder, "No thank you. I forgot my spectacles." That ought to shut him up, she thought, heading for the horse, from the left.

"Why, sweet Addie, I do believe you have a sense of humor!"

She stopped, glaring at him over her shoulder. "You're a sick man."

He shrugged.

Mumbling, she walked up to the horse. It stared at her with big brown eyes that she didn't trust. She held the halter so the rope loops would slide over the animal's nose.

176

A smug little smile appeared on her face. It didn't take a genius to figure that out. She started to slide the halter on, and the horse threw its ornery head up and out of reach.

"Dadgummit!"

The toad's deep voice rang out. "Slip the lead rope over his head and talk sweet to him."

Addie looked at the halter, trying to see the "lead." She tossed the long end over the horse's neck and looped it through the rest of the halter. It worked. Now she had to talk to it. "Nice horsey," she muttered. "Let me put this little rope on your nose like a good . . . boy."

The devil scrunched up its fat pink lips and bared its long, yellow teeth.

"If you bite me, you obnoxious beast, I'll—"

"Uh-uh-unnnh . . ."

Addie jumped and looked guiltily over her shoulder. He stood right behind her, shaking one long, tanned finger. He had heard every threatening word.

"Talk sweet."

"It wouldn't do any good. It hates me!"

"Give me your hand."

"Why?"

"Do you want to learn to ride?"

"Yes."

"Then stop questioning me and do I say." He held out his hand, callused palm up. "Give me your hand."

She shifted the halter to her left hand and placed her hand in his. The second their skin touched Addie looked up at him. His exasperated expression was gone. He stared at their hands with an odd, surprised look. She looked down. Her small, pale hand looked even whiter and smaller next to his. The yellow calluses on his fingers stood out, and those silly goosebumps raced over her skin again.

He cleared his throat, then lifted her hand and placed it on the horse's warm neck. In his deep, quiet voice he said, "Stroke him."

She did, but she wasn't thinking about the feel of the horse. His hand still covered hers and he guided her movement, slowly taking her hand up near the animal's ear and dragging their hands down its long neck. She could feel his

177

rough hand; his arm brushed hers as he moved her hand, and the heat from his tall body made her feel suddenly flushed and damp, except for her mouth, which for some crazy reason had dried up.

"Whisper what you want," he bent down and said into Addie's ear, but he didn't let go of her hand.

What did she want? She'd forgotten. It was awfully hot, and her clothes felt suddenly tight. She exhaled.

"Tell him what you're going to do to him." He released her hand, but he didn't budge. She could still feel him, just a fly's shadow away.

"Here, horse, I'm going to put this thing on you." The animal glared at her. "Real easy, I promise." She slowly slid the halter over the horse's nose, then held it in place and looked at Mr. Creed. "I can't reach that thing that goes over his head."

"It's called the crownpiece. Here." He leaned over her and his stomach rested against her back. She could feel the hard buckle of his belt. She shut her eyes and gritted her teeth until the heat passed. He handed her the rope strap and she clipped it to the small metal ring. Her hands shook a bit.

"Reward him," he told her.

"How?" she whispered.

"With some sweet words and soft strokes."

"Nice horse," she croaked, and patted the animal's neck.

"Stroke it. Don't pat it." He touched her shoulder, slowly running his burning hand down her arm. "Like this."

She held tight to the lead, but felt her legs melting and almost fainted. Then she remembered to breathe.

"Remember," he whispered into her ear, "always stroke something long. It feels better."

She couldn't swallow, couldn't speak. Her mouth was too dry.

He finally stepped back and cleared his throat, loudly. "To lead him, walk beside his neck. Like this." He grabbed her shoulders again and she tingled. Addie could have sworn that he rubbed them before he turned her so she was facing the same direction as the horse.

"Now push forward on the lead."

The horse walked about five feet and then stopped. Addie pushed on the rope. The devil didn't budge.

"Talk sweet," he reminded her, returning to his leaning spot by the tree.

She tugged on the rope. "Move, you obnoxious, mule-headed beast," she muttered out of the corner of her mouth.

It snorted.

"Cluck at him!"

She turned and gave Mr. Creed a withering look. "Chickens cluck, not humans!"

"Use your tongue. I *know* you can," he shouted, and with his hands cupped around his mouth, he "clucked."

The horse almost yanked her arm out of the socket when it took off toward its owner. She trotted alongside, wishing vile curses down on the beast. It stopped in front of the tree and she tried to catch her breath, wondering what had ever possessed her to try to do this, and with this horse.

"Not bad." Her instructor ambled over. "Now the saddle."

"What?" she screeched.

He raised his hands in the air. "You have to learn to saddle the horse."

She didn't say one word. She just burned.

"I told you before. If you want to learn to ride, you'll have to learn everything. A horse isn't going to be sitting there, all saddled and waiting for you to put that white butt of yours on it."

"Would you please stop talking about the color of my— my derriere!"

"All right. The horse won't be waiting for your round, little ass."

She swung her fist right at him. He caught it.

"Uh-uh-unnnh. No hitting the teacher."

"You have a dirty mouth."

"That didn't keep your tongue out of it the other night, did it?"

179

She jerked her hand away and stormed off.

"Give up?"

She skidded to a stop. Without turning around she yelled, "Where's the saddle?"

He didn't answer her, and the silence thickened. She finally turned. He pointed at it, lying on the ground all the way over by the barn. She stomped over to it, madder than she could ever remember being. And it must have helped, because she grabbed each end of the heavy saddle, lifted it and trudged over to the horse and the toad.

Sweat dripping down her temples and her ribs, she closed the distance between them and dumped the saddle at his feet. "There's your dadgum saddle!" She dusted her hands and glared up at him.

"Wiry little thing, aren't you?"

"Let's get on with it."

He held out a striped blanket. "Here, lay the blanket on his withers."

"His what?"

"Withers." He placed his hand on the animal's back, near where the mane stopped.

She tossed the blanket onto the horse. It slid off the opposite side and plopped on the ground.

"Lay the blanket on, don't throw it."

She marched around the backside of the horse and the animal tried to kick her. She screamed and jumped back, losing her balance and landing on the ground in a puff of dust.

"That beast tried to kill me!"

He leaned his elbow on the horse's withers and gave her a look that told her she'd done something really stupid. "Don't walk behind a horse unannounced—"

"Great," she interrupted. "Next time I'll bring my footman."

"Cute, Little Miss Pinky," he said, "but if you don't want that big brain of yours spread all over the farmyard, I suggest you listen.

"Number one," he held up a finger, "let a horse know you're coming by talking to him and putting your hand on him. Horses kick to protect their blind spot. Number two."

180

The second finger popped up. "Keep your voice calm. Screeching at a horse will only get him more excited."

"I don't screech," she declared with her nose up. "Crows screech."

"Crows caw. Don't walk in front of the horse when you lead him. Don't mount near a barn or a fence, unless you want to lose your big brain. And don't," he held up a hand to shut her up, "argue with the teacher."

"I hate you."

"Good, now put the blanket on him."

Addie dusted off her knickerbockers and grabbed the blanket, keeping her head as far away as she possibly could. She circled the front of the horse in a wide, ten-foot radius, then placed the blanket on the horse and waited.

"Now drag the blanket back a few inches," he instructed.

She pulled the blanket back almost exactly three inches.

"More."

"You said a few."

"More," he gritted.

"A few is three. You said a few. How do you expect me to do what you say if you don't say it right?"

"Pull the damn blanket back five inches!"

She ignored his swearing and pulled the blanket back another five inches.

"That's too far."

"You said five inches! I pulled it back five inches!"

He muttered a second, then said, "Push it up two inches."

She jerked the blanket back up the horse. "Well, I do wish you'd say what you mean. First three inches, then five inches, then two inches . . ."

He mumbled something.

"What?" She turned and planted her hands on her hips. "What was that about giving me ten inches?"

"Forget it!"

"Now . . . I'm supposed to move it ten inches?" she shrieked.

"I said forget it, and I thought you didn't screech."

"I don't," she said. "That was a shriek."

"Banshees shriek," Montana corrected.

"Banshees wail."

"Put the damn saddle on the horse!"

"How? I can't lift it that high!"

"Pick it up."

She did, and he picked them both up. "Now put it on the blanket!"

"I can't, these foot things are in the way!"

"Stirrups. Flip them over the seat."

"Now the strap thing with the metal ring is in the way."

"The cinch. Move it and set the damn saddle on the blanket!"

"Stop shouting in my ear." She set the saddle down on the horse. "There, I did it. Now put me down."

"Gladly." He dropped her.

Her boots hit the hard ground and she could have sworn that she heard her bones ring. "Ouch! I bit my tongue!" She glared at him. "You are no gentleman."

"You're right, I'm not." He adjusted the saddle a bit and then ordered, "Cinch the saddle."

Addie bent down and pulled the belt thing through the metal ring.

"Tighter."

"It'll hurt him."

"No it won't. Pull the latigo tighter."

"What's a latigo?"

"The thing in your hand."

"It's all puffy."

"The latigo?"

"No."

"What is?"

"Your horse."

"That's normal. Walk him in a circle."

"Why?"

"Because I told you to!"

"Fine." She grasped the lead and slowly walked the beast in a small circle, remembering what he had said about how to lead the animal safely. She stopped after a few circles and looked at him expectantly.

He was purple again. "Tighten it another notch or two."

She wanted to ask him if he meant one or two, but decided that that would just prolong the argument. She tightened it two.

"Buckle the other one." He pointed to another strap that hung loose behind the fattest part of the horse's stomach.

She grabbed it and pulled it through the buckle just as hard as he'd made her do the cinch.

Addie had never heard a horse scream.

"Jesus Christ!" He shoved her back away from the bucking horse and released the strap, talking to the animal in a deep, calming voice.

Addie bit her lip. She hadn't meant to hurt it. Even though she didn't like it much, she would never intentionally hurt an animal, even a mean horse like this one.

"What the hell did you do that for?" He stared at her as if she'd done it on purpose.

"I'm sorry. I didn't know. I—"

"Forget it. Just don't use your 'common sense' anymore, okay?"

She nodded, feeling bad and staring at the poor, mean beast. Its eyes narrowed when it returned her look. Its eyes weren't kind like the cows', who hadn't glared at her at all, even when she'd forgotten to milk them and when she'd slapped one of them on the rump.

"This is a bridle. Loosen the halter from his nose and leave it around his neck. Understand?"

She shook her head. He heaved a ponderous sigh. "I'll do it then, this one time only. You watch closely."

He slid the halter off the beast's nose and then put on the bridle, telling her what the headstall and the bit and such were and how to watch out so one didn't get bitten. She argued with him until he did it three times, telling him that's the only way she could remember the whole procedure.

"There are two ways to mount," he told her.

"Teach me the easy one."

"They're both easy."

"Well, which one do you use?"

"I twist the stirrup and stand near his shoulder."

"Then teach me the other one."

He looked like he was mentally counting. "Stand even with the saddle and face the horse."

She did as he told her. Her nose was level with the cinch ring.

"Hold the reins in your left hand." He watched her. "Okay, now put your hand firmly on the horse's neck and grab the saddle horn."

"Is that this handle up here?" She pointed to the leather knob that stuck out of the front of the saddle.

"Yes," he said with a smile, "that handle is the horn."

"I wonder why it's called a horn?"

"Grab it."

Addie dropped the reins and grabbed the handle with both hands.

"No," he yelled, exasperation threading his loud voice. "Put the reins in your left hand, place it on the horse's withers, grab the horn in your right hand, put your foot in the stirrup and mount."

"I'm confused."

He grabbed her hand and plastered it onto the horse's neck, then he took her right hand and closed it around the saddle handle. Holding out the foot thing, he told her, "Put your foot into the stirrup."

Addie put her right boot in it and then kind of hung there, straining to reach the high saddle handle and balance on one foot.

"Damn!" he swore.

"Now what's wrong?"

"Put your left foot in the stirrup, unless you want to sit in the saddle backward."

"Oh." She changed feet.

"Brace your knee against the horse and spring up into the saddle."

She waited a moment, eyeing the tall horse. "You lifted Rebecca."

"She knows how to mount. I just helped. You have to learn this first—" He stopped talking. After a long pause he asked, "Jealous?"

"Hardly!" Addie sprang upward so fast she almost went over the other side. The horse started shifting backward and the saddle wobbled. She dropped the reins and held onto the handle with both hands, her left foot in the holder thing and her other leg dangling next to it.

"Throw your right leg over the saddle," he ordered.

She did it. "Done. Now stop this thing, will you!"

"You have to learn to control the horse. Where are the reins?"

She leaned over the left side of the horse and looked down, both hands still gripping the handle. "Down there." She slowly released the handle with her left hand and pointed at the reins draped down out of her reach.

"Not much good, are they?" His voice dripped with sarcasm.

"Oops."

He handed them to her. "Now dismount."

"I just got up here!"

"You learned to mount and now you'll learn to dismount. Get down."

"How?"

"The same way you got on."

"Oh." She thought about it for a moment, then she dropped the reins, gripped the handle with both hands, swung her right leg over and fell onto the ground.

"Stop laughing!" She stood and dusted off her derriere.

"How's your little round butt?"

"None of your business! Can I get back on?"

"Be my guest." He bowed slightly.

Addie picked up the reins, put her left hand on the withers, grabbed the horn with her right hand, foot in the stirrup, and she mounted perfectly. "There." She grinned down at him. "Now what?"

"Sit erect."

She threw her small shoulders back and her chin went up.

"Good. Now slide your feet deep into the stirrups, heels down. Good. Hold the reins above the saddle horn . . . no, like this." He threaded the leather reins over her fingers. His other hand came to rest on her thigh. She gasped, and stared at his hand. Her leg almost burned beneath it.

"Now rest your right hand on your thigh, like I did. Now lean forward a bit."

This was easier, like cycle racing. Addie leaned forward like she did when she rode, with her nose practically touching the handlebars. Her nose was an inch from the animal's mane. The horse walked forward. Her nose hit its neck.

"Not that far forward! I said slightly!"

Addie straightened and bounced in the saddle as the horse trotted in a circle around Mr. Creed. "You said 'a bit,' not slightly!"

"What the hell's the difference?" he shouted back. "I didn't tell you to bury your nose in his mane!"

"How do I stop him?" She and the horse bounced along.

"Pull back on the—wait! *Gently* pull back on the reins." Then she thought she heard him say something about learning his lesson.

The horse stopped and Addie giggled. "I did it!" She turned to him. "That was good, wasn't it?"

"So-so."

Her nose shot up. "I stayed on and I stopped it."

"You might have stayed on, but there was enough daylight showing to blind a bat."

"What's that supposed to mean?"

"You bounced all over the saddle. It's called seeing daylight, get it?"

"Oh." She was thoughtful for a moment. "Well, how do I stay down? It's the horse that's bouncing, not me."

"Move with it." He grabbed her hips in both hands and slowly moved her back and forth on the saddle. Addie stopped breathing.

His movements slowed and his expression changed. She began to sweat.

Then his voice came out, soft, deep, low. "Ride on your crotch."

"Pardon me?"

"Ride on your crotch," he repeated. "You do know what that is, right?"

She nodded, but kept her eyes and her red face straight ahead. His hand rubbed the inside of her thigh and she jumped. "What are you doing?"

"Checking for space." His hand grazed the inside of her thigh and down her calf.

She didn't breathe. "Why?"

"Your thighs and upper calves should always be in contact with the horse."

"Why?"

"To keep your balance in the saddle." He started to go around to the other side of the horse.

"Don't! The other leg is fine. I understand." If he touched her like that again, she'd just die.

"Okay then, ride." He slapped the horse on its backside and it took off.

Addie bounced and bobbed in the saddle, managing to hold the reins and her double-handed death grip on the handle. The more the animal bounced, the more she wished she had her corset. This was worse than riding her cycle over the trolley tracks.

"Kick him into a lope," he shouted.

Addie bounced along. "H-H-Howww?"

"With your heels!"

She shut her eyes—she was getting dizzy from all the bouncing—and jabbed her heels into the horse. He stopped, but Addie bounced some more.

Mr. Creed ran over. "Why'd you stop? I told you to kick him."

"I did."

"Then why'd he stop?"

"Don't ask me. It's your horse." *Even has your personality,* she thought as she watched the animal lower its head and eat some more grass.

Tipping his hat back, he looked at Addie as if she were lying.

"I did kick it! Just like this!" She kicked the horse.

Its head flew up, its ears went back, and off it took at a full gallop. Addie hung on for dear life, trying to remember everything he'd told her. The horse was fast, and no matter how hard she tried to press down, she still flew all over the seat of the saddle. She kept kicking it but it still wouldn't stop. She gripped the handle with both hands. God only knew where the reins were! She kicked it again.

She could hear the toad yelling but she couldn't understand a word he said.

Gravel splattered and crunched. The horse picked up more speed—until it neared the road. Suddenly its front legs skidded out. It ducked its head and stopped dead.

Addie didn't. Over she flew, head first. She hit the ground and sprawled on her face. Her mouth was filled with the dry, metally taste of gravel and her elbows rang from the jarring. A curtain of black hair blocked out the light. She shook her hair over her shoulder and looked down the drive. Mr. Creed ran toward her. She spit out the gravel and pushed up on her hands.

"Are you okay, boy?"

Addie sat up on her sore behind and watched, stunned, as the toad examined his ornery horse, cooing and rubbing it like a worried mother. She stared at her hands. Her palm had gravel stuck to it, and when she glanced at her leg, she saw the long scrapes that marred her boots. Her castor-colored stockings with the diamond inserts were torn in three places, and one black stocking supporter dangled from the side of her knickerbockers. The white linen shirt she'd ironed so precisely was filthy. Her arms ached, her derriere felt battered, and, oh my God, a cuff link was missing!

She examined the gravel for the little silver bicycle bell. When she couldn't find it she panicked and scurried on her hands and knees, digging through the gravel in search of her precious cuff link. She sifted the gravel through her fingers, hoping to find it.

"Dadgum, ornery, obnoxious beast!" she muttered, canvassing the area where she'd landed.

A pair of dingy, gray-brown boots crunched in front of her. "You okay?"

Addie grabbed two handfuls of gravel and dust. She didn't look up. "Just ducky! Move your foot!"

"What are you doing?"

"Looking for my silver cuff link."

"Oh." He was quiet for a moment. "Is that it?"

She tossed her long hair out of her face and looked up.

188

He pointed to a silver sparkle sitting in the gravel just a few feet away.

"That's it!" Addie crawled to it. She just reached out for it and the horse moved its snout. "Oh noooo!" she shouted, and the animal's fat, pink lips closed over it.

She stood and grabbed the bridle. "Don't you dare!" She shook the metal part of the bridle, trying to get the horse to spit out the cuff link.

"What are you doing?" he asked.

"He ate my bicycle bell!" She jerked on the bridle. "Spit it out, you beast!"

"Here, I'll get it." He grabbed the bridle and spoke quietly to the horse, stroking its long nose. Then he placed his palm under its mouth and it obediently spit out her cuff link. He handed it to her, still stroking the mean horse. "Good boy."

She pinched her cuff together and slid the link into the hole, straightening the bar pin. She tugged on her cuffs and breathed a sigh of relief, then she groaned. Every muscle in her body ached. She wiggled her stiff shoulders and then rubbed her sore fanny.

"What me to kiss it and make it better?"

"Go kiss your horse!"

"That was a stupid thing to do."

"Pardon me?"

"It was stupid. You could have hurt Jericho."

She gasped in outrage.

"You could have been hurt too," he conceded, "kicking him into a full gallop like that."

"You told me to kick him!" She glared up at him.

"I just meant kick enough to get him moving a bit."

"That's not what you said. You said 'kick him into a lope.' "

"But I didn't tell you to keep kicking him."

"I thought he'd stop." She looked down at the cuff link, examining it for teeth nicks.

"I know horses, Miss Pinky, and they don't stop when you kick them."

"Yours did!"

He looked at her like she was fibbing.

"This is all your fault," she informed him, pulling her cuff into place.

"You wanted the lessons."

"That animal hates me, and you can't communicate! You say one thing and I do it and then you say I did it wrong and I just did exactly what you said!"

He shook his head. "I can't communicate?" he said, amazed.

"No, you can't."

"I know what I'm saying. If you can't understand simple English, then that's your problem. Like I told you before, get yourself a book."

She dusted her hands and clothes off. "That's a good idea. At least a book can get its point across."

His look grew angry. "Oh, I think I can get my point across." He stepped toward her.

She raised her face and glared up at him. "When pigs fly!"

His hands shot out, grabbed her and slammed her up against his chest, lowering his head at the same time. His mouth hit hers. His hand wrapped into her hair and he gripped it tight, holding her mouth to his and muffling her protests.

She wanted this. She shouldn't have, but she did, and soon she was lost. Her hands gripped his shoulders, squeezing hard, because she wanted the kiss to be hard, faster, even deeper. His mouth left hers and she moaned. It sounded so loud, yet she couldn't stop the sound. She let her head fall back and her lips parted more with each of her deep breaths. His tongue dove into her ear, kissing it as thoroughly as he had kissed her mouth. A thrill shot through her, stronger, more impelling than winning a cycle race.

His lower body moved in a slow circle, rubbing her. She had some odd urge to rub back. The instinct grew the more he kissed her ear, licked her neck, and whispered. His mouth traced her chin, then up to the corner of her open mouth. She sucked in a breath. His hand moved down the front of her and spanned her left breast, moving in the same slow circle as his hips. She groaned, and his tongue teased across her lip line, flicking and taunting.

"Get the point?" he whispered, his lips hovering above hers.

She didn't understand. His hips pushed into hers. She opened her eyes under the heat of his. "What?" she whispered, her eyes settling on his lips.

He grabbed her hand, his eyes boring into hers. He shoved her hand against the buttons on his pants and held it there. She gasped and tried to pull her hand away. He pressed harder against her palm, his hand gripping her wrist so hard that it felt bruised. She cried out, frightened. This wasn't a game or the kind of challenge she could handle.

"Don't," she moaned, shaking her head, suddenly frightened and wanting this to stop. She was scared of what this man did to her, of what he made her feel, of what he made her forget. "Please, I—"

He let go of her hand and pushed his knee upward, against her crotch. His hands gripped her head and he pushed it back, covering her mouth with his. He rammed his tongue against her lips, pushing his palm hard against her jaw until she opened her mouth. His tongue breached her lips and filled her mouth. His hips beat against her, and his one hand held fast to her head, using the force of his mouth to pin her. When she was lost to the pleasure of his mouth, his hand left her head and both hands grabbed the backs of her thighs and jerked her knees up on either side of his hips. His hands closed over her bottom and he groaned. He thrust up hard against her, rubbing, as if he could burn through their clothing.

She was scared, both of him and herself. This wasn't right. She pushed at his shoulders, trying to break free of the kiss. He wouldn't let go. She had to get away, so she moved her hands to the muscles of his upper chest and she gripped the skin with both fists, twisting. He released her hair and she pulled her head away. "Let me go!"

His eyes were glowing and his breathing was ragged. He looked as if he were in pain.

"Please," she whispered and her voice cracked.

He grimaced and let her slide back down to the ground.

The minute her feet touched the ground she backed away, farther and farther, never taking her wary eyes off him. He just stood there, hands knotted into fists at his sides, his breath just beginning to slow, his look still so hot that she burned. He hadn't uttered a word, and his silence frightened her almost as much as her own emotions. He could make her forget everything, this angry man who stared at naked ladies. Right now, the way his eyes bored into her, she felt naked, so she turned and ran as fast as she could, trying to run away from him, from what he made her feel, and from herself.

13

ADDIE STOOD ON THE PEDALS AND PUSHED DOWN AS HARD as she could. The cycle's wheels moved like molasses through a muddy, low section of the road. Her tow cart hit a rock and the metal milk cans clanged together. The bike wobbled and she tried to pedal forward. Her legs weren't strong enough. With a squishy oosh, her feet sank into the warm mud. She grimaced. *My six-dollar, hand-turned, Dongola kid shoes!* The damp mud oozed through the common-sense buttons. *Dadgummit!*

She peeled open her eyes. The mud christened her shoes ankle high. She popped one foot out of the mud, examining it. It looked like she'd stood in a fudge vat. She shook it and a few clumps of brown, sticky gunk flew off with a plop. The stuff was all over the hem of her skirt too. She gave up. She sank her foot into the soft, wet ground and, with both gloved hands gripping the handlebars, trudged the bike and cart up the small grade.

The morning sun glowed down, making her wish she'd left for town later in the day. Then the sun would have had a chance to dry the few muddy patches left on the road. But she'd left bright and early, thinking the cooler air boded better for the milk she carted behind her. She glanced back to check on the milk cans, but her gaze caught a distant wagon on the road, heading her way. Good, she thought, a friendly California neighbor who would no doubt assist a distressed lady into town. The wagon neared and she could hear the jangle of the harness.

Addie released the handlebars, steadying the bicycle between her calves, and she tucked up a few loose strands of damp hair under the crisp Milan straw of her Carmen hat. Then she grabbed the short brim, tugging the hat down twice. She patted the trim of silk hyacinths and cardinal-colored velvet ribbon that cascaded from one side of the hat. With a welcoming smile she turned back to face her fellow traveler.

It was the gruesome twosome—the toad and his bucking horse. She groaned, cursing her luck.

He pulled the wagon to a stop, the horse exactly even with her cycle. "Well, well, Jericho, look who we have here. It's Little Miss Pinky . . . and her big brain." He smiled, although Addie thought of it more as a baring of teeth.

"Hit a little mud, huh?" He enjoyed this, she could see it written all over his face.

She didn't say one word. She gripped the handlebars, pretending they were his neck. With her hands strained tight, she shoved the cycle forward. It moved in inches.

"Not speaking? Tch-tch-tch, that's a shame. Isn't it, Jericho, old boy?"

Addie gave the horse a furtive look. His pink lips wiggled up. She could have sworn the horse grinned.

His owner rested his elbows on his knees and kept talking. "You know what? I would have thought anyone with so much 'common sense' would have known that you can't ride one of those contraptions in the mud."

She moved a good five feet out of pure cussedness.

The harness jangled again and the wagon and horse meandered forward.

"Need a *ride*, Miss Pinky?"

She crested the top of the rise, milk cans clanging with each shove of the cycle. Her head was down, her chest heaved from exertion and anger, and her arms and legs ached as much as her saddle-sore bottom. She looked up, ready to send him to blazes, when one of the elastic stocking supporters that jimmy-rigged her cart broke. The cart pitched down on one side, the milk cans clattering together like country church bells.

"Oh, noooo!" She dropped the bicycle and moved toward the tilting milk cans. Two stoppers tumbled onto the road with a gush of spilling milk. Addie knelt in the road, hugging the cans while milk poured down the front of her green and red calico shirtwaist. A moment later a man's strong hands gripped the can handles, pulling them both upright and away from her small body.

"I've got 'em," he told her in that deep, bone-melting voice, now devoid of its baiting tone. He stood behind her, his tall body looming over her while he held the cans upright. "Get the stoppers and clean them off."

She scrambled out of the mud and reached under him to retrieve the metal stoppers. The mud was drier at the crest of the rise, so the stoppers weren't even half as muddy as her shoes or hem. She looked around for something to wipe clean the stoppers and found nothing. She turned her hopeful eyes toward him.

He stood watching. "Improvise," he said.

She reached beneath her seersucker skirt and grabbed a handful of the deep cambric ruffle on her underskirt. She wiped the first stopper. She checked the top for any speck of dirt, and finding it clean, started to straighten. She saw his gaze, locked right on her exposed, stockinged legs. She dropped the skirt and shot up, embarrassed.

"I could use one of those." He nodded at the broken, pink elastic stocking supporter. Then he looked right at the spot where she fastened them to her stockings. She could have sworn that he could see right through her skirt. She spun around and drew up the front of her skirt and under-skirt, unfastening one of her supporters. She straightened and wiped flat the wrinkles in her skirt, then turned and held out the garter by its elastic strap.

"Red?" He plucked it from her outstretched hand, his face all smirky. Then, just before he turned back to the cart and cycle wheel, he humiliated her. He whistled.

She wanted to crawl under the mud. Instead her nose went up. "They match my hat."

His look turned hot, and it boiled over her body.

"I can do that," she volunteered.

He ignored her and started fixing her makeshift hitch.

"Did you hear me?"

"Um-hmm," he answered, completely absorbed with his task.

"I said, I can do that." Her voice went up like her nose. "You can go on." *Please*, she thought, *just go*.

He snapped the garter to the tow cart, appearing to test the hold. "And leave you stranded?" He blessed her with that hot look of his. "Never . . . sweet."

Addie eyed the wagon seat. It was one narrow plank of wood just big enough for two adults. Town was another eight miles, and she was sure that it would feel closer to a hundred miles if she were sitting next to this man on that little seat. She turned to make some excuse, but she was too late. The tailgate was down and her milk cans were in the wagon. Mr. Creed heaved the cycle and cart onto the bed and then chained the tailgate into place.

"Please put my cycle back down here." She couldn't think of a good excuse.

He frowned at her.

"I need to . . . uh . . ." What did she need? She looked everywhere but at him. She settled for a bad excuse. "Uh . . . to . . . promote my muscle tone."

Faster than a flea's sneeze he swung her up into his arms. He tossed her lightly and her arms looped his neck. The hand that supported her back squeezed her torso. "Your muscle tone feels mighty fine to me." His grin was bare inches from her face.

His other hand gripped the back of her thigh and she squealed. "Stop that! Put me down!"

"Gladly," he said, as he swung her up and tossed her into the wagon seat.

She landed with a soft, but fanny-aching thud. "Oooh," she moaned under her breath, dying to rub her sore bottom. Stubborn determination kept her hands on the seat. She would not let him know she was saddle sore.

She started to tell him to please put her back down, but he hopped up into the seat, settling against the iron rail that served as a backrest. Then he stared at her, as if daring her to say something.

She refused to look at him, so she stared at his elbow, propped on the side rail right next to the red-painted Studebaker Bros. emblem. She couldn't think, but ohhh, could she feel. His hot gaze almost melted through her straw hat. Her hands flew to its brim, tugging it down and swiping the red velvet ribbon out of her face. She raised her head, staring straight ahead, and she squirmed a bit in the hard seat.

"Sore?"

Her mouth tightened. The man could read her mind.

"Of course not!" she lied. "I'm perfectly fine. Just dandy, in fact. Let's get this thing going. I don't have all day, and my milk might sour."

"Looks like you're wearing most of it."

Her gaze went to the wet front of her shirtwaist. The fabric clung to her chest.

"Cold?" the toad asked, a smile in his voice.

Her arms clamped over her chest. With her mouth tight, she aimed her face upward, away from him and right at that hot sun. "Yes. Let's go!"

He unwrapped the reins from the brake stick. She heard him mumble something about her "prissy" face being enough to make the milk sour.

This time she looked at him. "If you don't like my face, then just put me down like I asked!"

He gave her a knowing look. "And have you tell the whole town that I'm no gentleman?" He shook his conniving head. "Not a chance, *sweet*." He snapped the reins.

They rattled down the road, his right side—from hard, hot shoulder to tough, fiery thigh—rubbing against hers.

Addie was *cold* all the way to town.

Montana tipped back his hat and leaned against the wagon, watching Little Miss Pinky stomp down the plank walkway. It wasn't easy to stomp and push that silly bicycle of hers too. She stopped, ignoring the odd stares of passersby. The woman acted as if that contraption of hers were a sight as common as bees in a flower garden. She leaned the bicycle between some nail barrels in front of Peabody's Mercantile and she slammed inside.

He couldn't hide his smile—the damn thing just kept itching at his mouth. Although he did manage not to laugh. His plan was working. He was sure that the woman was getting close to her limit.

A week ago, had he passed her on the road, he would have foolishly driven right past her. He could be hot-headed. But he was learning . . . And was it worth it. He'd taken his own sweet time getting that wagon into town, purposely rubbing his leg against hers. Every time he did, he could feel her attempt to move into nonexistent seat space. He'd bet her right side was marked from plastering her hip against the metal side rail. Tomorrow that white skin would be black and blue.

He'd snapped Jericho into a faster speed and she'd almost flown head first over the foot rest. It was perfect. He'd thrown his arm around her small shoulders and hadn't let go once, no matter how much she'd wiggled around.

The gasps were the best, though. He had slowed down, until they were meandering along, then he'd relaxed his hold, letting his fingers dangle and innocently brush over the top of her right breast. He was careful to do this only when the wagon bumped over ruts. She sucked in a breath every time. Not once did he break down and look at her, not even the first time his fingers grazed her. He'd felt her startled look, heard the sharp whoosh of her gasp, but he had stayed as calm as a skunk in the moonlight. He'd kept his eyes on the road and just whistled.

But now he had things to do, so with a quick, lithe movement, he shoved off from the wagon and walked in the opposite direction, heading for the old grange hall. A large group of men stood outside the tall, red-brick building, and from all the commotion, Montana assumed their topic was a heated one. As he neared, he recognized John Latimer's dark head in the center of the group. He spoke just as Montana reached the ring of men.

"Come on, Herbert, we can't go running off half cocked over this thing, you know that," John said.

"Look, Latimer, you didn't just get your best grain downgraded to number three. That was top-grade wheat. I could have paid off my mortgage with that crop. That railroad-bought bastard running the grain elevator stole my life when he downgraded that wheat." The man whipped his straw hat against his knee. "You know who the hell's gonna get my profit, don't you? The railroad and the elevator operators! Christ, man, I just lost my whole crop! It's the same as having it burned, only those railroad robber barons burned it! How the hell am I supposed to meet my mortgage, let alone feed Bea and the kids?" The stocky, fair-haired farmer ran his gristled, work-worn hand over his tanned and troubled face.

Montana could remember that same worried look—the downturned mouth that signaled anger but also hinted at failure, the strong brown forehead creased with fear and a need to survive, and the moistness misting around the man's eyes, which screamed despair and disappointment. This man was damn scared and ready to break. His father had worn that look for the last year of his short life. Montana would never forget it.

He continued to watch the man, trying to concentrate on the present and drive the memory of the past from his mind. The farmer needed help.

Wade Parker stepped out from the shadowed entrance of the grange. "Schultz is right. We need to do something. I just came back from Sacramento. The rate commission can't do anything. Gordon and Doyle are the only two commissioners who aren't already owned by the railroad. There's no way to get a bill through the legislature until next year." He shook his dark head in disgust. "We'll have to try on local levels. I can't get any action going through government channels. In California, the railroad owns just about everyone."

The men began to drill Wade with questions. Herbert Schultz, the poor farmer who was about to lose everything, leaned against the brick wall of the grange, listening to Wade. As the crowd closed in to hear the news from the state capital, Montana moved closer to John Latimer.

"Wade's the lawyer for the local farmers association," John told him. "We've tried to get the railroad's freight rates regulated, but every time it looks like we're gaining, the railroad manages to either buy someone off or sway the vote."

"The Supreme Court upheld the right to regulate the railroads," Montana commented, staring at the crowd of farmers that seemed to be ready to tackle the railroad single-handedly.

"I guess you know more than I'd thought." John gave Montana a surprised look.

Montana backtracked a bit. "If I'm going to be a farmer, I need to know what's going on. It's in my best interests to be knowledgeable." He smiled at John. "After all, it wouldn't do for me to plant hay if cotton's going for five dollars more a bale, now would it?"

"Guess you're right. What's your crop?"

"Wheat. Winter wheat. I'm here to buy the seed and a good drayage team," Montana said distractedly. His gaze was captured not by the crowd and their heated plans, but by the small, gristled farmer who walked down the street, his hand crushing the straw hat—a symbol of the farmer's pride, his hunched shoulders screaming defeat, his head hung in dejection and failure. Montana's gut wrenched. He prayed to God the man didn't have a son to see his father's devastation.

"That's what most of us are planting. Jenson's just got the seed in from Chicago. Herbert Schultz might need to break up his team. He's had eight Morgans. He might be able to get by with four." John nodded at the defeated farmer.

"I don't profit from another's bad breaks." Montana spoke with determination.

"You'll probably be saving his farm. No one else needs those horses. We've all got a good team, but you decide." John waited.

Montana watched the man for a moment. "What are we waiting for, then? Come on, let's see if I can't change that man's luck."

The two men turned, heading for the farmer, but they were stopped when Wade Parker called out to them. "You two going to be here for the association meeting Tuesday night? The railroad and the grain operators can't stop us! We're going to raise less grain and more hell!"

John called out, "I'll be there!" He turned to Montana. "How 'bout you?"

Montana glanced back at the poor farmer, then he turned and said, "Sure. There's nothing I like better than raising a little hell."

Addie hunched over and looked out through the frosted print on the front display window of Peabody's Mercantile. Three men stood in the center of the street: John Latimer, a smaller man whom she didn't recognize, and Mr. Creed. It was odd, but those long legs of his looked perfectly normal, yet on the wagon seat she'd have sworn they were hard fire. After all, she'd just spent the longest half hour of her twenty-four years on a small wooden wagon seat with one of those thighs rubbing her until she boiled inside like a vat of fruit jam.

The glass fogged slightly, dulling her view, so she moved over. He tipped his hat back, a gesture that was now familiar to her. She could see his profile, his strong jaw, and the hard, carved lines of his face. His long, curly hair was tied with a leather strip, right at his neck. Lately he'd had it tied back every time she'd seen him. It made him look less . . . wild, more civilized. Although he wasn't civilized, that she knew. In fact, the man was a real stinker. *Cold, indeed!*

"I've got your total here, Miz Pinkney."

Addie shot upright, her hand on her heart. "Uh, yes. I'll be right there," she told the proprietor. She was just being silly, standing there watching that man instead of browsing through the mercantile. She shuffled through a stack of cloth bolts and felt as if she'd just been caught with her fingers in the jar of peppermint sticks. Unable to resist, she looked outside again. Mr. Creed and the short man shook hands, the man looking happier than he had earlier. People seemed to naturally like Mr. Creed, and it puzzled her.

The merchant cleared his throat loudly. Addie rammed a few strands of loose hair back under her fine hat, plastered a smile on her flushed face and spun around, marching past the mother-of-pearl button display and over to the long oak counter that dissected the town's only general store.

The room was crammed with merchandise. Signs and posters advertising everything from curative soda water to electric belts colored the paneled walls. Wood and glass cases filled with jewelry, hairpins, and personal toilet items lined the west side of the store. On the shelves behind the counter, hundreds of bottles—blue, amber, and dark brown—covered almost every square inch of space. A rainbow of tins—red, blue, yellow, and orange—containing powders, tobacco, cocoa, and every spice imaginable, were stacked like bricks on a long, marble-topped, iron display rack that stood between the counter and the east wall. A huge, red coffee grinder with a grinding wheel bigger than the ones on Addie's bicycle sat bolted to the end of the oak counter-top. Next to it were oversized glass jars with bright tin lids. They were lined up like toy soldiers on display. The fine, clear glass showed their colorful contents, everything from red and black licorice whips to giant green pickles. Addie's mouth watered.

Behind the counter was Mr. Seth Peabody. A tall man—everyone was tall except Addie—he was blessed with bright blue eyes and a head that was as bald and shiny-white as a newly laid egg. Icepick-thin, with a high, midwestern voice, he stood at the counter, greeting everyone as if they were his oldest and dearest friends.

Seth Peabody had a face with character—a long, hook nose, no chin, and more teeth than Mr. Creed's horse. And he was one of the kindest men Addie ever had the pleasure of meeting. He'd told her how he'd respected her aunt, whom he had considered one of the best "gall durn" women in Muledeer County. Honest, hard-working, and would do anything for someone who wasn't as "blessed" as she.

He flipped through a few green receipts. "Here's the total credit of the milk, three dollars and seventy-two cents. And remember, I'll buy your eggs, just as soon as you get that chicken farm running." He gave her a horse smile. "I've got your list filled, one apple parer, a pound of Morton salt, four nutmegs, two Mexican cinnamon sticks, one tin of red cayenne pepper, one spool lavender cotton thread . . ." He looked up and asked, "You want Clark's or J. P. Coats?"

"Clark's," she answered, her gaze captured by the variety of fragrance atomizers that lined the case in the front of the oak counter.

"Got it." Mr. Peabody turned and plucked a small wooden spool of thread from a wooden display case behind him. Then he went on, "One bottle of indelible ink, five-pound slab of bacon, one cured ham, White Lily Face Wash, Dr. Rose's Dyspepsia Powder. That's it! Anything else?"

"The ice?" Addie reminded him.

"Ah yes, Ben Richards will start delivery Friday, and he'll be out there every fourth day. How's that?" He stuck his pencil behind one large ear and looked up from the receipt.

"Fine, thank you." Addie stepped back to look at the items in the glass cases in the front of the long counter. Her muscles twitched. "Do you have a good liniment?"

"Dr. Silas Camphor Muscle Restorer. Use it myself, every time the missus gets me to reorganizing the display case." He laughed and plucked a tall, brown bottle off the crowded shelves behind the counter. He added it to her purchases, then he paused, looking a bit sheepish. "Do you need these delivered?"

"I'd planned on using my cycle and cart, but it might be easier if Custus brings them out. The road's still a bit muddy."

"Uh, well, there's a little problem." Seth Peabody

looked as if his collar had just shrunk. "Custus is a bit, ah, set in his ways. He got put out with me and quit this morning."

"Oh. Did he go back to work for the railroad station?"

"Nope. Jess Spindle, the stationmaster, said if he ever saw Custus McGee again he'd tie him to the track and hope his hard head didn't derail the express."

Addie had to laugh. "He's a character."

Mr. Peabody looked at her, amazed. "You're just as kind-spirited as your aunt was. I can get these out to you later today. The missus will be in this afternoon, and she can mind the place while I make the delivery." He started to remove her purchases and set them in a crate.

"Wait." She held up a hand, her face suddenly thoughtful. "You say Custus is out of a job?"

He nodded.

"Where can I find him?"

"Now, Miz Pinkney, I don't think you ought to be—"

"Custus and I deal fine together. Besides, I need to hire someone to help with the farm."

"What about Mr. Creed?"

Mr. Creed is the reason I need Custus, Addie thought. "We need more help." *And I need a protector.* "Now where can I find Custus?"

Seth Peabody scratched his bald head. "If you're sure . . ."

"I'm sure."

"He's down at the livery, giving Bud Hinckle hel—uh, what for."

"Thanks, just box these items up," she said, opening her money purse and paying the bill. "Custus and I'll pick it up on our way out of town."

"Whatever you say, Miz Pinkney." He watched her go, then added, "And . . . good luck."

Addie closed the mercantile door, then the smart click of her heels echoed down the wooden walk. This was the perfect solution. She would hire Custus as a farmhand. Between Mabel and Maud, and the chicks and the turkeys, she hardly had time to breathe. This would solve her problem. But best of all, Custus was the perfect answer to her problem with Mr. Creed and his hot, tricky hands. Those hands had become a real problem. They could make her forget her own behavior. In fact, everything about the man seemed to light something inside her. His hands, his voice, his tongue.

There went those goose bumps again. She rubbed her upper arms as she walked. There was no way he would be able to chase her with Custus there. And no chance that Addie would get herself into another one of those sticky situations. Custus would serve as the perfect chaperon. She didn't need good luck. She'd already found it. Finally, she could get on with her farming and forget about her troubles with Mr. Creed. Tonight, she thought, tonight I'll finally get a good, safe, and secure night's sleep. With that comforting thought, Addie went off to hire Custus McGee as her protector.

The night air was still as a stone. Not a breeze, not a chill, not a cloud moved above Montana, just a full, fat moon that glowed like a stockman's lantern and an ink-black sky filled with bushels of stars. He turned the loaded wagon onto the gravel drive and drove to the barn.

He'd made a good deal for the drayage horses, and he'd ride out to Schultz's place and bring the team back tomorrow. He unhooked Jericho, leading him over to the water trough, and as he pumped, he thought about plowing his field with the team, something he'd wanted forever. He left his horse to his drinking and grabbed a tarp from near the barn, snapped it up and over the bags of grain seed he'd bought.

On a whim, he walked out into the moonlit field. Hunkering down, he pulled his hand through the clumps of dry dirt. His dirt. He closed his fist and the clump changed to a fine powder that sifted through his hands. It was late and the dirt cool. No warmth from the sun clung to the land, but he didn't need to feel the warmth. Knowing this handful of rich earth was his, Montana Creed's, warmed him more than a dozen suns.

Rubbing his hands on his flexed thighs, he looked over the field. Acre after dark, rich acre lay fallow, begging for the seed that would prove its worth, awaiting the water that would help the soil drive its very essence into the crop. He would soon plow this field, digging the metal coulter into the dirt and turning it so the seed had a fresh womb in which to thrive.

For Montana, farming was like giving birth. The farm was a fertile belly of land that grows with the miracle of new life and springs forth with hard labor. His wheat would be his child, conceived in love and tended with a father's pride. It would be the best wheat he could nurture because its strength would come from virile land. His land.

And her buildings. He swore and stood, ramming his hands in the back pockets of his denims and kicking a rock back across the farmyard. He had to get rid of her. He was close to driving her off, real close. He was sure that if he could just catch her off guard one or two more times, she'd be long gone.

Leading Jericho to the barn, he put him in the stall. He was heading for the bunkroom when he remembered that he hadn't tied down the tarp on the wagon. He almost left it and went to bed, but he remembered how fast the Pacific storms could blow over those hills. He couldn't afford to lose that seed.

Behind the barn Montana uncoiled a hank of rope from a rope pile and took it back to the wagon, where he secured the cover. He wrapped the rest of the rope around his elbow and shoulder as he went around the barn, returning the rope to its original stack.

He rounded the corner of the barn and saw it—the open window—his invitation. He changed direction, prowling toward the back of the house. He peered in, half expecting a small, fireball of a body to barrel into his chest. He smiled at the memory. She was sound asleep, lying on her stomach, her face turned away from the window. Long black hair trailed across the bed, and he could follow the lines of her small body, round little butt and all, underneath the thin, lacy sheet. His palms itched.

This was just too good an opportunity, and he was no fool. He knew this was his last chance to scare her off. He wouldn't pass it up. Some guilt-ridden little speck of decency deep within him cried *No!* But that was all the more reason for him to climb in the window and into Little Miss Pinky's unsuspecting bed.

If he wanted this farm and his crops, he couldn't afford to care about the consequences. He couldn't afford to care about what happened to the woman when she was gone. He couldn't afford to admit that there was something about her that made him want to whack her prim little butt and hold it, all at the same time. For some reason he needed to bait her just to watch her reaction. It was a game that kept his blood flowing quicker, and he liked that. But the games had to stop, because this might be his best and only chance to rid himself of her. This would be the last game he'd have to play with her.

Montana bent down and pulled off his boots. Then, determined to scare the courage right out of her, he silently crawled in the window.

14

Oh my God!"

The toad was in bed with her! His hands clamped onto her wrists and he held her, on her stomach, pinned to the bed. He didn't say a word, and it scared her to death.

"Let me go!" She bucked up with her backside, but he collapsed full length on top of her, his hands still gripping her small wrists. His lips brushed the side of her face, so she turned into her pillow, trying to get away from his mouth.

"I'm going to teach you something else, sweet Addie." His teeth nipped at her ear, right through her hair. "How to ride . . . me."

His lips grazed her cheekbone.

She lifted her head and yelled, "Get off mfmpgh—" She buried her face in the pillow, muffling her screamed threat. It was the only way to escape his seeking mouth, which was everywhere. Again she pushed upward with her fanny and batted against hips. He bore down with his hard groin.

Chin stretched up, she let loose with a scream so loud it sounded like hell turned upside down. She couldn't move the lower half of her body, and she tried, over and over. Her breath plowed through her throat. She squirmed; she jerked back on her wrists; she twisted every free part of her body, all the time yelling into the bedding, commanding that he stop.

He didn't.

God! This was horrible. He was so much stronger than she. She tried to fight. He overpowered her. She struggled and pushed, but she couldn't move. Hushed tales she'd heard raced through her mind. She'd heard that men defiled women. She knew that was what he intended. Oh God, but she didn't even know what it meant. The word *rape,* some kind of intimate cruelty, was always whispered. It should have been screamed!

Addie began to shake. She couldn't stop.

But he stopped.

His breath no longer brushed through her hair, his lips no longer chased over the sides of her face, searching for skin, his hips no longer pressed her deep into the feather mattress. Her breath still skipped past her lips in short little fear-filled gasps. Her shoulders hiccuped with them.

"I want you, Addie, and the only way you'll stop me from having you is to leave." His voice was deep, clear, and not whispering his frequent taunt. This was a threat, and it was as real as death.

She swallowed, trying to moisten her dry mouth. From his tone she knew that this man would do as he threatened. *Oh God,* she prayed.

His knees bracketed her hips and his hands still clamped tight on her wrists; then he used one hand to hold them in a hard and painful grip against the bed. His other hand closed over her shoulder and he pushed her over onto her back. She tried to bring her knees up through the tower of his thighs, but he was too quick. He straightened his legs, burying his hips against hers and pinning her again.

Addie stared up at his chest, which loomed above her. She looked higher. The mouth that could smile with such charm was pressed into a thin, determined line. With each deep breath he took, his nostrils flared and the strength in his face was all there, showing even harder. There was a cruel edge to his look. He wasn't human; he was all stone, except for the harsh yellow eyes which fixed hers.

"You can get out or get laid—you decide."

Her rapid panting stopped, then grew shallow, turning into sobs.

Tears of fear burned into her eyes and she squeezed them shut, locking out the horror of what was happening. The drops spilled over and trickled past the corners of her tightly squeezed eyes, running down over her temples. The sobs kept coming, poured out like the tears. She cried so hard she could hardly catch a breath.

He groaned, and released her wrists so fast it was as if they'd suddenly caught fire. His elbows grazed her ribs and sank into the mattress. Her wet eyes stared at his hung head, watching as his hands rubbed his forehead as if he were in pain.

"Don't cry," he groaned through the wall of his hair. It hung down to her chest, hiding his face.

"Please don't hurt me." Her voice was a mournful wail.

"Don't cry. I won't hurt you." He lifted his head high and shook his hair back. One hand still shadowed his eyes.

Her sobs quieted to hiccuping sounds and sniffs.

"Just don't cry, please, Addie." He rubbed his eyes with his thumb and finger.

She sniffed, and he finally looked at her, wincing at the sounds she made. The hardness was still there, but it was only the hard cut of his facial features, not a hardness that came from within.

"I don't want to hurt you. I thought I could go through with this game. I can't."

His hands threaded into her hair, tenderly, and he held

her head, his thumbs wiping away the dampness on her temples while his fingers caressed the back of her head.

She still wheezed a bit. "Y-You thought you could r-rape me?"

"No, goddammit!" He turned his head away and stared at the wall. "I thought I could scare you away."

"Oh," she said, and the crying started all over again, this time because he didn't like her.

"I can't do it," he admitted, and his breathing deepened. He rolled off her and laid next to her. Still she cried. He groaned again and gathered her into his arms.

"Please, sweet, don't." His hands slid in soothing, circular paths on her small back. He pulled her even closer to his chest, resting his chin on the top of her head, holding her with all the gentleness, all the care, with which one holds a heart-broken child. Over and over he reassured her, "It's okay, sweet. It's okay . . ."

Montana Creed held her in his strong arms, soothed her with his deep voice, and Addie cried herself to sleep.

She stirred in his arms. Montana was almost afraid to look down at her for fear he'd see her tears—the ones that drove a schism through his gut. He swallowed, and her head nestled closer. The heat of her breath spread a burning path on his neck. Her small nose, the one that was always airborne, pressed against his Adam's apple. His left arm was numb, but it was the only numb thing from his neck down.

Her knotted fists rubbed slowly against his shirt. He swallowed again, and she twitched. His breath came a little faster and he closed his eyes, searching for control.

She moved her head away from his neck, and he could feel her looking up at him. He didn't trust himself to look back, so he kept his eyes closed, waiting. His mind didn't play fair. He remembered her naked back and all that black hair against her white skin. It had looked like coal in the snow. But coal was hard and this little woman was softer than the feather bed that held them. Snow was cold and her burrowing body was warm.

"Are you asleep?" she whispered up at him.

Knowing he could no longer avoid her, he prayed for strength and opened his eyes. The red edges of her lids and puffiness around her eyes told of her tears. That old feeling of helplessness welled up in him. Two small crease lines from the crinkled sheet marred her right cheek. He wanted to trace them with his fingers, or better yet, his tongue. Her lips were more swollen than her huge, dark eyes, and she stared at him.

No woman had ever looked at him like that, with such a need, such emotion that he couldn't have turned away from her if he'd been offered the world.

There was love in her huge, innocent dark eyes, and it scared the bloody hell out of him. He could feel the pull of it, and he prayed for control. Then her small hands splayed over his chest, unconsciously moving, making him more aware of the taut, invisible cord that drew them closer and closer. Their lips touched. His prayers went unanswered.

Holding her head in his hands, he drove his tongue between her lips. He needed to taste her, now. She answered his stroke with her own, so he drove to the back of her mouth, pushing and swirling, running over her teeth. Just her flavor sent his body into a taut, hard heaven.

When her small arms closed over his shoulders and under his hair, his hands moved from her head, down her neck, her shoulders, over her back, and they rubbed. His palms needed filling, so they closed over her bottom, pulling her even closer and squeezing the softness. God, how he had wanted this.

His mouth left hers and she moaned, her open mouth tracing up his cheek as he kissed a path across her soft cheek. He raised one hand, pushing her long hair aside, and he licked one long stroke up to her ear. "Sweet Addie, please don't stop me, not now."

Her only answer was to grab handfuls of his hair and pull his mouth back to hers, already open and seeking. Her small tongue played over his teeth and then flicked inside, beckoning his in a stroking match. He answered her, giving her the whole, hard thing, making it fill her mouth like he wanted to fill her body. She sucked it, and his hands closed over her breasts. He didn't hold them as he had her bottom, instead he used his palms to lightly abrade her hard nipples. He wanted to see them, their color, roll them between his lips, draw them into his hot, wet mouth.

He flicked open one of her buttons, held his breath, slowed his tongue and waited. One of her fingers inched inside his shirt and played with his chest hair. He moaned against her mouth, and she flicked open his button. His hands went crazy then, roaming over her ribs, her breast, frantic to get to her, and God help him, her small hands began to mimic his. He pulled away from her mouth; she stared up at him through eyes so black they made the night look pale. Her lips, wet from his kisses, parted, and her breath came in small pants that fed his excitement. He undid her buttons, watching her expressive face.

By the third button she'd closed her eyes, yet her chest rose and fell as if it called to him. He bent to her ear and buried his tongue. Her body bucked against his and she gasped so loud he did it three more times just to hear her.

Licking her ear and her neck seemed to excite her, for her motions quickened. He kept doing it, until he was caught in his own trap. Her hands had opened his shirt and they ran up, combing his body hair from stomach to just below his neck. Wadding the neck of her nightgown in his fists, he pulled it from her shoulders and jerked it down under her back. Her nipples met his chest, and he almost lost control.

Ramming his hands into the mattress, he pressed up, pulling his chest away, and he watched her while he fought for control. Her eyes were closed and her head turned to the side. Threads of her black hair twisted like ribbons over her pale shoulder, and others spilled onto his hands. His gaze followed the taut tendon of her turned neck, down to her collarbone, where a few blue veins showed through her skin. At this moment he didn't dare look lower, so he threw his head back and stared at the ceiling.

Long minutes later her small hand trailed up his straining arm. Just a second more and he'd have command again. He closed his eyes, counting in Spanish, and when in control again, he looked down. With her lips parted she watched him, and her other hand slid up his forearm. He could see that she wanted his mouth again. He moved down and atop her, and on his elbows he held his chest above her. He stared at her breasts with their dark, tight nipples and lowered his head until his tongue touched the hard tip. When he drew it into his mouth and sucked, she cried out.

Arching her back, she reached out and pulled him closer, so he filled his mouth with more of her. Minutes later he did the same to the other one. Her hands shoved the shirt from his shoulders and tore it off as he licked the undersides of her breasts. Then his tongue licked the long length of her torso, up her neck, before driving into her ear again and again. Her fingertips roved his chest and furrowed and tugged through the springy hair. He took both of her hands and guided them above her, lacing his fingers through hers, pressing their joined hands into the mattress, and watching as he rubbed his chest over hers in slow, eternal movements.

He lowered his head. "Give me your tongue." And she did, for what seemed like hours. He didn't want this to end. It was a hot, slow savoring, and he wanted it to go on and on, but his body wanted more of her. He could feel the metal buttons of his jeans holding him back. *Hold me longer,* he thought, *because I want to taste more of her.* He unlaced his hands, drawing his fingertips over the inside of her arms. She moaned. He nuzzled her ribs, dragging his damp mouth over each rib while his hands kneaded her breasts. Then he pulled her gown down farther with his teeth. He traced her navel with the very tip of his tongue and nuzzled her clothing lower, sucking a circle of little marks on her belly. Her hands closed over his, pressing them harder into the softness of her chest.

He grabbed both sides of her clothing. "Lift up for me." She did, but her eyes were still closed. He knelt between her legs, looking at her naked body, its pure, white skin that had to be soft as the clouds in heaven. Her long coal-black hair spread out about the pillows.

He unbuttoned his pants, shoved them down and kicked out of them. He placed a hand on each ankle and rubbed up her legs, spreading them wider. Over and over he traced the insides of her legs, each time just brushing her cleft with his fingers. She moaned every damn time. Soon she arched her hips up, begging for a touch. He gave it to her with his mouth. She screamed and pushed at his shoulders.

"No!" she cried out in a groan, and he stopped.

Their eyes met. She shook her head, a pleading look on her face.

She wasn't ready for this. He circled his fingers on her thighs, calming her and exciting her at the same time, and when he looked back at her, she was staring at him with a look of wonder and fear.

"We're going to do this, Addie." *Please woman, don't back out now.* He moved up so his chest was even with hers and he kissed her, deep and slow, long and stroking, caressing her soft chest with his until he felt her surrender. Then he pressed down with his body. His groin hit the bed between her legs and he bit back a curse. She was so small her body was shorter than his. He crawled up farther so he could press against her. When he met the warm moistness he craved, he pushed against her and slowly circled his hips.

He had to ease his way into her, for he knew she had no experience. So he circled his hips to teach her the pleasure motion, used his chest hair to taunt her breasts and his tongue to stoke her passion.

Deep inside he burned to mate with her. Everything—the unblemished smoothness of her white skin, the lure of her woman's smell, the unique flavor of her mouth—drove a hot, carnal flame through his body. He grew harder, felt close to bursting, and he craved the feeling more than anything in his whole life.

He moved down, lips touching, and mated with her open, seeking mouth while his fingers moved in to rub her cleft and toy with the seed of her. He could feel her rising. The thighs that held his hips began to quiver; her legs stiffened and her hips moved up as if they were seeking. He moved his finger to the top of her seed, rubbing faster. She screamed into his mouth the moment she came.

"Again," he whispered in her hot ear, and he put his finger inside her, driving in and almost out for minutes that seemed like long, impassioned hours, and he watched her shake her head as if she couldn't believe it was happening again. She was lost to the way he played her body. This one little woman who had known no man had more natural passion than all the women he'd ever bedded, and seeing what he could do to her made him feel like he held the world in his hands.

Her hips began to move down on his finger, responding with the motions of mating. He could feel her virgin's barrier, so he pushed at it, hoping to stretch it and make the breaching easy. She pulled up and slid down his finger faster. He inserted another finger, moved them in a tight circle, and her release squeezed around them, throbbing. Sitting back on his heels, he opened her farther, removed his fingers and pressed inside. He slid in inch by tight inch while his mouth moved over her ribs, her neck, her mouth and forehead. His elbows rested on either side of her shoulders and he entered her more, touching the barrier.

He stopped. It was impossible for his mouth to reach hers without moving out of her. Her hands scored his chest, pleading, and when they hit his nipples, he threw back his head. Her hot little arms wrapped around his waist, and he drove home.

She gasped and stiffened, but he didn't move. He stayed there, poised above her and buried within her, and he watched her face. Her look held no pain, just confusion and what looked like a little wonder. He pulled almost out, and he could reach her mouth. He whispered against her lips, "Again."

Her eyes widened in understanding and he began to move, slower than he ever thought he could. She was so hot, so tight, that he had to go on, harder than he planned. Now she moved with him in perfect synchronicity. The friction grew hot, burning as he swelled toward release. He drove in as she drove up, and their breaths raced out and seemed to wrap around the room, over and over. Her lips closed over his distended nipple and she sucked hard at the same moment he felt her deep contractions. One more dark thrust and he spilled in splendid agony.

When his vision cleared and his breathing slowed, he was

still on his elbows above her. They shook slightly, but he was amazed he had any strength left in his arms. This little bit of a woman had drained the life from him, and when he looked down at her, he felt the pull of something else, something elusive that held him to her. His long hair hung damply and hid the confusion that he knew was on his face.

There were just the two of them, together, joined at this moment in time, and God help him, no one else but her mattered.

She didn't move, didn't say a word, but her lips still held his nipple. She had fainted—a little death. He'd felt it too, when she'd sucked on his chest, that freefall over the edge of passion. As he gathered her small, warm, stirring body into his arms, wrapping her hair over them, Montana looked down and vowed that he would never make love to a tall woman again.

15

THE MORNING SUN GLARED THROUGH THE OPEN BEDROOM window. Hot and bright, it lit right on Addie's face. She grunted and buried her face in the pillow. It smelled like Montana Creed. She turned back toward the sunlight and pried open one eye, then the other. She inched an arm out from under the sheet and rubbed her eyes, trying to focus. When she did glance down, her bare bosom stared back.

Air whistled past her lips as she sucked in a breath, suddenly remembering *everything*. A quiet snore called out from the other side of the bed, and she stiffened. A groan burst from her lips. Her whole body ached. She licked her dry lips and they stung, so she ran her fingers soothingly over her mouth and chin. His beard stubble had rubbed them raw.

He stirred next to her, and her eyes popped wide open. She held her breath for a long second and eased over an inch closer to the edge of the bed. When she moved, every muscle beneath her waist screamed out and she winced. She felt black and blue. She plucked the sheet in her finger and thumb and pulled it up, peering down at what she was sure would be her bruised body. There were marks, all right. A small circle of walnut-sized bruises surrounded her belly button. She remembered how they got there and blushed so red her face felt on fire. She dropped the sheet as if scalded.

Good Lord, what had she done? Her dark eyes shuttered closed, but that couldn't block out what had happened. It didn't stop the confusion she felt, the shame, and the guilt, because the fact remained that Adelaide Amanda Pinkney had been intimate with a man, a man she wasn't married to.

"Mornin'," he whispered into her ear as he turned.

Addie almost flew off the bed, but his arm snaked out and pulled her back against his warm, hairy, naked body.

"Don't!" She pried his arm off her and scooted over to the very edge of the bed, jerking the sheet up to her chin so hard that she completely uncovered him. She didn't want him to touch her now. It just reminded her of what happened after he'd crawled into her bed, and she didn't want to be reminded, didn't want to feel guilty. What she wanted was to cast the blame elsewhere.

"What's the matter with you?" He frowned at her.

"This is all your fault!" She glared at his face, afraid to look lower than that blasted dimple on his chin.

"My fault?" He sat up and looked at her as if she'd grown horns. Then a cocky grin replaced his puzzled look. "What's wrong, Addie," he teased, "embarrassed?" He grabbed the sheet and jerked it and her into his arms. His lips buried into her neck. "Don't be embarrassed, sweet. I've seen every inch of you. Hell, I've tasted every inch of you."

"How dare you remind me!" She slipped from his hold

216

and scrambled out of the bed. She grabbed a hold on the sheet and yanked it with all her small might. It flew off him and billowed around her. She wrapped it over her naked, aching body and glared at him. "Cover yourself!"

"Why? You've seen all of me." He knelt in the middle of the bed, facing her in all his proud and naked glory. "Every damn *inch!*"

She grabbed a pillow and flung it at his naked hips. "Cover yourself! I don't want to see you! You did this to me. You chased me and confused me and kissed me and . . . and everything!"

"And you loved it," he dared as he held the pillow across the front of his hips.

"I did not!" she lied. "You seduced me!"

"Three times?" Sarcasm dripped from his words.

She threw a brush at him. He caught it.

"Can't face it, Miss Pinky?" He tossed the brush aside, his face no longer teasing but angry, really angry. "Can't face that you liked what I did to you? Hell, little lady, you were hot enough to burn a hole in the bed." He crawled off the mattress and bent to get his pants.

She clutched the sheet tighter, feeling scared and hurt and confused. "You've been chasing me everywhere." She didn't yell anymore; now she spoke barely above a whisper. "It's not my fault."

"Great!" he said, stepping into his pants and then standing there all mad and handsome, not even bothering to button them. "It's my fault, then. I'll take the blame." He shrugged into his shirt. "It's my fault you wanted it. I forced you to wrap your legs around me and moan. I made you use your tongue like that, didn't I? Oh, and I made you cry 'more . . . please' over and over, right?" He jammed his shirt into his pants.

"But I've never done it before!" she accused, pulling the sheet tighter, as if it could protect her from his words.

"Then I guess I'm one hell of a good teacher. It's too bad you didn't learn to ride a horse as well as you learned to ride a man."

She stiffened at his bluntness and unconsciously backed into the corner. "Leave! Get out!"

"I seem to recall telling you that last night, remember?"
He headed for the door.

She remembered. It had scared her to death.

He stopped at the door and turned his scorn-filled eyes on
her. "I told you you had two choices, and you made yours.
Little Miss Pinky didn't get out, but she sure got—"

She rammed her hands over her ears to block the word,
and she shut her eyes to block out his face. She stood there
naked and shaking, the sheet now a white pool at her feet.
When she opened her eyes, he was gone, so she sank to
the floor and cried.

Montana stormed through the barn doors, scowling.

"Wooo-eeee! Looka that face. What's wrong, bust your
nutcrackers?"

"What the hell are you doing here?" Montana glared at
old Custus, perched on a short stool milking one of the cows.

"The little missy hired me."

Montana swore and then began to pace. "The little
missy" was his problem. Everything was all fouled up. Stupid fool, he'd gone and really slept with her instead of
sending her off. He'd really messed things up now. He had
thought he could control the situation between Addie and
him, but somehow in the dark of night, with her in his arms
smelling all sweet and homey, all his plans, all his control,
had flown out the window. And now he'd never get this
place. He'd blown the best plan yet to scare her away.
Muttering himself to hell, he glanced at the old man.

Custus ignored him, chomped down on his stubby cigar
and went on milking. A few minutes of oral silence went
by; the only sound in the barn was the sound of the milk
hitting the pail and Montana's teeth grinding. Then Custus
began to hum.

It got on Montana's nerves. He kicked at the hay on the
barn floor and spun around. Listening to the old man hum
off key, he wondered what had been behind the hiring of
Custus. "Hired you to do what?"

"Just what I'm a doin'." Custus stood and bent down,
pulling out the milk pail and setting it aside. He leaned
against the feedbox and grinned at Montana. "A-milkin' . . .

an' a-feedin' them there smelly old chickens . . . an' a-cuttin' wood . . . an' a-helpin' ya. She said somethin' 'bout when I weren't a-helpin' 'er I were ta be a-helpin' you.'' He rolled the stub to the other side of his mouth and crossed his arms across his chest and waited for his words to soak in.

Montana had a hunch he knew what she'd been up to. "When did she hire you?"

"Yesterday, in town."

Little Miss Pinky had hired herself a chaperon—in the form of an old coot named Custus McGee. "Stupid, damn woman," Montana mumbled.

"Yup. She must be." Custus walked over to the hay pile and picked up a pitchfork. He stuck it into a bale of hay and then leaned on it. "Ya might wanna do up yer pants."

Montana looked down at his open fly. Damn if he didn't feel his neck flush. He fumbled with the buttons. Then he went back to his pacing, only this time he ran his hand through his hair every time he spun back the other way.

"Whatcha mutterin' 'bout?" Custus broke up the hay bale.

"The little missy," he answered sarcastically.

Custus dug the pitchfork into the hay and started flinging it into Jericho's feed trough. "Well, I got two greenbacks bet on ya."

"What are you talking about?"

"There's this here kitty in town. Ever since the judge ruled, most ever'one's been a-bettin' on whether you or the little missy'd come out on top."

"I'd say I've come 'out on top' more," Montana said, remembering last night. "But that's not my problem now," he admitted.

"What is?" Custus asked around his clenched cigar.

Montana unloaded. "I tried every damn thing I could think of to get this place, and she's blocked me every time. I can't buy the place from her. She's got some harebrained female notion about making her fortune here. She won't leave, even at gun point. I've tried everything and finally, last night, I . . . well, let's just say I blew my last chance. She's beat me, dammit, and it's rightfully my land!"

219

The old man stared at him for a moment, then he leaned on the pitchfork again and asked, "Why don't ya jus' marry 'er?"

Montana stopped pacing and looked up, stunned. "What did you say?"

"Get them taters outta yer ears, boy! I said, why don't ya jus' marry 'er? As 'er husband, the whole place'd be yers." He shook his bearded head and grabbed the milk pails, heading for the open barn doors. He walked past Montana, still talking away. "I don't see what yer all riled up 'bout. Seems downright simple ta me." He stopped and barked, "Now there ain't no reason ta swear at me, boy!"

"I'm not swearing at you. I'm swearing at me, stupid me." Montana stood there, unable to believe that his problem could be solved so simply.

Custus mumbled again, and Montana watched him leave, milk pails swinging alongside his squat old body. He wondered why he hadn't thought of this himself. It was the perfect solution, he thought, mentally listing her qualifications.

She'd be a great wife, except for her cooking. He grimaced. But she was an entertaining little thing, and he was certainly never bored around her. For a city woman, she was a fine, hard worker. He smiled. Both in bed and out. Hell, he figured he'd have no problem living on baked apples and long, hot nights in that feather bed.

That thought triggered the memory of last night and a certain moment that passed between them. For a brief instant she had looked at him as if he held her heart. That look had done something to him. It had touched a place he didn't want touched. He didn't want to care about her, but he did. He'd tried to get her off the place before this happened, before he cared enough to wonder about her after she was gone. And now he wouldn't only wonder about her, he'd probably worry about her. The damn fool woman would probably go read some book about ranching and get herself killed trying to brand a calf.

Hell, it was probably his duty to save her from herself. It was hard for him to admit that she'd gotten to him, so he blocked out his thoughts of how she'd made him feel last night. Instead he concentrated on her looks. He liked the feel of all that dark hair, and her body might be miniature, but it was about as close to perfection as he'd ever seen. Her legs were shaped perfectly, her white skin—which he'd first thought of as citified—was softer than anything he'd ever felt. She responded to him last night like a match to dry wood. And she was pretty. Her small nose fit her pale little face perfectly, and she had great lips. His blood ran just a bit hotter when he thought about her mouth. And those big black eyes were more interesting than blue ones. They were harder to read, and there were times when they held secrets—secrets that he wanted to uncover.

Like a little tick, this bit of a woman had wormed her way under his skin. So he figured he might as well make her part of his life. She already had a damn good grip on him. She sure could make him mad. There were times, like this morning, when he had to hold back to keep from throttling her. Instead he had throttled her with his cruel words. He frowned. He shouldn't have used those words with her, and the fact that he had used them bothered him. The only people who had ever angered him that much had been men, so in his red haze he'd lapsed into men's crude terms. For some harebrained reason, she could really piss him off. The woman got to him, but at least he wasn't bored.

In fact, he'd probably have missed her prissy little face and airborne nose if his other plan had worked. Marriage was much better.

Now that he'd given it some thought, he realized that was probably what had her all lathered up this morning. It made sense. He was a fool for not seeing it right away. She expected him to marry her. After all, they'd already had a consummation.

That was it. No wonder she was so hysterical. Women always equated sex and marriage, so why should she, a little pistol of a librarian from Chicago, be any different? When he hadn't mentioned marriage by morning, she must have been fit to be tied. No wonder she'd tried to shift the blame to him. She'd felt guilty. In Montana's mind, there was no one to blame. What they had done was a natural act—acts, he added the plural—and the best damn natural acts he'd ever had.

Well, now he had the answer to his problem. All he had to do was go back in there, tell her he'd marry her, and everything would be fine. Of course he'd have to apologize for his harsh words, but he reasoned that if she wanted marriage, she'd forgive him.

He grinned, rubbing a hand over his chin and feeling that for once everything was going to work out. He winced at his rough chin. He needed a shave and to clean up a bit. If he was going courting, he should look the part. So Montana went into the small workroom where he'd made his bunk and set about getting himself ready. He was going to give Addie exactly what she wanted, and then he'd have exactly what he wanted, the whole damn farm.

Addie squinted at the oval mirror. It didn't do any good. She bore the signs of what she'd done last night as sure as if she wore the word *unchaste* blazoned across her chest. Grabbing the blue bottle of facewash, she put some on a cloth and scrubbed her face for the fourth time. Now her whole face was bright pink, even the whites of her eyes. Turning her head this way and then that, she wondered if her lips would ever look the same again. She stretched them over her teeth and dabbed some petroleum jelly on the puffy, red parts. As she leaned to the left, a small little purplish-red bruise just below her ear glared back. Good Lord! It was just like the ones on her stomach.

Quick as a lick, she buttoned the high lace collar on her shirtwaist. It didn't cover the mark. She jerked the long black hairpin from her topknot and pulled her brush through her heavy hair. She heaved a relieved sigh. Her hair covered it, but she'd have to wear it down. Grabbing the long sides, she twisted them and tucked a comb in just above her ears to anchor the rolled twists. Then she grabbed a big black sateen bow and pinned it to hold the sides back low on her head. The long hair that hung below covered the neck perfectly; except with her black hair held down by the bow, Addie looked twelve.

But she wasn't twelve. She was a woman with whisker

burns on her chin, puffy, overkissed lips, and an ache between her legs that wouldn't let her forget what she had done. It was no use trying to look normal. She'd never be normal again. She couldn't ignore it, though she'd tried. She couldn't cover up what had happened with a starched, lacy shirt, a prim black skirt, and undergarments that were pure white.

No matter what she wore, Adelaide Amanda Pinkney would never be *pure* again. And God help her, but that was a hard thing to face.

She sank to the bed, her shoulders sagging and her tense hands folded in her lap. The sunlight bled through the window, caught a rainbow from a prism that dangled from the bedside lamp and spilled color onto the white cotton rug atop the hardwood floor. The distant sound of Mabel and Maud lowing drifted through the open window, and the smell of dirt and chickens and eucalyptus whisked in on an occasional breeze. Everything around her was exactly the same. The eucalyptus trees still bent softly in the west wind, their leaves crackling together. The cows still bawled and munched and slobbered along in the grazing field behind the trees. The rich, brickish dirt in the north field still lay there, turned and awaiting seed.

Inside the bedroom it was still the same. Cotton curtains still framed the windows, and the holland roller shades coiled at the windows' tops. The rug was the same, despite the rainbow light, and the bureau hadn't changed except for new layer of red dust. But Addie had changed. She'd given away her woman's gift to a man she barely knew, but loved. She finally admitted it.

She did. She really loved him, this wild-eyed, long-haired, rude man who towered above her, whose smile could make her stomach jump, and whose wonderful hands could make her forget everything. Except what he made her feel.

But she hated him too, hated him for being the one man for her. She hated him for making her face what she'd done, hated him for making her admit that what happened was just as much her doing as his, and hated him for being so crude. But most of all, she hated Montana Creed because he didn't love her back.

In the harsh morning light Addie had to accept last night. She had tried to blame him for her actions, and all she'd gotten for it was a crude recap of exactly what she had done. No one had ever spoken to her that way, and it hurt that the one person who did was the man to whom she'd foolhardily given the gift of her body.

Never, not one time, did he say the word *love*. Oh, he'd said *want* and *need* and *crave* and all those words, but he hadn't mentioned love.

She had ached to tell him she loved him, wanted to say it over and over. And she had . . . mentally. Every time he moved his body in hers she had shouted a mental litany of love. But that hadn't eased the aching need to hear him say he felt that way too. So she'd not said the words. Fear of rejection, and her pride, wouldn't let her utter them.

He was proud too, and that thought triggered another. Could that be why he had been so angry and rough this morning? Maybe he was waiting for her to say them. Like the light rainbow, a spark of hope spilled through her. Some of her despondency fizzled away. Maybe he had needed time to realize his feelings too.

It was possible. She tried to remember if he'd ever once looked unsure last night, as if maybe he had been waiting. The only time she could remember was when he'd begged her not to stop him, and she hadn't.

It would be just like the toad to make her say she loved him first.

She stood and paced the small space between the bed and the bureau. Unlike a few minutes earlier, when her shoulders sagged in despair, there was life in her step and a distinct conviction in the sharp click of her heels across the floor. She'd made up her mind.

At the mirror she fluffed her hair about her shoulders, then pinched some color into her cheeks. She pinned on her silver watch, tugged down her starched cuffs, wiped the wrinkles from her skirt, and somewhere, found the courage she needed. Addie marched out of the bedroom, knowing that she had to tell him she loved him.

She had just reached the dining room when she heard a knock on the front door. She stopped, then circled the mahogany table and pinched back the dining room curtain. Montana Creed stood, rocking on his heels on the front porch.

Her heart beat a bit faster and the room was just a little warmer. She checked the front of her starched shirtwaist, flipped the watch pendant over so the face was up, and walked to the door with a composed air she was far from feeling.

Staring, with silver-dollar-sized eyes, she opened the door wide and gestured for him to enter. He walked in and her courage flew out. She closed the door and stood there, trying not to wring her silly hands. He stood in the parlor completely silent, and he looked wonderful. All dressed in black, he was hatless and his hair was damp and tied back. The dimple on his chin looked as fresh-shaven as his cheeks, and his strong neck, the one she'd buried her face in over and over, strained just a bit tighter. He was as tense as she. He fidgeted with the silver buckle on his belt, then shoved his hands in the back pockets of a pair of dark denims. He looked everywhere but at her.

The air in the room was heavier than her plaster biscuits, and her mouth drier than that burned hunk of roast beef. He took a deep breath—she held hers—and finally looked at her. "I'm sorry about this morning. I was pretty hard on you, and I didn't mean to be so crude."

He was apologizing. He'd never done that. "You were, but I wasn't . . . I mean I wasn't very nice either. I'm sorry too."

The silence grew. Then he said, "We need to talk."

She nodded.

"Can I sit down?"

"Oh, yes, of course." She walked over near the sofa and he followed her, then went over to the armchair and stood in front of it, waiting. She stared at the buttons on his chest for the longest time. He cleared his throat. Her gaze shot up. He looked terribly uncomfortable, then she realized he was waiting for her to sit. She plopped down on the sofa so fast she bounced. She settled in, her small hands gripping the carved wooden edge of the sofa, while he eased into the chair and bent his never-ending legs, resting his elbows on his knees and gazing at the floor.

How did you tell someone you loved them? She thought about blurting it out, but that didn't seem right. And they were both being so formal. Finally, she opened her mouth and looked up.

"I—" They both spoke at the same time and immediately shut up.

Addie toyed with the lace on her cuff, then looked up again. He looked as if speaking and marching to the gallows were one and the same.

"You go first," she told him.

He stared at his clasped hands. "Let's get married."

She stared at his bowed head, her mouth gaping. My God, he did love her! A smile spread like rainbow light across her face. He loved her, wanted her to be his wife, forever. Addie felt as if the sun had just risen inside her.

He finally looked at her. "What do you say?"

That deep voice sent silly goose pimples all over her again. She vaulted from the sofa right into his arms. "Oh yes! Montana, yes!" She buried her head in his neck. He loved her!

His arms closed around her and she heard him say, "We'd better do it soon."

"Yes," she said into his wonderful, strong neck. She settled against his chest, her fanny perched on one knee and her arms locked around his neck, and she smiled shyly. "Now tell me why." She had to hear him say the words.

"Why soon? Well, because—"

"No, silly." She grinned at him. "Why you want to marry me." Her finger traced a button on his shirt.

"Uh . . . because of what happened."

"And . . . ?" she asked expectantly.

"Well . . . because it's a good idea."

Addie frowned. "And . . . ?"

"Because it's . . . it's proper!" He sounded angry.

Getting this man to say he loved her was like turning water to wine. He scowled at her, and she really didn't appreciate it. All he had to do was say the words.

226

"Don't scowl at me, and since when have you cared about being proper?"

"After what passed between us, it's only right."

"You mean all the *feelings,* right?" she hinted.

"Well, yes, it felt good."

"You are so hard-headed!" She stood and planted her hands on her hips and glared at him, certain he was purposely doing this. "Why can't you just say it!"

"What!" he yelled back.

"That you love me!" she shouted.

"I don't!"

Her whole world died. It became nothing but a big, black empty hole, and she wanted to climb right into it. He didn't love her. After last night, after everything they'd done, he didn't care. Her veins felt suddenly empty, and her heart did too, but her chest was so painfully tight that Addie wondered for an agonizing moment if she would faint. Her hand had flown to her mouth when he'd shouted at her. She touched her lips and swallowed, trying to focus on something, anything in the room. She turned, her little body stiff as a tree, and moved toward the long parlor window.

I will not cry! Her chin went up and she took deep, cleansing breaths while she stared out the window at nothing. Then it hit her. If he didn't love her, why had he just asked her to marry him? He had said something about propriety. He offered marriage only because he thought he should. Good Lord, what a horrible reason. It made her feel like a heavy weight hung around his neck, holding him down. She wanted to vomit.

Still staring out the window she said, "You don't have to marry me, just because of what happened, Mr. Creed."

"I want to marry you."

She spun around and stared at him, not understanding him at all. "Why?"

He began to pace. "Because it's just simpler! It'll be easier on both of us."

Now she was angry. "I told you that you didn't have to marry me to ease your conscience!"

"I'm not, dammit!" He glared back at her.

Her eyes narrowed into little suspicious slits. "Wait just

227

a minute here," she said, slowly walking around the small lamp table. "If you're not trying to ease your guilt—"

"I don't feel guilty," he interrupted.

"Fine, neither do I! And Lord knows you don't care, you made that quite clear . . ."

"Now, Addie—"

"What is 'simpler'?" Her hands landed on her hips. "You want a cook, don't you!" she accused, crossing her arms and waiting for the truth.

His neck was purple again. "If I wanted a cook, I wouldn't marry you. You haven't made a decent meal yet."

"You toad!" She grabbed the stereoscope and heaved it at him. He dodged it and started toward her. She scurried behind the table. "You want a slave, to sleep with and to cook and clean house—" She cut off her sentence and gasped. *The house, and the farm. That was it.* "You weasel . . . You want the house!"

He couldn't look her in the eye. His guilty face told her she was exactly right. She grabbed the box of glass slides and bombarded him with a handful of them. "You seduced me to get the farm!"

Two glass slides shattered against the west wall.

"I did not," he defended, backing to the door. "It was an accident."

She felt as if he'd slapped her. "Get out!" Her finger pointed at the front door.

"Gladly," he yelled back, then stormed toward the door.

"Wait!" she called, marching over to him. She bent and picked up the stereoscope. "Here, take these . . . these hoochy-koochy pictures with you!" The box of slides and viewer rammed into his stomach and she shoved him out the door. "Don't you ever, ever come into my house again!"

Silent and purple, he stood there, returning her look glare for glare.

"I hate you!" She slammed the door before he could see her angry tears.

16

THE KITCHEN DOOR SLAMMED AND ADDIE JUMPED. A stack of mason lids clattered over onto the kitchen worktable.

"Where ya want these here fruits?" Custus ambled through the back door, spilling a trail of dark berries from one of the large tin buckets he lugged inside.

"Set them on the sinkboard, please." She continued to sort through her aunt's canning paraphernalia, counting the lids and making sure she had the same amount of wide-mouth jars. Straight and precise as slats on a picket fence, she lined up her canning tools: the jar wrench, rack and lifter, and *Mrs. Sarah T. Rorer's Instructions and Recipes.* The cracked, ragged paper cover on the book was tainted a yellow and stained with splatters in different shades of brown, a testimony that it was favored and well-used.

Addie thumbed through the thin pages until she found the recipe she needed. With a determined step she headed for the sinkboard, but stopped midway when she saw Custus leaning against the sink, idly staring.

"Them there berries is late and the peaches is early. That means a mild winter," he informed her with typical McGee authority.

She smiled. "This is California, Custus. The winters are always mild."

"Just proves me right, then," he said in his rasp of a voice, and then he plucked a handful of ollieberries from the bucket and popped them into his mouth.

Passing him on her way to the stove, she said, "Supper'll be a little late because of the canning. Help yourself to the cornbread over on the table." She nodded toward the icebox as she lifted a large pot of boiling water. "The butter's in the icebox." She lugged the pot over to the sinkboard, set it down and then dumped the peaches into the scalding water.

"Yer friend said ta remind ya that he wouldn't be here fer supper since he done gone ta them there Latimers' place."

Addie's hand closed a bit tighter over the wooden handle of a long fork.

He shuffled across the room toward the kitchen table and dragged a chair out, making enough noise to wake the dead.

The loud, scraping noise was welcome. It covered up the sound of her teeth grinding. "That man is not my friend," she informed him.

Custus grumbled under his breath, and she ignored him and jabbed the fork into a peach, her mind flashing with the grating image of Montana Creed's hands on Rebecca Latimer's waist. With a sharp knife she peeled the peach, strip by strip, and pretended it was Montana Creed's skin, or Rebecca's face.

Never in all her days had she peeled fruit so fast. She filled the jars with whole peaches, ramming them inside so soundly that they probably wouldn't need the steam packing. As she stabbed a cinnamon stick into each of the jars, the peach juice slurped. The sound was almost as loud as Custus's chewing. She shook her head. His manners were as gruff as his voice. She reached for the tall, brown brandy bottle and her hand hit empty air. The bottle had been there a moment ago. A belch sounded from behind her. She turned and found the bottle, tilted against his mouth.

"Custus McGee! Give me that brandy right now!"

He lowered the bottle, swiping the back of his hand over his mouth. She snatched the bottle out of his hand and tried to shame him with a stern look. His white-bearded face creased into a big grin and his eyes glistened like sun on glass.

She had to laugh. "You silly old coot. Ought to be ashamed of yourself, swilling my canning brandy like it was water." The almost-empty bottle thudded onto the work-table. "Especially when there's a perfectly good bottle of

Napoleon brandy sitting on the tray table in the dining room."

It was the first time she had heard Custus McGee laugh. And it was something. Mabel and Maud bawling in a train tunnel would have been quieter than the bellows from the old man's mouth. But it made Addie smile. And she needed to smile, because every so often her mind would flash with the image of Montana holding Rebecca Latimer, and if she smiled, the hurt in her heart and her pride might not cut so deep.

Two hours later a deep bowl filled with black-eyed peas and ham, cooked to perfection, sat on the kitchen table. It had given her great pleasure to make the meal since Montana wouldn't be there to eat it. Addie twisted the jar wrench on the last of the canned peaches, tightening the lid with such force a winch wouldn't be able to open it. She set it with the others just as Custus brought in the milk, mumbling.

She turned. "Is something the matter?"

"That there sun set afore the west wind came." He frowned, looking as if the world had come to an end.

A perplexed look creased her small face. "Is that bad?"

He nodded, shuffling into the pantry. "Snakes," he called out before the hinges creaked on the cellar door and she heard the hollow clomp of him descending the stairs.

He was the most superstitious person she'd ever met. What on God's green earth could the wind and sun have to do with snakes? Don't ask, she told herself, sweeping up an armload of brandied peaches and heading for the pantry. The small cellar door angled out from the pantry's south wall, and the splatter of pouring milk echoed up from the cellar. She kept the large milk cans down there to keep them cool until she could get the milk to Mr. Peabody.

"You need some light down there?" she called out.

A white head popped up from the stairs. "No sirree! Th' light might wake them there snakes."

Her eyes grew. "Are there snakes down there? Real snakes?" She'd been in the cellar at least five times this week.

"Most likely, and if'n there weren't before, there'll be now," he told her with conviction. "An' them there devils like ta slither inta them there cool, dark places."

Her skin crawled and she turned her eyes on the peaches that filled her arms. She had intended to store the jars in the cellar with some of the other foods and supplies that wouldn't fit on the full pantry shelves. She even had the labels marked on the wooden shelves in the cellar's far corner: 634.019, brandied peaches; 634.055, ollieberry jam.

The milk buckets clanged against each other as Custus climbed through the cellar door. "Did ya know that if'n ya kill one of 'em there rattlers and cut it up, it still won't die till the sun sets?"

Her nose wrinkled and the color drained from her face. Did the pieces wiggle around? She stared at the dark cellar and then looked at the peaches again. She remembered the reason for his snake foreboding. She was being silly. Sunsets and wind and snakes sounded like a foolish superstition. He probably wore garlic to ward off the vampires.

She descended the stairs. The only light in the room came from the open doors, so she paused for a moment, letting her eyes adjust to the darkness. It looked the same, no slithering reptiles curling across the dirt floor. She placed her foot on the second to the last stair, and the wood creaked.

Addie jumped back up two stairs so fast she almost tumbled backward.

Dadgummit! This was stupid! She threw back her small shoulders and marched down the steps. Four leaps on tiptoe and she was at the corner shelf, stacking the mason jars in their proper position. Every so often she'd pause and listen for the sound of snakes. Silence greeted her. Finally she laughed at herself and turned to leave. The stopper was off one of the milk cans, so she walked over and plucked it off a crate and recorked the can. She turned and her elbow tapped against something and it thumped to the dirt floor. Then she heard it. The rattle.

She grabbed the wooden stair rail and vaulted over it. Her skirt caught and the sound of tearing cloth, scurrying little female feet, and one hell of a scream hung in her wake. She all but flew through the cellar door and around the pantry, skidding to a heaving stop right in front of Custus and a light-haired stranger who stood next to him.

"Snake!" she gasped between breaths. The men ran past her and she sank into a chair, sagged back against the kitchen table.

A few minutes later the stranger reentered the room. "Pardon me, ma'am, but your father asked me to find out where exactly you saw the snake."

"Over by the milk cans," she told him, and he disappeared before she could tell him that Custus wasn't her father. She wondered who he was, but only for a minute, because she heard Custus yell that he'd found it.

Addie relaxed and then debated whether she should leave the room. She wasn't sure she wanted to see the dead snake. The thought made her freeze, then peer toward the window. It was dark outside, so she relaxed. The snake would die, and hopefully they wouldn't have to cut it up. She cringed.

A short time later the men came into the room, Custus leading with his hands behind his back. "I got yer snake."

The sound of the rattle pierced the room.

It must still be alive! "Kill it!" She squeezed her eyes tightly shut and crunched up her shoulders, waiting.

It rattled again and she was ready to run from the room when she heard the distinct sound of a man's laughter. A second later Custus's belly bellow filled the room.

She pried open one eye. He held a plump, pear-shaped gourd by its neck. She sat straight. He shook it and the gourd rattled like a snake.

Addie turned beet red, while her hired hand and a complete stranger laughed at her. She crossed her arms and waited for them to finish. Tilting her head so she didn't have to look at them, she tucked some hair up into her bun, then picked at the tear in the hem of her skirt and waited. She lost patience. "This is all your fault, Custus. Walking around here mumbling about snakes and sun and cool places. And I don't think it's that funny!"

The other man snorted, and she blessed him with a glare. "And who are you?"

He swallowed his laughter and said, "Like I was about to tell your father—"

"He's not my father, but that doesn't matter, because who are you?"

"Oh, sorry. My name's Murdoch, Will Murdoch, and I'm looking for a friend of mine. Montana Creed. I understood that this was his place."

Addie jerked a bit straighter. "This is *our* place."

The man was stunned. "How'd he find the time to get married?"

"He didn't." She'd set him straight.

The man blushed. "Oh."

Custus snorted, and she realized what this Murdoch fellow thought. She glared at Custus, then said, "It is not what you think! We both own the farm. The buildings are mine and the land is his."

Mr. Murdoch appeared thoughtful, then he grinned one of those same male smirks that Montana did whenever he found something especially humorous. They had to be friends.

Addie's nose went up. "Mr. Creed is visiting a neighbor, but you can wait if you'd like."

The man's eyes drifted over to the table and he stared at the food.

"We have plenty, Mr. Murdoch. Wash up at the outside pump and then you can join us." Addie lifted the cool supper and went to the stove to reheat it.

An hour later the three of them sat at the kitchen table in companionable and replete silence. Addie had changed her opinion of Will Murdoch. He was a nice man. He and Custus had spoken about everything from grain farming to water rights. He'd made sure to include her in every conversation, and his interest in her opinion was genuine. He treated her on an equal level, intellectually, which made her estimation of him rise like hot air. He'd told her of his four sisters—all but one were younger than he—and Addie could tell he cared about his family.

But now Custus had decided she should get an in-depth description of exactly how silly she'd looked during the snake incident. So she sat there, listening to her hired hand's droll description of how she'd looked and watching Will Murdoch valiantly try to keep from exploding with laughter. Finally, when Custus said her scream was loud enough to peel the wallpaper, Addie gave in to her own laughter.

"You're terrible," she told him, biting her lip. "I guess I did look a little silly . . . but I still have you to blame, talking about cutting snakes into pieces and all."

"There's one borned ever' minute," Custus said. "Just make sure, little missy, that there's no witnesses when ya make a jackass outta yerself."

She tried to look put out but couldn't. He was right. She must have looked awfully foolish.

"It's a good thing Montana wasn't here," Will said.

"Why?" she asked.

"He's got a thing about snakes himself," he answered, and then went on to explain. "Can't blame him, though. His ma was killed by a rattler when he was ten. His pa was gone and Montana came in from the fields and found her. I guess by then her leg was all puffed up and blue-black. There wasn't anything he could do but hold her hand until she died. He told me once that she cried the whole time."

Addie closed her eyes, thinking about what a horrible thing that would be for anyone to experience, much less for a ten-year-old boy. When she was ten she had two loving parents and a secure and protected life. She hadn't had to work in farm fields. She had school and leisurely Sunday walks in the park and the joy of eating ices on a hot summer's day. All that had changed when she lost her father, but she had been older when she was forced to fend for herself and learn to deal with that empty part of her life. At ten that would have been difficult.

There was a hard edge to Montana Creed that she hadn't understood. There had been times when he was kind—like saving her chickens—and there were times when he seemed to like to spar with her, and last night he'd held her and made her feel that he'd die if she asked him to leave her bed. But there were also the times when he'd grow cold and harsh. At those times she almost hated him. Well, she amended, maybe feared was a better word than hate. She hated him because of what he made her feel and do. She feared him because she didn't understand the cruel streak inside him. After what Will had just told her, her fear lessened. Montana's past might be the key to what she didn't understand.

She pictured him as a boy, at his mother's side, and imagined his young face and yellow-gold eyes. Then one of the men clattered his silverware against a plate, startling her out of her daydreaming. Her gaze shot up and met a pair of burning gold adult eyes. Montana stared at her through the window. Surprised, she blurted out, "Montana . . ."

Will jumped up and was out the back door by the time she and Custus had risen from their chairs. Custus followed him out the open door, but Addie lagged behind. After this morning she felt used, and angry because she had let herself fall in love with him when all he wanted was the farm—and her body for a night. He really hadn't even wanted her body. Addie closed her eyes. This morning he'd called sleeping with her an "accident." When she remembered that, the pain sliced through her like a serrated knife, cutting into ragged pieces both her heart and her precious pride.

She bowed her head for a second, trying to handle the biggest mistake of her short life. Straightening, she stacked the plates and carried them over to the sinkboard, banging them on the counter. *Damn him!*

Montana walked in the back door. She looked up and right through him before turning back around and scraping clean the plates. Will and Custus followed, and she could feel their stares. She couldn't very well ignore them all, so she turned and leaned against the sinkboard, wiping her hands on her apron.

The deep voice she loved and hated cut through the room. "I've offered Will a place to stay in exchange for helping me plant the wheat." He looked as if he were expecting an argument.

She refused to give him one. Besides, she actually liked Will Murdoch. They could use the help, and the better the crop, the higher her split of the profits.

"Fine," she said.

"Thanks, Miss Pinkney," Will said. As he grabbed his hat off a hook near the door he added, "Thanks for the meal too. It was one of the finest meals I've ever had."

Montana turned and looked at his friend as if he'd lost his mind.

"Yep, best black-eyed peas and ham I ever et," Custus agreed, then told Will he'd show him where the men slept.

Addie went back to the table and heard Montana mutter something that sounded like "no wonder." She gathered the rest of the dishes, acting as if he wasn't there.

"Hettie asked about you," he told her.

She didn't say a word.

"She wanted to know if you were coming to the women's meeting at the church tomorrow night. They're planning something to support the grange."

"I heard." She filled a tin tub with dishwater and dumped in the dishes.

"She wondered if you needed a ride to town." He paused. "I told her I'd take you."

Addie broke a plate. She turned and pinned him with the coolest look she could muster. "Don't do me any favors."

He returned her look. "I wasn't. It'll save them going out of their way. They'll have a full wagon to boot."

"Fine." She turned back to banging the dishes in the tin tub.

"I'll pay you for Will and my meals." He had to raise his voice over the racket she made with the dishes.

She gave an irritated sigh and turned around again. "I don't want your money."

His neck turned purple again. "Why the hell not?"

Addie held her head high, despite her vulnerable insides, and said, "Because, Mr. Creed, if I took your money I'd feel like a harlot."

He looked as if she'd slapped him, and he searched her face for a moment. She didn't flinch, didn't even take a breath. A second later the door slammed shut.

And then she cried.

*　　*　　*

Addie's squat heels clapped like clogs on the hollow plank steps of the Four Corners Presbyterian Church. The jangle of a harness signaled that the wagon had pulled away. She refused to look back, even though it took every ounce of her willpower. Custus and Will had ridden in the back of the wagon, leaving the minute wagon seat for Montana and her. She had been prepared for the ride, but not for the feel of his hands spanning her waist when he lifted her onto the seat. The other night his hands had spanned her bare waist just like that, lifting her over and over.

From the moment he held her again, she had been aware of Montana. He talked with the other two men and she had felt the timbre of his voice flow like blood through her. His arm brushed hers and chills blistered on her skin; his scent assailed her senses and brought to mind the one thing Addie wanted to forget—their bedding.

Now, when she paused at the church door with her hand on the cool brass knob, Addie tried to push the man from her silly mind. *I'm okay,* she thought, opening the door and entering the vestibule.

She was wrong. Rebecca stood a few feet away, as if she'd been waiting there. She glanced at Addie and then spoke to a gathering of the younger women. "I dreamed of Montana last night." Then she sighed for effect.

Addie straightened her shoulders and sailed right by. "I'm sorry to hear you're having nightmares, Rebecca."

Lizzie giggled—God love her—which got the others doing the same. She latched onto Addie's tense arm and introduced her to the other women. In a matter of minutes she relaxed, for the women were kind and made her feel as if she'd known them all for years.

Standing in the small, narrow church for the first time was an odd experience for Addie. It was filled with the women of Bleeding Heart, most of them strangers until a few minutes ago, and yet she felt such a part of them. Children whooped and cried and ran in wild, chickenlike circles around the wooden pews, yet there was an odd sense of peace that prevailed within the whitewashed walls. A huge, cherrywood pump organ stood to the left of the altar as proud and straight and dominant as Eden's apple tree. Deep red hymnals were stacked at the end of each pew and a great, gold-edged, black leather bible lay open on a plain pine stand near the pulpit. The room was spotless and smelled of candlewax and almond oil and pine tar, except for an occasional whiff of lavender water or verbena perfume worn by its occupants. The rich knotty-pine floors shone like glass in the warmth of oil lamps and flickering candles. The Four Corners Church was a small-town monument to its residents' pride and faith. And as Addie settled into a pew, with Lizzie at her side, she became one of them.

She smiled. She was home.

By eight-thirty the wives of farmers and the town's businesses alike had told of how the railroad, with their escalating freight rates and crooked practices, were bleeding profits, savings, and in some cases destroying the property of people throughout the state. The railroads owned— through blatant practices of graft and bribery—the large newspapers, the law enforcement agencies, and many of the regional courts.

It didn't take long for the plans to be made. Two weeks from that night, the town would host a barbecue and dance, just like on the Fourth of July. It would be held at the grange hall, and the proceeds from the food and the dance would raise money to help sponsor the grange's legislative bid for state and local regulation of the railroad.

Each woman volunteered her share, everything from a pot of baked beans and a whole, butchered cow to Martha Bickerson's promise of her husband's fiddling and Annie Pearson's offer of all the liquid refreshment, coffee, lemonade, sarsaparilla, and—some of the women groaned—beer.

Hettie leaned to Addie and said, "Let's bring the fried chicken. I've got plenty of cockerels, and some of your aunt's layers are old enough to slaughter."

Addie's stomach dropped. She hadn't planned on slaughtering any chickens for a while. Her face reflected her thoughts.

"Lizzie'll come help you," Hettie added.

Anxious to please, Addie agreed, and they started a list. Then Rebecca popped off sweetly, "I'll make my apple cake, Mother." She paused and looked at Addie. "Montana said he loved apple dessert."

"Fine, Becky," Hettie said distractedly while she kept writing on an offering envelope.

Lizzie leaned closer to Addie and whispered, "Becky almost crammed the whole cake down that poor man's throat."

Addie giggled, then grew thoughtful and leaned closer to Lizzie. "Did he really say that?"

"What?" Lizzie asked.

"About the desserts."

Lizzie nodded.

Then Hettie stood and announced, "The Latimer women and Addie Pinkney will bring . . ." She glanced at her list. "Ten fried chickens, five jars of brandied peaches, one apple cake, two loaves of molasses bread—"

"And three apple pies," Addie spouted off without a thought.

Lizzie laughed out loud and Rebecca's beautiful blue eyes narrowed to ice chips.

The challenge was on.

Montana didn't hear a thing Will or Custus said. His thoughts followed his eyes, and they were locked on Addie's behind. He watched her go up the front steps of the farmhouse and go inside. A small bit of light glowed from behind her as she closed the front door, blocking her from his thoughtful gaze. Of their own accord his eyes drifted to the front window. The shades were up, and he watched her remove her shawl. Her arm reached up to hang up the shawl and his eyes locked on her small body. She was such a tiny thing. Bending down, she picked up the lamp and disappeared from view. The strangest thing happened. Montana felt sad.

He had no idea how long he stood there staring at the dark house. He only knew that when he turned toward the barn, both Custus and Will were gone. By the time he crossed the barn, checked on the horses' feed and water, he could hear the snores coming from the small room off the barn where the men bunked. Ducking under the low doorway, he went inside. A dim lantern burned in the corner.

The light was necessary since the room was still filled with the menagerie of tools left by Addie's uncle. Montana had removed the bigger tools—the wheelbarrow, a few coulters for the plow, and an old thresher—the first night he'd slept there. The next day he'd pulled out what he needed and then piled the duplicates and others in the corner. They still sat there.

Custus had built a wall cot in the right corner, and Will had his bedroll on the opposite side. The old man snorted a loud snore, then turned over and slept more quietly. Montana sat on his cot and pulled off his boots. He stripped and stretched out on top of the rough woolen blanket. It made him itch. He tried to ignore it, and the memory of Addie's fine, crisp sheets, but he failed because the memory set the direction of his thoughts. Montana couldn't get her off his mind.

During the grange meeting he'd been plagued by flashes of her—images of black hair and white skin, of a small, proud nose that shot up at the blink of an eye, and the words she'd spoken. *I'd feel like a harlot,* she'd said, and it had hit him like a fist in his gut. For the first time in Montana Creed's life he was ashamed of his behavior. He wanted this farm, wanted it more than anything, but he had to accept the fact that he wanted her too.

But she wanted love, like most women. Hell, he didn't even know what the word meant anymore. He'd loved his parents, they had been his youthful world, but when they died, so did any vestiges of that love. There had been women in his life, mostly tall, buxom women who had whet his appetite and who knew he would leave when the appetite was satisfied. But with Addie it was different. He was still hungry.

Lacing his hands behind his head, he stared at the rough rafters above him. He'd messed up, handling that damn marriage proposal about as well as she handled his horse. He wanted the farm, but he wanted her too, and if that meant marriage, then he'd do it. Hell, if she left now, he'd never have a moment of mental peace. Exactly what he'd been afraid of happening, had—he cared what happened to Little Miss Pinky.

The problem now was that he had to find a way to get her to forget what happened. He needed another plan, and had a hunch that seduction probably wouldn't work twice. Although, there was the old adage that if something worked once, it just might work again. He'd have to be less aggressive, that he knew. This time he'd ease his way into it, because he didn't want to chase her away. This time he wanted to catch her.

17

"PARDON ME?" ADDIE WAS SURE SHE'D HEARD HER WRONG. Lizzie couldn't have said *that*.

Lizzie was bent over one of Addie's feeders, examining the chicks. She straightened and repeated her question. "I asked if the chicks have been sexed."

Addie's face was bright red. "Aren't they too young for . . . for, uh, that kind of behavior?"

Lizzie's burst of laughter rang clear through the chickenhouse, letting Addie know immediately that she'd said something stupid again.

"I'm sorry for laughing, Addie, but you looked so horrified. Sexing means separating the cockerels from the pullets, male from female."

"Oh," Addie said on a sigh of relief, before muttering a quiet "thank God" under her breath. Then she added, "The book didn't say anything about that."

"That's okay," Lizzie told her in a cheerful voice. "I'll teach you and you'll be a—" She stopped and gave Addie a wicked grin. ". . . sex authority in no time."

I already am, Addie thought, covering her fallen face with a false smile.

"Here's what you do." Lizzie bent over and picked up a chick. "Grab a hold on its feet, like this, then hold it upside down, like this." She dangled the cute little chick by its feet and the chick popped its head up, trying to peck at the girl's fingers. "There, see it bring its head up and try to peck me?"

Addie nodded.

"That means it's a male, a cockerel."

"Oh," Addie said, thinking it figured the males would peck. Then she asked, "What do the females do?"

"They just dangle there." Lizzie rolled her eyes.

"You're kidding."

The girl shook her carrot-red head.

"That's not very liberated of them," Addie said, remembering that once Montana's hands were on her, she'd acted pretty passive herself. She bent and grabbed a chick.

"Chickens aren't very smart either." Lizzie picked up another one. "We'll need to mark them. Do you have any leg rings?"

Again Addie didn't have the faintest idea what she was talking about.

"Red twists of wire to put on their legs," Lizzie explained with the patience of a true friend.

Addie snapped her fingers. "I saw something like that in the cellar. I'll be right back." She ran into the house and to the cellar doors. Then she skidded to a stop. Tentatively she pulled the doors open, suddenly sure that her cellar would be a teeming snake pit. She grabbed a lamp and lit the wick before she descended the stairs with the same speed as Custus on a slow day. Holding the lamp out in front of her, she eased down the stairs, her eyes whipping from corner to corner on snake patrol.

She reached the last step and looked for the glass jar with the red twists that she'd spotted on one of her first trips down there. It sat by the milk cans. With her heart throbbing in her ears, she ran over, grabbed the jar, and was back on the steps before she had a chance to take another breath. She listened. There was nothing but silence, so she calmed herself, ascended the stairs and rejoined Lizzie.

"Are these them?" Addie held up the jar.

"They sure are." Lizzie plucked a fingerful of twists from the jar and began twisting her wires onto the leg of a chick she took out of a feed box hung near the door.

Addie started to work. She bent, dangled, and marked chick after chick.

"Addie . . ." Lizzie said a few minutes later.

"Hmmm?" Addie twisted the tie on her latest cockerel.

"All the chicks I've checked are cockerels." Lizzie stared at her. "That's unusual."

Addie stopped. "So are mine."

"Where'd you buy these chicks?"

"On the Livermore road. A big, broken-down place that belongs to—"

"The Potters." Lizzie finished the sentence and leaned against the wall of the henhouse, shaking her head. "You got taken, Addie. Those two are almost worse crooks than the railroad."

Addie gaped at all her chicks. "You mean these are all cockerels?"

"Probably." Lizzie's face was all sympathy.

"Dadgummit!" Addie began to pace the little room, dodging chickens as she walked. "What am I going to do with all cockerels? That means none of them lay eggs!"

"Cockerels are fine eating," Lizzie told her cheerfully.

"Lizzie, even those three men out there couldn't eat that many cockerels."

"You could sell them," she suggested.

"That's true. At least they aren't completely worthless." Addie stared with defeated eyes at her chickens, the ones that would never produce a single egg. Then she looked at the jar of twists. "Do you think we need to mark them all?" She couldn't keep the hope out of her voice.

Her friend slowly shook her head.

"That's what I thought," Addie said. "Let's go."

The two women left the henhouse and walked across the chicken yard. When they reached the gate, they heard loud

244

hammering, some wild gobbles, and Custus swearing the air blue.

"Dadburned, gull darn, cursed piece of crap! This here thing's 'bout as worthless as a pail of horse slobber." The hammer sailed across the yard to the accompaniment of guttural turkey screeches.

Addie picked up the hammer, and the women exchanged amused looks before joining the scowling old man at the turkey pen he was repairing.

Addie approached him. "What's wrong, Custus?"

"I'll tell ya what's wrong. That dadblamed hammer's too big fer these here nails!" He banged a fist against the pen post and then muttered, "Shoulda knowed somethin' a-like this'd happen. That there south door of the barn stayed open on its own."

Lizzie, wearing a baffled look on her face, looked at Addie, who held her hand up to stop the question she knew was coming. "Just wait a second."

"Ever'one knows that's a sign of them haints."

"Haints?" Lizzie leaned toward Addie and whispered.

"Haunts. Custus is a bit superstitious," Addie explained. "Would a smaller hammer help?"

" 'Course a smaller one'd help. I already told ya that this here one's too big."

"I remember seeing a whole slew of hammers in that workroom in the barn. Isn't that where you're all sleeping?" Addie asked.

"Well, since I been a-sleepin' in that there room, there ain't been no hammers," Custus said with all the tact and kindness of a charging bull.

"I'll be right back," she said, spinning on her heel and disappearing inside the dark barn. She went into the workroom, but didn't see any hammers in the tools that were piled in the room's cluttered corner. She crossed the barn and found a small area of equipment and tools behind a stack of hay bales. Everything was in crates, with no rhyme or reason to how they were stored.

"How can he find anything in this mess?" she muttered, fumbling through each crate until she finally found a smaller hammer.

"I ain't got all dadblamed day!" The peal of Custus's grouchy voice echoed through the barn's rafters, so Addie left the mess of tools and took him the smaller hammer.

She walked back into the bright sunlight and was momentarily blinded. When the spots cleared she saw Montana and Will leaning on the top rail of the turkey pen, talking to Lizzie. Addie slowed her approach, but her heartbeat sped up and her stomach took a little, aching leap.

Montana towered over the pen, with one long, tight leg resting casually on one of the lower rails. His hat was tipped back and she could see the dampness on his tanned face. Some of his brown hair had slipped from the rawhide strip he used to tie it back; it curled around his ears and neck. His shirt-sleeves were rolled up, exposing the thick, brown hair on his forearms as they rested on the top rail of the pen. She remembered running her hands up his arms of steel when he strained above her on the bed.

With that thought, Addie's temperature must have risen ten degrees, and she felt every single degree. She couldn't tear her eyes away from him, and didn't even try, because it was fruitless. She loved him, whether he loved her or not, and there wasn't a thing she could do about it. So, unknowingly, she caressed him with her eyes as he quietly stood watching the turkeys with Lizzie and Will.

"Oh, there she is!" Lizzie waved at Addie. "Come on over and see this, Addie!"

She walked up to them, following Lizzie's pointed finger to where the turkeys gathered in the middle of the pen. She could feel the heat of Montana's look, but she wouldn't allow herself to look at him, at least not just yet.

A turkey hen pecked at the seed on the ground, and a big tom turkey, all nutty brown, paced in a circle around the hen. His chestnut-feathered tail fanned out like an Elizabethan collar and his chest puffed out twice its normal size. He scratched at the ground, sending dust up behind him, and then a loud gobble pierced the air. The hen glanced up once, looked bored and resumed her eating.

"What's he doing?" Addie asked.

It was Montana's deep voice that answered, "Courting the hen."

Addie didn't budge.

The tom paced back and forth, puffing and scratching and lifting his proud tail, then he strolled past the hen and drooped his wings until they dragged on the ground. Lizzie's laughter was contagious. It was the silliest thing Addie'd ever seen. The tom puffed, drooped, fanned, and gobbled over and over while the hen ignored his dramatics.

It was something to see, until she felt the warmth of the sun suddenly blocked from behind her and looked up, laughing. Her smile melted away in the heat from Montana's eyes. She looked around and saw Lizzie and Will talking near the barn. She and Montana stood alone, watching the turkeys.

"Looks like she's not interested," he said, nodding toward the hen but never taking his eyes off Addie.

"Looks like he's too *obsessed* with his goal," she shot back.

His gaze pinned her. "Maybe he's lonely."

Needing to escape those eyes, she turned around and rested her arms on a low rail, pretending to watch the bird's courting ritual. Then she whispered, "Maybe she thinks he's only going to use her."

There was a long silence, then the crunch of boot heels on the gravel as he walked away.

It was broad daylight when the train was robbed. It rolled down the track, past a grove of old, tangled sycamores that lined the dry riverbed. Rattling wheels and the spit of the steam engine drowned out the thunder of the horses. Their hooves pounded with the same cadence of the engine. Down the dry riverbed on a cloud of brown dust the two horses and riders paralleled the train track.

One rider leaned out from his saddle and grabbed the handrail on the back of a rusty car. He pulled out of the saddle and his horse veered off toward the trees. Hanging from the handrail, the man fought for a foothold, his boots scraping against the side of the rusty rail car. His long body shook with the vibration of the racing train and it looked as if he would fall.

But he began to swing, back and forth, lifting his hips

higher and higher until his foot hooked over the top of the rail car. Pulling himself up, he gripped the roof rails and waved to the other rider, signaling he had made it.

The cattle in the car beneath him moaned and lowed, blocking out the thud of his boots on the metal roof as he ran. Reaching the end, he jumped; his long legs hit the next car and his knees buckled. The train sped up a grade, and the man slid back and almost over the edge. His hands grabbed the guide rails on the roof and he crawled along the car until he reached its end. He hung down over the coupling platform that joined the two cars.

And he let go.

His boots landed on the back platform, and in a flash he turned her coupling wheel and unlocked the back cars, letting them roll slowly down the grade as he applied the handbrake. The cars came to a stop, and the tall man leaned indolently on the platform rail, tipping his hat back and watching his companion ride up and jump from his mount. The shorter man shot off the lock and slid open the door, disappearing inside. There was another gunshot, and he emerged a few minutes later with a wooden box, its shattered lock hanging at a cockeyed angle.

A small cloud of dry dust billowed up when he landed on the ground. He glanced at the tall one, leaning against the rail, cool and calm as could be. "Like you said, no guards, and as far as I can tell, it's about ten thousand dollars." Then he added in a tone filled with scorn, "Apparently ten thousand is too little to guard, just another day's graft to those bastards at the S.P."

The tall man jumped from the platform and whistled. A few seconds later his horse loped out from the shelter of the trees. He mounted, then turned to the other man and said, "Yeah, but I've a hunch that the Schultz and Harrison families can use the money." And then the men rode south.

The next morning Addie stood in the chicken yard, flinging feed to over one hundred chickens that were physically incapable of laying eggs. She still had her aunt's layers, but half of them were into their second season and, according to Lizzie, ready for slaughter. At least she'd have plenty of meat, and she could sell the others and use the money to purchase a new batch of fall chicks. That brood she'd buy already sexed. Addie squirmed. It was hard for her to even think the term. She finished the feeding and was heading toward the gate when she heard it—a deep, loud male bellow.

"Goddammit to hell!" Montana shot out from the barn, a hammer in each hand and his face purple.

"What's wrong?" she asked, closing the latch on the gate.

"You were in the tools!" he accused, shaking one hammer high in the air.

"Oh that," she said with a wave of her hand. "You've been so busy that when you were gone yesterday I thought I'd help. You don't have to thank me." She started for the barn, swinging the feed pail by her side.

"Thank you? I ought to . . . never mind." He hurried after her and caught up just as she entered the barn. "I can't find anything."

Addie stopped and put her hands on her hips, wondering why he was making such a big deal of this. "I left you a card catalog."

"A what?"

She sighed for patience. "A card catalog." She marched over to the area where he'd put that mess of tools. She pointed to a small wooden box. "See, right here." She flipped it open and thumbed through the cards, ignoring his muttering.

"Every tool is labeled and in its proper order on the wall. It's really very simple." She then went on to explain to Montana exactly how the Dewey Decimal System worked. It was great, just like being back at the Mason Street Library teaching a class of schoolchildren the wonders of cataloging.

She finished up by asking, "Now what tool did you need?"

He had this odd, blank look on his face. After a minute's thought he said, "A wrench."

"Okay, see . . . you look it up under W—it's alphabetical—and then you pull the card." She pointed to the heading printed neatly at the top of a crisp white card: WRENCH. "See, technical sciences are the 600 category, subcategory 91, for construction materials, then the decimal point, thought up by Mr. Dewey, and the next restrictive subcategory, 0235, for hand tools, under W."

He made a noise that sounded like a grunt.

"I know it sounds confusing, but it's really quite easy. Then up here . . ." She pointed to the wall and turned back around to explain the numerical placement. He was so close that the first thing she saw was his shirt pocket.

Instinctively, she stepped back and butted against the small wooden table that was wedged up to the wall. She started to move left, but his arm suddenly leaned on the table edge. When she looked right, his other arm was there. He had her pinned.

"Addie . . ." he whispered, his head lowered and his eyes on her face. One look at his lips, parted and nearing hers, and she was lost.

His arms pulled her against him and then gripped her fanny, slowly sliding her up his hard body while his mouth took forever to descend. She could feel his breath, all warm and teasing as it brushed over the top of her head, getting closer and closer. She wanted to taste him, wanted to feel his lips upon hers, making her melt.

The trail of his breath moved closer to her mouth. She watched his lips, and as his face neared, her mouth parted and her eyes drifted closed. She could almost feel his lips touch, just one breath away . . .

"Leave . . . the . . . tools . . . alone." And he let her slide back down to the ground.

Her eyes flew open and narrowed. "You toad!"

He just laughed louder. "Hot little thing, aren't you?"

"I hate you!"

His gaze locked on her chest. "I can tell."

She looked down. Two little beads puckered beneath the bodice of her thin cotton dress.

Her arms covered her chest and she spun, stomping away, but just before she left the barn she yelled, "I'm cold!"

18

THE AIR STOOD STILL, NOT A BREEZE AROUND TO COOL THE heat from the noonday sun. The cows lay in the shaded corner of the field, occasionally twitching an ear. It was too damn hot even to swat at the flies. A hawk wheeled down, plucking up a luckless rat and soaring back into the cloudless sky that was a true, yet illogical blue. It was a stupid color for sky. Water, cool and wet, was blue. Ice, when it was truly cold, was blue. But a sky that propped up so hot a sun shouldn't have been blue. Today, Montana thought, the sky should have been red.

He dropped his hat on the pump post and let the cool well water run over his head. It felt so good. He straightened, letting Will step under the spigot. While Montana pumped, Will doused his blond head and let loose with a whoop. "Damn but that feels good!" he said, voicing Montana's same thoughts.

"I don't know what's better," Will said, shaking the water from his hair. "The cool well water or the smell of that fried chicken."

Montana turned toward the kitchen door. "It smells good, but that doesn't mean it'll be edible."

"Come on, Montana, ease up on her. She's not that bad a cook." Will gave him an exasperated look.

"You showed up on a good night."

Will slicked his wet hair back. "You've been snapping at everyone all morning. What the hell's the matter?"

Montana continued to scowl at the farmhouse. "Nothing. This weather puts me on edge, is all." He turned and grabbed his hat. "And that woman is a bad cook. Christ! She could find a way to ruin an apple."

Will followed Montana to the house, mumbling, "Anything that smells like that can't taste bad."

Montana started up the steps. "Just keep thinking that and maybe you'll fool your stomach." He opened the back door and stepped inside, placing his hat on the wooden peg by the door.

The kitchen was almost hotter than it was outside. Lizzie Latimer and Addie scurried about the hellhole of a room like water drops on a hot griddle. Lizzie ran to the sinkboard, grabbed something, then ran back to the stove where Addie stood, fork in hand, over four big cast-iron skillets. She handed Lizzie another fork and then both women set to turning the chicken that sizzled like the weather and smelled like heaven.

Montana silently watched Addie as she stabbed the chicken and turned it over. She wasn't cold now, he smiled to himself. Her black hair hung halfway down her back, and it was damp and curly all around her flushed face. She raised her hand and swiped the sweat from her forehead. Her pink shirt clung to her damp body, outlining her breasts and narrowing to a waist that was so small it was almost doll-like.

Will cleared his throat, and Montana would have liked to have killed him for it, because it gave away their presence. He could have lingered a bit longer, unnoticed and looking to his heart's content.

"Where's Custus?" Addie asked, not looking at Montana.

He made sure he was the one to answer. "He'll be in in a minute."

She didn't say a word, but Lizzie, who had been welcoming Will with a delighted smile, didn't ignore either of them. "Dinner's on the table. You two go ahead. We need to finish this chicken for tonight."

Montana walked over to his chair. He didn't have the time or the inclination to play gooey eyes like Will and Lizzie were doing. It took him a minute to realize he was staring at Addie's butt. What he wanted was to eat, to lie down near a cool, shaded stream and make love to Little Addie Pinkney, not necessarily in that order. Instead, he jabbed a hunk of ham and shoveled some scalloped potatoes on his plate, expecting at least one of them to make his stomach churn.

Neither did. The ham was moist, instead of dry as usual, and the potatoes didn't stick to the roof of his mouth like flour paste. He eyed the biscuits, unsure if he was strong enough to lift one, so he watched Will pluck two from the plate—with one hand. Montana grabbed three before they disappeared. Custus joined them and the men ate silently while the two women finished their cooking.

"This was great." Will leaned back in his chair when he had finished. Montana scooped up the last bite of biscuit and mentally agreed. He hadn't had a meal like this since he'd eaten at the Latimers'.

"Thank you," Lizzie said, shyly smiling at Will. "Addie let me fix dinner while she cut up the chickens."

"No wonder," Montana said under his breath, and received a prissy smirk from Addie.

Then she twitched across the room and opened the icebox, pulling out a bowl of chipped ice and a fresh pitcher of iced tea. She set them on the table and then went back to the stove. A few minutes later she and Lizzie both sagged back against the worktable, big glasses of iced tea in their hands.

Addie set hers down first, eyeing the huge platters of fried chicken. "We're finished."

"Mama said this morning that it figured she'd offer to make fried chicken on the hottest day of the year." Lizzie walked over to the table and leaned near Will to get the pitcher of tea. She refilled their glasses and walked back, taking her sweet time about setting the pitcher down.

Montana watched Will stare at Lizzie, about chest high, and then squirm in his chair. He stood and announced, "Time to get back to work."

Will all but shot out of his chair, his eyes still on Lizzie, who was standing at the sink cleaning pans. Custus still sat, intent on slowly picking his teeth. Montana nodded and he finally creaked up.

They headed out the door, but Montana stopped next to Addie and said, "We'll be in early. I figure we should leave for town by five."

"Fine," she mumbled, bent over some contraption that she was trying to clamp to the edge of the worktable. Curious, he waited long enough to hear her swear under her breath.

"Here, let me do that," he offered, moving in to readjust the butterfly nuts so the thing could clamp onto the table edge more easily. He tightened the nuts and then tried to wiggle the thing. It was clamped tight. He eyed it, then asked, "What is that thing?"

"An apple parer," she answered over her shoulder just before she disappeared around the corner of the pantry. A scraping sound called from the back room, and then her butt came around the corner, followed by the rest of her, bent and dragging a crate of apples into the kitchen.

She straightened with an apronful of apples which she dumped onto the table. She jammed an apple onto a long, metal fork that protruded from a crank wheel. Then she slid a hook over the end of the fork and secured the apple. Then she grabbed the wooden handle and cranked the wheel. It worked like a lathe. The apple spun with each turn of the crank, and a paring cutter moved against the apple and peeled away the skin. She swung the cutter aside and twisted the apple counterclockwise, and it came away peeled and cored.

"Well, I'll be . . ." Montana was surprised. He'd never seen one of these contraptions. He remembered his mother sitting on the porch and peeling apples by hand.

"You need some help with those pies, Addie?" Lizzie called out over her shoulder.

Pies? Not pies. He groaned at the thought. He couldn't help it. He loved apple pie, and the mere thought of Little Miss Pinky making one was almost a sacrilege.

"No," she answered. "I can handle these." To Montana's horror, she peeled more apples.

He stood there a moment, then remembered he had things to do, besides which, he didn't think he could watch the desecration. As he walked to the door he thought of the ways she could ruin an apple pie. The crust could be like her biscuits, he thought with horror. Other than that, he didn't think there was much she could do wrong. Just apples and spices and sugar and salt . . .

He stopped dead, his mouth already puckering. He sneaked a peek over his shoulder. Lizzie was drying the dishes and Addie was busy with the apples. His hand shot out to the salt crock that sat by the stove. He snatched it and hid it in front of him, grabbing his hat and beating it out the back door. This way, he reasoned, heading for Will and the horses, the pies would have a fighting chance.

Addie pinched together the crust on the very last pie. One was still in the oven and the other one sat on the open windowsill, cooling. They were perfect, she thought with a satisfied smile. She popped the last one in the oven and began to clean off the worktable.

Lizzie came through the back door swinging the empty garbage pail. "It's amazing how much garbage chickens can eat. She continued over to the sink, washed the pail and poured another glass of tea. Sagging back against the sinkboard, she rested an elbow on the edge and said, "I wonder where Mama is. Isn't it after three?"

Addie glanced at her watch pendant. "Almost three-thirty," she said, bending to remove the second pie from the oven. She set it on the sill, next to the first one. "Lord but it's hot. I wonder if these pies will even cool." She shook her head, unable to believe they'd gotten everything done.

"I'm drenched," Lizzie commented, plucking her bodice fabric away from her damp body.

"I want a bath, a cool bath," Addie wished with a sigh.

A wagon jangled and crunched down the drive. "Oh, there's Mama!" Lizzie said, standing on her toes to peer out the kitchen window. "Oh, rats! It's Becky."

Addie looked down at her clothes. Sweat ringed her sleeves and ribs and there was chicken fat and flour all over the front of her apron. She took off the splattered apron and peered down. She still looked as if she'd melted.

Lizzie grabbed her things and turned to Addie who was

wiping the sweat from her forehead. "It's hot in here, but that's preferable to what I'll have to put up with for the next half hour. There's the heat, the dusty road, and—God give me strength—Becky's whining." Lizzie walked to the back door and went on, "I've never understood how two people as good-hearted and sweet as Mama and Papa could end up with a daughter like her."

Addie laughed and followed her outside.

Lizzie leaned over and whispered, "Do you think maybe the doctor dropped her?"

Addie smiled. She really liked Lizzie.

Lizzie straightened, a deadpan look on her face. "I guess not—that might have knocked some sense into her."

Both women approached the wagon, and Addie wanted to hide. It must have been over a hundred degrees outside, but Rebecca Latimer looked as if she just stepped out of an icebox. Didn't she sweat?

"Hello, Adelaide. Where's Montana?" Rebecca scanned the farmyard.

"Hi, Rebecca. Yes, I'm fine, thank you." Addie couldn't resist.

Rebecca gave her a cool stare. "Cute." Then she turned to Lizzie. "Come on, I don't have all day. It'll take me at least two hours to get ready for the dance." She turned to Addie and blessed her with a phony smile. "I've got a beautiful new blue dress and—"

Lizzie plopped on the seat and cut in, "And it'll take her the full two hours to get her corset laced tight enough to squeeze into it."

Rebecca ignored her sister and went on, "Montana told me how stunning I look in blue."

Addie was just biting back the urge to tell her she'd be glad to turn her black and blue when Montana and Will rode in from the field. They rode up and Montana dismounted, slapping that obnoxious horse of his on the backside and then watching it head for the water trough. Will reined in next to Lizzie. "Are you all off?"

"I guess. Becky's in a hurry—umph!"

Addie saw Rebecca jam her elbow into Lizzie's side, and then she said, "I'm just so excited about the dance. Aren't

256

you gentlemen?" She directed her question straight at Montana.

He glanced up. His face and neck were dusty from his field work and sweat glistened from the chiseled bones of his face.

"I'm looking forward to that chicken," Will said, a typical hungry male look on his face, which had the same sweat dirt on it as did Montana's. His smile, though, was only for Lizzie.

It made Addie wish a man—one man—would smile at her like that. She glanced at Montana. His eyes weren't on Rebecca, perched so pristinely on the wagon seat, like she figured. They were on her. She hooked some damp hair behind her ear and said, "Thanks, Lizzie, for all the help."

"Anytime," Lizzie answered, climbing onto the wagon and settling next to her sister. "Let's go, Becky. It'll take you a year to get into that dumb dress."

Addie grinned and Rebecca gasped, then sat a bit taller on the seat and looked right at Montana. "I'll look forward to that dance you promised me." She gave him a meaningful smile.

Montana smiled back.

"Well, see you all tonight." Rebecca snapped the reins and drove toward home.

"I'm going to go get myself a nice, cold bath," Will said, dismounting and leading his horse toward the trough.

Addie turned and started to leave but Montana asked, "Can you still be ready by five?"

"Of course I can be ready. I'll have you know I'm never late." She raised her nose a notch. "What's wrong? Worried that you might miss your dance with Rebecca?"

His mouth tightened a bit. He waited a moment, searching her face; then a stupid grin lit his face. "Jealous?"

"Hardly," Addie said, walking toward the back door.

A tinny, scraping sound, like dragging tin cans, sounded from the back of the farmhouse. Addie stopped just as that devil of a horse nudged an empty, bent pie tin across the farmyard.

"My pies!" she screamed, running around the corner and

heading for the windowsill. The sill was empty, but her foot hit the other tin. It too was licked clean.

"That horse from hell ate my pies!" She spun around, her fists knotted at her sides.

Montana stood in the yard, examining his stupid horse. She grabbed the tin and marched over to him.

"You have to do something!" she told him, waving around the pie tin.

He glanced at the tin and her, then he scrutinized the horse. "Do you think he'll get sick?"

"What?"

"Maybe I should send Custus for the veterinarian," he mumbled.

"I'll have you know those were perfectly good pies!"

The horse raised its freckled lips, belched and smacked.

"He ate those pies on purpose," Addie accused, waving her finger at the thing.

"I doubt that," Montana said, his face serious, then he gathered the reins and led the horse toward the barn. "Animals have an innate sense of self-preservation."

She gasped so loud her throat ached, then she spun the pie tin right at Montana's grinning head.

"And so do I." He laughed, ducked, and disappeared into the barn.

Montana slunk an inch lower in the tin tub. The well water was cold, but it felt damn good. He was so sweaty that the dust clung to every bit of his exposed skin, and when he had removed his hat, his hair had a circular dent from the crown. His head had looked like a peanut.

Bending forward, he dunked his head in the water and used a bar of soap to get a good lather. A few minutes later he was clean, so he lounged back in the tub, his legs flung over the end, and just let the water soothe him. In the bunk room, Custus was singing some bawdy song about the real kind of dancing a man liked to do—on a mattress—and every so often Will would join in. Montana smiled at one particularly lurid verse. He shook his head and sank lower. The next thing he knew he was mentally acting out the verse with a tiny, black-haired woman who had skin as white and soft as a new cotton bud. God, he could almost feel it . . . It was a damn good thing this water was cold.

Something had to happen, and soon. He hadn't had much chance to seduce her. There were just too many people around. No, he thought, seducing her wouldn't work. He needed another plan. Propping his elbow on the edge of the tub, he sank deeper. What he really needed was some way to get *her* to want *him*. Maybe if he ignored her completely . . . Suppose he danced with every woman in the grange tonight except her. Or . . . Montana's eyes took on a decidedly wicked gleam, he could dance with Rebecca. He remembered her reaction to Rebecca, and he grinned. Yep, that was it. Every time Rebecca Latimer was around, Addie got twitchy.

He liked her twitchy. Her nose went up, her eyes were like black fire, and boom! she was in his arms—right where he wanted her.

Addie strained to reach the last few covered buttons on the back of her dress. She finally got them. She backed away from the dresser to widen the scope of the mirror, and she twirled, sending the skirt of her lilac figured silk dress into a full bell. She smiled at her reflection; she couldn't help it. The deep purple lapels were trimmed with lace jabots of a lighter shade. Bodice gores crossed in front, taking the shape of a basque jacket—with its tight-fitting waist and center point. In this dress her waist looked smaller than a choker.

As the skirt settled from her twirl, the silk rustled and the lilac lace jabots that trimmed the left side spilled downward like water over a deep purple moire silk inset. The dress was so feminine, and against the white of her skin and the black of her hair, it looked as if no one else in the world could wear it.

Sent to her by her Aunt Emily, the dress had been delivered the day before her college graduation. "We're with you in our hearts," the note had said. Addie had cried for two full hours, lying on her lonely bed in the women's home, hugging her purple graduation dress and wishing some of her family were there in person. The crying spell had purged that rare bout of self-pity.

The next afternoon she'd donned the dress, and a smile for her long-dead father, and she graduated with her head held high. No one knew that Adelaide Amanda Pinkney, the small, quiet girl at the top of Melvil Dewey's School of Library Economy—class of '92—was lonely and scared and vulnerable. No one knew her heart ached with the need to have someone who loved her there when they called her name; someone to be proud of her when they placed her rolled diploma in her hand; someone to hug her when the other girls were hugged by their families.

From that moment on, the dress had become Addie's pride dress. And like a knight who dons his armor, she wore it to protect herself when she was most vulnerable.

Tonight she was an open wound. She loved a man she wanted to hate, and who didn't love her. In a foolish moment of passion, she'd given him her marriage gift, and he only wanted her farm. She wanted him to value her, not her farm.

Twisting her black hair up high on her head and securing it with an ivory comb, she took one last look in the mirror. The woman who stared back didn't look wounded. The color of the dress tinged her skin to a pearly white. Her black eyes almost glowed. She left the room, gathered the food baskets and walked out the door, heading for the wagon, her head held high. Tonight a smile masked her face, a determined walk hid her shaky legs, and her pride dress covered her wounded heart. Tonight no one would know.

19

On the notes of a fiddle, laughter rode out the open windows of the grange hall. The light spilled out too, forming long, boxy shapes of yellow on the dark cool dirt of the alleys. Within the red-brick walls, light shone from a few sweaty, bald heads in a group of men who sat near the wood stove. Their faces were brown from working in the fields, where the sun burned down and had no favorites. But their brows were white as milk from wearing the cool, protective covering of a straw hat.

In this tight corner the bite of ancient wood smoke mingled with that of bay rum, beer, and human musk. Custus stood among the group, sucking on a cold cigar stub around which rolled a stream of gruff curses that caught Addie's attention. She smiled, wondering if he was having a rough time keeping up.

When they'd first arrived she had stood nearby, listening to the talk of farming and animals and the men's simple pastimes of dominoes, fishing, and dove hunting. She learned that durham wheat grew best in California as a late crop, and cows which eat too many pine needles can abort their calves or die. She learned that no less than five men called themselves town champion of a domino game called sniff, that Seth Pearson shot the most doves last September—although Eli Whittier argued that point. But what Addie really discovered was that in this group, the first liar didn't stand a chance.

"I was a-passing by Mule Ear Creek the other day an' I sawed a trout that were leastways four pounds," Custus'd bellowed to the men.

A few men had snorted their disbelief, but Harlin Perkins, the blacksmith—a small-town title that encompassed locksmith, gunsmith, harness maker, and shoemaker—begged to differ. "I ain't never seen no four-pound trout in these parts, McGee." He gave Custus a look of pure skepticism.

Custus's face said he wasn't moved, nor the least worried about the men's doubt.

"How'd you know it was four pounds?" Harlin challenged.

"Weeeell . . ." His cheeks colored to a rosy pink and a grin of devilment lit his lips. "I could tell by the *scales.*"

The group erupted with groans and laughter. Custus must have grown a good inch, and Harlin Perkins bought him three beers. Addie had walked away certain that if lying were truly a sin, then none of these men were destined for wings and harps.

She'd moved to another crowded corner where the air swelled with lemon verbena, lilac, and rose water, and it was here that Addie still stood with the other women, watching the dancers strut by.

Will swung Lizzie in a full circle right in front of Addie. The skirt of the girl's blue dimity dress rustled against a wealth of white petticoats that fluttered into view for a circular second. His hand spanned her waist as he swung her, and Lizzie's laughter sang with each exaggerated swirl. Her face was flushed pink and her green eyes sparkled. In the lights of the grange room her bright red hair picked up golden highlights that made it look like a winter fire. Addie thought her friend was lovely, both inside and out.

She could see the look of adoration on Lizzie's sweet face and she frowned, not wanting her to be hurt. But then she chanced to look at Will, and his expression mirrored her friend's. There was nothing to worry about there. Those two were falling in love fast and at an equal pace.

She felt relieved, but just a bit emptier than the moment before. Then she saw Montana and Rebecca, and Addie stood as stiff as a clothesline post. Unconsciously she shook the skirt of her pride dress, tugged down its tight sleeves, and rested her pale hands on the small, snug waistline. Her chin went up an extra inch as they spun by, tall and striking on the small dance floor, swans in a crowd of ducks. She felt ill.

Becky talked with Montana as they danced, and Addie noticed that her nose was almost even with his mouth. When he stood close to her, her nose was even with the middle of his broad chest. It made her feel . . . Lilliputian. Rebecca fluttered her dark lashes as they danced by again. She appeared about as coy as a fox prowling around a chicken coop.

The tune changed to a country waltz and, afraid to watch again, Addie turned and joined in a conversation between Hettie and Annie Pearson. A minute later a tall shadow blocked the warm touch of light behind Addie, and she sucked in a quiet, tentative breath. Someone touched her shoulder and she turned, her black eyes wide with expectation.

"May I have this dance, Miss Pinkney?" Wade Parker held out his hand and smiled down at her.

She masked her disappointment. "I'd love to, Mr. Parker." And off they swung in the circle of dancers, his big hand spanning her lower back as he danced her past Montana and Rebecca.

One hour and six dances later, none of them with Montana, Addie stood behind a long table groaning with food, and she served the chicken to an eternal line of men that passed by, plates in hand. Lizzie spooned up some potato salad and served it to her father. John moved to Addie and she smiled up at him. "Light or dark or both?" she asked.

"Both, please." His blue gaze followed her hand as she speared a meaty breast and a leg with the thigh still attached and dropped them on his full plate. He smiled his thanks and moved on. Addie knew that Will was next, followed by Montana. She tried to calm her bubbling insides but she couldn't. He hadn't danced with her once, and he'd danced with every other young woman and with Rebecca at least four times. He had purposely excluded her; Addie knew that, but the knowledge didn't make the swallowing of it any easier.

Will now stood in front of the chicken platters, but he

wasn't looking at the food, he only had eyes for Lizzie, who returned his look. Addie watched her scoop up a big glop of potato salad and lift it toward Montana's plate, never taking her eyes from Will. She turned the spoon and, to Addie's delight, the potato salad landed on Montana's tanned hand.

"Landsakes, child! Watch what you're about." Hettie stood on Lizzie's other side, and she grabbed the spoon from Lizzie and scraped the salad off Montana's hand and shirt cuff.

"Serves him right," Addie muttered and immediately felt the heat of Montana's look. She gave Will his chicken, two breasts, then stood with the fork up as Montana moved in front of her.

She didn't say one word, she just stabbed the fork into the platter and put the almost meatless chicken neck on his plate. The silence hung around them like fragrance. He didn't move on, just continued to stare at her.

"More?" she asked with feigned innocence. She jabbed a chicken back and dropped it on top of the neck. She could have sworn she heard the grinding of teeth, and she sincerely hoped so.

"I'd like some dark too . . . please." His words were spoken through clenched teeth.

Addie blessed him with her brightest smile. "Certainly." She stuck the fork into a wrinkled little gizzard and scraped it onto the edge of his plate.

She could see the knuckles on his hand whiten. He didn't move. The only sound around them was a distant cough of embarrassment from someone in the line behind him.

To break the tension, she forked another gizzard and put it on his plate.

"Again," he said in a deep, bedroom voice that had nothing to do with wanting more chicken.

Addie turned so red she thought she'd burn up right there. Her head shot up and she was captured by his look—a challenge.

Her hand jabbed at the chicken on the platter and lifted it toward the plate. His eyes left hers and locked on the fork, poised above his plate. Addie looked down. Two little fried chicken hearts were speared on the end of her serving fork.

He smiled, and before she could move, he plucked them off the fork and moved on. She wanted to chuck the fork right into his horrid black heart. Instead she gave the next lucky man three plump breasts and two thighs.

When all had eaten and the main meal was put away, desserts of every kind lined the table. Elbow-high chocolate cakes, lemon pies with golden meringues, and crispy thick cobblers sat on the damask-covered table that looked ready to buckle under the heavenly weight. Addie's one apple pie sat right next to a Sierra-high angel food cake with dark chocolate icing drizzled over it like a black waterfall.

"Here, Addie, help me write numbers on these squares." Hettie handed her a stack of larges squares and a pencil.

"What are these for?" Addie asked, following Hettie's example and writing her numbers, twenty-eight to fifty-two on the squares.

"A cake walk."

Lizzie came and grabbed the finished squares and, with some of the other women, placed the foot-square cards with giant numbers in a circle on the dance floor.

Karl Bickerman, fiddle in hand, stood at the podium. "Well now, gents. The ladies have come up with a grand way to make some money for the anti-railroad lobbying fund, now called the BTBFB, Beat the Big Four Bastards." Chuckles echoed around the room and he waited until they died down. "Like I was saying, the ladies have decided that if we gents want any of that devil's temptation setting on that table over there, then we're gonna have to pay and perform for it." Now the men groaned. "There'll be a cake walk, although in this particular case it'll be a dessert walk, since there's more than just cakes on that table. It'll be a dollar a card. Line up, men, and the missus, here, will take your money."

The men lined up, some laughing and some grumbling, but all of them came up with the money. A few minutes later ten men pranced in a circle of white cards to Karl Bickerman's scratchy but lively fiddling. The women clapped and the men performed, most of them not prancing but stomping, their feet being more accustomed to fields and plow furrows than fancy footwork. When the fiddling stopped, each man had to stand on a square, and then a number was picked. The man with that number won the dessert that Martha Bickerman held for display.

Eventually Will, John, Custus, and Montana were all in the circle. Martha held up a dark molasses-colored tube cake and Lizzie leaned over to Addie and whispered, "That's Rebecca's apple cake."

The music started and so did the men, John Latimer stomping with his farmer's boots, Custus rolling along in a kind of lurching gait that was so slow it held up all behind him. Will and Montana strolled right past him, earning themselves a string of curses. The music stopped and Addie prayed. Karl pulled a number out of his hat and called out, "Eight! Number eight."

Addie held her breath while the men shuffled back, checking their squares. This time, God answered her prayers. Custus's hoot of triumph filled the room and he rolled forward to get his prize. Lizzie elbowed her in the ribs and nodded into a back corner. A pouting Rebecca plopped into a chair, crossing her arms and sulking like a three-year-old.

The game went on three more rounds and then Addie's pie was the prize. Montana still hadn't won, but she knew she couldn't dare hope he'd win this time. It was just too much to ask. She watched intently as the music played for what seemed like ten times as long as the others. Then suddenly it stopped, and so did the men. Karl pulled out the number. "Number two!"

The next thing she knew, Montana was holding up his square. He'd won! And Addie felt like Moses' mother. Martha handed him the pie and he walked in Addie's direction, an unsure look suddenly creasing his face. He passed by her and then stopped and turned.

"This isn't yours, is it?" His face now wearing a look of impending doom.

She smiled.

He groaned, right out loud, and she wanted to bop him.

"I'd better take this outside," he mumbled and strode for the doors.

Addie spun around and grabbed a fork off the table and marched after him. He'd eat that darn pie or she would bop him! She pushed open the back doors and stepped out into the night. It took a moment for her eyes to adjust to the change. Then she spotted him, sitting on a rail on a tall, wooden water cistern.

Her small feet ate up the distance between the two structures, and in a blink she stood before him, the fork in her outstretched hand. "Here!"

His face looked liked a condemned man. He took the fork, grimacing.

"Eat it," she said, crossing her small arms and tapping an impatient foot.

He stuck the fork in the pie as if he expected it to explode. When it didn't, he raised a forkful to his lips, Custus speed, and then closed his eyes tightly and took the bite.

His eyes popped open in surprise. "Hey, this is great!" Then he shoveled a huge bite into his big mouth and chewed like Mabel and Maud.

"Of course it is," she said in disgust, plopping down on the wooden rail that linked the cistern legs. He had eaten half the pie by the time she got the nerve to look at him. He had more regard for that silly pie than he had for her. "Remember the black-eyed peas and ham?"

He looked up, his mouth still full, so he nodded his head.

"That was the only meal I didn't . . . uh . . . doctor."

He swallowed and gave her a speculative look. "Doctor?"

A little smile quirked at the corners of her mouth. "Ruin."

He put the fork in the pie tin and set it on the cistern pump. "The broken egg yolks and dry ham?"

She nodded.

"The raw mashed potatoes?"

She nodded again.

"The leather roast?"

Another nod followed.

He was silent for a thoughtful minute, then asked, "What did you put in those biscuits?"

She grimaced, then with an apprehensive, wide-eyed look, she turned and faced him. "Plaster of paris."

There was a pregnant pause, then he burst out laughing. "Addie, Addie," he said shaking his head. "You're the burr under my saddle."

She rested her elbows on her knees and propped her chin in her hands. "It's your own fault."

"How do you figure?"

"It just is," she evaded, nervously smoothing the skirt of her pride dress, not wanting to get into the things he'd done, especially the things they'd done together and the way she hurt because of them.

They sat there, each staring at nothing, saying nothing.

"I asked you to get married," he finally said, staring straight ahead and opening all Addie's wounds.

She took a deep breath. "You wanted the farm."

He let his hands fall between his bent, propped knees and he stared at the ground. "I still do," he admitted, and she stiffened and her breath whistled past her tight lips.

She started to stand, but he grabbed her and pulled her back down. His hands gripped her small shoulders and he turned her to face him. He looked her square in the eye and said, "But I like you, Addie."

"Like me?" She could have hit him. "Like me!" Instead she twisted out of his arms. "Well, whoop-dee-doo! Lucky me." She shot upright and glared at him. "What you like is that I have no more morals. You like my farm, my buildings, and you like to sleep with me. That's what you like!"

He was mad now too, she could see it, but that didn't stop her. "You like to crawl in my bed and my body but you don't like me!" she cried, poking her finger against his chest.

"That's not what I meant, Addie, I—"

"Why, you don't even like me enough to dance with me, damn you to hell!" She started to walk away, but he lifted her right off her feet.

"Put me down!"

"No."

She scissored her feet, trying to get him to put her down. "Stop it!" he ordered.

"Go to hell!"

"I've already been there."

"Well so have I," she spat, "and you were right there with me!"

He dropped her legs, letting them dangle down, and pulled her against him. She started to kick at the air, and one strong arm clamped under her bottom and the other across her shoulders. His eyes said he'd had enough. "That was heaven, Addie, not hell."

Then his mouth closed over hers. She refused to open her mouth, even when he stroked her lips with his warm tongue. She squirmed against him, but his answer was to hold her even tighter. His lips still moved against hers but she wouldn't open, not for anything, even the lure of his taste. She just couldn't. She couldn't be that weak.

They exchanged glares—pure challenge. His thumb and finger held her chin and he tried to pry her mouth open. She ground her molars together and wiggled enough to get one arm unpinned. He applied more force to her chin, so she grabbed the tied hank of his hair. The more pressure he applied, the harder she pulled. His eyes heated to gold; her eyes cooled to black.

"You . . . stubborn . . . little . . . witch," he gritted against her mouth.

Her answer was to yank harder, and his lips left hers, but his eyes didn't.

"Let go," he commanded.

"Put me down," she countered.

He gave in. His arms loosened and she stopped pulling his hair. Her feet hit the ground with a soft thud, and she backed away, still freezing him with her eyes. She adjusted her dress, then lifted her proud head. "If you can't dance with me, you can't kiss me."

He ran his hand through his hair in frustration. "I was wrong, Addie. I'll dance with you. I wanted—"

"It's too late. Go dance with Rebecca." With that she turned, swishing her pride dress as she walked back inside, her head held high and heart sunken low.

*　　*　　*

Montana had met twenty-year-old mules who were easier to deal with than Addie. He'd given her time to cool off, but time only seemed to make her madder. He'd tried to ask her to dance, but she'd pretended he didn't exist. She'd looked right through him and turned and asked Hettie Latimer if she could help her.

He knew now that his plan tonight was another bad one. He stood back and watched her, fussing about behind the food table and fiddling with an ice cream maker. The way she twitched around, one would think making ice cream was right up there on the importance level with electing a president.

She worked with the other women, picking the ice . . . He shook his head. She was really mad, if her actions were any indication. She hacked so hard at the ice block that Montana was getting a headache. She lifted the bowl of ice—she had twice as much as the others—and dumped it into the bucket.

He thought about approaching her again, but he looked at the icepick and decided against it. Besides, something told him that he could keep on asking her to dance but get the same result as he would singing psalms to a dead horse.

The small band—two fiddlers, a guitar, and a banjo—broke into a lively Virginia reel. He had to give it one last try. He'd start out by apologizing . . .

Montana crossed the room, worming his way through the crowd until he stood in front of the table. She was just snapping on the top on the ice cream maker.

"I'm sorry, Addie," he said.

She ignored him and banged the lid down a bit harder.

"Please dance with me."

"Why, I'd love to, Montana," Rebecca cooed, appearing out of nowhere.

Addie looked up then, but it was too late. Rebecca had his arm and pulled him to the dance floor. He tried looking helpless by shrugging at Addie, but she just stuck her nose up and started turning the crank on the ice cream machine.

They joined the line of other dancers just in time to hold hands and follow the line of dancers under a bridge of hands. Montana held both of Rebecca's hands and they schottisched up the line. He kept looking over at Addie, but her nose was stuck up so high she couldn't have seen him unless she had eyeballs in her nostrils. He gave up, and do-si-doed around his partner.

The reel was one of the livelier dances, where everyone talked and laughed and strutted. Will was dancing with Lizzie, and both men started trying to outdo each other, dipping and swaying, shuffling in fancy steps around their partners. Everyone laughed, except Addie. When Montana finally slowed down, he glanced in her direction. One arm hugged the ice cream machine to her chest, and her small chin rested on top. But it was her right arm that got his attention. It cranked the ice cream maker faster than a spinning weathervane in a gale wind. Her hair curled here and there about her small, flushed face, which was in one of the best scowls he'd ever seen. She was really mad.

One more turn around Rebecca and the dance ended. He managed to un-cling Rebecca and he headed for the table, but Will stopped him.

"Harlin and Custus are getting together a fishing party for tomorrow at Mule Ear Creek, so he won't be home till tomorrow, and I thought I might go on with the Latimers. John could use some help with that new well and—"

"And it'd give you a chance to see Lizzie," Montana interrupted.

Will grinned. "You need me for anything?"

Montana clapped Will on the back and said on a laugh, "Naw, you go ahead." He watched Will cross the room and then turned back toward Addie. She was dishing up ice cream to a line of kids and adults. As if bidden to, she looked up. He plastered an innocent smile on his face and waved. Her nose was up before he could blink, and he laughed all that much harder. There was no love-light in those narrowed black eyes. Yes, she was mad. But that was okay by him, because he had a whole, long, wagon ride home with just the two of them. If he couldn't change her mind by then, well . . . he'd just keep on driving the wagon, clear to Tulare if he had to, until she gave in.

He made his way over to the beer keg and bought his second beer. Leaning against the back wall, he watched her serve up her ice cream. He raised his glass, toasting what was to come, but she never noticed. Her nose was too high.

"I can get up there by myself, thank you!" Addie told Montana, jerking her arm out of his grip. He stood back, so she grabbed the wagon seat and the foot rest and tried to pull herself up. She couldn't quite get enough oomph.

He snorted.

"I can do it," she quickly assured him again so he wouldn't help her. She tried again, and this time she pictured him dancing with Rebecca. She vaulted up so hard she almost landed facedown on the seat. She pushed upright and wiggled into position, her right hip smashed against the seat rail to give him plenty of room.

He walked around and hopped up onto the seat. He unwrapped the reins and pulled back on the brake. The horses started to ease away.

"Wait!" She grabbed his arm. "You can't leave. What about Custus and Will?"

"They're not coming." He snapped the reins and the team took off, jarring Addie against the back of the seat.

"What do you mean they're not coming?" She gripped the side rail and gaped at him.

"Custus is staying in town. He's going fishing tomorrow, and Will went with the Latimers. He's going to help John with his new well." His voice held a smile. "It's just little ol' you and big ol' me."

"Ducky," she muttered, "just ducky." Then she decided that those were the last words she was going to say. She felt like Red Riding Hood with the wolf.

They drove along the dirt road. The only sounds were the clatter of the harness, the soft thudding clap of horse hooves on the dry dirt road, crickets in the night, and the horrendous drumming of her dadgum heart. Common sense told her that he couldn't hear it, but it thumped so loudly in her ears that she was sure he could.

Then he began to whistle. She did her best to ignore it, until she recognized the tune. It was "A Man Without a

Woman," and he was doing it on purpose. The verses began to play in her mind like the tune:

A man without a woman is like a ship without a sail,
Is like a boat without a rudder,
Is like a fish without a tail.
A man without a woman is like a useless, empty can.
But if there's one thing worse in the universe,
It's a woman, I said a woman without a man.

He whistled the final line loud enough to send the horses into a canter. He pulled back on the reins and slowed down the team.

"If you want a woman, I'm sure Rebecca would be glad to oblige," Addie snapped, then could have bitten her tongue off.

"I don't want Rebecca."

Addie squirmed a little and only succeeded in accidentally brushing against him. She then sat as still as the night. The silence continued. Then some ornery little devil in her made her say it. "That's right, Rebecca doesn't have a farm."

He pulled on the right rein and the wagon hit a deep pothole that lifted Addie a good five inches off the wagon seat. Her fanny slammed back down so hard her teeth hurt. She gasped but refused to let him get to her.

"I don't like Rebecca."

"You liked her enough to dance with her all night."

"I asked you to dance and you refused."

His voice was quiet and so reasonable that she wanted to scream. She didn't want reason, she wanted a fight, and by God she'd have one. "You looked just like that silly tom turkey." She waited for his response.

He was silent.

"Rebecca stood there swishing her skirts, and you shuffled your feet like a turkey scratching around a hen."

Still nothing.

"You puffed your chest out and swaggered all around her like that turkey courting dance, dipping your shoulders like wings and weaving all over."

Not one word.

"I was waiting for your tailfeathers to fan."

He pulled back on the reins and jammed back the brake so hard that she was surprised it didn't break off in his hand. He was down from the seat in a flash.

"What are you doing?" she asked, a little panicked.

He stood in front of her. "Get down."

"No." She slammed her back against the seat and crossed her arms, staring straight ahead, scared to death he was going to throw her off the wagon and drive off without her.

"You are so damn pigheaded." With that gruff pronouncement, he hauled her off the seat.

She kicked and squirmed, and he set her on her feet, but his hands held her shoulders. She glared up at him. There was no way she'd let him know that she was scared. If he was going to abandon her on this dark, dirt road, like the lowlife he was, well fine. She'd fare better against snakes and scorpions and such than she would with him.

"Dance with me."

Now she was silent.

"Dance with me, Addie," he repeated.

She didn't know what to say, so as usual she said something dumb. "There's no music."

He held out his arms and began to whistle a waltz, "After the Ball."

She just stood there feeling small, and silly, and confused.

He stopped whistling. "Please."

It was the craziest thing she'd ever experienced. One moment she stood there, the next she was in his arms, waltzing to a whistled tune on a dry dirt road. She only reached his chest, pocket high, but his hand was warm as it held hers, and his arm pulled her close enough to touch bodies. He hadn't held Rebecca like this. Addie smiled, closed her eyes and swirled like a princess in a fairy tale, one where her toad had turned into a prince.

The moon was the only light in the black night sky. She glanced up at Montana and saw his profile outlined in the moonlight. They swirled in a half turn, and the moonlight shone on his face, revealing his features. They were all there for her to see: the long nose with the rugged bump, his chiseled, whisker-shadowed cheeks, his deep-set golden eyes, and a jaw strong enough to defy death.

She loved that face, and right now it was kind, relaxed, but still so strong—except for that dimple in his chin. She smiled at her thoughts and leaned her head against his chest. His heart beat a tattoo in her ear, sounding like percussion added to the whistling of the waltz. It was the most romantic, most wonderful moment of her whole life. Over and over they spun down the road—a dirt road, but that didn't matter to Addie because in Montana's arms, she felt as if she were dancing on moonlight.

Addie snuggled a little deeper into the soft warm bed. She didn't want to open her eyes and ruin it—the memory of last night. No one would have believed it, Montana Creed and Adelaide Amanda Pinkney dancing on the road at midnight. And last night, on that dirt road, she really and truly lost her heart.

Oh, she loved Montana before, she had to have, otherwise she'd have never let herself go that night in her bedroom. Yes, she loved him then, but now she adored him, enough to accept that he didn't love her in return.

He had said he liked her, which had insulted her at first, until she realized that it was quite an admission from a man like him. Maybe liking her would be the best she'd ever get from him, and she had to decide if that was enough.

Right now, when she savored last night's end, it was enough. To have danced with her like that was a girl's dream come to life. Then he'd put his arm around her on the last part of the drive home, he'd walked her to the front door, held her for the longest time and then kissed her, only kissed, before he said good night. It was special, the sort of moment one cherished.

It was enough for Addie. She threw back the covers and stretched out of bed. The holland shades glowed from the morning sunlight. Grabbing the small crocheted ring on the shade, she pulled down, releasing the catch, and the lace-covered shade flapped up. From the nearby grove of eucalyptus trees some mourning doves cooed, and in the distance the gurgling, flutey song of a mockingbird answered back.

The hills were even golder than the week before, and they rolled like yellow waves across the western horizon. Above them stood the oak- and pine-covered ridges, so dark a green that they appeared to demarcate the warm gold land from the ice blue sky. No rattling trolleys, no smudged gray sky filled with ash and smoke, no stench of human waste existed in her new world. Just birds, blue skies, and the sharp, clean scent of eucalyptus. The locals called their farms the home place, but for Addie this was a place to call home.

She smiled, her thoughts as dreamy as her mood. She dressed slower than usual, because her mind would drift and dream. She felt younger, more alive today, and the practical part of her said, "snap out of it, silly girl." Her shirtwaist was a soft, feminine shade of lavender, trimmed with lace, but her skirt was no-nonsense black. She brushed her hair, deciding to wear it down with a big black bow, but to offset it she slid her small feet into a pair of squat, practical shoes. But even the practical shoes couldn't keep Adelaide Amanda Pinkney from all but floating out of the room.

She fetched the fixings for breakfast, the eggs from the basket near the cellar door, ham from the meat barrel, plump red potatoes to fry with onions, and the ingredients for biscuits, less the plaster of paris. She smiled. He'd been a good sport about that, and she intended to make up for her bad meals, especially since he now knew the truth. And a good breakfast couldn't hurt her cause either. After all, there was that old adage about the way to a man's heart.

Addie set the ingredients on the worktable and went to light the stove. There wasn't any stove wood. Custus must have forgotten to bring it in. She crossed the kitchen and descended the back steps, her shoes clicking like impatient fingernails on the stairs. She all but skipped over to the woodpile and began to stack stove wood in her arms, humming "After the Ball."

She felt the warm heat of Montana's look, and smiled as she turned, arms filled with sticks of rough, splintery pine.

He leaned on the water pump, his red shirt half undone, his hair wet from dunking his head, but best of all he wore that warm, delighted smile—the one Addie had wished for, and now gotten.

"Want to dance?" he asked around that smile.

"There's no music."

He began to whistle, and her heart swelled so, she thought it might burst from her chest. She reached to grab one more piece of wood and his whistling stopped.

"Don't move, Addie!" His voice was no longer teasing. It startled her and she straightened.

"Don't move!" he shouted.

She froze, then heard it. The rattle.

She didn't move; she didn't breathe; she didn't blink. She did pray.

She caught a flash of red from the corner of her eye. He'd run into the barn. The snake rattled again. It was a beady, black sound, and it was so close it sounded as if it were in her ear. Chills raced down her back, her arms. The wood felt like iron, so heavy she wondered how long she could hold it, and her breath. The rattle went on and on.

A gun exploded. The bullet whizzed past her ear. The rattle stopped.

Montana pulled her arm so hard she dropped the wood. He held her tight, so, so tight. "Are you all right?" His voice was barely a rasp.

"Yes." She shook, so she held him even tighter, her small arms gripping his waist. Her face was buried against his chest.

"I didn't think I'd get back fast enough. God, Addie, but that was close." He dropped the gun, and before it thudded to the ground, his hands clasped her head, tilting it back. "God . . ." he whispered just before he kissed the fear right out of her.

His tongue dove deep into her mouth, stroking, as if testing to see if she was real. Then he left her mouth and pulled back, but kept kissing her face, her eyes, her temples. "That was so close . . ."

"I'm okay, Montana. I am." She heard all his past

demons in his poignant voice and felt as if she had to soothe him.

"You don't understand." He murmured against her lips.

"Yes, I do." She pushed away a bit and looked up at his face. "Will told me about your mother. I do know, and I'm okay."

He didn't say a word, he just held her, rubbing his hands over her small back, resting his chin on her head. She listened to his heart slow down until it beat at a normal rate.

"I care, Addie. I care so much. I didn't want to but I do. Please marry me."

She pushed away from him and looked up. "I love you," she told him.

He looked as if it was painful to speak. "I've never been in love with a woman. I don't know what it's like." His hands fell away from her, but he continued to look at her as he spoke. "I don't like to care about things, Addie, because when you care about something, something always happens to take it away. I don't know about this love business, but I know that I care about you."

He laughed a bit cynically. "Believe me, I fought it every step of the way. I do know that I don't want you to go. I know that I want to hold you, sleep with you, and make love to you over and over. I know that I'd like to try to make this farm a success, but I don't want to do it alone anymore. I want to do it with you. This should be our place, not your buildings and my land, your well and my water."

He turned and began to pace a short line in front of her. "I promise I'll be good to you. I'll provide for you and help you. I'm a hard worker, Addie, and I'll try not to let you down if you'll marry me. That's the best promise I can make to you, but I think we could have a good life. I'll try. Is that enough?" He stopped and looked at her for the first time since he'd started pacing and listing his qualifications as a husband.

There was a long silence.

"I'll always dance with you, Addie." He smiled a tentative, anxious yet teasing smile.

Lord but she loved this man, and she didn't think she

278

would ever get another proposal like this one. She cared more about Montana then she did about the farm, but she wasn't sure he did. Before she answered him, she had to know. "Will you agree to sign a contract about the farm?"

"What kind of contract?"

"You can deed me half the land and I'll deed to you half ownership in the buildings and improvements. Then it will be our place, legally and in writing." She held her breath. His answer would determine hers.

He smiled. "If I agree to the contract, will you agree to marry me?"

She smiled. "If you'll agree then I'll agree."

Then he laughed, but to her joy there was a tinge of relief in that laugh. "You're still the little burr. Should we count to three and then both say yes at the same time?"

"Yes," she said.

"Yes, you agree to marry me?"

"Uh-uh. Yes, I agree to count to three." She didn't want to make this too easy for him. After all, he did dance with Rebecca.

"One . . . two . . . three . . ."

Neither of them said a word, but they both laughed.

20

WHERE DO WE SIGN?" ADDIE ASKED LEVI HAMILTON.

"You sign here and Montana signs here. Then you'll both get a copy, and I've kept an extra here for Wade when he gets back from Sacramento." Levi looked at both of them. "I'm glad you two finally got this sorted out. Although working on Sunday is against my principles. Why did it have to be done today?"

"I was afraid she'd change her mind," Montana told him.

Addie handed the contract to Montana. "Here, you sign first." Then she grinned.

With an exasperated shake of his head, Montana took the paper and signed his name to the line where she pointed. She knew she was gloating, but she couldn't help it—and he did dance with Rebecca.

He handed the paper to Addie, and she signed it, but just to worry him, she took her sweet time. When she finished, she handed the contract to Levi and he witnessed it.

"Okay. It's official. You each own half of the other's property. Montana owns half the buildings and improvements and Addie owns half the land."

"Good," Montana said, turning to Addie. "Now will you marry me?"

Levi choked, then sat on his desk in a coughing fit.

"Yes," Addie answered, patting her lawyer on the back.

Montana grabbed her hand. "Good, let's go." He pulled her toward the door and over his shoulder he said, "Thanks, Levi. Send those copies out to the farm, will you?" And he pulled Addie out the door.

"Don't you think we should have stayed to make sure he was all right?" she asked as Montana lifted her onto the wagon.

"He'll be fine, and I'm not waiting." He jumped up, sat, and the team took off toward the Four Corners Church. They careened around three sharp turns, with Addie gripping the rail on the wagon seat, before he reined in and ran up the church steps. The doors were locked.

"Goddammit! Since when is a church closed on Sunday?" Montana sulked down the steps.

"That was either very brave or very stupid," she told him.

"What?" he asked, climbing into the wagon.

"Standing on the church steps and cursing," she said, adding dryly, "and on a Sunday no less."

He just looked at her, then asked, "Where would the preacher be on a Sunday afternoon?"

"At home, or possibly having Sunday dinner with one of

the parishioners." She adjusted her skirt. "We could wait unt—"

"No," he said, snapping the team into motion. A few minutes later they were at Reverend Fromer's home. Again Montana jumped down, then unlatched the small, white gate that opened onto a walk lined with a rainbow of velvety petunias and towering snapdragons. Up the front steps he loped and knocked on the red, wooden frame of the screen door. He rocked impatiently on his heels, waiting, and probably cursing the porch air blue, Addie thought. But she was secretly thrilled that he was so anxious. She watched him rock on his heels, mumbling, and she smiled.

After he'd killed the snake and they had agreed, in sorts, to their plans, he'd rushed her through breakfast and into the wagon. The next thing she knew, Montana had tracked down her lawyer and coerced him into drawing up the contracts. Apparently, from Levi's reaction, Montana hadn't told him about their marriage.

Another set of loud knocking rattled the Fromers' door. The reverend could be gone, and then they'd have to wait. If the truth be told, Addie really didn't want to wait either. Montana turned, his shoulders down just a notch, and the front door opened. Addie could see Mrs. Fromer's white bun through the screen. The woman was wiping her hands on a white towel while she listened to Montana. Then she turned and peered over his shoulder at Addie, who waved a quick, guilty little wave. She'd missed the service this morning. The two of them stood on the porch, spoke a moment more, then Montana came back to the wagon. He was smiling that cocky male smile of accomplishment.

"We're to go to the church. The reverend's working on his cistern pump and he'll meet us there in about a half hour." He hopped up and away they went again.

Forty-five minutes later they were still waiting, Addie sitting on the front steps of the church and Montana pacing a rut into the dirt. The Fromers' buggy pulled up and the reverend helped his wife down and then unlocked the church doors.

"Sorry I took so long. I can't seem to get that pump working," the reverend said, pocketing the big brass key and pushing open the doors. "I brought the missus here as a witness. She said you were somewhat . . . uh, anxious that the ceremony be performed today." He turned toward them.

Addie wondered if a preacher could tell if you'd sinned. His face sure looked as if he knew exactly what had gone on between Montana and her. She felt herself flush.

"Neither of us has any family left, so there was no reason for a wedding." Montana put his arm around her shoulders and pulled her close to him. "Besides, Addie here is a romantic. Today is the day her parents married, and she thought it would be special if we married on that day too," Montana lied, saving her moral face.

He gave her shoulder a quick, affectionate squeeze and added, "Isn't that right, sweet?"

Addie prayed for forgiveness and nodded.

The reverend smiled. "Let's get started, then." He turned and walked down the aisle and up to the front of the church, where he reached behind the podium and took out a book. He stood just to the left of the huge pipe organ and told them to stand in front of him and join hands.

As he spoke the marriage words, all kinds of thoughts ran like jackrabbits through Addie's mind. Was she making the right decision? Montana had said he liked her, cared for her, but was that really enough on which to base a lifetime? A home? Children? She looked up at him, so tall, his face so chiseled, his jaw so hard. She was scared.

As if ordered by fate, or because of some eerie ability to read her mind, Montana squeezed her hand just a bit tighter. She glanced up again and he winked. That was all she needed. If he spent a lifetime draping his arm around her, dancing in the moonlight, and winking, well then, it was enough.

"Do you . . ." The reverend paused and looked at Addie with a question in his eyes.

"Adelaide Amanda Pinkney," she answered.

"Do you, Adelaide Amanda Pinkney, take . . . ?"

"Montana Bartholomew Creed."

She tried to stop it, but a little snort of laughter escaped Addie's trembling lips. *Bartholomew?* That was the name of one of the twelve disciples. She got the giggles, imagining a dimple at the last supper.

Montana squeezed her hand really tight and she bit her lip. Then she realized that the minister, his wife, and Montana were all looking at her expectantly.

He repeated, "Will you, Adelaide Amanda Pinkney, take Montana Bartholomew . . ."

She grinned again.

". . . Creed as your lawful, wedded husband? To have and to hold, from this day forward, in sickness and in health, till death do you part?"

"Do I have to go first?" she asked.

"Addie . . ." Montana warned.

"Well, I don't see why I have to go first," she argued, not yet forgetting about the way he danced with Rebecca. "Can't he go first?"

Montana sighed and told the reverend to ask him first.

"This is highly irregular," the reverend said, glancing back and forth between the two of them.

"So is my bride," Montana said.

This time Addie squeezed his hand too tight, and out of the corner of her eye she saw him smile.

The reverend shook his head and said, "Will you, Montana Bartholomew, take Adelaide Amanda for your wedded wife? To have and to hold, from this day forward, in sickness and in health, until death do you part?"

"I will." Montana's deep, princely voice said the words of her dreams.

The reverend turned to Addie. "Will you, Adelaide Amanda, take Montana Bartholomew as your wedded husband? To have and to hold, from this day forward, in sickness and in health, until death do you part?"

"I will," Addie said, but the words came out in a croak. God had a sense of humor. Here she was marrying Montana and *she* sounded like a toad. Addie bit back an embarrassed smile.

"Do you have rings?" the reverend asked.

She stood quietly waiting, wondering what Montana would do. She knew he didn't have time to get a ring. But he surprised her when he pulled out a small ring from his pants pocket. She breathed a sigh of relief, then quickly slid the nickel chain of her small chatelaine bag off her wrist. In her nervousness, the chain clinked and rattled. It sounded as loud as a train in the tense quietness of the small church. She snapped open the clasp and dug through the small bag, pulling out her father's wedding ring. It was special, and she looked at it for a moment before she tentatively handed it to the reverend.

Montana took her hand again and she stared at their clasped hands. Within seconds they both wore their rings, rings that would bind them together for a lifetime. Addie felt her throat tighten with emotion, and for a brief second she felt as if her family were there, standing just over her shoulder, watching with approval.

The spell broke when the reverend pronounced them man and wife.

She looked up at Montana. He was smiling that smile— the one she'd longed for and could now experience for a lifetime. But then he bent down and gave her a chaste peck on the cheek. It was a cool and empty kiss that left her completely baffled. Addie would have thought after the way he'd hurried that he would have picked her up and plastered his lips to her as soon as the ceremony was over.

The Fromers congratulated them, and she found the strength to don a phony smile on her face. No one could tell how she really felt—worried. Montana had half the farm now and they were married. Maybe that was all he wanted. Maybe his caring was all an act. Addie had a horrid sinking feeling in the pit of her stomach, like she'd just swallowed a bundle of dynamite that would explode any minute, sending her into shattered pieces.

She turned her blank eyes to Montana. He had pulled some silver dollars from his pocket and handed it to the reverend, who shook his head. "Do you know anything about cistern pumps?"

"Yes," Montana answered.

"Good, then instead of a donation of money, how about if you help me get that pump running instead?" Reverend Fromer waited for his answer.

Montana looked as if the man had asked for his left arm.

"I might be willing to say a little prayer in your behalf about missing all those Sunday services." The reverend offered the bribe without a bit of shame in his voice, which also had just the right amount of authority in its tone. He had them.

Montana agreed. So for the next two hours Addie sat in the Fromers' parlor, listening to Mrs. Fromer and mentally giving Montana Creed, her new husband, all kinds of nefarious reasons for tricking her into marriage. By the time they had eaten with the Fromers, at their insistence, and had passed through town, it was dark. And so was her mood.

They passed the town jail, a brown-weathered, splintery, old building with a sagging porch roof. It was the last building in town. Montana made the turn onto the road that led home. She was so down that she didn't even notice at first that he'd stopped the wagon. Then it hit her and she looked up. "Why'd you stop?"

"For this." He pulled her up and into his arms so fast she hardly had a chance to take a quick breath before his mouth closed over hers. He kissed her like he'd waited for an eternity, like she was rain to his drought, like he'd die if he didn't. His hands roved over her small back, pressing her closer. His tongue was long, thick, warm, and rough, and it overtook her mouth, filling it, melting her. By the time he pulled back, she had stopped all conscious thought.

"I've been wanting to do that since the church, but I didn't want them to think we'd been intimate, Addie. After all, we have been living on the same place. People will talk, but they can only speculate. They can't be sure, besides which, in public we've been acting like enemies and not lovers. I think my rush to marry told everyone that we've been sensible, and that damn chaste kiss took every ounce of willpower I could dig up," Montana explained, laughing without humor.

Her smile was so bright it made the rising moon look dull. She threw her arms around his neck and kissed him just like he'd kissed her. Within minutes her back was wedged against the seat rail, his body over hers and his hands all over her chest. The corner of the seat back poked into her shoulder and she grunted in pain. He pulled away, his breath in rapid pants. He rested his forehead on her chest while he fought for control.

"Give me a minute," he said, his voice a begging rasp.

The night sounds were suddenly there, crickets chirruping, the west wind rustling the grasses that lined the road, a distant shout from the end of town, the slowing of his breath. Then his arm moved beneath the small of her back and he pulled her up with him as he straightened. They both sat there for a long, heavy minute, before he spoke. "I think this is a little too public for what I had in mind."

He turned to her, the inklings of a smile on his tension-thinned lips. She tore her gaze from his mouth to her clasped hands. She needn't look into his eyes, for she knew what she'd see. She could feel the heat of them anyway. She didn't speak, but a relieved sigh escaped her mouth when he snapped the wagon into motion.

The ride home had never seemed so long. Montana drove up to the front of the house, stopped and jumped down. His hands covered her waist and he lifted her off the wagon, pausing when she was just above him. He pulled her close and let her slide in unyielding inches down his chest, his stomach, his hips. He stopped when her face was just a kiss away, and his hot eyes singed into hers, as if he were trying to read her soul. Her arms linked around his neck and she closed the infinite gap. Her lips brushed his, teasing. Her tongue licked the crevice where his lips met. He groaned. She smiled.

She rubbed her smooth cheek against his, loving the gritty feel of his night beard. It felt rough and hard, and she loved that difference between them. She drew her lips lazily across his temple, and his arms wrapped around her, holding her so tightly she could barely breathe.

Then his hand splayed across the back of her head and his tongue thrust inside her mouth, forcing hers into submission just by size and strength. While he filled her mouth, imitating what they both strived for, he let her slide down farther, until he could rub his groin against her woman's bone. She rubbed in counterpoint, a natural reaction that was uncontrolled and driven by some part of her that was all instinct. That same part of her swelled like some stormy force and her legs spread slightly. His mouth left hers and moved to her ear.

He whispered in her ear, telling her exactly where he wanted to be. As if to make his point clear, his hip rotation changed to an upward thrust, bumping against a part of her that needed touching so desperately. She cried out and held on tighter while he gently beat against her.

"Sweet Jesus, Addie . . . I swear I'm going to take you right here."

From somewhere she found the strength to push on his shoulders. Their upper bodies separated. His hips slowed, then stopped, and he set her down. He gave her a long look before gently brushing aside some black hair that had fallen around her face.

"Go inside. I'll unhitch the team and be there in a minute." He turned and started to loosen the wagon harness.

It took a minute before she could will her legs to move, then she was up the stairs and inside by the time she heard the barn door squeak open. She closed the front door with her back and leaned against it for support. With her eyes closed and her head back, she drew a deep breath, then another. She pushed away from the door and walked toward the bedroom, not bothering to light any lamps.

She stared at the bed, swallowed hard, and went to the windows and slid them open. She sat on the ledge of one and looked into the dark bedroom. This was no longer her bedroom, it was theirs. For the rest of her married life she would sleep with Montana in this room.

Before she had a chance to think anymore, the hollow sound of his boots called out from the short hallway. Then he stood in the doorway, watching her, waiting. Slowly she pushed away from the window and stood. His eyes never left hers, yet he began to unbutton his shirt. He stopped after the last button. Addie raised her hand to her high collar and undid the little bead buttons of her shirtwaist. One by one she slipped them through the buttonholes until her shirtwaist was undone. He raised one arm and undid a cuff. She mimicked his action. He undid the other, and so did she. He pulled the shirt from his pants and shrugged out of it, letting it fall to the floor. With her eyes on his bare, hair-matted chest, she removed her shirtwaist.

He unbuckled his belt; she unbuttoned her skirt. He pulled the belt through the loops and tossed it to the floor. She let her skirt slide down and stepped out of it. He came toward her. When he stood barely a foot away, he smiled. "You should have gone first this time. You have more clothes."

Addie smiled as he bent and pulled off a boot. Then she looked at her button-top shoes. "I need a buttonhook."

"Take something else off," he said, his deep bass voice tinged with a taunt.

She undid her corset cover and he pulled off the other boot. She let her underskirt fall to the pile of clothes that surrounded her. He pulled off a sock. She looked down. She wore her corset, dark stockings and supporters, and her drawers. She counted. He had one sock, his pants and underwear. She smiled and reached underneath the knee band on her drawers, trying to get to her stocking supporter.

"Those frilly drawers next," he said. It wasn't a request, it was a demand, and that sent a thrill right through her.

She'd do as he asked, but not too fast. She ran her hand down her stomach to her waist. As slow as possible she drew one finger over the waistband, pausing to play with the ties that held the garment on.

"Addie . . ." he warned.

She looked straight into his eyes, smiled, then pulled the tie loose. The drawers didn't fall to the floor, and she didn't move, just let them hang about her hips, right where her corset stopped and bare flesh was all that was left.

He pulled off the other sock and said, "Push them down . . . and take something else off."

She pushed them down and stepped out of them too. Cool air chilled the place where she was so hot, damp, and almost itching with the need to be touched. Now she stood in her corset, ending mid-hip, her stocking supporters hooked to her corset and her dark stockings. She supposed that she should have been embarrassed, standing there with her womanhood and thighs exposed, her breasts and calves covered, but she wasn't. One look into his eyes and Addie saw her own female power.

His gaze went slowly from her head to her breasts. He paused, then slowly let his gaze drift downward. He stopped when his eyes lit on the shaded, curly-haired place where her legs joined. Part of her melted and flowed to that very spot.

He undid his pants, taking even more time than she had taken untying her drawers. And just like she'd done, he paused, not pushing them down. Her gaze drifted down. He'd cheated, he wore nothing else. The trail of thick curly hair moved down his chest, his flat, rippled stomach, down his belly. It was so thick where his pants hung open that she couldn't see any skin beneath. Then she remembered how his hair had rubbed low on her belly when he'd made love to her. Every time he had moved into her, the hair had rubbed against her skin. She wanted to feel it again.

He stepped out of his pants. "Where's your button-hook?"

She couldn't speak, so she pointed to the dresser behind him. He turned and her eyes scanned the back of him. He was beautiful. His shoulders were wide and muscular, as was his back. His waist and hips were narrow and his buttocks tight. At the small of his back the body hair started again, only much sparser, and it spread over his buttocks and thickened on the back of his thighs and down his long legs.

Just when her eyes were on the backs of his thighs, he turned and Addie found herself looking at the male part of him. She didn't turn away; she didn't blush; she was curious and wanted to see him. He didn't move, just stood there and watched her as she looked at him.

Long seconds later he closed the gap between them and knelt before her, unbuttoning her shoes. His hand rubbed a slow pattern on the back and inside of her calf. He pulled her foot free and treated the other leg to the same stimulating treatment. When he'd pulled off the other shoe, he still knelt, rubbing his hands up and down her legs. It took every ounce she had to stay standing.

His fingers snuck beneath her front stocking supporters and he unsnapped them. "Turn around," he ordered.

She did, and he released the back supporters, slowly peeling away her stockings and rubbing every inch of skin revealed. His hands clasped her hips and he turned her again. He started at the bottom of her corset, unhooking the hooks from the eyes. She could feel his knuckles grazing her skin. The corset fell away.

Immediately his lips roved over the creases on her ribs while his hands stroked, feather light. She shivered and her hands gripped his shoulders, kneading them as he increased his caresses, building the part of her that yearned for him. His tongue flickered over each nipple, then he sucked and pulled at them before dragging his wet tongue over the undersides of her breast, across her ribs, her hipbones. His breath blew against her wetness, cooling the fire that burned in her cleft. God help her, she had stopped him before, but not now, now she wanted his mouth there. She closed her eyes and begged the want away.

His hands closed over her hips and he walked her back until she stood against the side of the bed, then he lifted her and set her on the edge. He wedged his shoulders between her legs, spreading them. When his mouth covered her she fell back on the bed, biting back her moans and gripping the sheet in her fists. He used his mouth there as he had on her lips, her ears, and her breasts, only not stopping until she peaked. Then his tongue was inside her, giving her love's most intimate kiss, and she cried a river of tears.

The throbbing continued over and over, and when she could finally open her eyes, he stood above her. His hands moved under her buttocks and he pulled her forward, sliding into her until it felt like he touched her soul. In slow, drawing motions he pulled almost out of her then in, out then in, never moving faster.

It was a slow death of ecstasy.

When she could take no more, she raised her arms, "Please . . ."

He buried himself deep and moved over her, pushing her gently up the mattress until his knees rested between hers and his elbows bracketed her shoulders. He was close enough now, so she kissed his chest, flickered his nipples, and when she sucked on one, he groaned and started thrusting hard and fast, over and over, building and striving and driving toward that peak of yearning.

They came together—he on a shout of triumph, she on a scream of love.

Addie awoke to the soft tickle of warm breath across her face. She opened her eyes and her husband smiled back at her. A little satisfied moan escaped her lips, and a deep, masculine chuckle followed it.

She turned and buried her nose in his chest, threading her fingers through whorls of brown chest hair. "I fell asleep," she announced.

"I know." His voice still wore a smile. "Can't keep up?"

She bit him.

"Ouch!" Montana rubbed his chest.

Addie pushed away. "It's hard to keep up with someone who's never . . ." She raised the sheet and looked under it. ". . . down."

"You're right, it is hard."

Addie groaned and Montana turned toward her, enveloping her in his arms, his chin resting on the top of her head. "You'll have to learn to live with it, Mrs. Creed."

That stopped her. He'd called her Mrs. Creed. She glanced at her left hand for a brief moment, staring at the gold ring on her third finger. He pulled back and followed her gaze. His left hand threaded with hers.

"It was my mother's ring."

"It's beautiful." The gold was shiny on the raised parts of the leaf design that circled the band. The recessed part was dark, almost black with oxidation. It made the leaf design stand out even more.

Addie turned their hands. "This was my father's," she told him, referring to the plain gold band she'd given him.

He looked at it for a long moment. "Thank you."

He pulled her into the crook of his arm and they lay there silently. The only sounds were the quiet ones of the late night, floating through the open window with an occasional whiff of eucalyptus.

"Montana?"

"Ummm."

"Who named you?"

A sigh of exasperation rent the air. Addie laughed.

"Didn't your parents tell you, Addie, that it wasn't nice to laugh at other people's names?"

She kept laughing. "I'm sorry, but you don't look like a Bartholomew."

"Oh. Well, what does a 'Bartholomew' look like?"

"Let's see . . . Well," she said, purposely looking very serious and thoughtful, "he should have black hair."

"Why?"

"So when his friends call him Bart, it'll fit him."

"I see. What else."

"He should have glasses, thick glasses."

"What else?"

"Pale eyes, and he should be really short, and have no chin."

Montana didn't look at her, but he continued to hold her. "What about Montana?"

"I like that one, it fits you." She snuggled closer.

"That's what my mother said. I was a big baby, over ten pounds, and Montana means mountain in Spanish. She was half Spanish, and so after my birth, which I guess was pretty tough, she named me Montana."

"What does Bartholomew mean?" Addie asked.

"Farmer." His voice changed, grew serious and a little bitter. "My father was a farmer, a sharecropper. His dream was to own his own place."

"What happened?"

"He died." Montana's voice was flat and cold. From the way he answered, Addie was afraid to ask any more. She could tell she'd get no more information even if she asked. But what little he had told her helped make her understand him a little better. This farm did mean a lot to him, of that she was sure. But their light mood had changed. It was tense and heavy, so she tried to lighten it.

"What about my names?" she asked. "What do you think someone named Amanda should look like?"

He was quiet for so long she thought he wouldn't answer her. Then he said in a curt voice, "Blond."

She was silent.

"Big, blue eyes."

Addie's lips tightened.

"Let's see . . . she'd have curly hair, a sweet smile, and . . ." He let the word hang there for the longest time, then finished. ". . . she wouldn't be too short."

Addie punched him in the ribs. "You toad!"

He laughed and rolled her onto her back, pinning her hands with his, clamping his long legs over hers. She gave him some token resistance, then stopped struggling and smiled up at him.

"Amanda means lovable," she informed him, her nose up a bit.

"And you are . . ." His mouth descended.

A huge banging crash split the air. Montana's head shot up, breaking their kiss. "What the hell?"

The crashing continued, sounding like a train wreck right outside the bedroom window. Addie whipped her head toward the window and she grabbed onto Montana.

Then the sound of Custus's voice, intertwined with Will's, rasped through the window. They were singing an absolutely awful, bawdy song about marriage. Once the song was done, Custus yelled, "Hey, ya two! Stop what yer a-doin' . . ." He chuckled. "We's a-givin' ya a shivaree!" He banged some more metal together.

Montana's forehead hit the pillow next to hers and she heard him groan. He raised his head and yelled. "Go away!"

"That was damn stupid ta get yerself hitched on a Sunday. I can't collect them there winnin's until tomorrow. An' didn't ya know gettin' hitched on a Sunday's bad luck?" Custus let loose with a loud belch, followed by a mumble that sounded like "Damn rotgut whiskey."

"Yeah!" Will yelled. "And with—hic—out us!"

"Well, ya know, Will, some people ain't go no sense. I bet they'd walk inta a river so's they could drink standin'

293

up." Will chuckled, but Custus howled with laughter, and Addie was sure she could hear him slapping his knee.

There was some whispering and it was quiet for a moment, then a loud cackling screech came in the window. "Don't wring 'er dadblamed neck, Will!"

"Sorry," Will said, then hiccuped.

Custus shouted out again. "Just bringin' ya some good luck. Ever'one knows that if'n a chicken cackles after the weddin', nothin' bad'll happen ta ya!"

It was quiet again, except for Addie's giggles and Montana's swearing under his breath.

"Ya didn't pass no white dogs on that there road ta town, now did ya?"

When they didn't answer, Custus went right on. "It's bad luck. Will, ya can get rid o' that there chicken."

"Where, hic?"

"Where the hell do ya think? In the dadblamed hen-house!" There was a pause. "Here, you bang these here pans and give me the damn chicken!"

Montana got out of bed. "Where's my gun?"

Addie sat upright. "You can't shoot them!"

Montana stopped, stark naked, at the doorway. "No, but I can sure scare the hell out of them." And he disappeared.

"Custus," Addie warned. "Please go to bed."

There was nothing but silence. She listened for the longest time, then thought she heard the clang of the chicken-yard gate. She waited.

Montana crept into the room, his pistol in his hand. He moved over to the open window.

"I think they've gone," she told him.

He pulled back the shade and pointed the gun out the window.

There was silence. Finally she was sure they were gone, so she settled back against the pillows.

"Ya know now that yer all married ya can cure warts with yer wedding ring. All ya have ta do—"

Montana fired.

"Goddammit to hell, ya shot my last cigar!"

Smiling, Montana set the gun down and crawled back into bed. They lay there a few moments, waiting.

"Come on, Will, uncover yer dadblamed, drunken head and get up off the ground. We'll leave them there ingrates alone. Shootin' my last gul-darn cigar when all's we was a-tryin' ta do was bring 'em some good luck!" There were two more hiccups and then the barn door slammed shut.

Montana's arm clamped around her waist, pulling her closer, and with a smile in his voice he asked, "Feeling lucky?"

"Sure." She laughed, holding her left hand up so she could admire the wedding band. She held it up in his face and added, "Now whenever I touch my toad of a husband, I'll be able to cure my warts." She laughed until his mouth shut her up.

21

THE NASAL, HIGH-PITCHED CRY OF A BLACK HAWK PEALED above the chicken yard. Addie tossed another handful of chicken feed and wadded the corners of her seed-filled apron into one fist, then she brought up a hand to shield the sun as she looked up. A barn swallow, blue-black with its chestnut-red head, chased a soaring hawk, pecking at its fanned tail, fluttering and then jabbing fearlessly at the bigger bird. It was a common sight, the persistent small bird, harassing the hawk for coming too near its nest in the barn eaves. But the sight always made Addie smile. When she and Montana had first seen the birds, he'd said the swallow was a feisty little thing, like her, pestering the heck out of that poor beleaguered hawk.

She tossed off the last of her chicken feed and dusted off her apron and hands. Then she looked at the south field, where only a few days before, golden wheat had rattled like dry grass in the soft westerly wind. Now the field was harvested, leaving it a sea of dirt and buckskin-colored stubble.

A distant shout, the clatter of the wooden machinery, and the rumble of thirty-three mules pulling the combined harvester clamored from the north field. Addie left the chicken yard and stood watching the harvest crew maneuver the Best Company combine over the last of their wheat crop. Montana had said that today they'd finish up the harvest and the crew would leave, moving on to the Latimers' place to work for another few weeks.

The crew, most of them members of the Blue family, arrived two weeks ago, a dusty parade of vehicles and livestock lumbering down the road from the Johnson place. It had been some sight. The harvest workers were in two freight wagons, followed by the cook wagon—a long rectangular wooden box atop a wagon bed. It looked something like a train car, except gray canvas covered the windows and a black stovepipe stuck up from the rounded roof. Behind it was a wide water wagon and three more supply wagons, filled with food for both the crew and the livestock. Bringing up the rear was the combined harvester, nicknamed Blue's Big Boy, and it was the biggest jumble of wood, metal, pulleys, and wheels that she'd ever laid eyes on. But when Montana had brought her out to watch the harvest, she'd been amazed.

Over thirty mules were lined up to pull the Big Boy, and he'd told her that sometimes the machine used as many as forty. She had watched the driver, an old mule skinner named George, who could outswear and outlie Custus, climb up to a seat perched on a ladder that slanted out over the mule team. It looked as if he were riding the prow of a ship. With only two sets of reins for guides, he led the team down the field, a sea of ripened wheat, and the huge spindly, wooden combine blade cut a thirty-foot-wide swath clear through it. The wheat was cut and threshed in one operation, and the grain poured from a chute into a bulk wagon that Custus, Will, or Montana drove alongside.

A job that used to take over thirty days to cut and thresh could now be done in half the time. When she'd spoken to

Mrs. Blue one day, the woman had told her how they used to hire over forty men to cut and thresh, but now, with the newer combined harvesters, the family could handle the operation with only two or three of the local boys as hired hands. From what Addie could tell, the invention of the combine had made life easier for the women of the Blue family. Cooking and washing for a crew of forty men working a filthy job had to be endless. Addie couldn't have done it.

She'd been washing Custus, Will, and Montana's workclothes for only two weeks, and she felt as if she never had a chance to breathe. They'd come in covered in a shroud of dark dust and chaff. Even after washing at the pump, they'd squirmed and scratched when the chaff crept inside their clothes. She had scratched herself silly just carrying the itchy, chaff-crusted laundry to the washbasin, then had to practically beat the black dust out of their clothes. She couldn't imagine doing that, plus cooking, for over forty men.

Of course if Montana'd asked her to, she probably would have slaved for a hundred such men. The past months together had been so special, and he'd made Addie feel special too. The smile she'd once longed for was something she now saw often. She'd be standing on a stool and he'd sneak up and lift her high in the air, tossing her and swinging her until she'd forfeit a kiss. Many was the time that the kiss led to more. He'd taught her body to sing, over and over, whether they were in the bedroom, up against a pantry wall, or even once, underneath that giant, crawling oak tree. They would touch, and passion burned between them, hotter and more intense than a prairie fire.

She'd learned so much, more than just the secrets of her body and his. She'd learned about men and women. Men didn't see things in quite the same light as did women, which made for some lively discussions. Sometimes it amazed her that they could match so well in bed since everything else they did seemed to be contrary. Montana was a morning person, up at the crack of dawn, hungry and ready to go, while Addie would burrow under the pillows and moan and groan until he would finally threaten to whack her on the backside if she didn't get up.

Addie tended to leave her clothes where they fell, figuring she'd pick them up later, but Montana hung everything up, except his boots, which he always managed to leave where she'd trip over them. Just yesterday she'd threatened to cook them and serve them for supper if he didn't keep them out of the doorways. He brushed his teeth with baking soda while she used peppermint tooth powder. His beard grew in a matter of hours, and there were times when he'd shave twice in one day, but if Addie took the scissors to her hair, he'd wince and groan, scared to death she'd cut too much off. And she knew why. He'd use her hair when he made love to her, wrapping it around them, around his hands to hold her where he wanted her for the longest time. There were times he'd walk up behind her when she brushed it, burying his head against it, and telling her he loved the way it smelled like lemon pie.

And he'd kept his word. At the Widermann wedding he'd danced with Addie the whole time, never once dancing with another woman, not even Rebecca Latimer. He'd done the same thing at the Fourth of July picnic, whirling her around the floor of the Johnson's barn, whistling in her ear and making her remember a moonlit dirt road on a warm May night.

Her memories were suddenly distracted by the rumble of a huge, laborious bulk wagon coming down the road. It turned on the drive and moved toward the space near the barn where the other wagons stood filled, tarped, and ready to transport to the grain elevator in Stockton. Montana jumped down from the seat, his face a grimy black mask and chaff clinging to his clothes and hair. He grinned at her, and his teeth shone bright white against his dirty face. "What are my chances of getting a kiss, Mrs. Creed?"

" 'Bout the same likelihood of Custus giving up swear words."

"That bad, huh?" He looked down at his dirty clothing and took a step toward her. "Guess I'll just have to steal one, then."

His arms shot out and Addie shrieked, dodging him and

running like a weevil toward the tree. She shot a quick glance over her shoulder and saw he was closing in, a white grin on his grubby face.

"Montana, don't you dare!" she threatened over her shoulder as she ran to the oak tree, her hands gripping its sides while she poked her head around the side of the trunk.

He stopped at the other side, laughing. "You move pretty fast for an old married lady . . . with short legs."

"I don't want that itchy stuff all over me! And I have long legs for my height." Her voice was indignant, but not too much so because she had to watch him, knowing he was going to try to jump her any minute.

"But you promised to obey me, remember?"

"You promised first, and I didn't make any vows about kissing you when you're filthy."

He straightened and said, "You're right."

He just turned and walked away, and Addie couldn't believe it. She moved out from the tree. "Where are you going?"

"Back to work." He waved good-bye as he headed toward the wagon.

She stood there for a moment, a little hurt that he'd dropped the chase so fast. She shrugged and walked toward the front porch, her shoulders down just a bit.

He tackled her from behind, rolling onto his back when they hit the dirt and absorbing the jolt. He held her firmly against him and grinned up at her.

"You toad!" she groused, having trouble hiding her smile. "Let me up." She pushed against his chest.

"It'll cost you."

Addie stared down at him. She loved him, dirty, grimy face and all. "Okay," she told him, then she gave him a quick peck on the chin. "There's your kiss. Now let me up." She laughed.

"Again."

She stopped laughing. The word was a trigger, and they both knew it. Montana pulled a hand from her back, stroked the hair out of her face and looked at her as if he were looking for something. He lifted his other hand so both hands cupped her small face, then kissed her gently, with only his dry lips. He whispered against hers, "Later."

Addic sighed, and suddenly he chuckled, pulled her face against his and rubbed the dust and chaff and dirt all over her clean face while she called him every name of any lowlife animal she could think of.

He finally stopped but still held her head while he scrutinized her face. "There, now you look like the wife of a wheat farmer." He sat up with her, ignoring the fist she jabbed in his ribs, then he stood and set her on her feet. With the afternoon sun glaring over his shoulder, she had to crane up to look at him. "The harvest is over, Addie, and we've grown the best damn wheat I've ever seen. Top grade. Let's celebrate tonight."

"How?"

"Pack a dinner for us and I'll take you someplace special." Excited and proud, he looked like a little boy who'd just won a fistful of firecrackers in a Fourth of July race. Just knowing he wanted to share his success with her made Addie feel light as goose feathers, and when he swatted her on the fanny and left to get back to the field, she floated inside.

The clink of gold coins tapped on the kitchen table. Addie stood back by the pantry, watching Montana pay the Blues for the harvest crew. He had pulled out a small sack of gold coins and now he counted them into stacks on the table. They had never talked about money. He always brought out his sack and paid in coin, gold or silver, never with silver certificates—paper bills. She'd thought of bringing up the money issue, of sharing their finances, but he'd always pull out the sack before she could ever reach into her bag. She wondered how long and hard he'd had to work for that money, and doing what. She wanted to ask him what he did before they met, but was still tentative about probing into his past when he was so private about it. He was still a mystery to her in so many ways, and it bothered her sometimes.

She had told Montana of her family, her college experiences, and her childhood. They'd even laughed about Hilary. There were times when they were with the Latimers that they'd all talked about her aunt and the uncle Addie'd never known. After those times she felt a bit closer to her dead aunt and uncle. Montana had always been a part of those conversations, but he never voluntarily talked about his past. She had asked him a few questions, but he'd always given her an evasive answer; even though he was aware that she knew about his mother's death, he still never spoke of it. When she'd try to bring it up, he'd change the subject.

There were times when he seemed preoccupied, and when the weather was hot, he was often moody and quick to anger. She wondered if he just didn't like the heat. After all, he'd nearly bitten her head off the first time she'd spoken to him. It'd been hot that day and so had his temper.

The one thing she knew always set him off was the subject of the railroad. Montana seethed whenever the S.P. was brought up, just like that first time when he'd burned himself with the hot coffee. He would just close up.

One time she came into the barn and heard Will and Montana talking about some incident when they were boys. They'd mentioned the S.P., but she'd only caught the end of their conversation before Montana had spotted her and changed the subject. It was natural to be curious, especially when he was so uncommunicative. They were so relaxed together in so many ways. And it bothered her that talking to him about himself was, as Custus once put it, "like trying to find hair on a frog."

Her parents had had such an open, loving relationship. She could remember them talking about so many things together. They'd had a very honest, open family life. There was nothing that she couldn't talk to her father about, nothing. If he were alive, she knew she could talk to him about Montana. But he wasn't alive, and neither was her mother. Yet she knew Montana cared for her. He was so good to her and he teased her, and when he made love to her, it wasn't an easy, calm thing. It was driven, and hot, and so consuming that she couldn't believe that his heart wasn't involved.

Maybe it was. Maybe he did care more than he knew,

but she also knew that until he could trust her with every-thing, open up to her, really tell her of his hurts and fears and doubts as well as his dreams, until then they didn't have love.

"Well, that's taken care of," Montana said, slipping his arm around her. "Have you got that supper packed?" He craned his head over to try to see the basket she'd set down.

"Yes, and it'll be a surprise too."

He smiled. "Burnt roast and lead biscuits?"

"Nope." She shook her head. "Dry ham and raw mashed potatoes, with chili peppers."

He grabbed the basket and tried to peek inside, but she slipped her arm through it and tucked the cloth tightly around the rim. She slipped her other arm through his, tapping her foot impatiently, and asked, "Are we going to stand here all evening or are we going for a drive?"

"Don't get all snippy, Mrs. Creed. I'll have you know that after I sell this wheat, you'll be married to a very prosperous farmer."

"And I'll have you remember that half that wheat is mine." Her nose shot up.

He rolled his eyes. "How could I forget? No one ever lets me forget about that ruling or our contract, and exactly how much money they won or lost because of me. And Custus is the worst." He led her outside and helped her into the wagon, then jumped up onto the seat. "But since half the wheat is yours, that just means I'm married to a prosperous lady farmer." He winked at her and off they went, rumbling down the dirt road and heading toward the western foothills.

Two hours later, after they'd eaten the cold fried chicken and all the fixings, Addie wiggled her shoulders against the white, mottled trunk of a giant sycamore. Montana opened one eye and stared up at her. "Back itch?"

She nodded, but continued to rub his temples as he lay with his head in her lap.

He closed his eye. "Must be the chaff," he mumbled with a smile.

"Lord, I hope not. I hope that's the last of that horrid stuff I see for a long time." She grimaced.

"At least till next year," Montana reminded her, then he groaned when she must have rubbed a good spot. "That feels great."

"Umm," she answered offhandedly, enjoying the beauty of the country hills.

The sun was just falling behind the hills and the air temperature had cooled. Spread before them like candy gumdrops was a field of wildflowers, pink bleeding hearts, yellow mule's ear, lavender foxglove, and purple monkeyflower. A nearby morning glory had wilted into limp, blue funnels that wouldn't open until the morning sun and dew awakened them. Bright pink bell-shaped blossoms on a vine of twinflowers crept around a crepe myrtle bush, and the sweet, honeysuckle fragrance filled the cool evening air. She took a deep breath. It was like breathing dessert.

The arroyo de Laguna trickled just a scant hundred feet away, and a few giant valley oaks clawed across the gentle, golden rise above them. Over the rise a group of black hawks floated and dipped near the trees, circling and searching for their night's food, and a small, buzzing swarm of mosquitoes and gnats hovered over the field of flowers.

Two mule deer loped up from the arroyo, and Addie caught her breath. The larger one, a light buckskin-colored doe, stopped. Her dark brown ears perked and her head tilted so her light gray nose was up to read the danger. With innocent, apprehensive black eyes she looked right at Addie and Montana, while the smaller deer nibbled on the flowers. Suddenly the doe barked a sharp baa, then twitched her tail, and both deer were gone so fast Addie wondered if she'd really seen them.

"They're beautiful animals," Montana said, staring at the spot where they'd stood.

She was quiet for a minute, then blurted out, "I love California."

He laughed.

"Were you born here?" she asked quietly, holding her breath to see if he'd answer.

His eyes were closed again and she continued to rub his temples. Maybe she could rub the information out of him.

"No," he finally answered.

"Where were you born?"

"Iowa."

Addie smiled. One-word answers, but at least they were answers. She waited a minute before she tried again.

"Have you always farmed?"

"Nope."

"What did you do before you came here?"

Silence. Then he said, "A little of this and a little of that." He raised his hand up and opened his eyes. He drew a finger lightly over her lips, rubbing back and forth, making her forget the next question. His finger traced a path from her lips, up her cheek, down her jaw, and his hand snaked around her neck and he pulled her down to kiss her.

A few minutes later she lay on her back, her dress unbuttoned, her breasts pushed out of her corset, her husband loving her right through the slit in her drawers. As always, her blood heated and her body dewed and suddenly she shuddered, clutching around him, holding him tightly as he found the same tide of release.

By the time the moon had risen, they were turning onto the familiar gravel drive of the farm. Montana pulled the wagon to a stop and unhooked his arm from around her shoulders. He hopped down, helped her and unhitched the team. Addie sauntered over to the back door while he took care of the horses, and stood waiting for him, not wanting the touching to end.

He didn't know she stood there. She could tell by the way he moved, never once looking her way. It was special, watching him move, watching his tall body as he walked the horses to the pump, where he watered them before leading them inside the barn.

Addie still waited, enjoying the clicking crickets, the sigh of the breeze in the eucalyptus, the crackle of drying leaves. The barn door squeaked closed and Montana said something to Custus, then closed the door. He started to walk to the house but stopped and turned back toward the grain wagons lined up next to the barn. He walked over to them, and she watched as he untied one of the tarps. He reached up inside the wagon and pulled out a handful of grain. He just stood there, holding it, looking at it.

She wondered what was going through his mind. His mood had lightened tonight. He was obviously happy. If ever there was a man who loved farming, it was Montana. She'd seen him do the same thing once with the dirt. He'd hunkered down and held it in his hand, like he was trying to make sure it was real and his. Was that what he was doing now? Possibly. He'd told her it was the highest quality grain he'd ever seen, and Bill Blue had said something similar. Montana had been so proud when the harvest boss had complimented him that her heart had skipped when she saw his face.

Yes, she thought, that is what he's doing. He's making sure it's real and not just a dream. And maybe that was why *she* needed to have him hold *her,* so she would know this was real, not just some wonderful dream that would disappear one morning. Or maybe she needed to have him hold her like he'd held the soil, like he was now holding the wheat. Yes, that was it. She needed to have Montana care so much that he had to hold her to see if she was real. Then she'd know she was loved, and they would both know this wasn't a dream.

22

Montana MANEUVERED THE FIVE-MULE TEAM DOWN STOCK-ton's Main Street. It was a bustling town, its dirt and gravel streets filled with vehicles of every kind. A fully loaded depot wagon emblazoned HOTEL CALIFORNIA rattled past him, luggage strapped precariously to the flat, black leather roof, and trunks and bags secured on the boot. The vehicle headed in a rush for the train station, where its passengers would unload and new guests would be taken to the prominent hotel.

Black broughams and Studebaker buggies clustered around the walkways of the Main Street merchants, and some boys, with short pants, caps, and bruised knees, chased an ice wagon, picking at the ice blocks whenever the wagon was slowed by traffic. Barreling a cross path directly in front of Montana was a wagon load of chickens, squawking and cackling in their cages while feathers flew and fluttered in the wagon's wake. Whenever he saw chickens he thought of Addie, buying and half killing all those cockerels. He chuckled to himself, shaking his head; some chicken rancher, getting her green self talked into buying all males. Even now they still had more chicken than he ever cared to eat. He rubbed his unshaven chin thoughtfully as he waited for a freight wagon to lumber by. Maybe he'd buy some beef cattle with some of the money from the sale of the grain.

Glancing over his shoulder, Montana checked to see if Will and Custus were still behind him. They had left Bleeding Heart the day before, each man driving a five-mule team pulling the double-bulk wagons full of wheat. At Mule

Ear, the halfway point, they'd stopped and made camp, catching a few hours sleep before continuing on the remaining miles to Stockton. The sound of Custus swearing a blue streak echoed from behind him. Montana laughed, thinking that at least he knew the old goat was back there. He spotted Will, waved his turn to both men, and slowly turned the team and wagons on the road that led to the grain elevator.

The harnesses clattered and the wooden wagon wheels groaned to a stop at the loading platform of the Avery Bros. Grain Elevator and Silage. White steam sputtered from a Chicago-bound train that was loading on the track that ran behind the elevator. Cattle thundered and bawled up a wooden ramp into a railed cattle car, and the smell of grain and hay and the sharp sting of cow dung sweltered through the hot, Indian summer air.

Will pulled up, followed a few minutes later by Custus, so Montana went up the platform and stood in line at the office where the elevator operator would weigh and grade his wheat. There were quality grades of wheat, from fine, high quality used for special expensive flours, down to poor, low grade wheat that was used for feed mix. The high grade wheat brought eight times more per bushel than the low grade. And for a farmer it meant the difference between prosperity and failure.

By the time Montana's turn came, he, Will, and Custus had been standing in the hot sun for over an hour. It didn't exactly make him overly tolerant of the cocksure little bastard of a operator, who took his sweet time getting out to the bulk wagons.

Montana untied the tarp and pointed to the three sets of double wagons. "Here it is."

"Yeah, yeah, what's the name?" The operator scribbled something on a clipboard, never lifting his weasely face up from his writing.

"Creed, from Bleeding Heart."

Then he looked up, his eyes roved over Montana, assessing him. "Untie all those tarps. I want samples from each wagon load."

Custus butted in, sarcasm dripping from his gruff voice,

"What the hell for? Ya think we done grew one kinda wheat for one wagon and another for them there others?"

"We've been cheated before. If you want to sell the wheat, you'll abide by our rules." The operator eyed all three men. He stood with his bandy legs spread in a belligerent stance, and his attitude said he didn't give a rat's ass if they bought the wheat or not.

Montana and Will untied the tarps, and the operator walked down the platform, scooping out samples of grain from every wagon. Then he left them and went inside for the grading and weighing.

Custus struck a match on his boot and lit a cigar stub, puffing and sucking on the ugly, brown tobacco until the fat tip glowed orange. "Throws up a load of dust for such a li'l sonofabitch."

Montana paced a few short feet of the platform. "He can afford to. Avery's the only grain elevator buying up here."

"Creed!" the operator shouted, waving Montana over to the office. "Pull those wagons up here and unload into the chute. We'll weigh the loads."

He turned to go back inside, but Montana grabbed his sleeve. "What about the grading?"

"We'll give you the grade after it's loaded and weighed. Then you'll be paid." He jerked his arm out of Montana's grip and looked up at him. "If you don't like the terms, take the load away. We got others waiting for you to unload. I ain't got all day."

"Jus' let me git one swing at 'im," Custus muttered to Montana. "I'll knock some sense inta the li'l fart."

"Leave him be, Custus." Montana moved to his wagon and mounted the seat. With a sharp snap of the reins, he pulled forward, then backed into the loading chute, where the grain emptied into the weight shelf and then to the elevator. He pulled the wagon away, unhooked it and backed the front wagon for the same weighing and unloading.

After unloading all the wheat, the three men stood waiting, Montana pacing, Will fidgeting uncomfortably and Custus practicing his punches. The office door creaked open and the operator walked outside. He handed Montana a piece of paper. "Here's the draft for your grain. You can cash it in at the Stockton Bank."

"Wait. This can't be right. My check should be seven or eight times this much." Montana looked at the small figure on the bank draft, a stunned expression on his face.

"Your wheat wasn't up to standard. We paid you for low quality. That's the best we can pay for that grade." The man turned back toward the office, obviously dismissing Montana as inconsequential.

Montana grabbed him and slammed him up against the office wall. "That was high-quality wheat, you bastard," he said through gritted teeth, twisting the man's collar. "And I've got witnesses."

The man's face turned purple and he twisted against Montana's grip. Then he suddenly threw his feet up and kicked Montana in the gut. Montana doubled and fell to his knees, gasping for air.

"Keep your hands off me or I'll tear up that draft. It's the best you'll get from us." He took a step back when Montana looked up at him, so angry he wanted to kill.

Seething, Montana knotted his fists, fighting for control. He lost. His fist shot up and clipped the man right in the chin. He could feel teeth rattle.

"Whoooeeee! Nail that there li'l fart!" Custus yelled, punching his own fists at the air, "Give it ta 'im!"

The operator shook his head and came at Montana, who shoved the man back before grabbing his shirt front and punching him over and over and over. He felt nothing but fury and the physical satisfaction of smashing the man's cheating face in.

The next thing he knew, Will had his arms, holding him back. "Stop, Montana, stop! You'll kill him."

Another man came outside, a rifle pointed at the three men, "Get outta here, or I'll blow yer head off."

Will pulled Montana away. Custus picked up their hats and followed them down the platform and over to the wagon. Will said, "There's nothing you can do, Montana."

He brought his hand to his face, rubbing it to calm himself down. His knuckles were red and bloody and hurt like hell, but he didn't care. They'd all but stolen his wheat, cheated him, and there wasn't a damn thing he could do about it, except maybe kill the bastard.

"Let's get the hell out of here," he said, grabbing his hat from Custus and heading for the wagons.

Halfway there he stopped and spun around, hearing the voice of the man who had taken his wheat, his profit, and his pride. He was slumped between two elevator workers, and he rubbed at the blood on his face. Montana could still feel the soles of the man's boots as they knocked the wind from his gut. He raised a hand and pointed at him. "I'll get you, you bastard. I'll get you." Then he turned back to the wagon, jumped on the seat and took off.

Two hours later he was on the road to Bleeding Heart, Custus and Will driving silently behind him. He'd cashed the draft, knowing that grain operator could cancel it and then he'd have nothing. But now he sat on the hard, wooden wagon seat, with the hot afternoon sun beating down. As he wiped the sweat from his forehead, his mind flashed with the image of his father, angry, just like he was now. He could remember watching his father prowl around the farmhouse, seething at the railroad for trying to steal his land.

He remembered both his and Will's fathers meeting with the men and planning to make a stand, a stand that would eventually take their lives. But what he also remembered were the few times he'd seen his father not looking angry, but looking defeated, like Herbert Schultz had when he'd almost lost his farm. He never thought it would happen to him, but now it had. He had failed just like those men, let himself be manipulated.

The wheat was fine quality, the best, and he knew that when it arrived in Chicago it would be sold as high quality. Then Avery Bros. and the S.P. would split the profit. And he had let them do this. God, what a fool.

He was tired, so goddamn tired, but he sat taller, throwing his aching shoulders back. He wouldn't let them slump. They wouldn't do to him what they did to the others. He'd fight back. As God was his witness, he'd fight back.

Addie pulled her hair back and tied it with a deep green

bow. Her long black hair hung down her back, the way Montana liked it. She smiled. He'd be home soon. Tilting up her watch pendant, she checked the time: six-thirty. The evening light had faded from the south windows, so she went to the shades and pulled them, walking away as they retracted with a couple of loud flaps. One last glance in the mirror, a quick pinch of her pale cheeks, and she left the bedroom, heading for the kitchen where dinner simmered on the stove.

Half an hour later the table was set, dinner was ready, and Addie paced like a nervous bride. She'd missed Montana. Last night had been the first night they'd been apart since their marriage. But it was for a good reason; actually, the best reason. By now he'd sold their wheat and was on his way home, probably busting at the seams with pride.

A horse rode down the drive and she ran to the window. It was him. She untied her apron and hung it on a hook before racing out the back door. Down the steps she ran, unable to keep her excitement locked inside.

"Montana!" she called and ran toward him, her feet moving so fast that gravel spit up in her wake. He dismounted and she flew into his arms.

"Addie . . ." he whispered, catching her and holding her so tight her ribs ached, but she didn't care. He had missed her.

She smiled into his warm neck, then looked up. "Well, how's the most prosperous farmer in the valley?"

His arms slackened and he let her slide to the ground, his face suddenly hard. He turned to his saddlebags, pulled out an envelope and slapped it into her hands. "Here's the money."

She jerked back a bit, his voice was so angry. Staring at the envelope, she noticed its thinness. Slowly she opened it and looked inside. There couldn't have been more than a hundred dollars, much less than he'd mentioned making the other night. He had uncinched the saddle and carried it toward the barn, his horse following behind him. He hadn't said another word, and acted as if she didn't exist. He moved with purpose through the barn, getting rid of the saddle, settling the horse in his stall and brushing him, much harder than usual. He didn't look at her, and she sensed he was doing it on purpose.

Something had happened, but what? And what could she do? She felt helpless, afraid to talk about the money and afraid not to. "Where are Custus and Will?"

"In town." He kept brushing his horse.

"The wagons?"

"I took them and the teams back to the livery." He stopped currying and looked right at her with coldness in his eyes. "I paid the livery, and Will and Custus." He walked past her. "That's all that's left."

"Montana, wait!" She reached out but missed him as he tossed the curry comb across the barn and walked out the doors, not bothering to close them.

Her shoulders fell and she slowly moved to the doors. The back door banged closed, and through the windows she could see him walk through the house. He stopped in the dining room and a moment later she saw him lift a bottle of brandy to his lips, drinking a long time, too long and too much. He must have been swindled by the granary. She knew from the women's meeting that the grain people had somehow managed to get in cahoots with the crooked railroad, but with Wade working so hard at the state capital, she hadn't thought they'd be affected. And Montana never mentioned the possibility of this happening to him.

He must be crushed, she thought, remembering how excited he'd been when the harvest was done. He'd been proud and happy, but not now. Now he was angry and defeated. She tried to think of something she could do to help. When her father had problems, her mother had been there for him, and she wanted to be there for Montana.

Slowly, she walked to the house, went inside and headed into the dining room. He was gone now; so was the bottle. She turned off the lamps and went into the bedroom. He lay on the bed, fully clothed, his boots against the coverlet like he had that time she'd dumped the water on him. He held the bottleneck in his fist and he stared right through her.

"Montana, tell me what happened." She sat on the edge of the bed.

He raised the bottle and swallowed. "There's nothing to tell."

She sagged on a sigh. "When are you going to talk to me?"

"I thought I was talking to you." He drank again.

"Please, let me help." Addie reached out and tried to put her hand on his.

He jerked it back and shot off the bed, bottle in hand. "How are you going to help? Can you make the the grain operator honest? Can you make the wheat suddenly reappear so I can haul it somewhere else to sell? How are you going to help? By putting labels with stupid, senseless numbers on all my troubles? Will that make it all perfect?" He bent over the bed, moving his angry, scorn-filled face closer. "Or maybe you'll just hop on that stupid bicycle and ride the hell away from a loser like me. That's what you ought to do, get the hell out!" He threw the bottle against the wall. It broke and a brown stain of brandy ran to the floor.

She felt helpless and hurt, but she knew he hurt too, so she didn't lash out, she just searched his tight-featured face, while her mind groped for something to say.

"Hell! You don't have to get out, I'll get out!" He left the room. Then the back door slammed, and a few minutes later he rode away.

Addie sat there, alone, empty and aching. She didn't cry. She felt too impotent. She loved Montana and she couldn't help. He wouldn't let her. All she wanted to do was hold him and have him need her, need to hold her. But he didn't. She stared at the broken pieces of glass lying on the floor, shattered like her heart, shattered like her dream.

23

THE S.P. WAS ROBBED AGAIN. THIS TIME JUST A FEW MILES from Bleeding Heart." John Latimer lifted a coffee cup to his lips, sipped, then set it down, his large sun-browned hands dwarfing it.

"There was some of them there railroad agents in them fancy suits and preacher-white collars sniffin' all over town when I picked up them supplies." Custus settled back against his creaking chair, chewing on what Addie would have sworn was the same cigar stub he'd been masticating for months.

"I heard," John said, then added, "They say it was the same two bandits that were doing all those robberies a while back. They got fifty thousand in gold."

"Whoooeee." Custus rolled the cigar to the other side of his mouth, shaking his head.

Addie finished pouring coffee into the other cups, and she paused over Montana's. His knuckles were bruised black and blue, except for some splits in the skin which had scabbed, and they were swollen something fierce. She winced and he looked up at her, his eyes completely unreadable. His face was still taut with stone hard anger, his lips in a straight, hard line, his eyes alert and suspicious; his neck muscles were tight, and she could see the blood pump through the veins there. Nothing had changed since the night before—except he was back home. Her pride wouldn't let her ask where he'd been, so she walked back to the stove and tried to look busy while she listened to the men talk.

Montana and Will had ridden back to the farm early that

morning. Both of them were covered with dust, unshaven, and broodingly quiet. Montana had gone inside, grabbed some clothes, and in passing, the only thing he'd said to her was a cold, "I'm back." He left her standing in the farmyard as he headed for the barn. Less than an hour later he emerged all cleaned up. Then Custus had returned with their wagon filled with supplies, and John Latimer had come over right afterward. There had been no chance for Montana and Addie to talk or be alone.

But it hadn't mattered that they couldn't talk because she had decided not to talk to him. Gripping the handle on a cast-iron pan a bit harder than necessary, she lifted it off the stove and went to the sinkboard, filling it with water from the hand pump. If he was bent on closing her out of his life, then nothing she could say or do would change his mind. The pump handle whipped up and down, water gushing like a flash flood from the spigot. *He* was the one who had to learn to open up. *He* had to let her into his life and his thoughts, even his pain, otherwise they'd never have a good relationship, and she'd never break through his hardheaded, close-mouthed barrier. The sound of the pan overflowing stilled her rapid pumping. She stared at the full sink basin a bit sheepishly, then glanced over her shoulder to make sure no one had noticed.

No one had. Montana still sat there hardly saying a word, but listening to John and Custus talk. There was to be another grange meeting. Wade had come back from Sacramento and there was news. Addie scrubbed the pot with a brush, but not too vigorously because then she couldn't hear them. The sinkboard was a distance from the table, and the kitchen window was open to let in a wisp of a breeze. Outside, John's team moved, shifted, and the harness jangled, and that—combined with the slop of a water-filled basin, the cackle of her chickens, and a distant bawl from Mabel or Maud—made her eavesdropping harder.

"Well, I've got to get back to the farm. The Blues are harvesting the last of the west field today. I wanted to let you know about the meeting tonight." John stood and picked up his hat.

"We'll be there," Montana told him. Addie wondered if she was included in that "we."

Then she got her answer.

"Hettie said she'll see you tonight, Addie," John said, and then he and the men went outside.

They stood talking, then John Latimer said something and clapped Montana on the back. Custus jabbered away and threw some mock punches, as if he were fighting with the air. She should have followed them outside and listened out there. John and Custus probably knew more about Montana's problems than she did. And that hurtful thought just reminded her of where she stood in her relationship with her husband. She stood locked outside, until he wanted to let her in.

The grange hall was packed; every person in Alameda County appeared to be there. Montana had gone outside a few minutes before with Wade, Levi, and Will. As Addie sat on a hard, creaky wooden folding chair, she looked around the room. Every chair except the one next to hers was occupied. Smoke and sweat and kerosene filled the hot, tight air and floated along the ceiling of the room like early morning fog. She pulled out a lace hankie from its hiding place beneath her tight cuff and fanned her damp face, absentmindedly listening to the surrounding chatter.

The chair next to her clattered and groaned as Montana sat down. Anticipation silenced the room as the tall, dark figure of the grange lawyer, Wade Parker, and the shorter figure of Levi Hamilton, moved toward the front. They threaded their way down the narrow, overflowing aisle, heading for the platform where the band had played the night of the dance. Now a wooden podium, slightly orange with varnish, stood alone, awaiting its speaker. There was none of the sense of merriment that had been present that night a few months ago. The only thing in the air tonight, other than sweat, lamp oil and smoke, was tension—straining, vibrating tension—and everyone there felt it.

Levi stood back a bit while Wade stepped up to the podium, clearing his throat before he spoke. "As you all know, at the last meeting we decided to try to raise more funds to build a people's railroad. It's a big job, but there's been support from all over the state. The ranchers in the valley are having the same problems with the railroad that we are. The freight rates go up daily and they're getting no more for their cattle than you are for your grain."

The room grumbled and Wade held up his hand to quiet them. "The farmers need grange-operated elevators so we can stop the practice of downgrading the grain. We have to have the People's Railroad to ship because the railroad won't ship for granary operations that they don't own. Right now the grain operators are in cahoots with the railroad, but they know that they're our only means of getting the grain to the eastern market. They'll use it to make as much money as they can. Although I understand in Stockton that that weasel, Charles Avery, is sporting a broken nose, about five less teeth, and a shiner swole up the size of a Pasadena orange. That might make him less likely to downgrade any wheat for a while."

There was laughter and a few men turned and looked at Montana. Addie glanced at his mangled fist, and now she understood.

"The plans are in motion. There will be five elevators operated by the Association of Farmers in Modesto, the Fresno Brotherhood of the Land, the two grange associations in Alameda and Costra Costa Counties; and the Northern and Central California Cattlemen's Associations have started the funding for the People's Railroad, which still needs more major funding. It will ship the grain and cattle to the eastern markets. Both the farmers and the ranchers will be assured of fair treatment." Again everyone started talking, so Wade banged a meeting gavel on the podium. "You haven't heard the best news, yet. Today the People's Railroad Fund received an anonymous donation of fifty thousand dollars."

Cheers erupted in the room and Addie could hear Custus's whooping above all the others.

"I think we'll have something to say about that money." A voice shouted from the back of the room and the place suddenly quieted. A wave of heads turned like wheat in the wind toward the voice. Addie tried to crane over the people

317

behind her to see who had spoken. Bootsteps pounded from the back and then five men in dark coats and white shirts walked toward Wade Parker.

Immediately, Montana stood, stepping over Addie to the side aisle. Frowning, she followed his movements with her worried eyes and saw him nod at Will and Custus. They mimicked his movement. The three men lounged against the window walls, watching. She caught Hettie's worried look and was sure it mirrored her own, then she noticed that John and some other men were in the same positions as Montana. The men looked itching for a fight, so she closed her eyes and silently prayed.

The short, swarthy leader of the suited men confronted Wade. "Where'd you get that money?"

"As I said before, it was an anonymous donation." Wade stood a bit taller and his shoulders arched back, straighter. He looked pleased, not the least bit intimidated. "And what business is it of yours?"

"We're agents for the S.P., except for Mr. Howell here, who's a federal marshal." The man nodded at a tall, ordinary-looking man who stood on his right.

Montana stepped up on the left side of the platform and slowly walked to stand behind Wade. John did the same. The room was silent except for the hollow thud of boots stepping on the platform, which matched the insistent pounding of Addie's heart. Will and the others followed Montana from the left and John's side filed up from the right. Then a wall of fifteen men, three times that of the railroad, was standing behind Levi Hamilton and Wade Parker.

Finally the railroad agent spoke, "Hand over that money."

With a knowing smile, Wade gestured to Levi. "Ask my colleague, here."

"First of all, it's been deposited in the grange association's account. Isn't that right, Collins?" Levi called out.

The banker stood. "Sure is, all nice and tight in the vault."

Titters of laughter ran through the audience.

"What makes you think it's the railroad's?" Wade asked

with a suppressed smile. It looked to Addie as if he was enjoying this.

"You damn well know that fifty thousand was stolen from the S.P. number seven, just after midnight last night. The train was only five miles outside of town when it was hit."

"That's too bad." Wade leaned casually against the podium and he smiled, making it obvious that he wasn't the least bit sorry. Then he said, "But I don't see that your loss has anything to do with our donation. Do you, Levi?"

"No," Levi answered to chuckles from the room.

The marshal stepped forward. "How was the donation paid?"

"Just appeared on my office desk this morning," Wade said with a straight face. "There was a note that said, 'For the People's Railroad Fund.' "

"Was the money in paper or gold?" the marshal asked.

"Gold." Wade didn't flinch. The whole room was well-aware that the money was the S.P.'s, but no one gave a hoot, because the railroad had, in some way, put the screws to almost every person in that room.

"The stolen money was gold." The marshal just stared at Wade.

"It's the railroad gold, Parker, and we want it," the agent said.

"Prove it." Wade smiled.

"We don't have to prove it!" the agent shouted. "It's obvious that's our money!"

"Just prove it and we'll be happy to give it back. Right, Levi?" Wade continued egging the railroad men on.

"Sure," Levi agreed. "Unlike the railroad, we don't want money that doesn't belong to us."

"Fifty thousand in gold was stolen last night, and suddenly fifty thousand in gold appears in your office? Anyone with a lick of sense can tell that's the same money!" The agent was shouting mad.

"Circumstantial," both lawyers said in unison.

There were snickers from some of the people in the room.

"You bastard! You know gold coin can't be traced.

Where else would you farmers get that kind of money?" The agent started to step onto the platform, and the line of men behind the lawyers moved forward. The marshal grabbed the man's arm and pulled him back, shaking his head while he quietly spoke to him.

Custus spit out his cigar stub. "Ya know what? I bet all them there farmers and ranchers that ya've been a-screwin' for fifteen years has been savin' up their gold, jus' a-pilin' it up. Can't ya picture all them there broken-down men and widows savin' and scrimpin'? I reckon over that many years it'd be about fifty thousand." He looked at Wade.

"Sounds logical to me," he agreed, and the room erupted with laughter.

"We'll get that money! The courts will see it our way," the agent threatened, then he turned to the others and said, "Let's get the hell outta here." And they filed out.

"Tell the S.P. that maybe they ought to ship paper bills from now on. They have serial numbers!" Wade called out after them.

The back door slammed shut and the room became silent, then someone started clapping and the whole grange filled with applause. Wade smiled, but then his face grew serious and he held up his hands in a quieting gesture. "We'll have to fight them in court, but I'm not too concerned. If we can get those bastards in court, we can win."

"What about the railroad-bought judges?" someone yelled out.

"The mood in Sacramento is changing, for the good," Wade answered. "The state legislature has followed Congress, and they've formed a regulatory commission to try to control the railroad. It's still pretty green, though, and their power is limited. The courts are where we need to get support, and I was assured that there is progressive movement in that area. And I'll not let them get their hands on that money. Levi's deposited it in the fund's account, and they can't touch it without a court order."

"Then we got 'em," someone yelled from the audience.

"With the money, yes, but they can cause other problems. They could do what they've done in the past," Levi warned. "They could hire thugs to start harassing the women, burn people out. When they tried to fight back in Tulare County, two of the men in charge had their homes burned and some others were beaten pretty badly. If tonight was an example of the railroad's plans, I don't think it'll stop with just a court threat, especially if they hear that we're trying to get the case tried by Judge Higgins. The railroad doesn't own him."

Montana stepped forward. "We won't let them threaten us. I'm willing to fight back." Addie cringed when he held up his bruised fists.

"We can't afford to back down now, we all have to fight," John Latimer agreed.

The other men shouted their agreement. It appeared to Addie that every man there was ready to stand up to the railroad, no matter what it took. But she wondered how many of their wives were scared, like she was. She looked at Montana, standing with the other men, his eyes glimmering with a need that she couldn't understand, and it scared her. There was no fear in any of the men's eyes; in fact there was a sense of challenge and excitement. But Addie didn't feel it; there was no thrill in this for her. When she looked at Montana and saw that he was just edging for a fight, her stomach tightened with fear. She didn't want him hurt, and she was darn scared he would be.

After a few minutes the room began to clear and she went up to the platform, standing back from the men with Hettie and Lizzie.

"You think this is a good idea?" she asked Hettie.

"We have no choice," Hettie answered. "I'll back my John in whatever he decides. He said Wade thinks we'll be able to beat them."

"I'm scared, Hettie," she admitted in a whisper.

"It'll be all right, Addie," Lizzie said brightly, slipping an arm around her shoulder. "Will won't let anything happen. He's ready for them, and so is Montana. I know they'll beat them."

She looked at Lizzie. Her green, adoration-filled eyes were on Will Murdoch. The girl thought Will could single-handedly turn the world. Addie wasn't that blinded by love. She'd heard about the railroad thugs, the beatings and the burning out of those who'd tried to make a stand against them, and she didn't want Montana to be one of the victims.

The men joined them, and Lizzie linked her arm through Will's. "You were wonderful," she heard the girl whisper, and Will grew a foot with pride.

Will turned to Montana. "I was worried for a bit. It was too much like Mussel Slough."

Montana nodded, but Addie was completely lost. She didn't understand what they spoke of.

"I thought they'd start shooting any minute," Will admitted.

"I wish they would have," Montana said, his voice as hard and cold as the wind off Lake Michigan. It bit right through Addie. He meant it. He really wanted a shoot-out with those men. Lord, what had happened to him? He was harder now than when they'd first met.

"Let's go," he told her, and she gave mechanical responses to the good-nights they received from their friends. Montana led her down the steps, and soon she was on the wagon seat, listening to Custus retell the whole horrible night in his excited male manner.

The entire way home she was silent, praying that her sense of impending doom was wrong. When they reached the farm, Montana helped her down and she went straight to bed. She could hear the men talking in the kitchen after they'd taken care of the team and the wagon. She covered her ears, not wanting to hear any more.

Sometime later, she felt Montana crawl into bed. He didn't hold her, didn't put his ever-cold feet against her legs, didn't even touch her. He just stayed on his side of the bed until his breathing was slow and even. But she couldn't go back to sleep. Instead she hugged her pillow and prayed over and over that God would make everything okay.

It was dawn when someone pounded on the door and woke Addie. Montana was still asleep, then the pounding got louder. He sat up.

"What time is it?" he said, rubbing a hand over his eyes.

"About five, I think." Addie started to get out of bed.

"I'll get it." He placed his hand on her arm to stop her and climbed out of bed, then he slipped into his pants. He crossed to the door but turned back and reached out to grab his gun belt, buckling it on as he walked through the hall.

That got her out of bed fast. She shoved her arms into her dressing gown as she ran after him. At the end of the short hallway she stopped and peered around the corner. Montana drew his gun and looked out the parlor window. Then he frowned, drew a hand through his hair and opened the front door.

"Montana Creed?" came a man's voice.

"Yes?" Montana held the gun poised in front of him.

Another gun clicked from outside, and Addie held her breath.

"I'm the U.S. marshal, and you're under arrest."

She gasped and stepped into the room.

"What for?" Montana asked.

"The robberies of the S.P.," the man said. Addie moved to stand next to her husband. Five more men stood outside, and the railroad agent was with them. "Put the gun away. We don't want any trouble. We've already got your friend."

Both Addie and Montana looked out into the dark drive, where a group of horses stood. A man had his gun pointed at Will Murdoch, who sat atop a horse, his hands tied in front of him.

"You okay, Will?" Montana called out.

"Yeah."

"Oh my God . . ." she whispered, looking into Montana's hard face. He turned his gun over to the men, and she grabbed his arm. "No!"

"It's okay, Addie," he told her, but the men pulled him away and wrapped a rope around his wrists.

"You come too, Mrs. Creed. We need to ask you some questions," the marshal said, poking Montana in the back with his gun, indicating he should go down the steps.

"Leave her out of this," Montana said, spinning around and standing threateningly tall above the smaller marshal.

He acted like he didn't care about the rope that held his hands immobile.

"Get on the horse, Creed. You have nothing to say in this," the marshal told him. "Take him away."

She watched them pull Montana down the steps and across to a horse. Three men held guns on him. A movement behind her caught her attention, and she turned away from the marshal. Custus stood inside with a rifle pointed at the open doorway. He dropped its barrel and said, "I'll drive ya ta town. Get dressed."

She ran out of the room and into her bedroom, where she dressed and raced back out. When she got to the porch, Custus waited in the wagon, but Montana and the men were gone.

She jumped into the wagon. "Where are they?"

"I sent them on. I'm gonna take ya there, then I'll see if I can catch that Parker fella afore he leaves fer Sacramenta." Custus slapped the reins, and the wagon and team sped toward town, Addie praying that it was all a bad dream.

It wasn't a nightmare, but everything she'd been told in the last two hours was.

She sat in a smelly little room in the Bleeding Heart jail—the building whose roof had looked like it was sinking toward the ground. It was dark inside and the floors were covered with dust and mud and what smelled like cattle dung. And she was in a waiting room; she could imagine what the cell that held Montana was like.

In this horrid little room she had finally found out about Montana's past, but he hadn't done the telling. The marshal told her of some incident almost fifteen years before. It was something called the Mussel Slough Tragedy. When he'd said the name, her stomach took a deep dive. She remembered Will referring to it the night before, and the tie-in made them look all that much more guilty.

Then she heard about the killings, and that the incident happened on Montana's family's place. She heard how his father and Will's had been shot and their land confiscated. Then she heard about all the train robberies that started late last year. With the telling of each incident, her hopes for her husband died more and more.

But Lord, it was all so awful she didn't blame him. Addie understood hatred, and fear. She hated horses because of what they had done to her parents, and that had been an accident. But the railroad had killed Montana's father, shot him in cold blood and gotten away with it. It was no wonder he hated them. Just hearing of the injustice of the whole thing made her feel the same way.

About halfway through the story, Custus had entered with Levi. Wade had already left for the capital. Shortly after that, two of the railroad agents came in and stood in back watching her. The mouthy leader from the night before was there. Up close he had little beady eyes and pockmarked cheeks. He was short and pudgy and his rabid, vengeful look made her skin crawl.

Now they all listened to the marshal, who seemed to be the fairest man there. "Will Murdoch and your husband, Montana Creed, both fit the description of the robbers. Along with the fact that they had motive from their families' involvement in the Mussel Slough incident, it's enough to have them charged and tried for the crimes." He paused a moment, then began to question her. "How long have you been married, Mrs. Creed?"

"Five months."

He thumbed through some papers. "You were married on . . ."

"May fourteenth."

"What were the dates of the robberies?" Levi asked.

The marshal checked a paper and read them off. Addie tried to remember back to see if any of the dates could have been wrong, but she was so shaken, she couldn't place any time or date. The latest robbery kept running through her mind. It was the night that Montana had stormed out and hadn't come home until late morning. Will had been gone too. There were earlier robberies, ones since they'd both been on the farm, but Montana had been gone a lot at first. He was always riding in and out, and she had tried to avoid him so much at first that she hadn't paid any attention to the length of his disappearances. Now she knew why he'd told her so little, why he'd been so evasive. And now she knew where his money came from and why he'd always used gold coin. Oh God, but after what she'd learned today she didn't blame him.

The marshal finished listing the dates and turned to Addie. "Can you tell us of your husband's whereabouts on any of these dates, Mrs. Creed?"

She paused and took a deep breath. "My husband cannot be guilty, Marshal. The night of the last robbery he was with me the entire night." Addie looked straight at the marshal, then she looked at her lawyer. Levi's mouth broke into an approving smile.

"She's lying!" The railroad agent glared at her.

The marshal scrutinized her for a moment, then he asked, "What about any of these other dates?"

She looked at Levi. He gave her a slight nod, so she turned the paper so she could pretend to go over it. All the other dates were before they had married.

"Get Mr. Creed and bring him in here," the marshal ordered one of his men.

A moment later Montana stood across from Addie, handcuffed. He looked at her, but she couldn't read anything in his eyes, except maybe a bit of forced pride. She wondered if the pride was there because of what he had done, or to cover up the humiliation of her seeing him like this.

"I understand you arrived from Chicago last April?" the marshal questioned her.

"That's right."

"There was a robbery on April eighteenth." The man awaited her response.

"He was with me." She didn't even blink.

"Uh, Mrs. Creed. I've been told about the circumstances at your farm. I understand that both of you were occupying the property, but how could you be sure he was there?"

She looked at Montana. Now he was glaring at her, but she didn't care. She loved him, and by God she would lie to save him. "He was in my bed, Marshal. I think I'd have been able to tell if he had left it."

There was a cough of embarrassment, but she didn't give

326

a fig. She glanced at Montana's hands, cuffed together. His knuckles, even the bruised ones, were white.

She turned to the marshal and smiled, as innocently as she possibly could.

"Unlock the handcuffs, Ned."

"You can't let him go! She's lying to protect him!" The agent argued with the marshal.

"My client knows she has to speak the truth here. Can you prove he's the robber, or that she's lying?" Levi said.

The agent didn't say a word. He turned fuming red.

They released Montana, and Addie asked, "What about Will?"

"Was he in your bed too?" the railroad agent sneered.

Montana jumped at him, but the deputy held him back. Levi helped Addie up and put her arm through his. "I'll take care of Will. Just get Montana out of here." He patted her arm as he led her outside. "You did fine, don't worry," he told her.

She turned around and saw exactly why she should worry. Montana was livid.

"I don't understand why you're so angry." Addie looked at her husband. He stared straight ahead, his face taut, but there was an angry twitch in his cheek.

"You're not going to say a word, are you?" she asked, still watching his cheek twitch. Then his hands tightened on the reins so hard that one fist began to shake. She didn't think he had a right to act all angry with her, especially since she'd gotten him out of jail. "I'd think you could at least say thank you."

Very slowly he turned his head. He seethed at her for a few more moments, which did no good because she just stared back, then he said, "Shut . . . up. "

"Fine," she said in a witchy tone, throwing her shoulders back and staring straight ahead. She could be angry too. Not a minute passed before she spoke again. The words were just itching to get past her mouth. "I saved your life and you tell me to shut up. Nice, real nice."

He swore. *That* word did shut her up.

Ten minutes of brooding silence passed before he turned

the wagon onto the gravel drive. He didn't stop in front of the farmhouse like Addie thought he would. He pulled the wagon over in the shade of the barn.

"What are you doing?" she asked.

He jumped down from the wagon and turned. "Get down."

She scooted over to his side of the wagon. Her side was blocked by the wall of the barn. His hands grabbed her waist and he pulled her off the wagon and set her on the ground so hard her teeth rang. "Get inside."

She looked up at him. He'd never ordered her around like that. "Excuse me?" she said, letting him know she didn't like it one bit.

"Get inside," he repeated through a jaw so tight the words almost vibrated.

Her nose shot up. "No."

The next thing she knew, she was flung over his shoulder, staring at his broad back while he stormed toward the farmhouse. "Put me down!"

He walked up the stairs, and she was sure he purposely jarred her, then he went through the house and into the bedroom. He dumped her on the bed and turned to walk out of the room.

"You bully!" she screamed, wanting a fight.

He stopped at the doorway. "I might be a bully, Addie, but I'm not a train robber." And with that he walked out.

She'd had an hour to mull her mistake over in her mind. At first, when Montana had left the room, she'd lain on the bed, stunned. He'd told her he was innocent. Guilt flooded through her. She hadn't believed in him, her own husband and the man she loved.

But the more she thought about the situation, chewing herself out, the more she realized that she really couldn't take all the blame on her small shoulders. If he hadn't been so close-mouthed and secretive about his past and all, she wouldn't have had reason to suspect him. So for the last fifteen minutes she had thought of all the reasons why her actions were perfectly justified, considering.

And now she was dadgum mad!

She stomped down the steps and headed for the barn. It

took a minute for her eyes to adjust to the barn's darkness. She could hear him milking one of the cows, so she stepped around one of Custus's loose barn chickens and walked toward the cattle stanchions.

A pail of milk sat to one side, and Montana sat on a stool milking the other cow, either Mabel or Maud, she couldn't tell which was which unless she was milking them. Then she could see that Mabel had a star-shaped group of freckles on her udder.

Addie stood at the end of the stall. The only sounds in the big barn were the occasional cackle and scratch of a chicken, the ring of milk against the tin pail and the creak of a wooden stanchion as the cow strained to get more hay.

"It's your fault I lied," she informed him.

He didn't say a word.

"See," she said, pointing an accusing finger at him. "This is exactly why I thought you were guilty. You won't talk to me!"

He finished milking and stood with the full pail. As he walked past her he said, "Because I don't talk I'm a train robber, right?"

She scurried after him. "Yes," she said when he stopped and set the milk down next to the other pail. "If you weren't so secretive about everything, I wouldn't have thought you had something to hide!"

He grabbed both pails and headed for the barn doors, with Addie marching right behind him.

"Don't you walk away from me when I'm talking to you!" She grabbed the back of his waistband and belt with both hands and tried to stop him.

He stopped for a second, then kept walking. She dug her heels into the dirt but it didn't stop him, he just kept right on walking and dragging her behind him across the barn. Her hands slipped and she fell backward, her fanny slamming on the hard dirt. She'd swear she heard a snort of laughter, and that really made her mad. He thought their marriage was a joke!

A nest for one of the barn chickens sat a few feet away. There were two eggs in it. She crawled over and grabbed one; then, taking aim, she yelled, "Damn you, stop!" And she let loose with the egg.

It hit him right in the back of the head.

He stopped. Very slowly he turned, yellow egg yolk and broken shell dripping from his hair.

Addie still knelt by the nest. "Don't walk away from me when I'm talking to you," she said, much less forcefully than before. Then she added quietly, "I don't like it."

She took her eyes off him for a second so she could get up, and never saw him move until it was too late.

He dumped a full pail of warm milk right on her head.

She screamed, then swiped the milk-soaked hair out of her eyes. By then Montana stood by the barn door, one pail still in his hand. "I'll talk to you when I damn well feel like it, and not until then. A man doesn't feel like talking when he realizes the woman he loves doesn't trust him." He left the barn.

The woman he loves?

He was in the kitchen before she caught him. He had set the milk down by the door and turned just as Addie raced through the kitchen door, dripping milk everywhere. "You love me?" she squeaked.

"Of course I love you," he told her in a tone that said she should have known it.

"You never told me."

"Jesus Christ, Addie, I married you, didn't I?" He still looked angry.

"All you ever said was 'I care,' not 'I love you'!" She planted her hands on her hips again. "See, that just proves I'm right. You never tell me anything."

"God, why do I feel like that hawk, with some pesky little thing pecking at me?" He rolled his eyes heavenward.

"Well, you don't tell me things." She marched toward him, her shoes making a loud squishing noise. She stopped directly in front of him, dripping. "Put yourself in my place. I don't know where you came from, how you got your money. You always paid for everything with gold or silver coin. You hate the railroad, but I don't know why, and you were gone with no explanation the night the train was robbed. Now what would you think?"

He stood there, quietly thoughtful. Then he gave a quick snort of laughter, as if now he understood. "I guess I would have thought the same thing," he admitted. Then he opened his arms and she was there, holding him as tight as her small, damp arms could.

She felt his chin rest atop her wet head. "I was so drunk when I left here that night, I fell off Jericho and slept by the side of the road. I woke up and was headed back here when I ran into Will."

"You could have told me," she said.

"We weren't speaking much, remember?"

She nodded, wiping little beads of milk on his shirt.

He continued, "I've lived all over California, working as a hired hand. I worked for some wheat-harvesting crews for a while and on a cattle spread near San Jose. My last job was near Tehachapi, baling hay. I always asked for my pay in gold because my pa didn't believe in bills. He got some bad paper money once when he was a kid and never forgot it.

"I hate the railroad because of what they did to him. He was an honest man, Addie, and he worked damn hard. He lost everything. We weren't wealthy, but to Pa the land meant wealth. Those railroad men have so much, mansions all over the state, enough money to buy congressmen and judges and newspapers. They didn't need to sell our land too, just like they didn't need the profit from our wheat." His arms tightened around her.

She moved against him. "I love you, Montana. I don't want anything to happen to you."

"Nothing's going to happen, Addie." He picked her up by the waist and started to kiss her, but she pulled back. "Say it," she demanded.

He smiled. "You are like that barn swallow, but I do love you."

Then she kissed him. Her arms wrapped around his neck and her fingers went instinctively to his hair.

"Ugh . . ." She pulled away and frowned at her hand. It was sticky with egg. She looked up at him. "Egg," she said.

331

He looked down at his wet shirtfront. "Milk," he said. They laughed.

"Do you care?" he asked her, looking at the egg on her hand.

"No." She pointed to the milk stains. "Do you?"

"No." And he carried her to the bedroom.

24

THE MONTHS PASSED QUICKLY FOR ADDIE. HER MARRIAGE was all she had dreamed of, and more. Wade Parker had gotten Will Murdoch out of jail. The robberies had always been done by two men, and without Montana, they had no case against Will. Public sentiment toward the railroad had changed, even in San Francisco, where the railroad barons had always had influence. The railroad was no longer viewed as the golden link between east and west. Now it was fast becoming likened to a grasping octopus, with its greedy tentacles wrapped around the people who could least afford to fight it.

Montana was very active in the work on the People's Railroad, as were many of the local farmers. Wade Parker had made inroads in Sacramento, and Levi had managed to get the court case on Judge Higgins's docket. It wasn't due to come to trial for months, but rumor had it that the railroad was running scared.

There had been an incident here and there, and Wade Parker was beaten up on one of his trips north, but the farmers and ranchers stood strong, and the lawyer now had a bodyguard—Will.

Montana, like some others, had planted a crop of barley, which they could sell in Southern California and transport themselves, eluding the railroad's crooked practices. And they'd bought a few head of cattle, because he was "damn sick of fried chicken." She'd bought more chickens, once she'd sold the cockerels for eating, but this time she'd bought them sexed. She could even say that word now without blushing, so she knew she was really a farm woman, about some things.

Others, well, they took some getting used to—like Thanksgiving. What a teary week that had been. They'd killed the tom turkey, the one she'd renamed Bartholomew. There had been a big turkey dinner with the Latimers, but Addie hadn't touched the meat. She'd felt like a cannibal. She'd never felt that way about the chickens, but there was something sentimental about that silly turkey.

Of course, Montana didn't think like she did. Addie suggested they cook Jericho, but he didn't see the humor in that statement. She thought it was pretty funny considering the animal had done nothing to change her low opinion of it—it'd eaten over a dozen loaves of bread, a cake, and the potato salad for a Sunday picnic.

On the drive home from the Latimers' Thanksgiving night, Montana told her she could never name a food animal again. But she ignored him, figuring what he didn't know wouldn't hurt him. Last week she'd named all the cattle.

But now it was late on a Saturday afternoon and the rich red soil of the new irrigation ditches formed small dirt frames around the fields. A clear, Pacific-blue sky met the buckskin-colored hills, and the hawks meandered overhead, searching for their evening meal. The air was still, no late afternoon breeze, nothing in the air but the distant bawl of a cow and the rumble and scratch of the chickens.

Another grange meeting was scheduled for that night, so Montana had come in early, bathed, and now stood in the barn as Addie rolled her bicycle from an empty stall.

"You're going to hold me to that silly bargain?" Montana gave her bicycle a look of dread.

"Uh-huh." Addie maneuvered it through the crackling hay that covered the dirt floor to where her husband stood, a twenty-eight-year-old man who looked at the cycle as a young boy looks at a spoonful of cod liver oil. Which reminded her . . . She unchained her lollipop-shaped oil can from the handlebars, then bent down and squeezed a few drops of cycle oil on the chain mechanism. She purposely ignored Montana's groaning because she was not going to let him get out of this. Biting back a smile, she stood. "There. Now you're all set. Where shall we begin the lesson?"

He grimaced at the cycle.

"Let's go outside." She rolled the cycle out the barn doors and waited. He didn't follow her, so she backed up and stretched her neck around the door. He still stood there frowning.

"Come on!" She stood there until he reluctantly followed her around to the back of the barn. Once behind the barn, she leaned the bike against the barn wall and checked out the ground, which was dusty but hard-packed, and much easier for him to maneuver the pneumatic tires.

"Now . . ." Addie took her instruction stance, lecturing finger raised shoulder high, her other hand propped on her small waist, her face serious. A little devil within her couldn't resist teasing him a bit. "Bicycles are very economical. You don't have to feed, water, or clean up after them. And they don't bite or eat apple pies."

"You're never going to forget about that, are you?" He sighed, a long-suffering male sigh.

"And the bread and the cake and the potato salad," she listed, then added, "besides, that horse hates me."

"No, he doesn't. He just needs to get to know you."

"He always lifts his lips and bares his teeth at me, like he's ready to bite."

"He's smiling at you, Addie."

"I know. He smiles just before he bites. Now let's get back to the cycle lesson. This vehicle is much easier than riding an old horse because you don't have to catch it first."

He shook his head at her.

"Well, you don't." She placed her hand on the seat. "This is the bicycle saddle. Unlike a horse saddle, it's light, there are no straps, and it's attached to the cycle until a new one is needed."

"How often is that?" he asked.

"That depends on how much it's used and whether it's ridden on rough roads. Out here, I'll have to replace it every year or so. Although this saddle is a custom-fitted, plaster-cast seat, and I'm not sure where I can get another," she said as she suddenly wondered where she'd get the bicycle supplies that she couldn't order from the Montgomery Ward Catalog.

"Plaster cast? What did you do, sit in a plaster mold?" He laughed, thinking he was being really funny.

Addie looked up. "As a matter of fact, I did."

He eyed her fanny and then he howled. "You could always sit in your biscuit dough."

"Are you going to be serious?"

"Give me a minute. The image of your butt in a bowl of plaster is a little hard to ignore."

She waited while he laughed. "Montana, you can try to be as obnoxious as possible but I'm not going to let you get out of this. You promised."

"I had a weak moment," he said, then added, "I was under duress."

"No," Addie said, "you just wanted something."

"That too," he admitted with a leer. "Wanna do it again?"

"Not now. I want to see you ride this bicycle," she said stubbornly.

"Okay." He grabbed the handlebars, straddled the seat and pushed off, his boots on the pedals and his long legs bent outward to avoid banging his knees on the handlebars. The bicycle was too small and he looked like a crab, a wobbly crab. But a few minutes later he'd mastered the cycle, despite its size, and he was riding it around the barn.

He rang the bell as he went past her. "Hey, this is fun."

"I told you so!" she shouted after him, watching her husband catch on to the fun of cycling. He had a great sense of control and balance. Probably from riding that ornery horse, she thought, remembering how he had looked on Rebecca's horse. He had ridden as naturally as if he'd been born on a horse. Addie watched him and soon he had the cycle swirling up dust around the barnyard. He whizzed around the back of the barn and tipped his hat at her, looking cocky and certain and male. He made another pass close by her, and suddenly he leaned out, wrapped his arm around her waist, and in one swift, sure motion lifted her onto the handlebars.

Squealing like a pig caught in a gate, she grabbed onto his shoulders. Once they had made two turns around the barn, she was feeling secure and laughing at the devilment on her husband's face.

"Now I've got you where I want you." He gripped the handlebars, bracketing her between his arms.

"You're crazy," she yelled on a laugh.

Montana's face leaned over hers and he kissed her.

So around the barn they rode, sparking on a bicycle. It was silly, it was fun, and it was the way their marriage had been ever since he'd opened up to her—more comfortable than an old shoe, more full than a lifetime of I love you's, more wonderful than a year of dreams.

The wind howled into the dark western sky. A storm thundered in from the Pacific, and before long there'd be rain with the wind. Eucalyptus leaves and bark skipped across the back of the farmhouse, and the chicken gate rattled like a thin bell. The giant oak groaned at a strong gust, and the music of the wind was the only other natural sound, because the birds had fled the upcoming storm.

But inside the farmhouse it was warm, and laughter floated on the music in the parlor. The tinny tune stopped, and Montana walked over to the roller organ where he switched the music roller and cranked the handle. The bellows filled and the gears that drove the music reeds wound tight. Soon the reeds pinged slowly in three-quarter time. A waltz rang out from the organ box, and Addie and Montana danced around the room to the melody of "After the Ball."

As he spun Addie past the front window, a loud thumping sounded on the porch, followed by a whinny.

"What the hell?" He stopped and bent to look out the window. Jericho was on the porch.

"What is it?" Addie placed her hand on his shoulder as he squinted through the glass.

"Jericho's out." He straightened, grabbing his hat and coat off the hall tree and shrugging into them. "Custus must have forgotten to close the barn door when he left. I'll be back in a few minutes." He gave her a quick kiss and went out the front door.

His horse stood in the shelter of the porch and nickered when he saw Montana. "Hello, boy." He stroked the horse's muzzle. "Kind of cold and windy out here, isn't it?"

He led the horse down the porch steps and across the drive. A distant banging rattled from the barn. He couldn't see the barn doors, but it sounded like them, open and banging against the barn wall. They rounded the corner and the doors battered again.

"Come on, boy. It's not much farther."

A few minutes later they were inside the dark barn. He slapped the horse on the backside to send him to his stall and then he turned and closed the banging doors.

Jericho snorted again and Montana turned, surprised to see that his horse wasn't in the stall. He always went straight there with just a slap on the backside. It was routine with them. He let his eyes adjust for a minute, then looked over to the worktable where they kept the kerosene lanterns. There was only one and they had three. He figured Custus must have left them somewhere, or maybe Addie had. Everytime she came near his stuff he couldn't find anything. Hell, the woman had labeled everything but the animals, and those she'd named.

He struck a match on the worktable and held it up to the lantern. The wick wouldn't light. He shook the lantern. It was empty. He swore and looked around for the kerosene can. It was gone too.

Mumbling, he looked around for the can and spotted it near the ladder to the hay loft. He walked over to it, calling Custus every name in the book. When Custus got back from picking up the feed in Stockton, Montana thought, he was going to have a talk with him about his carelessness. He bent and picked up the can. It was empty too.

His guard came up and he slowly perused the room. There was a wet pool in the hay a few feet away. Montana squatted down. It smelled of kerosene. Two drops hit his shoulders and he looked up to the hay loft. Two more drops fell from above. Very slowly he straightened. Silently, he climbed the ladder.

Addie checked the time. Montana had been gone for forty-five minutes, and that was awfully long, even to curry the horse and check on the other animals. Of course, once he'd gotten into the barn, he'd probably managed to get sidetracked. More than likely he was messing up the worktable again. She had tried to get him organized, but he just didn't understand her numbering system and he refused to use the card catalog.

Another eternal fifteen minutes and she had had it. As she opened the back door, the wind snatched it from her hand. She paused on the back porch to shrug into her coat. The barn doors were closed. He was probably inside, fiddling around. She made her way across the farmyard, the leaves and twigs dancing at her feet in a whirling circle. She bent her head to block the dust from her eyes and she pulled on the barn doors. They were latched from the inside.

"Dadgummit!" She banged on the doors. "Montana! Let me in!"

Nothing happened. She went to the narrow side window and tried to see inside the barn. It was dark, and that bothered her. Montana should have lit the lantern, and he would have, especially if he had gotten sidetracked. In back the barn doors only had an outside latchbar, so she hurried around to the other side. She turned the corner and tripped, slamming to her knees on the hard, cold ground. She pushed up and looked over her shoulder.

Then she screamed.

A man lay on his back, his head bent at an unnatural angle. She crawled closer, her breath held in fear. She looked at him and closed her eyes, a sigh of unrepentant relief escaping her lips. It was the railroad agent who'd had

Montana arrested. From the cold stare of his eyes, she knew he was dead.

"Montana!" she screamed, looking frantically around the area. The loft doors crashed against the barn and she glanced up. The dark hole of the loft stared back, its doors swinging and clapping in the wind.

"Montana!"

Nothing answered back but the howl of the wind.

She searched and searched, then saw him, lying next to a stack of baling wire. She ran and stopped above him, afraid to look and afraid not to.

He lay sprawled faceup, his hip turned oddly. Still panting with fear, she stared at his still face, tears rolling down hers.

"Oh God, don't let him be dead." Her prayer disappeared in the wind.

She knelt near his head. His eyes were closed. "Montana." Her hand stroked his cold cheek. His eyes opened and his lips moved, but any sound that came out was windstolen like her prayer.

"Oh God, Montana, please . . ." She held his head and cried.

His lips moved against her cheek. He was trying to speak.

"G-G-Get h-help . . ." he rasped, then winced in pain.

"Let me get you inside, love, please." And she started to try to get her arm under him.

He groaned, "N-Nooo," still gasping for breath. "D-Don't move me . . ."

"Okay. All right." She nodded, so panicked, so scared. His eyes were closed. Dear Lord, she had to get help. She shot upright and shrugged out of her coat, tucking it around him.

"It'll be okay, my love. I'll get help, I promise . . ." She stood and started to run, but stopped and turned back. "Montana, don't you dare die!"

She ran into the barn, heading straight for her bicycle, but then she stopped. The cycle was too slow on the dirt roads, and the wind would hold the speed back.

Jericho whinnied and she turned, knowing she had no

339

choice before she ever focused on the horrid animal. The horse was faster.

She plucked the halter off the wall and approached the horse. Its eyes followed her as usual, as if it were looking for a nice meaty piece of white flesh. Okay, she thought, now just be calm. She tried to remember what Montana had taught her. Talk sweet, he'd said.

"Nice horsey . . ." She moved closer. It ran to the other side of the barn.

"Dadgummit!" Maybe if I move slower, she thought, easing toward it. When she was a few feet away, she held out the halter. "See, Jericho, all I want to do is slip this on your nose. Okay?"

It snorted and pawed the dirt floor.

"Sweet Jericho, nice horse, just let me . . ." She almost had the rope on his nose, and he threw his head back and off he took.

They faced off, a good twenty feet between them.

"Look you! Stop this! Montana needs us and I don't have time for your obnoxious games!" She was going to cry, and she wasn't sure if it was because she was more scared, angry, or frustrated. She swiped at her eyes and glared at the horse. "You will not stop me," she said, determined to catch the horse. And once determined, she didn't back down, so she walked closer, reciting over and over that it couldn't stop her because she was more stubborn than it could ever be.

The horse bared his teeth.

"I swear if you bite me, you dadgum beast, I'll bite you back!" It snorted, but didn't nip at her. She cursed and prayed at the same time, and just as she had the halter over the horse's nose, it threw its head high out of reach and shifted backward. Then it looked right at her and smacked those big, freckled lips like it had every time it ate her food.

Food . . . the cake! Addie turned and ran to the front doors and unbolted them, running full bore across the windblown farmyard. She slammed into the kitchen, grabbed the apple cake from supper, and was back in the barn in little more than a minute.

Panting, she walked over to the horse, stopping about three feet away. She set the cake down.

"There." And she moved back, grabbed the halter and waited. So did the horse.

"Come on . . . eat that cake . . ." Jericho didn't budge, just stood there flicking its tail.

"Oh God." Her hand covered her mouth. What was she going to do? She looked over her shoulder to where she had left Montana. Her heart tightened so that she thought she might just fall apart, right there, but she couldn't, he needed her. She looked at the horse, remembering the animal was so contrary. So she slowly moved toward the plate, appearing as if she were going for the cake.

It worked! The horse moved faster, beating her to the plate and planting his muzzle in the cake. She dropped the halter and lugged the heavy saddle over to the horse. With a wide stumbling heave, it landed on Jericho's back. Gasping, but not hesitating, she buckled the strap things, making sure she did them right—that part of her lesson she hadn't forgotten. By the time she finished, the horse was swabbing the plate with his big tongue. She picked up the halter and tried again. The horrid animal curled its lips and nipped at her.

"Damn you!" She slapped Jericho so hard her hand stung.

He threw back his head, shook it and, mane flying, he loped past her, out the open back doors, disappearing into the darkness.

"Oh nooo!" she cried, running outside, but the animal was nowhere to be seen.

Through a sea of tears she turned toward Montana, looking at his still figure. Defeated, she went to him, just needing to touch him. She knelt beside him, brushing the hair off his face. "Don't die," she whispered, "please, please . . ." His eyes opened; hers teared more. His eyes glazed with pain, then slid closed, and she hung her head in her hands and sobbed, "Don't die, don't die," for what seemed like forever.

Something soft nudged her back and she looked up. Jericho stood over her, nuzzling her. She held up her hand to fend off the bite she expected but was too upset to care about. Jericho licked her hand, as he'd always done to Montana. The horse stared at her. Her sobbing quieted and she stood, holding her hand out again. The horse licked it again, then nuzzled her hand like a lonely old hound dog. She stood and ran for the halter. The horse actually followed her, then stood perfectly still while she slid it into place.

"Oh, thank you," she prayed, hugging the horse at the same time. She grasped the handle thing and mounted, perfectly, except the foot holder things hung down too far for her feet to reach. They were adjusted to Montana's long legs. She didn't dare waste any more time, so she grabbed the halter rope and the saddle handle in both hands, and saying one last prayer, kicked the horse into a gallop. They sped past the doors and into the night with Addie bouncing and holding on for dear life as she yelled, "Don't die, don't you dare die!"

25

"His hip is broken." The doctor snapped closed his leather bag and cleaned his spectacles on the hem of his coat.

"He'll be okay?" Addie prompted, twisting a hunk of her skirt fabric into a knot. She looked at the older man's serious face and waited for him to tell her that Montana would be all right.

"I'm not going to lie to you . . ."

At those words, her insides crumbled like old brick.

". . . There's spinal damage of some sort. He fell almost thirty feet. He told me he caught that railroad agent trying to set the barn on fire. They struggled and fell out the hay doors. He's damn lucky he didn't end up dead like the other fella." The doctor put his spectacles on and looked Addie square in the eyes.

She stared at him but didn't see him, all her senses dulled, except the sense of sound. With dread she listened.

"He can't move his legs, Mrs. Creed."

She sagged back against the chair back and closed her eyes. After a numb moment she asked, "Is it permanent?"

He shrugged, "I wish I could say for sure. We just don't know. Once his hip heals, we'll have to see how he does." He stopped and placed a gentle hand on her shoulder. "I'm sorry."

She lifted her pale face and nodded, accepting his words given in kindness, but they both knew the words were impotent. Being sorry wouldn't help her husband walk.

The front door clicked closed after the doctor, and Addie stood staring at her hand on the glass doorknob, feeling so vacant. She released the knob and walked over to the chair, resting her hand on the back for support. She couldn't seemed to grasp a single one of the feelings that raced through her. She wanted to run to Montana and hold him; she wanted to hide until everything got better; and she wanted it to be yesterday, forever. Part of her wanted to cry and never stop until everything was back the way it had been. But she didn't dare.

What she needed was to get herself under control, no sad faces, no tears, just positive confidence. Montana needed that from her, and she had to go in there to him in a moment. With a deep breath and a few eternal seconds of strength-gathering, she walked through the room, down the hall, and stopped outside the bedroom door. She rubbed her eyes for a second, then pinched her cheeks to make sure she didn't look deathly pale. Then, to help, she thought of the man she loved dancing with her on a dirt road—the memory always brought a smile of love to her lips. Hopefully, that would be what he most needed to see, a loving smile. Then she opened the door.

He stared out the window, a listless, vulnerable look on his face. There were black circles under his eyes and the bones of his cheeks appeared even sharper. His eyes closed, and his face strained with an instant of pain. She could see the deep breath he took, then held. *Oh God, don't let him hurt like this.* Slowly his chest deflated and his eyes opened. He looked right at her.

She smiled and walked over to the bed, then sat on its edge. She covered his large hand with hers. "Hello, love."

He turned away.

She rubbed his hand slowly. "Can I get you anything?"

"A new pair of legs." He laughed without humor.

"Montana, I—"

His hand jerked from beneath hers. "Don't say anything. There's not a goddamn thing you can say, so don't try. Just don't goddamn try."

She sat there, searching for something to do, or say, to help.

"I love you," she whispered, willing him to turn and look at her instead of out the window.

"Leave me alone." He didn't move his head even a fraction of an inch. If he had, the wall of tension he created would have seemed breachable. But he didn't move, didn't look at her. It was as if he couldn't stand to.

Quietly, she left the room, closing the door behind her. Then she sagged against a wall, aching with a hurt so crippling that she thought her own legs might give way. She gasped for air. She fought the tears. Then she pushed away from the wall, rushing into the kitchen. She threw up in the sink pan, over and over, until nothing was left inside her but the gagging heaves of her sick stomach.

Finally her stomach settled into a tight ball. She leaned her head down and slowly reached up and pumped some water into the sink. She splashed the cool water on her hot face and rinsed her mouth.

Her hands gripped the counter and her tears came, rushing like a spring flood. She slid to the floor and cried, letting loose the grief she'd tried so hard to hold back. There was no longer a reason not to grieve, because the dream was gone.

"I've told you before, I can feed myself! My hands aren't crippled!" Montana grabbed the fork out of Addie's hand,

344

and she stiffened, as she had almost every day for the past two months.

His hip had healed, but there'd been no change in his legs. He still couldn't move them, couldn't feel a thing from the waist down. She wished her heart were as paralyzed as his legs. Then she wouldn't hurt, day in and day out. Montana was angry, so, so angry, and since she was the only one there, he often took his anger out on her. It took every bit of love, every bit of strength she had, not to let him get to her, or at least not to show it.

There were days when he was sullen, there were times when he ranted about the railroad, blaming them for destroying his family and him, and there were times when he lashed out at her. Today was one of those days.

"I have some news," Addie said, unsure of how he'd react. He scowled at the tray of food on the bed. He hadn't touched any of it since he'd jerked the fork out of her hand.

"If it's another one of those cheery stories of yours, keep it to yourself. I don't feel like being cheered up." He jabbed the knife into a piece of roast and sawed the bejesus out of it.

"I doubt if this will *cheer* you up," she said, unable to keep the sarcasm out of her own hurt voice. "The federal marshal has issued warrants for Will and Wade. For the train robberies."

He swore, then muttered thoughtfully, "So they finally found out."

"You knew?" Addie was stunned.

He nodded.

"You knew that Wade Parker was related to one of the men the railroad killed?"

"Sure I knew, that's why I never said much. What did I owe the railroad? Hell, if I would have known about this," he waved a brisk hand over his legs, "I'd have joined them."

She stood and walked over to the dresser, biting her lip and pretending to straighten the bottles and boxes on it. The only sound in the room was the clink of silverware. At least he's eating, she thought, feeling half eaten herself.

Not a day went by that he didn't chew her up and spit her out.

"When's the trial?"

She turned. "They haven't caught them yet, just issued the warrants. I heard that Will and Wade have been hiding in the foothills, and it seems that the railroad and the marshal can't find them." She thought she saw a glimmer of a real smile, so she went on. "Custus told me that the ranchers and farmers the railroad cheated have been helping them, hiding both bandits and warning them if the railroad gets too close."

She stepped closer to the bed. "Custus says it's getting to be quite a joke. The newspapers are making fun of the railroad's ineptness and rooting the bandits on. They've become heroes to most everybody."

He did smile then, but it was short-lived.

He put his hands on the mattress to try to shift his position and the tray wobbled. Suddenly the milk glass tipped and fell onto the plate, sending milk and gravy and roast all over him, the bed, and onto the floor.

"Shit!" He grabbed the tray and flung it against the wall. She stood in stunned horror. The dishes crashed and broke, and the food that hadn't spilled, splattered up the wall, on the ceiling, on the floor.

Her hand dropped from her mouth and she slowly walked over to the mess. She bent and picked up the tray, then without a word she stooped and began to stack the broken dishes on the cracked, wooden tray.

"Leave it and get out." His voice was ice.

She ignored him and picked up the rest of the pieces. Standing, she looked at him and said, "I'll get some clean sheets."

"Don't bother. Just get out!"

She turned and silently carried the tray out of the room.

Montana heard the barn doors close, then the crunch of gravel as someone walked across the drive. Heels clicked on the wooden steps, a woman's heels. It was Addie.

The sounds haunted him, reminded him that he was

chained to the bed, unable to see anywhere except the small environment of the bedroom and the narrow view from the windows. He couldn't stand, couldn't work, so Custus and Addie did it all. She was working twice as hard as she usually did just to keep up with the farm.

Where he had once been strong, capable of almost anything, now he was nothing but a lump in her bed. He couldn't even control his simplest movements without spilling food or knocking over a lamp.

But worst of all, he was no longer a man.

His head hung back against the pillows, covered only that morning with crisp, clean cases. Addie changed the bed every other day, either to keep him comfortable or because of some spill or accident. Every time he looked out the window, she was hanging out laundry or lugging the heavy milk pails with a yoke across her small shoulders. She was the strong one now, and every time he looked at her he was torn between wanting to hold her and draw some of that strength or wanting to send her away from the humiliation he felt. And every hour of every day he wondered if he could go on.

He loved her; with every bit of his rotten, crippled soul he loved her. But he could never be the man she deserved, the man she needed. He couldn't provide for her. He couldn't love her, give her children. God, he thought, he couldn't even hold her the way a man holds a woman. His mind flashed with his favorite image—her love-filled face looking up at him as they danced on a moonlit night. It had been a simple thing that had made her happy, and he'd vowed he'd never forget it. And he hadn't.

Now it haunted him, because though he hadn't forgotten, he was no longer capable of giving her that one, simple pleasure. He would never dance with her again, and that thought stood as a symbol of all the "nevers" that faced them. Addie deserved better, and deserved a chance for a life without the burden of him. But he wondered if he could exist without her. Probably not, and that was what was so hard. While his mind told him to drive her away, his heart wouldn't let him.

The door opened and she came into the room, a tub of

steamy water lugging down her small arms and some towels draped over her shoulders. He watched her bump the door shut with her hip, then she crossed over to give him a bath. Every muscle that still worked in his useless body tightened with humiliation. He hated this, hated himself, and hated her for still loving him.

To breathe around all that hatred was suddenly a struggle; he panted, his fists tightened. She walked toward him and set the tub on the edge of the bed, completely unaware of the rage that consumed him.

He grabbed the edge of the tub and shoved it off the bed. Water rushed everywhere, and Addie screamed. The tub clattered to the wooden floor. She looked at it in horror, then looked at him as if she expected to see some animal.

He leaned out and his fingers bit into her soft arms. He squeezed harder, bringing tears to her big, dark eyes. Through gritted teeth he spat, "Get out!"

"What did I do?" she whispered, looking like a frightened deer. Then her mouth trembled and she cried, "What do you want from me?"

He squeezed harder. "I want you to get out, leave, for good!"

Her hands went to her mouth in horror and tears bled from her wide, hurt eyes. His guts twisted but he steeled himself against it, wouldn't let himself give in to it.

"Get . . . out!" he shouted.

And she did.

Montana had heard her crying. The sound had torn through him, made the functional parts of his body tighten and flinch with each sob. Then he'd heard the clatter of her digging through the hall closet. She had walked into the bedroom, grabbed her purple dress and left the room. When she came in again, she wore the dress and her head was held high. Then she packed some clothes, shoving them into her cloth bag.

With every item she stuffed into her valise, he wanted to leap from the prison of his bed and beg her not to leave him. But he loved her, so he wouldn't do it. Instead he'd struggled to turn onto his side, pushing his weight with only the strength of his arms, not an easy task, but determination and his pride gave him added strength. He faced away from her huge, dark eyes, the ones rimmed red from her hurt, the ones that no longer had warmth within them. But at least they no longer held pity either.

Then she'd left the room, her dress swishing softly and the sound of her heels clicking on the floor, a familiar sound that he'd never hear again. He'd closed his eyes, foolishly thinking it would stop the emotion from rising into them and spilling over. Through a damp blur he'd watched her walk across the farmyard and disappear from view. A minute later the wagon jangled past. She was gone.

And with her went the joy in his life, the one gift he'd been given and now had to give up. Like the slide scenes on a stereoscope, his mind flashed with her image, flying out the bedroom window in only her nightdress to land on his chest in a ball of indignance, the flurry of her small feet pedaling that cycle of hers with a cart full of canned beans bouncing behind, her face fused with enough determination for ten men, and the Little Miss Pinky who mounted Jericho backward. He laughed, but then the smile faded. He swallowed the hard lump of emotion that ached in the back of his throat.

All he would now have were the memories: her indignant nose and the way it shot up like a scorpion's tail whenever she was mad; the silky brush of her long black hair; her taste—sweeter and spicier than baked apples; that odd mix of vanilla, honeysuckle, and lemon that he smelled whenever she was near; and the look of love in her eyes whenever she'd gaze up at him. She would look at him like that and he could almost believe that he could walk again.

Almost, but not quite. But none of that mattered now because she was gone, and he swallowed that lump again, holding the pillow as tight as he would have held her—and then he cried.

26

THE TRAIN RATTLED ON THE TRACK, SLOWING; ITS BRAKES squealed and the steam blasted out, disappearing into the fog that lingered on the station platform. Addie stepped from the train, pulling her cape a bit tighter around her cold shoulders. The temperature was so different here, at least twenty degrees cooler than home. She walked along the wooden platform, making her way to the gate where the other passengers left and found conveyances into the city. She stopped momentarily, having forgotten the bustle, the crowds, and the noise of city life. A moment later her hand covered her nose. She hadn't forgotten the smell, especially when it rode in on the cool, damp fog to remind her why she'd left city life.

Bending, she picked up her valise, then straightened and pulled from her pocket a small piece of paper with an address written on it. A brisk walk to the street corner and she looked up and down the busy streets, seeing wave after wave of horsedrawn vehicles, hearing the rattle of steel-rimmed wheels as they crossed the trolley tracks, the clatter of a thousand horse hooves, shouts and bells and whistles all confined by tall, red-brick and graystone buildings that stood like prison guards up and down each knobby-paved street.

A small boy hawking a damp wad of newspapers barged up to her, shouting something about the fall of the "giant octopus." Addie gave him a nickel and he smiled a toothless thanks, slapping the paper into her gloved hand and barging on to his next patron. She stepped back into the safety of a stoop, set down her valise and opened the paper.

The tentacles of a cartoon octopus crawled across the front page, but the body of the creature was crushed underneath a boot branded *Congress,* and the headline blared in huge black block print: STATE LEGISLATURE APPROVES FORMATION OF STATE REGULATORY COMMISSION!

She closed the paper and ignored the tightness in her chest, for the railroad always brought to mind the image of Montana, lying on the cold ground in front of the barn, his face pale and pained. That image always made her shake with protective anger for the man she loved.

Taking a deep, damp breath, she tucked the newspaper under her arm, picked up her valise and walked up the street toward a cab stop. Now it was empty, the train passengers having hired the awaiting cabs and depot wagons that had been there only minutes before. She stood under the post that marked the stop and waited for the next free vehicle. She checked the address again: 627 Mason Street.

Mason Street. The same street name as in Chicago . . . She had first seen that as a good omen, or strange coincidence; whatever, this San Francisco address was her destination, and her last hope.

Before long she sat in a black leather cabriolet as it made its way through the hilly streets. The cabby pulled to a stop in front of a large, five-story, pink-brick building with curly iron grates and gray, wide-slatted shutters. He helped her down and she slipped the fare into his hand, never even looking at him because her eyes were drawn to the impressive building. She unlatched the gate and walked up the stone steps until she faced the huge double doors. A pull-chain style door chime dangled next to the sidelights in the door, and she pulled the chain firmly and waited, trying to ignore her fluttering stomach. She nervously smoothed a few imaginary wrinkles from the skirt of her pride dress, then listened for some sign of movement from within.

An older woman in a white nun's habit slowly opened the large door and eyed Addie curiously.

"I'm Mrs. Creed, I believe I'm expected—"

"Yes, yes." The woman smiled and nodded repeatedly as she stepped back and waved Addie inside. With a quick look back over her shoulder, she watched the cabby pull away, then she took one last look at the building, grabbed hold of her skirt and stepped inside, knowing that the knowledge held within this one impressive building would determine her future. And Montana's.

"Don't ya get so all-fired stubborn with me, goddammit! I fixed them there beans and ya'll eat 'em by God or ya'll wear 'em!" shouted Custus, just before he ducked to miss the plate of beans and bacon that sailed at his white head.

"Get out of here! Just leave me alone!" Montana glared at the old coot. His warden. They'd given each other nothing but trouble for a week, and it had been a dark, dreary prison of a week since Addie'd left, a week that felt to Montana like years of solitary confinement.

"Ungrateful whelp," Custus muttered. "A-laying in that there bed, makin' ever'one as miserable as yer rotten self! Chasin' off the little missy with all yer dadburn hollerin'." He turned to Montana. "Well, ya ain't gonna chase me off. I kin be jus' as stubborn. I done got more years of practice at it. An' I promised 'er I'd take care o' ya!" Then he picked up the tin plate, scooping the mess of beans into it before turning. "I oughta make ya eat these." He waved the plate in front of him.

"You're right Custus, he ought to eat them." Addie stood in the doorway, her arms crossed like a frustrated mother.

At the sound of her voice, Montana's head jerked up. Life suddenly sparked through him. His heart thudded like a schoolboy and he had the overwhelming urge to grin with relief. Sitting up, he drank in the sight of her.

Thank God she's back. Since she'd left, each hour had been a year, each day a decade. Heaven help him, but he needed her. And she was back. He had to bite his lip to keep from telling her the hell he'd been through since she'd left. But he couldn't do anything but look at her. A wealth of feelings soared through him all in one confusing yet joyous instant.

God, but he wanted to hold her to see if she were real. The need to touch her swelled within him, and the need to feel her, to smell her, to taste her, and he wanted to run to her, and for one infinitesimal second he almost thought he could, but it passed. He sagged back against the bed pillows, knowing he couldn't run, couldn't even walk or stand. He waited a moment, expecting some of the life he'd felt at the sight of her to slip away. It didn't.

"What are you doing back?" he finally asked, his voice purposely hard and snide, something that took a great deal of effort since inside he still sang because she was standing there.

She leaned against the doorway, appearing not the least bit affected by his remarks, even smiled a small quirk of a smile before she said, "It's good to see you too."

He stopped himself from wincing, and since he couldn't seem to come up with anything mean enough to say to her, he decided to be silent. A few pregnant seconds meandered by, then he found the strength to glower at her.

"Well, here's what we have to work with," she said to someone behind her as she stepped into the bedroom.

A big bear of a man came into view. He had graying blond hair, a nose as big and misshapen as an Idaho potato, and a mouthful of grinning teeth that were whiter than a country snowdrift. His cheeks were apple-red, looking chapped by the sun and wind, and his gray suit fit his wide shoulders like an oat sack. But the thing that caught Montana's attention was what the man held in his mammoth fist—a black leather doctor's bag.

Montana swore loudly.

"This *gentleman,* with the four-letter vocabulary, is my husband, Dr. Karlson." Addie looked at the huge doctor as if they shared a private joke, and that really pissed off Montana.

"I told you to leave!" He gave Addie the angriest look he could muster. "I don't need another doctor! I just need to be left alone!"

"If you'll leave us alone, Addie, I'll examine him." Dr. Karlson walked toward him.

"What in the hell are you doing calling my wife by her first name?" Montana suddenly felt strength run straight to his fists. He also felt the intense need to bash the man's potato nose into his face.

The doctor pulled up a chair and sat down, dropping the

bag next to him. Then he leaned back and silently scrutinized Montana until he could have sworn the big man could read his belligerent mind.

"Do you want to walk again, Mr. Creed?"

"No." Montana gave him a look filled with the same sarcasm as his voice. "I want to spend the rest of my life in this damn bed."

The man smiled, and Montana had the feeling he'd heard those words before. The doctor waited a moment then said, "I promised your wife I'd examine you. I will not let her down, so you can cooperate or—"

"What's my wife to you?" His upper body stiffened with jealousy.

The big man was silent. Montana wanted to kill him, and wondered if maybe he could pull himself to the edge of the bed so he could try.

"Your wife is a friend, and in one short week is someone I've come to respect. I want to tell you something, Mr. Creed. Your wife sent me a letter about you." The doctor pulled a crumpled up piece of paper from his coat pocket. "Listen to this:

"Dear Dr. Karlson:

I am writing to you about my husband, whose back was injured from a fall. This has been really hard on him because he's a young, strong man who is used to doing for himself. I have heard that you have a clinic where you teach people to walk again. I would like to come to visit your clinic for the purpose of learning your techniques. I want to teach my husband to walk again. He's a proud man who won't be easily handled. If I can learn, then maybe I can help him without his knowing it. That might save his pride and our happiness. We have a small farm in Alameda County, only half a day from San Francisco. It seems since we're so close that maybe God had something to do with this, and I hope you'll agree.

Awaiting your response,
Mrs. Adelaide A. Creed
Bleeding Heart, California"

354

Dr. Karlson folded the letter and put it back in his pocket. Then he looked Montana straight in the eye. "She doesn't know I brought the letter. Your wife wanted me to examine you and let her know if there was any chance of the techniques working for you. She didn't want to get your hopes up, she said." He stood, locked his huge hands behind his back, and paced slowly.

"You know, Mr. Creed, I don't think there's a man alive who wouldn't give everything to have a woman like her. From the minute I agreed to help her, she jumped into learning everything with more determination than I've seen in patients who wanted to walk more than anything in the world. Addie was like that. She wanted this for you, more than anything in the world. When I told her that you were lucky to have her, she just laughed and said she was the lucky one, and that she loved you."

Montana continued to stare at the tantrum-stained wall, feeling loathesome and small and petty. He didn't even know if he could look this man in the eye. He didn't want to hope that the doctor could help. He was too afraid, because if it didn't work, he didn't know if he was strong enough to deal with the defeat, again. The knot in his gut twisted and he closed his eyes for a brief, settling moment. Addie's face smiling up at him on a moonlit night flashed through his mind. Somehow he dredged up the nerve to look at the doctor. "What do I have to do?"

"Let me examine you, and then we'll talk."

Montana jerked the covers off his bare, useless legs, scowling at them. They looked the same as they always had, long and muscled, but the muscles didn't work. His gaze moved upward to his thighs, still looking powerful from years of working and riding. He couldn't tighten them. Then he stared at his flaccid genitals, and was filled with a desperate feeling of hopelessness and weakness. He couldn't feel anything, do anything; in fact it was as if everything below his waist belonged to someone else. After a long moment he looked at the other man. "Go ahead."

Dr. Karlson closed the bedroom door behind him and turned to Addie.

"Well?"

"There's a chance," he told her. "He has some sensation below the injury, which indicates that this could very well be temporary. But I told him what he had to do. You can't do it for him, Addie. You can stimulate the muscles, you can massage them and help him, but you can't do it alone. He has to try himself. He has to learn to use those muscles, and you've seen firsthand the pain he'll go through."

Addie nodded, remembering the struggles of the people in Dr. Karlson's clinic. Men who cried from the pain of struggling to stand up, one woman who was drenched with sweat from only a fifteen-minute session on a bar walker, a child who laughed and giggled all day because she was finally ticklish again on one small toe. That child's joy had been the catalyst for the patients of the clinic. Within two days most of them had progressed farther because of the hope given them by the little girl's laughter. And Addie wanted Montana to hear that laughter.

Dr. Karlson rolled a high, cane-backed invalid chair into the hallway. Addie put her hand on his arm. "I'll take that inside."

He searched her face for a moment, then asked, "Are you sure you're up to it?"

"You think it'll be that bad?" she asked.

He nodded, a tinge of a smile playing at his lips. "Remember Ezra Crowley?"

She shuddered. "Don't remind me. I didn't know such words existed." The man was a banker who'd fallen down a flight of stairs. He'd arrived at the clinic the day before Addie had begun her brief training stint, and Dr. Karlson had sent her to the older man for a baptism by fire. It wasn't easy, but by the time they'd left this morning, Ezra Crowley was racing down the corridors in his invalid chair, pinching the nurses and sending the nuns into hiding.

"I've left your husband the book with the exercises. It's lying on the night table. He didn't touch it while I was in there. He had some questions, most of them doubtful and challenging. It's going to take him a while. I've met his type before. He's about as hard-headed as they come." Dr. Karlson gathered his things and waited.

"I know," Addie said walking him to the front door. "Custus will take you back to the train station." She held out her hand. "Thank you, for everything."

The big man smiled back at her. "You're pretty special, Addie." He gave her hand a pat. "It's too bad you're already taken."

She laughed. "You wouldn't have time for me if I wasn't. Besides, Melda Potts has a fancy for you, I think."

Melda Potts was the female version of Ezra Crowley, and the good doctor laughed, then waved good-bye and walked to where Custus sat in the wagon.

Addie closed the front door and walked to the hallway. She grabbed the invalid chair, took three deep breaths and rolled it into the bedroom.

"Goddammit, Addie, get that thing out of here!"

27

ADDIE SETTLED A LITTLE DEEPER INTO THE STUFFED CHAIR, dislodging the tooled-leather book that lay open in her lap. The crisp pages fluttered closed and she sighed. She couldn't concentrate. Pulling the spectacles from her nose, she let them drop, the chain around her neck keeping them within easy reach. She rubbed the bridge of her nose and let her head drop back against the lace tidy that protected the chair's back. It was late, and the crickets chirruped from outside and an occasional rush of the wind in the eucalyptus leaves spilled indoors, like they used to, before their world fell apart.

It had been another long day, one where Montana's moods had been mercurial. She had cracked open the door and seen him thumbing through Dr. Karlson's book. The sight had given her such hope. Maybe he would try. But when she'd gone inside and tried to massage his legs, he'd bullied her almost to tears. She didn't know how to deal with him. One minute he'd be pensive and quiet, and the next belligerent and rude. She'd only had a week of training, and while some of the patients had acted like Montana, she wasn't as affected as she was when it was the man she loved who was doling out the hurt. She closed her eyes and vaguely felt the edge of sleep start to fall over her.

The crash of breaking glass sent her reeling out of the chair. She ran to the bedroom, where she found Montana struggling to sit upright while he stared with disgust at the shattered remains of the bedside lamp, now burning on the floor. She grabbed a pillow, beating out the flames before they spread. Then she stood there silently, clutching the smoky pillow to her chest and remembering the spills from before. She awaited Montana's violent reaction. It didn't come.

Curious, she looked at him. His eyes were on the spill, staring blankly, his shoulders and neck muscles ridged with tension, and she followed the ridges down his arms to where his hand held the sheet in such tight, knotted fists that his knuckles were stark white and his hands shook. All of his pride was slowly being destroyed, eaten away by his inability to control his body. The angry tension he felt was born of shame, the shame that he could do so little for himself.

She ached for him, ached for him to walk that cocky, arrogant walk that had set her teeth on edge when they first met. She ached for him to dance, like a mating turkey or on a quiet moonlit road. She ached for him to ride like a stormy wind on Rebecca's horse or to pedal her cycle around the farmyard, his long legs sticking out like a rock crab. But God only knew if it would ever happen, so she moved closer and placed her hand on his white-knuckled fist.

Montana turned his troubled, hurt, fear-filled eyes toward her. She stepped closer and, Lord above, he finally reached for her. "Oh God, Addie . . ." He pulled her against him, burying his face in her neck, and he held her as if she were his miracle.

He whispered her name over and over against her neck, and she felt him swallow several times. She swallowed too, but her tears came anyway, spilling down her flushed face as she rocked with him.

"I'm only half a man, Addie." His voice was a raw rasp, but the words in his admission bored straight to her heart.

"Not to me, my love, and even if you never walk again, I'll still love you. No matter what happens, you'll still be my husband—only dying can change that, and if you die," she sniffed a short laugh through her tears, "I'll kill you." His arms tightened around her and she took a deep breath, just letting him hold her and draw from her what he needed.

Long moments later Montana pulled back, still holding her in the close circle of his arms. "I might not ever be able to give you children."

It killed her to see him like this, scared and human and vulnerable. And she knew he was most vulnerable with her. His doubts were about them, not just him. Now more than ever he needed her reassurance, so Addie shrugged, ignoring the fantasy image—brown-haired boys who loved horses and little wisps of girls who loved books—the children they might have had. "I have my chickens, the cattle—I named them, incidentally," she admitted with a tentative smile.

He looked down at her, exchanging smiles. "I know." Then his face grew serious again. "I won't be able to make love to you, the way a man was meant to love a woman."

"You can hold me, and as long as you still love me in your heart and your mind, that's enough for me."

He was quiet again, then he took a deep breath. "When we married, I made you a promise." His eyes, still unsure, searched her tear-streaked face. "I'll never dance with you again." His look told her how important that one thing was to him.

"Oh Montana . . ." She shook her head at him. "It's not the dancing, or the physical loving. And children are gifts from God anyway. It's the needing, the holding, the loving from deep within that's important. It's having someone to talk to, to share things with. It's not being alone anymore, and it's knowing that you're loved by someone, just because you're you."

She placed her right hand in his and her left hand on his shoulder, positioning their upper bodies as if they were standing, getting ready to waltz across the room. She looked up at him, her chest lightly touching his. "Is this really any different just because our legs aren't moving?"

Relief and love and tenderness freed the tightness in his face, and he even smiled again.

"There's no music," she said, just like she had on that moonlit night. She snuggled her head against his chest and soon his chin rested on her head and his hand squeezed hers. They both remembered. Then his chest rose and fell with a few deep and ragged breaths.

A moment later he whistled their waltz, until they both drifted to sleep.

* * *

"Open this for me, would you?" Addie handed Montana a mason jar with a towel around its lid.

Montana turned the tight lid and handed it back to Addie.

"Thank you." A secretive little smile quirked about her lips before she turned and left the room, her steps as spritely and happy as if she had just won a blue ribbon for chicken raising.

An hour later she marched back in, carrying all the fixings for a bath. She spent over an hour washing him and rubbing his dead muscles over and over. Then she left again, still smiling.

It wasn't much longer before she came in to change the sheets. Instead of rolling him around like a Christmas sausage, she made him lift up, use his arms and strain to pull his body around so she could tuck in the sheets. This time she whistled her way out of the room.

He wasn't stupid. He knew what she was doing, though he wondered if her antics were all in vain. He'd read the book Dr. Karlson had left. It had pages about muscle stimulation, massage, and instructions explaining why it was important to keep the patient moving and keep up the strength in the upper body and arms.

A month of this and he'd resigned himself to her manipulations. In fact there were times when he laughed to himself. She was so proud of her sneaky therapy that he let her continue, sometimes just to see how far she'd go. She was the light in his black life, and no matter how hopeless he believed his situation to be, he would never try to send her away again. He needed her, and there were times when he actually believed that even useless as he felt he was, she needed him.

There was a companionship between them. Sometimes she'd just be sitting next to the bed, reading, yet they were together and the sense of peacefulness they shared was a whole new kind of emotion for him. The only chigger in their relationship was the invalid chair.

It sat like an Armageddon next to the bed, waiting. Addie had prudently stopped suggesting he try it, although he saw her gaze drift toward it more than once. He probably should have appeased her, but the chair was the one thing that still horrified him.

Montana felt, deeply, that if he sat in that chair, then he was accepting his paralysis as final, that he'd never walk again. He still wasn't ready for that acceptance. He needed the one internal speck of hope that flickered in the recesses of his mind—the hope that maybe the doctor was right, that maybe he could walk again, be whole again.

But he seldom let himself think of that hope, especially when he looked at his lower body and the useless appendages that weighed him down, kept him in the bed. When he looked at them, his rational side told him the hope could never be, and for the first time since Addie's return, Montana slumped back into desolation.

Addie stood over the stove, stirring the corn syrup and sugar and such that would boil into candy. She'd come across the taffy recipe in her aunt's book and she'd had the best idea. Pulling taffy was a great upper body exercise, and she intended to put it to use on Montana that very day. She had to keep him busy, otherwise he might fall into that depressive slump again. He'd been becoming more and more quiet the past day or so, and that worried her.

She turned the candy in a pan to cool, pulling a spatula through it again and again until it was cool enough to handle. She grabbed the butter that would keep the candy from sticking to their fingertips and, with the pan of taffy propped on her hip, she left the kitchen.

She slowed in the hallway, puzzled by the odd sound that came through the half-open door of the bedroom. It was a muffled, slapping sound. Very quietly she moved to where she could see into the room.

What she saw was so awful that she almost dropped the candy.

Montana sat in the bed, the covers pulled aside. But that wasn't what shocked her. It was his actions and, oh God, his tortured, angry face. Over and over his fists punched into his legs, socking them as if he could beat them into working again. His face was contorted and thrown back, and tears streamed down his cheeks. The more he beat his legs, the more he cried.

And so did Addie.

She stepped back from the door, afraid a loud sob might escape her. She didn't want him to know she'd seen him. It would kill him, but seeing him like that almost killed her. She glanced down at the candy, her great idea. It now seemed stupid. For the first time she wondered if maybe there was no hope. She had told herself she had enough belief for both of them, but that belief was sagging. The longer there was no progress, the more her hope dimmed. But she couldn't take the chance that he might see her doubt. Montana still needed her faith, even if she had to hide the fact that it was weakening.

So she left him alone, left him to beat out his anger, and she walked into the other room, sat in the big chair and cried. Then she tried to conjure up the image of Dr. Karlson's clinic and of the young girl's face, her elation and the hope it inspired, because right here and now, with the sound of Montana's fists pounding his numb legs, Addie desperately needed some hope to cling to.

The ache woke him up. It was a battered and bruised ache that had a distant familiarity. Montana hadn't felt that ache since the last fight he'd been in. But instead of swelling through his jaw, the pain was in his thighs. He sat up, his eyes riveted on his lower body. He jerked off the covers and stared at his legs.

They hurt, they actually hurt.

His breath labored and his throat tightened. He swallowed. The hope burned bright, a torch within him that yesterday was only a spark. He touched his leg and felt a bruised pain. And suddenly Montana was crying, deep wracking sobs of relief that he couldn't control, and didn't want to, because his legs hurt, thank God his legs hurt . . .

28

HIS EYES BURNED AND HIS RELIEF WAS SHORT-LIVED. WITH the bright morning sunlight came the fear and insecurity that shattered some of Montana's hope. His mind told him that he must have dreamed the pain, that maybe he wanted it so bad that he thought he felt it. He rubbed his hands down his legs. There was sensation. They still hurt. He pressed on one of the black and blue bruises. It was sore, but still he doubted, mostly out of the fear of killing off the last bit of hope that he'd ever be whole again. In the bright morning light he doubted, because he was human.

God, he wanted to believe he could walk again. But he was so damn scared.

The barn door banged shut and Montana could hear the meter of horse hooves, followed by Addie's laughing voice. His gaze skipped from his legs to the window, where he could see her leading Jericho out of the barn.

Addie and Jericho. Miracles did happen.

She stood in the farmyard, playing the game he had always played with his horse. He watched Jericho prance from view while Addie stood there grinning. Suddenly the charge of pounding hooves clapped up the drive, faster and faster. Then Jericho flew into view heading straight for his little wisp of a wife. And she stood there, black hair tucked into a neat little bun, her white shirt looking as crisp as fried chicken, her arms crossed, and she was smiling without a bit of fear in her face or her stance. Jericho stopped less than a foot in front of her, and she laughed. The horse whinnied and threw back his head, mane flying, as if he was answering her laughter.

His wife and his horse had made their peace. Not once since the accident had she ever referred to Jericho as "it," which was something she'd always done before. Now she treated his horse even more motherly than she had the other farm animals. If he hadn't already named his horse, Montana was sure that Addie would have, although the horse's name fit. For his little wife, the wall of fear had come tumbling down.

He watched her hang on Jericho's bridle, using him to steady her as she bent and dusted off her shoe. Her shoes weren't prissy new anymore. They were scuffed, and he'd noticed the other day that they were beginning to wrinkle, like his old, comfortable boots.

Addie belonged here.

No longer was she a prissy little librarian who'd come west on a whim. Boy, had he pegged her wrong. Now he knew why she'd come here. They had talked about it. She had a dream, just like he had. She'd been alone and needed the roots that the land gave a person. She'd had her doubts and her fears, but she'd up and left Chicago, determined to make those dreams come true.

And she had. Now Addie could plow a field, milk the cows, wring a chicken's neck with the best of the farmers' wives. She could shoot a snake, drive a wagon, and even harness a team. And she could ride a horse. This little woman who'd been so afraid of horses had overcome that fear. She'd told him about her parents, of her father's death and her mother's crippling. He understood her. After all, he'd had some fears of his own. Snakes, the land, and the railroad. He understood how hatred and fear could combine into something that controlled your life . . .

Montana didn't move, didn't breathe. He just thought about that for a long pensive moment. Then he groaned, realizing for the first damn time that he was still letting those things control him. He glanced at his legs then back at Addie, who stood by Jericho, stroking his neck and probably sweet talking him. His little wife was stronger than he was.

He'd spent most of his life clinging to his hatred of the railroad and fighting to have what he thought was so important—the land, his own land. He fought with his very soul not to end up like his father, a failure. It was a hard thing to admit, thinking that the father you loved was a failure. And that was what he, Montana, had thought for all those years. But Addie would have never thought of his pa as a failure, because he had tried to build a place for his family. He'd tried.

Montana had been so scared of failing that he had failed. Yet here was Addie, a little wisp of a woman, who'd given up everything familiar to her to come west and build her dream—a dream he'd forced her to fight for every step of the way. She had overcome every obstacle he'd thrown in her path. She'd even won his respect, and then his heart.

And what had he been doing? Sitting in this bed, mired in self-pity and fear and not even trying to fight. His wife had faced a big battle—a battle with herself. She'd won. She'd faced that deep fear of horses she'd harbored since childhood, and she'd overcome it, because of her love for him. And what had he fought for? Not much.

Oh, he'd fought for the land, the right to sell his grain freely, the farmers' railroad, but he hadn't fought for the things that really mattered. He hadn't fought the fears that made him give up. His wife never gave up. She was a little barn swallow pecking at the black hawk that was five times her size.

Montana closed his eyes in shame. She was the strong one, and lying in bed letting his fear and doubt keep him there was the equivalent of giving up. But she hadn't given up. Like Dr. Karlson had told him, Addie had fought to help him. And he in turn hadn't even tried.

He looked at the invalid chair, then at his wrinkled old boots, sitting abandoned in the corner, as if they were of no use. And that had been how he'd viewed them, of no use, because he hadn't been willing to fight to use them again. He made her fight his battle. She was the strong one, willing to fight for *his* will to walk.

What a fool he'd been, a stupid damn fool! He took a deep, resolved breath, dug his fists into the mattress and pulled his body toward the edge of the bed.

It took half an hour to get close enough to pull the chair

parallel to the bed. He panted from the exertion of dragging the dead weight of his lower body. Sweat poured down from his temples and beaded on his chest. His neck and shoulders ached from straining. He fell back against the pillows, and when his eyes closed, Addie's face, filled with determination, flashed through his mind.

From somewhere, either in the depths of his mind or in the depths of his heart, he found the strength to maneuver himself into the chair. Then he rolled around the bed, banging the rails as he learned to push and control the large wheels. He managed to roll to the other night table, and he picked up the book and laid it open in his lap while he gathered the strength to try.

It was then that he realized he wasn't doing this for himself, he was doing it for Addie. Someday he would dance with her again, hold her again and, God willing, make love to her again. It wasn't fear that drove him on, nor determination, nor pride, it was love, and there was more drive and will and grit and faith in that one emotion than in anything Montana had ever believed in before. He finally had found the strength he needed. It came from his heart.

The morning sun crept over the eastern foothills, dying the gray sky a burning pink, the few clouds a deep violet. It was dawn, and Addie's favorite time of day. She stood on the porch, leaning against the wooden rail, and her gaze moved to the giant oak tree.

It had been over a year since she'd come to the farm, over a year since Montana had stood under that tree, pointing his gun at her. It seemed like ten years and it seemed like yesterday.

The birds awakened and sang in the cool morning air. A rooster crowed and the distant cackle of chickens hummed from the chicken yard. Mabel or Maud bawled from the barn, and Addie could hear Custus swearing at the cows. Soon he'd be bringing the morning milk into the kitchen where she'd make butter from the cream. It was Wednesday, and she always made the butter on Wednesday.

Through the open windows she heard the soft, rolling hum of wheels across the parlor's wooden floor. It was

Montana's wheelchair. She knew the sound well, since it had been so much a part of their lives in the past months. The front screen door creaked open, and she turned just as the wheels rolled out the front door.

The chair was empty. Montana stood behind it pushing it through the open doorway. He turned and smiled at her. "Think it's about time we got rid of this thing?"

She looked at him, standing so tall and straight, his shoulders back, his face all hard angles except for that wonderful dimple in his chin. Then she remembered what he had gone through, remembered his face contorted with pain as he tried to stand alone, remembered his determination when his legs gave way over and over. All he would say was, "I can do it. For you, I can do it." He'd sworn that she was his inspiration, and that anger and self-pity wouldn't help him walk, but having her there with him could; so she had stayed in the room while he'd tried.

There were times when it had been so hard to watch him. Sweat would pour down his face as he struggled to stand, only to stumble or bonelessly collapse to the floor. She had wanted to run to him, help him, hold him, but she hadn't, for his sake. And he'd tried that much harder, pushed himself that much further. Other times the muscles in his face would strain and his fists would whiten, his breathing would deepen as he tried to find the courage to let go of the walker bar and take his first steps, alone and unaided. Yet as hard as it had been to watch his pain, she'd stayed there as he'd asked her to do, praying for him and for the strength she needed to mask her reaction. She refused to let her fear or doubt or concern show on her face.

It paid off. She was there when he stood for the first time, there to see the pride on his face when he did walk. And remembering those moments still brought joy to her heart and a tightness to her throat.

And now, when she looked up at him, the love he felt for her shone in those yellow eyes—the same ones that had frightened her so much the first time she'd looked into them. Every time he looked at her, those eyes held his heart. Her throat ached, and she swallowed so she wouldn't do something stupid like cry.

He pushed the invalid chair out onto the porch and stepped around it, his right foot still carrying the inklings of a limp. His boots tapped an uneven, hollow beat on the wooden porch and that awkward sound made her heart rise to her throat. She loved the cadence of his footsteps and never, ever failed to listen for it.

And this time, that sound did make her cry.

Montana's arms linked around her, holding her as if he needed to see if she were real. Then she felt his chin rest on the top of her head. Her silly tears dripped onto his arm, and he turned her around, tilting her chin up so he could look into her face. "What's wrong?"

She sighed as she looked up at him through her blur of tears. "Nothing really, I'm just being sentimental."

He smiled then, that male smile of indulgence. "Are you going to cry for the next seven months?"

She sniffed. "Probably. It's my prerogative, as an expectant mother." Her nose went up a notch.

"So I've heard." He paused for a moment, then asked, "Can expectant mothers still dance?"

"Only if they have music."

He took her hand and placed it on his shoulder, then took her other hand in his. His lips touched hers for a brief instant, then he pulled back and began to whistle. A moment later they waltzed along the wooden porch, her cheek against his chest, his chin resting atop her head; and neither of them cared that they moved a little slower, nor that their turns were not so wide and even, the dips not so sweeping, nor that Montana's steps were a bit uneven. They didn't care because the dreams they once thought they'd have to surrender now danced on.

Others, well, they weren't as lucky. The People's Railroad was fraught with delayed funding, operating decisions, and ironically, government regulations. For over two years Wade and Will continued to elude the authorities, hiding in the foothills, aided by a network of sympathizers. The S.P. was still entrenched in the manhunt, desperate to catch the robbers who had now become folk heroes throughout the state.

A reporter for a San Francisco paper was able to interview both Will and Wade, and he printed the interview much to the chagrin of the railroad. Their own agents, numbering in the hundreds, couldn't catch the two men, yet a reporter found them and got an interview. Despite the humor of the situation, the interview humiliation made the railroad intensify the search. Eventually they caught Will, leaving the back of the Latimer barn where he met Lizzie. He was arrested. Wade wasn't so lucky. He was killed in a shootout a few miles away.

But support for Will Murdoch was massive. Hundreds raised funds for his legal battle, but even public opinion couldn't save him. He was sentenced to life in prison by a railroad-owned court.

Then the winds of change blew westward, and it wasn't long before the S.P. was "derailed" of its power. The rise of the Progressive Movement and the increase in regulatory power given by Congress to the Interstate Commerce Commission undermined the railroad's political machine.

A few years later a Progressive reformist was elected governor of California and Will Murdoch was pardoned. Addie, Montana, and Lizzie were there when Will walked free. In a matter of days the town of Bleeding Heart had its own celebration out on the Creed place, which had quadrupled in size and was one of the most profitable farms in the state.

The farmhouse had grown too. It was three stories high, with a skylight, turrets, and gables, and a round window that was the talk of the town. Music played from a white pavilion that stood in the west corner of the property. In that pavilion the town would gather to celebrate Admission's Day and the Fourth of July, for it was said that the Creeds threw the best damn celebration in the valley, maybe in all of Northern California.

And nobody missed these gatherings, not even the newly elected United States senator, Levi Hamilton, who had managed to get four farm bills through Congress his first month. He was a local hero. The Latimers' bright redheads were among the crowd—John, Hettie, Rebecca, and the boys, Abel and Amos. Lizzie stood by Will, her new husband, and with them stood their nine-year-old daughter Amanda, who had met her father for the first time the day he walked out of prison. You couldn't miss her carrot-red hair, her mother's glow in the girl's green eyes, and her father's grin.

The five Creed children, three boys and two girls, streamed through the crowd. Art, the oldest, and the spitting image of his pa, was already the best horse rider in the county. Josh was different. He had blond hair and black eyes, a superstitious nature, and a wicked sense of humor honed to precision by his idol, old Custus McGee. Josh also collected toads. Robert, the youngest boy, had skipped three grades, loved books, and had a tendency to label everything, even his older sister Lillian's prize chickens. They were an active bunch, who managed to raise a little hell themselves. But they were good kids, loving kids, raised by parents who loved and respected them and never failed to let them know it.

The music stopped and Old Custus McGee left a group of arguing, crooked old men, half of whom had no hair. He moved through the crowd, as slow as a snail on a greased log, and he called all the children to the starting line of a cycle race—a favorite event in Bleeding Heart. Anxious and giggling, the children lined up, excitedly waiting to take off, their bicycles side by side.

But one child was missing, and no one noticed that five-year-old Emily Creed, the youngest child, didn't ride in the race. She had rolled her little cycle, with its custom-fitted saddle, near some bushes and waited in the shade of the eucalyptus trees, twisting her black hair impatiently and watching the goings-on. With the blast of a gun, the race began, the other children taking off to cheers and laughter, dirt and gravel spitting up in their wake.

Emily watched, then turned her gaze toward the pavilion, where her parents danced a waltz to the band. It was a familiar sight for her. She rolled her eyes. Her parents always danced.

Little Emily Anne Creed didn't care about dancing or the

race or the cycle. She had other things to do. She moved over to the giant oak tree that stood so proudly in the front drive, and she bent down, picking up a heaping plate that she'd hidden there earlier. Then, plate in hand, she skipped across the gravel dirt, her little shoes making a light, melodic crunch.

Around the barn she traipsed, her long black hair flying out like a flag behind her. She reached the back pasture, her yellow eyes glowing like golden nuggets, and she grinned, a determined, stubborn little grin that showed the slightest hint of a dimple in her small chin. She ducked under a fence and walked across the grass, past the cows, past the mules, and over to a pond. Once there she laughed, a bright, cheerful child's laugh that rivaled the music of the pavilion band. Then she set the plate down and fed her mother's apple pie to her best friend—a plump, old horse with pink, freckled lips.